A Council of Wolves

AN ANGLO-SAXON MYSTERY

A Council of Wolves

AN ANGLO-SAXON MYSTERY

by

ELIZABETH SPRINGER

Characters

In Wessex

Edwin – *newly-appointed reeve of Wimborne*

Molly (Lady Molgifu) – *Edwin's bride*

Edmund – *Edwin's older brother, an ealdorman (governor) of Wessex*

Aethelwold and Aethelhelm – *aethelings (princes), sons of Alfred's late elder brother*

Alfred – *King of Wessex*

Bert – *Edwin's groom*

Bishop Aethelheah of Sherborne – *Edmund and Edwin's maternal uncle*

Bunny – *kitchen maid*

Cnapa – *Eng's assistant*

Eng – *cook at Wimborne*

Eormengyth – *Abbess of Wimborne*

Father Ingeld – *priest of Wimborne*

Fram – *Hana – Alfred's chief spy*

Henna – *Molly's maid*

Lullus – *Steward of King's hall at Wimborne*

Osgar – *a West Saxon nobleman*

Red, Stapa, Stig-rap – *Edwin's horses*
Sebbi – *Molly's dog*
Winfred – *interim cook at Wimborne*

In Mercia

Aethelhun – *Abbot of Buckingham*
Aethelred – *young Ealdorman, related to King Alfred's wife*
Aethelwulf – *Aethelred's uncle, lord of Buckingham*
Beornoth – *Ealdorman and cousin of former king Burgred of Mercia*
Buntel – *a poacher*
Ceolwulf II – *king of Mercia*
Cynric – *Aethelwulf's gamekeeper*
Deorlaf – *Bishop of Hereford*
Helmstan and Garmund – *Aethelred's retainers*
Waerferth – *Bishop of Worcester*
Wulfsige – *nobleman of Mercia, related to a saint and a king*

Chapter 1

On a hill facing Offa's Dyke, King Ceolwulf's tent rose higher than the others around it. Its red and yellow panels rippled in the rising breeze of an early October afternoon.

The king motioned to the physician to open the tent-flap. From his sickbed, the king could see them: four warriors waiting by the entrance, trying to avoid being whipped by the royal standard flapping on its pole. Their hair was plastered to their foreheads and they carried their battle helmets in their hands.

The king watched as these dirty, dishevelled men—the chief nobles of Mercia—ducked their heads and entered, one by one: the young upstart, his clever uncle, the arrogant fool, and the useful one.

The tent was dim inside; the heavy royal fabric shaded out the brilliant sun that had broken through the clouds late in the day. It also muffled the sounds outside of the Mercian army rounding up what remained of the Welsh prince Rhodri Mawr's defeated forces.

The king lay on his narrow wooden field bed, tucked up comfortably with brightly-embroidered coverlet, and a pile of fat white goose-feather pillows to cushion his head against the twin carved dragon-heads holding the headboard on either side.

King Ceolwulf II turned his head toward his visitors. He tried to turn his body, but gasped in pain; the physician laid a steadying hand on his shoulder. "Please lie still, sir," he said in an undertone.

"Ealdorman Aethelred," the king addressed the young upstart, who had not yet seen twenty winters. "Make your report."

Flushed with success, the young man plunged into a detailed explanation of his tactics, the terrain, and an estimated number of combatants. The king cut him off. Looking at the older man beside him, the clever uncle, he said, "Lord Aethelwulf, teach your puppy of a nephew when to stop yapping."

Aethelred, the young man, closed his mouth abruptly in a tight line and stood at attention, staring over the king's head, as if the tent were not there to break his line of vision. Only a sudden pink flush in his ears betrayed his mortification.

His father's brother Aethelwulf was speaking. "Our offensive was also successful, my king," he said smoothly. "We drove the enemy back over the Dyke and slaughtered most of them before they could reach the forest."

The king's eyes moved to the arrogant one, Wulfsige, dark of hair and proud of bearing. "Report."

This man took a sharp breath of air through his nostrils before speaking. "My sword sang and made many Welshmen food for the crows, my king. But I insist that you allow me to take my men and drive the enemy into the western sea. If we leave their path back to Mercia a scorched ruin, they will not readily return. My strategy—"

Ceolwulf had caught one word of this speech, and it was enough. Time to whittle down this man's growing arrogance. "Insist?" he rasped. He took a wheezing breath, and continued. "You may give yourself airs because of your royal lineage, Lord Wulfsige, but never forget that I am the king, and you are not."

Wulfsige's face flashed a look of pure hatred as he met King Ceolwulf's gaze. The king was the first to look away: in disdain. He turned to the fourth dishevelled warrior, the useful one, and said, "Well, Ealdorman Beornoth; and you?" The king knew that arrogant fool Wulfsige would not miss the emphasis he gave to his rival's title; for all his pride in his ancestors, in point of fact Wulfsige was outranked even by him.

"Sir, my part of the line held well," the red-faced, sandy-haired man replied. As he said this, he adjusted his sword belt, which his belly had caused to sag, and the scabbard fittings made a jaunty little clink.

"And?" the king prompted.

"And?" Beornoth repeated blankly. "Er, and, there was a great slaughter." Brightening, he added, "And one of my men killed Prince Gwriad."

"Count on Beornoth to give me some proper news!" King Ceolwulf exclaimed, sitting up straight in bed. He spoke too vehemently, however, because he then said, "I feel—I—" and sank back on his mountain of pillows, too light-headed to move.

The physician hovered close, felt the king's pulse, made quick adjustments. Ceolwulf could hear the voices, as if from far away. "The king has lost a great deal of blood from a leg wound, gentlemen," the physician was saying. "He also suffered two or three broken ribs which may be pressing on his lung on the left side."

"Will he recover?" asked Beornoth.

"He has an even chance," replied the physician. "He needs rest, complete rest. He is not old; he is hale enough to regain his strength in time."

"How long will it take?" one of the men asked.

"It will be a couple of weeks till he can be safely moved," the physician said. "I am treating his leg-wound with a plaster of herbs." There was a sound of rummaging on the small table next to the bed. The table also held a roll of bandage, a corked earthenware bottle of some drink, and a tiny glass bottle with some liquid in it.

"This," the physician said of the tiny bottle, "is a sleeping-draught. As you have seen, the king is still very much animated by his duties and the events around him. For his wound to heal and his body to regain strength, he must rest. Three drops of this syrup in a cup of mead will help him sleep through the night. It is a powerful sedative, however. No more than three drops must be given, or he may be troubled by strange visions."

"You are the physician. Why are you telling us this?" Wulfsige asked dismissively.

"I am telling you, gentlemen, of the king's condition so that you may rest assured that he is receiving proper care and may, with God's help, recover in due time. You four are his closest counsellors and will probably be expected to stay close at hand during his recovery—even to tend him when I cannot be at his side. I may be coming down with a bit of a cold myself."

Though his head swam, Ceolwulf's mind reached out and clung to one idea. *Recovery. Yes, must recover. Can't leave Mercia to these fools.* The king's eyelids fluttered, his chest rose and fell mightily, and he opened his eyes. He blinked, and his gaze was sharp again.

"Are you four still here?" he croaked. "Clear off! Back to your duties!" As they turned to go, he called after them, "No, wait. I want Beornoth. Come here, Ealdorman. The rest of you are dismissed." As they passed through the tent-flap again, one by one, he began rapping out orders: "This bandage smarts. Can't you change it yet? All right, lift it and have a look, then. Beornoth! I want to play a table game. Bring that board over here. The pieces are in that box. No, not that one, you oaf...."

In the days that followed, the king continued to rest unwillingly and mend slowly. He drank up news of the camp more thirstily than medicine, questioning each of his lords closely about the activities of the others during their visits to the royal tent.

Lord Wulfsige did not get to muster an overwhelming force to drive the Welsh into the western sea, leaving Gwynedd a scorched wasteland forever; but he did conduct some very effective clearing and raiding operations in the territory just over the Dyke.

Lord Aethelwulf rode east as far as Lichfield to secure provisions, and his young nephew the Ealdorman gained valuable experience as senior commander of the camp. It fell to him to decide which forces to send home and which to retain, and how to keep those forces occupied while they waited. It would not do to leave the wounded king without a suitable force so close to the border, but even Mercia could not afford to keep so many in the field after the battle had been won. Aethelred did it all very efficiently and received no commendation whatsoever—the king was not of a mind to encourage upstarts, and besides, no one notices such things unless they are done badly.

Much to the king's satisfaction, useful Ealdorman Beornoth stayed, for the most part, at his bedside. He soon learned how to make the king's sleeping-draughts and apply fresh herbs to the bandage when the physician was taking his brief rest in his little adjacent tent. Every now and then, when even Beornoth needed a rest, Aethelred would tend the king; and when Wulfsige and Aethelwulf returned to in camp, they took their turns. The dosing and bandaging were not difficult; the king could eat for himself, and he had several servants who took it in turns to bathe him and attend to other bodily needs.

One day following a stretch of cold, wet weather, the wound became hot and red and the king ran a fever. The physician tended him to the point of exhaustion. Aethelwulf, dropping in to report on the delivery of the supplies, sized up the situation and sent the physician to his bed. Aethelwulf himself would take the first watch; the other three noblemen would take it in turns to sit with the king until his medicines took effect. The king heard all this; he twitched his hand and nodded. Even in his feverish state, he claimed the right to give his consent to the plan.

◆

It was a very dark night, a new moon, and the clouds hid the stars. The wind whipped the treetops and caused the royal tent to flap and creak all night long. The king was feverish, but sleep would not come in spite of the drops in his mead. He had a vague memory of a familiar voice holding a cup to his lips and murmuring, "Drink this, sir." He drank. He dozed and woke; he was not sure what he dreamed. Again a shadowy figure came in the tent. Who was it? He could not remember. The figure did not speak. Then one of the pillows was pulled roughly from under his feverish head. The pillow beneath felt cool. That was better. But now the other pillow was on his face, pressing against his nose and mouth. He opened his eyes but the pillow was there, too. He could not breathe. He tried to turn his head, but pain from his wounds shot through him like lightning, as if someone were sitting on him, holding him down. Panic began to rise above his clouded senses, and he tried to fight. He flailed with his arms; his uninjured leg kicked out to no avail. No air; he was becoming faint. His lungs screamed for air. Suddenly, out of nowhere, he saw the painting of Christ in Judgement on the wall of Tamworth church. It seemed to get bigger and closer until it was no longer a painting on a wall but a reality that filled him with terror. Then the king's arms and legs fell limp and moved no more.

Chapter 2

In Wessex

It was not the first wartime wedding in Wessex; nor would it be the last. After so many years of danger and privation a short, uneasy peace had descended, and everyone was ready for something joyful to look forward to. The bridegroom, Lord Edwin, had seized the moment of peacetime to claim the hand of his childhood sweetheart. This was Lady Molgifu, known to her family as Molly.

Edwin sneaked a sidelong glance at her sitting next to him at the high table. She was not a legendary beauty, even in her rich red gown, new linen headdress fastened with jewelled pins, and hints of her reddish-blonde hair peeking out underneath. Her nose and eyebrows were very straight, suggesting acuity of judgement and a trustworthy character; but her brown eyes twinkled with merriment and her cheeks were flushed with good humour. Her figure gave the impression of plumpness without being discernibly fat.

What had he to offer such a bride? Edwin was the obscure younger son of a famous warrior and the quiet younger brother of a brash, outgoing ealdorman. He found he had little of his own to add to the tales of recent valour now being exchanged at the feast. His brother had led armies; he had served King Alfred in his exile by gathering scraps of intelligence for the Athelney stronghold, and such small favours as reading books or telling riddles by the campfire at day's end.

The Danes had left the land, and the girl he loved now sat beside him as his wife. At this moment, though, at the culmination of so many long-cherished hopes, he was left with a cold and clammy feeling of inadequacy. After the feast they would go to his new posting at Wimborne, a royal estate near the south coast. And there, all at once, he would be a husband and a royal reeve, having no experience in either office. He would rather die than disappoint the King, or Molly. She treated him like a hero. The King seemed to think he could do anything. They would, he feared, soon find out that there were wiser, braver, better men they could have chosen.

◆

In a land ravaged by war, it would have been a lean summer anyway. To save up for the feast, the bride's household had eaten coarse brown bread all summer to keep enough fine white flour for the wedding-cake. Newly-made cheeses had been kept under lock and key, and butter and honey banned from the table as if the family were in a perpetual fast. The calves and pigs were marked out from birth and fattened with every ounce of fodder that could be spared. And enormous vats of ale, cider and mead had been brewed to make sure the three days of the feast were jolly right to the end. The chill autumn air had given an edge to everyone's appetite; so when the marriage agreement was sealed and the church's blessing given, all that remained was to settle in and enjoy the revelry.

But no wedding, however long in the planning, can come off without a hitch. The feast had progressed to the presentation of gifts, when there was a sound of clattering hooves in the yard and a panting, travel-stained rider stumbled into the hall.

Edwin looked over the heads of the company seated at the long tables on either side of the hearth. There was something familiar about the rider, even through the haze of the fire. The man looked around, saw Edwin, and there was a flicker of recognition. Then he glanced at the company and, for the first time, seemed to notice that it was a wedding-feast. He hastily combed his hair with his fingers.

Edwin motioned for the man to approach, and he did so, followed by Molly's father.

"Hana, what's the news?" Edwin asked in a low voice, as the man came near.

"I've got news, all right," replied Hana. "I was hoping to find you here, but—I didn't know this was your wedding day. Of all the luck."

Edwin suppressed a rising sense of dread. "Don't worry about it. Just tell me what is going on."

Hana looked out across the tables and saw dozens of guests staring back at him expectantly. "I'd better sit on it until you're done with the gifts. Let's not get everyone worked up. Just slip away as soon as you can with your brother and come meet me somewhere private."

The gifts were presented with due ceremony. By prior arrangement, Edwin and Molly both feigned delight at the pair of hideous heirloom glass beakers Molly's mother presented to them. Edwin's gifts to Molly were a set of half-a-dozen cups made from Danish silver (his share of the spoils of war) and a well-trained guard dog named Sebbi. He was a handsome heavyset creature with hazel eyes and a brindled-and-white coat.

It had taken Edwin months to raise and train him for her. Perhaps a stout, well-trained guard dog is not the most obvious wedding present, but Edwin knew that when he was away this was the best means of procuring peace of mind about his wife's personal safety. Since the spring, Edwin had been able to visit several times and teach Molly how to handle him.

Looking back, these visits were among the dearest memories of his life. He was permitted to take Molly on long walks with Sebbi through the fields and meadows of her father's estate. The way she looked on these walks is how he would always remember her, the red-gold plaits of her hair glinting from beneath her headdress and the golden wheatfields beyond, the promise of a new beginning after so many lean and terrible years. They certainly did train Sebbi creditably, but the dog was the only witness to the kisses stolen at opportune moments, and Sebbi was too loyal to tell tales.

After another round of toasting Edwin caught his brother's eye. Asking Molly to excuse him for a few minutes, he left the table and made his way to a small room at the side of the hall. Hana had been watching and met the brothers there.

"Where have you come from?" asked Edwin.

"Cirencester. You're the only stop on the road to Winchester I knew I could trust. What I am going to tell you must stay between us until we get to the King."

Edmund said, "All right, what's going on?"

"Guthrum's on the move," whispered Hana.

Edmund swore.

"It looks like he's heading northeast," Hana said, "toward eastern Mercia."

"Guthrum and his army have been up there at Cirencester

for a year, hanging over us like a storm-cloud. Maybe they are finally leaving for good." Edwin's tone hovered between hope and doubt.

"Do you think he's really going to keep to his bargain?" scoffed Edmund. "He hasn't shown himself to be honour-bound by any oath before. I didn't trust Guthrum when he made peace with us after his defeat at Edington; and I don't trust him now."

"Nor do any of us," Hana agreed. "But I haven't told you all. Before Guthrum left, he had a falling-out with two of his chieftains. The word is that the chieftains split off from Guthrum's army with a smaller force, somewhere between fifty and a hundred men, and we don't know where they are going."

Edwin began to pace in small circles. "So even if Guthrum takes his army away towards the east, keeping to terms, we've got another small army of Vikings running loose on the borders of our country."

"And what if they both turn south? They could start from opposite ends of the loaf and devour Wessex between them," said Edmund.

"And there's another thing," Hana said.

The two brothers, absorbed in contemplating the news about Guthrum, looked up in surprise.

"While I was at Cirencester, I met up with the physician for King Ceolwulf. A mate of mine is friends with a cousin of his—never mind. Anyway, Ceolwulf is dead and nobody is talking about it. Even the physician didn't want to talk about it. Scared out of his wits, and barely made it to his cousin's house before collapsing from fever. He said the king had been wounded in a battle with the Welsh up there. He was getting better. But one morning the man came in to tend him and he was dead."

"A fine story! How do we know it's not some Mercian ruse? Or maybe the physician did it himself—if he is really a physician!" Edmund huffed.

"I did some checking. He was the Mercian king's physician all right," said Hana. "He only told his cousin because he was afraid he was dying. Then his cousin told my mate, who told me. I went and talked to him. I'm convinced—Ceolwulf really is dead, though whether by battle or murder I couldn't say. Now the lords of Mercia are all riding to Buckingham for a council to decide the kingship. It's vital we get this news to the King tomorrow. I was hoping to spend the night here and get a fresh horse from Lord Sigebert, er, your—" Hana raised his eyebrows in a question.

"Father-in-law," Edwin nodded. "As of today."

"Yes, your father-in-law, so we could get to Winchester by tomorrow night to inform the King."

Edwin's heart sank. The joy of his wedding feast, three long-awaited days of making merry between past years of war and future years of service, shattered to bits. He stood stock-still, expressionless, trying to absorb the disappointment while running down the list of all the preparations that would have to be made. Luckily Edmund was doing the same thing without the added blow of being denied his wedding-feast.

"Well, brother," said Edmund, and Edwin had enough presence of mind to be grateful he didn't call him 'little' for once. "I suppose we are going to have to break it to everyone. It will take us all day to reach Winchester if we start out around dawn tomorrow." Edmund had about twenty men with him.

At Edwin's invitation, Hana went back to the hall and took a seat at the mead-bench. Then the brothers went to find the bride and her parents.

"What's this? Of all the times to be called away! Had you no idea?" Molly's mother began at once.

Her father only said, "Hph'm!"

They all knew what that sound meant. He was, in one clearing of the throat, resigning himself to the change in plans and working out all the arrangements to be made. His orderly mind was already composing the speech he would presently make to the wedding party, directing the servants to begin preparing supplies and saddling horses before the break of dawn, trying to figure out what to do with Molly.

"But what about the guests? What are we going to do with all the food? And what is Molly going to do now?" Molly's mother was saying.

"Now, now, my dear," her husband said. "I can see that this is not going to be the most common sort of wedding feast. We are going to have to say farewell for a short time to Edwin and Edmund and their party, as they are called away on very important royal business" (he said firmly, eyeing his wife), "but in the meantime many of our guests have travelled from all around the shire. They cannot be expected to go home tomorrow. Let us continue as planned, and give our guests the feast they came to enjoy."

"But what about Molly?" she persisted.

Edwin turned to Molly, "You can certainly stay here with your parents until I return. I have no idea how long I will be gone, but I will try to get word to you if I can find out. But if you want to, you can go to Wimborne and await me there. What would you rather do?"

All eyes turned to Molly.

"Well—" she paused. "I suppose I've been saying goodbye to my old home all summer. Everything's packed up. What will you do with me if I stay here?" she smiled at her mother and father. "I don't even know how long it will be." With the boldness of youth, she said, "I will travel to Wimborne as planned after the feast."

"Marvellous!" beamed Edwin, as her mother gave a little wail of dismay. Molly's father, who seemed to have suspected this was how his daughter would make up her mind, said, "Well then, we'll just have to work out how to get you there."

"My uncle should be passing that way," said Edwin. "I'm sure he would gladly see you safely to Wimborne after the feast. I'll have to take Maca and Aeddi and my groom, Bert, with me. Lullus, the new steward, can stay for the feast and go back with you too."

"That's settled then," said Molly's father. "And you and Ealdorman Edmund," with a motion of his head towards the latter, "will be leaving with your men at dawn?"

"I'm afraid so, sir," said Edwin.

With that, the family party made their way back into the banqueting hall, where their absence had begun to be noticed. With a sign, the father of the bride called for silence and gave his speech, explaining the situation in as much detail as he thought necessary. Well-fed and merry though they were, the news brought a certain pall over the company. Their host wasted no time in bringing on a singer with a harp and refilling drinking-horns, so soon everyone was able to suspend their disappointment while listening to a tale of the exploits of some long-dead hero.

Chapter 3

The door opened slowly, and a shaft of dim, flickering light pierced the blackness. A low whisper called out, "My lord." Edwin was already awake and sat up expectantly. The servant tiptoed into the room and handed Edwin a candle. Silently, so as not to awaken Molly, Edwin edged out of bed and began to collect his clothes, pulling them on quietly as he went. He had just located his comb when he glanced back at the bed and saw her sitting up.

"There's no need for you to try and creep about, you know," she said, yawning. She turned her face towards him, pale in the dim light, and smiled a sleepy smile.

"You could sleep a little longer. We're not leaving just yet," said Edwin.

"Well, of course I have to get ready, too. I can't be in my nightgown when you give me my morning-gift." With that she pulled on her dress and wound her braids up at the back of her head, and pinned her headdress firmly in place. Edwin looked at her and his heart melted; she looked beautiful. "Come here, my lady, I have something to tell you," he said.

She came over to where he was standing, and he enfolded her in his arms. "Now let's not start that again," she said, giggling. At that moment the servant brought in some water for washing and the couple devoted themselves to preparations for the day.

Molly's morning-gift turned out to be a mill on Edwin's family estate, a piece of property that he had inherited from his mother apart from Edmund's larger share. Molly was to have the mill and its income; the deed was witnessed by Bishop Aethelheah and Edmund. The presentation of the morning-gift had been planned as a late-morning event at the wedding feast with all the party reassembled, but it turned out to be a hurried affair, finished by candlelight in the presence of a handful of people in just a few brief minutes.

When the cavalcade was ready and mounted, the household and the guests who were awake and dressed assembled at the door of the hall to see them off. Edwin and the rest started down the road at a spanking trot; the horses were fresh and excited to be out in company. No one spoke for a long time. Many of the men looked rather grey and hung over. As for Edwin, his military training enabled him to keep his outward expression in check; inside was another matter entirely.

As the morning wore on, the horses got steadier and the men began to perk up. As they entered the forest of Selwood, jesting and conversations among the rear guard echoed through the trees. Edwin's own companions Maca and Aeddi, the captain of the Wimborne guard and a guardsman the latter had brought with him, resisted every effort he made to draw them into conversation.

The woodland eventually gave way to open land as their route led them over the downs and onto Salisbury Plain. At midday they stopped to graze their horses and take refreshment. Edwin was impressed at the martial punctuality with which Edmund's men dismounted, ate, remounted and formed up to continue on their way. Maca and Aeddi did not want to be the last men ready, but Edwin noticed their slowness and fumbling. "Not as well-drilled as the warriors," he noted to himself, and resolved to inspect the guardhouse when they returned.

On the second leg of the journey, with a straight Roman road before him and the winds across the downs whistling in his ears, young Stig began to surge ahead again. Fram easily kept up, trotting merrily alongside. Clouds had been gathering since midday, pushing a thick grey blanket across the clear autumn sky. A few miles more and the first drops began to fall; soon it was raining steadily. The men pulled their hoods up over their heads. The horses shook their bridles and swished their tails as rivulets of rain began to trickle down their bodies.

The rain continued the rest of the afternoon, and the company lapsed into silence. Edwin, for one, was glad. In all the bustle of the sudden journey he had almost forgotten it, but the King was bound to ask if Edwin had a new riddle for him. It was a sort of tacit competition between them; Edwin always tried to compose a riddle that would stump the King, and the King so far had guessed every one. Now he began to rack his brain for a fresh attempt.

The scenery, what he could see of it through the rain, was not much inspiration. Rain dripped from the eaves of soggy thatched cottages. In the fields, cattle huddled under distant trees. Wet brown leaves were ground to pulp beneath the feet of the horses, and a chill began to seep into Edwin's bones. He tried to think of warm, dry things but the damp had penetrated even into his thoughts. If he were to compose any riddle, it would have to be about something cold and wet.

As Edwin and the others approached Winchester in the evening gloom, they could make out clearings in the forests on either side of the road, tree stumps receding into the darkness bearing mute witness to Alfred's feverish rebuilding efforts. Up ahead they saw the palisade gates at the entrance to the town. The main thoroughfare led directly towards the royal hall and the Minster, which loomed up through the rainy evening. The horses' hooves made sloppy sounds in the mud as they drew near to the King's hall.

Chapter 4

When the horses had been led away and the men ushered in for the evening meal, Edmund and Edwin were called aside by the steward of the royal household.

"My lords, I am to take you to the King's private room," he said as he conducted them through the main hall to a separate apartment behind the dais. The room was furnished with an oak table and benches arranged neatly around a brazier. The room was redolent of the pleasant smell of fresh-hewn beams and wood smoke.

"The king will be with you shortly," their guide said, and withdrew.

A small group of Alfred's faithful were there, men who had remained with their King in exile during the dark days of Danish occupation. Edwin knew them all. Lord Osgar, hero of the battle of Winchester, was telling a humorous anecdote, mead-cup sloshing as he gestured and laughed.

"Edmund!" Osgar said. "And Edwin! What are you doing here? I thought you were busy getting married."

Then Osgar saw Hana come in behind them, and he shed his jovial manner.

"Why don't you warm up with some hot mead," Osgar said as a servant brought in cups for them. The brothers felt that they had never been so glad to see a drink. It flowed down Edwin's throat like a tingling river of gold, warming his chilled bones.

At last the King entered the room. He was in his prime, just thirty-one, but the cares of leading a war-torn kingdom had marked him. All in the room pretended not to notice, but Alfred did not look well. They all knew about the mysterious affliction that ravaged their lord in curious fits and bouts every now and then, only to disappear as mysteriously as it had come.

Alfred sat down in his chair at the head of the table with a studious attempt at ease. He glanced round with chagrin at his men's concerned faces. He said cheerfully, "Now, Edwin, too bad about your wedding-feast. I suppose you left the bride and her family well?" The other men also murmured their congratulations and best wishes to the bridegroom, and sat down.

"You three look exhausted," said Alfred. "And we have much to discuss. Let's go ahead and eat before getting down to work." The King turned to the servant behind him and said, "We'll have our meal now, I think." The man withdrew, returning shortly accompanied by two kitchen-maids carrying baskets of bread, butter, and bowls of a savoury-smelling beef and onion stew. Ale-horns were filled and the men all ate with appetite.

When everyone had eaten their fill and the dogs lay contentedly at their masters' feet, the King turned to Hana.

"So Guthrum is on the move," he prompted, lacing his fingers. All eyes were on the old spy.

"Yes, my lord. When I left Cirencester he was moving east with all his men. My trackers will let us know if he moves south."

"Good. Let us hope that Guthrum intends to keep the

promises he made to my face at his baptism."

"Do you trust him, then?" Edmund asked.

The King shrugged. "Not yet. He may be no different from many other Danes who make gestures toward religion and peace when they judge it to their advantage. Very soon we will know his intentions. Let us pray for peace, but be ready for war."

Hana said, "There were also rumours of a break-away band of Vikings. They were traced as far as Banbury but no farther. Whatever Guthrum's intentions may be, this other lot is dangerous."

"But Banbury is well over the border into Mercia," someone spoke up. "King Ceolwulf would surely be able to defeat such a small force."

"This brings us to the point," continued the King. "Our last news of King Ceolwulf a few weeks ago was that he was moving west, probably because of the unrest on the Welsh border. Since then we've been unable to get any news from western Mercia at all."

"King Ceolwulf was never anything but Guthrum's puppet. Most likely he and Guthrum are meeting to cook up something against us," one of the men said.

"Not likely," Hana broke in. He relayed the news of Ceolwulf's death and the council at Buckingham he'd already shared with Edwin and Edmund in confidence.

The room erupted into surprised speculation. The King hit the table with his palm, bringing the men to order. "We must act immediately. If no one is in control in the west, Guthrum will be tempted to seize back the territory he ceded to Ceolwulf three years ago."

Osgar nodded. "But any unfriendly neighbour to the north is bad for Wessex. As much as we have spoken of the Danish threat, we would be no better off with a hostile Saxon king forming alliances to our disadvantage."

"My lord, what do you propose?" Edwin asked the King.

Alfred knitted his brows. "We will send an embassy to Buckingham without delay. Edmund, you will lead the mission and take your men. Your lineage and rank will command respect from the Mercians, and your following will lend military weight to your words. Lord Osgar, you will use all your skills—and all your widespread connections with friends and kin—to see that everyone comes away from this council feeling that they have gained something. I want no accusations of West Saxon coercion if I can avoid it. Lord Edwin, you must return to your old job of 'scent-hound'. Be my eyes and ears at the Mercian court. Find out what Ceolwulf and his council are up to. I expect a full report from you on your return."

"What are we looking to accomplish, my lord?" prompted Edmund.

"The interests of Wessex are to ensure a peaceful neighbour in western Mercia and to contain Guthrum to the east. I am not going to stand by and let my dear wife's homeland be taken over by Norsemen. Mercia is large—it is rich—and it is our near neighbour. If King Ceolwulf has been overthrown, there will be a mad scramble among all the other competing royal families. The challenge will be to either back the contender who is friendliest to Wessex, or to convince whoever is already in place that an alliance with us is worth his while."

The door was pushed open and a seven-year-old boy burst into the room. He was followed by a girl of about ten, wearing a very neat and expensive dress of blue-purple wool trimmed with bands of woven silk, carrying an earthenware jug of steaming mead. As the girl went round carefully refilling mead cups, the boy climbed onto the King's lap.

"Now, Edward," said the King, "I am sending some men to Mercia. Which way do you think they should take?"

"If you want them to go fast, they had better take the north road out of Winchester and then that little road to Reading. From there they can get a boat to take them up the Thames to Dorchester, and from there to Buckingham."

"Well done," said Alfred with a smile, tousling the young prince's hair.

"What are they going to do in Mercia?"

"I'll tell you later. But I want them to visit the Mercians and find out how they are faring."

"Are they going to see King Ceolwulf?"

"I don't know, son. Perhaps they will need our help with their kingdom."

"You can send me up there, Father. I'd soon sort them out," called Aethelflaed from the other side of the table.

"I know you could, my girl," smiled Alfred. "You would make short work of them all."

Edward turned to Edwin with an eager face. "Have you a riddle for us?"

"Yes, indeed," replied Edwin with a smile. He took another swallow of mead and stood to speak his riddle:

My realm is the sea with my many companions,
I wear a mail-coat of silver on my breast,
But I delight in slipping from my enemy's grasp
And I fight hard against those who would capture me.
My sliminess makes a decent man recoil,
And an Englishman is happiest
When I lie dead before him.
Say what I am.

There was silence in the room for some time. Edwin sat back down. As he watched the faces of his audience, he had to smother a gleeful grin. He could see that they were all thinking of the same solution, the one he had wanted the riddle to mislead them to. The King looked at him with a sharp twinkle in his eye, showing Edwin that he knew the answer.

One of the gruff old warriors was the first to speak. "Danes. I know you want us to say it, young scoundrel, but Danes is all I can think of. The sea. Mail-coats. Fighting. Sliminess. It's got to be the Danes."

Edmund was tapping his foot. He found riddles, especially Edwin's, tedious.

"No, Breca," Aethelflaed said. "Edwin's put out a red herring for us this time."

Osgar yawned and said, "Edwin, dear boy, you might have done better to save this riddle for next Friday."

After so many hints, young Edward and the others could not fail to hit upon the real solution to the riddle. When everyone had gone back over all the ambiguous lines once again, the two eldest royal children scampered away as quickly as they had come. Edwin caught a glimpse of a nursemaid at the door waiting to take them to bed.

When the door had closed, the King was ready to get down to business. He leaned forward and spoke in a low voice to Edwin, Edmund and Osgar. "You are the only men of rank I can trust absolutely that are able to accomplish this mission. If Ceolwulf has been deposed—and if this council at Buckingham has been called to elect a new king—I authorize you to extend the offer of West Saxon friendship to the new leader. He may have the protection of Wessex if he consents not to style himself as king, but to bear the title of Ealdorman under my nominal authority."

Edwin concealed his surprise behind a slow nod. This was another way to take a kingdom!

Chapter 5

The rain had subsided to gently-falling mist by the time Maca and Aeddi and the rest of the men were finished eating and drinking. The table boards were taken away and the floor cleared, and the men began to unroll their bedding along the edges of the hall. The two guardsmen from Wimborne were relegated to a draughty corner away from the hearth, the best spots already having been allocated to the higher-ranking men in the entourages of Edmund and Osgar and other noblemen.

Aeddi had been sullen and silent all through dinner. Even the horns of ale he had drained had not lightened his mood or induced him to laugh at the jests that crisscrossed the table as the men ate.

Having set out his bedding, Aeddi made the excuse of having left something in his saddle-roll and a side door was unbolted for him to go out to the stables. Maca followed him, ill at ease. As he emerged from the building, he saw Aeddi peering around in the darkness at the various outbuildings rather than starting directly across the stable yard on his stated errand. "Aeddi!" hailed Maca in a hoarse whisper. Aeddi whirled to see his superior officer behind him. "Where are you off to?"

"None of your business," Aeddi growled with an oath. They were out of sight of the hall now, between the stables and an outbuilding.

"I think I know your business," sneered Maca. "You stupid young hothead, what do you think you can accomplish? Are you going to take on the entire palace guard single-handed?"

"I don't have to," said Aeddi. "All I need is one good chance." He put his hand on his seax sheath.

"Then you'll be dead. What will that accomplish?"

"He'll be dead too. And the poets of years to come will sing songs about me. When the usurper's out of the way, Prince Aethelwold will be able to take his rightful place on the throne of Wessex."

"You fool!" hissed Maca, trying hard to keep his voice in a whisper. "You know it's only a matter of time anyway. No need to spoil things now. All we need to do is to be ready!"

"With old men like you it's all talk and no action. Think of the opportunity. Here we are, in Winchester, right in the Ki—in the royal hall. I can't let this chance slip away. It's now or never!"

With these words Aeddi surged forward, attempting to move away from Maca. But his captain was just as quick and grabbed his arm. In a moment they were grappling with each other, rolling in the mud in the darkness.

Maca was able to get in one solid punch before Aeddi grabbed his neck and began to throttle him. Blood from Aeddi's nose began to drip hotly on Maca's face as he tightened his grip on Maca. Maca desperately fumbled for his knife. Aeddi took a hand off Maca's throat to parry Maca's hand away from his knife-sheath, which gave the older man time to roll to one side and escape Aeddi's grasp. He coughed and gagged in the mud as his breathing returned. He started to rise, but Aeddi surged towards him again. With his knife drawn, Aeddi leapt upon Maca who was just rising from the ground, and it took all Maca's strength to keep the blade at bay. He rolled, taking Aeddi with him, and now Maca seized the advantage. Sitting atop his attacker, he levelled another punch at Aeddi, so hard that it dazed him. Maca was able to snatch the knife from Aeddi's hand and fling it far away into the darkness. Aeddi finally regained his wits with a shake of his head and this time, even his captain's superior weight holding him down was not sufficient to contain the rage of the sinewy young assassin. He wrenched himself from under Maca's body and sprang to his feet, drawing Maca's own knife from his belt as he did so. Maca took hold of Aeddi's legs, trying to bring him down once more. Before he could do so, Aeddi plunged the knife into his neck and Maca fell instantly to the ground.

This disturbance had not gone unnoticed. A stable hand who had gone outside to dump some refuse at the back had heard angry words passing between the two men. Suspecting trouble, he had crept back to the stable to get help. A crowd of grooms of all shapes and sizes appeared just in time to witness, but not to prevent, the fatal blow. They fell upon Aeddi and dragged him bodily into the hall, while three of their number lifted Maca and followed slowly behind with their lifeless burden.

◆

Edwin, exhausted but with his mind still full of the king's assignment, was stunned when the news reached him of the killing. His mind raced in search of a reason for the violence that had erupted between Aeddi and Maca.

He realized how little he knew about either of them. Maca,

to the best of his knowledge, had worked on the royal estate his entire life. Starting as a guardsman, he had eventually been promoted to captain of the guard and had held that post for at least ten years. He had always conducted his duties to the satisfaction of his superiors; there had never been any complaint. He had assented with no sign of reluctance when Lullus, the new steward of Wimborne, had asked him to provide an escort to and from his new lord's wedding.

Aeddi he knew less about. Presumably from a local Wimborne family. He had apparently volunteered to come along when Maca was looking for a guardsman to go with him on the journey. Had Aeddi intended to harm his captain from the start? Or had they quarrelled? Perhaps some boast or some woman. Perhaps Aeddi had been too drunk to know what he was doing (a dangerous tendency in a guardsman, Edwin reflected).

"And the killer has said nothing?" he asked the man who had come with the news.

"Not a word, my lord," said the man. "Just glares, and when we tried to make him talk, he spat in our faces."

"The King will have to be told," said Edwin, tight-lipped. His own men had violated the King's peace and shed blood at the royal residence! He felt at that moment that he would rather take on the Danish army than face the King with such news.

"The King has already retired, and is not to be disturbed; so his steward told me," was the reply.

"Then I suppose it will have to wait till the morning. The prisoner is secure for the night?"

"Yes."

"And nothing could have been done for Maca?"

"No, my lord. He bled out immediately and was dead by

the time the stable hands reached him."

"Thank you. You may go."

Edwin sat down. Thoughts and questions kept rising in his mind like fish coming to nibble at the surface of the water. Aeddi would certainly be put to death according to the law. He would also forfeit all his possessions to the king, though Edwin could not imagine that his property would amount to much. What would he, Edwin, say to King Alfred? There was no pretty way to announce that one of his men had murdered the other on the King's own premises. He began to run through scenarios of how to approach the King and what he would say. There was no doubt that this would mean a critical delay in setting off on their mission. Edwin suddenly burned with anger towards Aeddi—not first because of Maca, but because the stupid fellow with his stupid quarrel had thrown a hindrance in the way of an international mission of far-reaching importance.

He soon realized that in his present state it would be pointless to try to sleep. There was only one way to prepare to face the King tomorrow. He got up, put his shoes on and crept through the hall full of snoring men to the door that led to the Minster.

Edwin tried his best to open the great iron-bound oak door of the Minster quietly, but everything sounded louder in the silence of the night. The bolt rattled and the door creaked as he crept in. Two candles were burning, one on either side of the altar, flickering on the glazed floor tiles. That was the only light.

Suddenly, out of the gloom, two guards emerged and took him by both arms. It nearly frightened the life out of him. "Who are you and where do you think you're going?" one of them growled.

"To pray. Er... Lord Edwin, reeve of Wimborne," Edwin replied, and suddenly he noticed the still, kneeling figure at the altar. The guards were searching Edwin for weapons. Finding none, they released him.

"Go in peace, Lord Edwin," they said. "But do not disturb the King."

Edwin crept forward and found a place distant from the King to kneel and pray. He had counted on being alone, so it cost him some time to settle and concentrate his mind to reverent prayer. He could see little of the Minster; its stone walls rose into dark oblivion above, and only the area around the altar was illuminated. He found himself praying, *The Lord is my light and my salvation; whom shall I fear?* What he dreaded most was the King's disappointment and disfavour. The lack of judgement he had shown in bringing violent brawlers into the King's hall loomed before him like a monstrous shadow. Alfred would surely dismiss him as a callow young thegn who could not keep his men in order. The King would wonder, and rightly, if this was someone who could be trusted on an international mission. He might even give his reeveship to another man and Edwin would be forced to return to Molly and the entire family in utter shame. The words of the Psalm still echoed in his mind, *Though my father and mother forsake me, the Lord will receive me.* Finally, the absurdity of his situation broke in upon him: here he was fearlessly begging help from the Heavenly King because he was in trepidation of an earthly king. Fortified by this reflection, he formed a resolve to see Alfred first thing in the morning. He opened his eyes, and to his surprise saw him sitting nearby, as if he had been waiting to speak to Edwin.

"My lord the King!" said Edwin in surprise.

"Couldn't sleep either, I see?" The King's voice was tired but friendly.

"Yes, sir, I—I certainly have plenty on my mind. But please excuse the intrusion."

"Not at all. Now what is on your mind, if I may ask?"

Here goes, thought Edwin. *I suppose it is pointless to conceal it from him now.* He forced himself to look up from the floor, where he had been staring at his toes like a boy caught in mischief.

Taking a deep breath, he said, "I regret to report that tonight, one of my two attendants, a guardsman from Wimborne, apparently quarrelled with and killed the other, the Wimborne captain of the guard. The offender has been arrested," he hastened to add. "But please accept my apologies for this blatant breach of your peace. I know there can be no excuse."

The King's face was grave. "This is indeed unfortunate news. Is it known what they quarrelled about?"

Edwin relayed the information he had been given. "If I had had any indication—" he began.

The King held up his hand.

"You forget that although these men were acting as your attendants, they are in truth my servants, as they belong to the Wimborne estate. Thus, the guardsman's breach of the peace is my responsibility. There is no reason your mission to Mercia should be delayed by this incident; we will try the man and carry out sentence here."

The relief for Edwin was overwhelming, and he thanked the King sincerely.

"Now it seems you are without any attendants for this journey," said the king.

Edwin waved this aside. "That was the least of my worries. My brother has men enough to spare. In any case I'm used to roughing it, as you know," he smiled, and the King smiled back.

"Good," said the latter. "Now go get some sleep. You have a long day ahead of you tomorrow."

Edwin bowed and thanked the King again, and did as instructed. For a few moments, as he lay down, he indulged himself with memories of Molly's embraces; but before he knew it he was deep in slumber and did not awaken until he heard the bell for Prime, his signal for an early start.

Chapter 6

At last the wagon was loaded, goodbyes were said, and it was time to depart. Molly's own baggage was supplemented by a purse of money from her father, pressed into her hand when no one was looking, and a basket of herb roots her mother presented from her garden wrapped in damp cloths and packed in sand. She had gone through all the nondescript little parcels with far more thoroughness than Molly could take in—names, properties, and the best way of cultivating and preserving each one. Molly honoured her for the gift, but could not help but feel a little embarrassed all the same; surely a king's estate would already have such things in its gardens? Cook had also sent baskets from the kitchen with provisions for the journey. Molly sniffed them with delight. Would the cook at Wimborne be anything like as good as the one she was leaving behind?

The journey to Wimborne was to be made in two days. Molly enjoyed the journey and Stapa's gentle ambling gait; much better than riding in the creaking wagon with Henna and their belongings, feeling every rut and stone in the road. Lullus proved to be a pleasant enough companion. He had been assigned as steward of the Wimborne estate at the same time that Edwin had been appointed as reeve. He was perhaps a few years older than the bride and bridegroom but had a boyish air. There was something of the monk about him, Molly thought—perhaps the earnest expression on his face. The thing about Lullus that struck Molly most of all was his memory for detail. He would surely be very conscientious in his work. He had little outside knowledge, however, and was uncommunicative about his background. And though he was generally a cheerful person, whenever Molly made a humorous remark he took it seriously and she had to explain herself.

The Bishop, however, was a lively conversationalist. Since he had practically adopted his nephew Edwin as his son, she was regarded as an honorary daughter. She knew that he was a scholar, but to her relief his conversation as they travelled was mainly of current events. Lullus also took a keen enjoyment in hearing the news of the kingdom, so the journey passed quickly.

The travellers stopped at a monastery for the night. The next day dawned bright and crisp, and they continued on their way bubbling with excitement. Lullus was the only one who had seen the royal estate, so Molly tried to get him to talk about it. She found his descriptions at once too detailed and too vague. He had plenty to tell about the production of the farms that belonged to the estate, the number of livestock and slaves, the perquisites in milk, wool, etc. that were owed to each worker at certain times of the year. Molly tried to take it all in, because after all, this was now partly her responsibility. But when she tried to get a straight description of what the estate looked like, Lullus' answer was a confusing exposition on property lines.

As the day wore on, the bright autumn sky began to cloud over. Soon it began to drizzle. The rain continued, sometimes blown about their faces by the wind, as they slowly made their way north-east. In the wagon, Henna got under one of the sheets that was covering their belongings. Sebbi licked the rain off his nose and trotted along gamely behind the wagon until Molly took pity and put him under a sheet as well. They continued to the creak of wagon wheels, the clop of hooves, and the snorts and sneezes of man and beast until Lullus pointed up ahead to a crossroads with a house at the fork. Beyond it were more high-pitched roofs—a settlement of some size. The terrain had flattened out, and off to the east Molly could see that the road led to a river ford.

"Is this Wimborne?" she asked excitedly.

Lullus shook his head. "Blandford. We will ford the Stour here, and then continue south-east for another eight miles or so to the King's hall. But the owner of this house offers shelter and ale to travellers. Let's stop here for a bit—we all need a chance to dry out."

The ale was good, and the mutton stew, which was mostly cabbage and onions with just a hint of mutton, was decently flavoured but exorbitantly priced. They also got brown bread but no cheese; cheese, they were told, was extra. Edwin's uncle, though, being a bishop, was given his food and ale for free and shared his cheese with everyone else. While the men exchanged news with the innkeeper—the same news that the party had chewed over the day before—Molly and Henna huddled drowsily together on a bench near the fire as their clothes dried. Before she knew it, Lullus was shaking her gently by the shoulder and saying, "My lady, time to get back on the road."

They spent the rest of the journey getting their clothes wet again. The horses and oxen seemed to have more spring in their step, however, and seemed not to care that the rain continued intermittently. They did mind fording the cold river, but that was soon accomplished; the horses splashed across quickly, but the oxen had to be prodded and pulled. The water, contrary to Henna's fears, did not reach farther than the axles of the wagon and none of the baggage got doused.

Their path led over flat open land. Lullus told the travellers to look out for the Rings; but none had any idea what these might be, until at length he pointed left through the rain and they saw a stepped hill rising from the land.

"What on earth's that?" asked Edwin's uncle.

"The Badbury Rings, sir," replied Lullus. "A fort built by the folk of long ago. Still big enough to be used in times of trouble."

From the Rings it was only a short distance to a building with crossed dragon gables and overlapping scale-like shingles. It looked finer than a regular hall, but at the same time less like a home. They stopped; the building was the guard-house of the royal Wimborne estate. The guards checked their credentials. "We've been expecting you, my lady," the guard said to Molly. "And Lullus the steward. We had also been expecting Lord Edwin." Molly explained the situation and introduced Edwin's uncle. The guards then escorted them down the path to the main hall.

What awaited them was not what Molly had expected. She had imagined a bustling establishment like her father's but larger and grander. A big hall would be at the centre of it all, golden light gleaming from the windows, smoke curling from the smoke-hole in the roof, neat outbuildings, trim servants, livestock pens and the endless cycle of firewood being chopped and water being hauled from the well.

Instead, against the weakening afternoon light fading westward from the cloudy sky, the hall was a great triangle of blackness. In the gloom it looked like a great dead monster, shaggy with thatch, fallen on its face in the muddy yard. The yard which (in Molly's imagination) should have been teeming with servants chopping wood, fetching water and feeding livestock, was instead deserted. Some distant bleatings and lowings reassured them that the place was not abandoned entirely. But it took some effort by Lullus and the guards to find anyone about to welcome them.

At length they were escorted, not into the hall, but into a dusty but spacious guest house with one large bed and one small one, several chairs, a bench and a table. A brazier had hurriedly been placed in the middle of the room to warm it; its heat had not yet begun to beat back the advancing chill. Lullus and Henna went to the kitchen to fetch food, while Molly and Edwin's uncle sat and waited.

No one knew what to say. Finally, feeling that someone must say something, Molly began, "I'm sorry. I don't know what is going on here, but this is not how I would want to welcome guests—" here her voice got wobbly and she stopped talking.

"I don't know why you should feel embarrassed. This cold reception isn't your fault, my dear," said Edwin's uncle. "The Wimborne people owe an apology to you."

"I still feel responsible somehow."

The light had faded and Molly closed the window. The coals of the brazier cast weird shadows on their faces and the world seemed to close in. There was life and comfort, just a little bit, here in the small circle of light and warmth, but beyond that the world seemed to dissolve into a vast, empty, hostile darkness. An owl screeched suddenly close by—it must have been sitting on the ridge of the roof—and nearly frightened Molly out of her skin.

At long last they heard footsteps and voices, and a knock

on the door. Lullus came in with a tray of ham, barley-cakes and cheese. Henna carried an earthenware pitcher of cider, and a pale, waiflike kitchen-maid followed with cups.

"Where are the other servants?" Molly asked the kitchen-maid after they had eaten. "Surely you are not here all alone?"

The girl almost cringed to be spoken to directly. "No, my lady, not alone—that is—most of the servants live out—but there's a few of us here."

"And why were we not taken into the hall?" Molly tried to make her voice sound kind and encouraging, but it was difficult to keep the note of insistence out of her voice; she was tired and really wanted to know.

"It's *disused*, my lady," replied the girl, as if this explained everything. This was the only reason she had been given, someone else's word for her to repeat.

"Doesn't anyone live there?" Molly persisted.

"Most servants live out." The kitchen-maid, alarmed at this prolonged interrogation, wrung her apron in anxiety. "Two grooms live in the barn yonder," she nodded her little pointed chin vaguely into the distance. "Gardener lives out. Brewer lives out. Cook lives out. I sleep in the kitchen. Housekeeper don't come no more."

"Why not?"

"She's ill, my lady." This was said with a sort of hopeless finality, as if there were only one person in the world who could set the royal hall at Wimborne to rights, and if she were ill, that was an end to the question.

"Very well," said Molly. "We'll look into that tomorrow. What's your name?"

"Bunny, my lady."

"Well, Bunny, please tell the cook that I will be ready to inspect the stores and receive the keys tomorrow after breakfast."

"Yes, my lady," replied Bunny doubtfully, taking the tray and departing. Lullus took his lantern and walked her back to the kitchen. He stopped by once again to ask if they needed anything else before retiring, with the Bishop and Molly's father's men, to another guest-house. Henna, exhausted from the journey and its jarring effect on her old bones, was sent directly to her bed in the corner. But even with the comforting sound of her old nurse's snores to soothe her, Molly had never felt so alone in her entire life.

Chapter 7

Weary, lonely and overwhelmed, Molly managed to cry herself to sleep that first night at Wimborne. She was glad Henna could sleep so soundly and leave her to her tears. Sympathy would only make her depressed; all she needed, she felt, was a good night's rest and everything would be right again.

When she awoke the next morning, she had a moment of panic waking to unfamiliar surroundings. Then the preceding day came back to her in a rush. At least the sleep had fortified her. The whirlwind of faces, places, sounds, and smells began to take their places once again in her mind.

Henna had opened the window and started a fire in the brazier. Today, sunlight streamed in and lit up the gloomy space. She looked around at the reeve's quarters where she and Edwin were to begin their married life. The bedstead, Henna's narrow bed in the corner, and the chests full of Molly's and Edwin's belongings were the only objects of note in the room apart from a table and bench. Edwin, Molly reflected, had gone from the austerity of the religious life to the austerity of the warrior's life in the field, and he would probably see nothing lacking in this bare little place. It would be up to her to bring an air of liveliness and comfort to their quarters.

Molly set about getting dressed. No one had made an effort to set up breakfast in the great hall. The Bishop came early to take his leave, and Molly gave him the remaining basket of food she had brought from home. For their own breakfast, Henna was supposed to go and get a tray from the kitchen again.

"That's going to be rather inconvenient in winter," remarked Molly, recalling that the reeve's quarters were at the opposite end of the compound from the kitchen. "I'll just add that to all the other things to confer with Lullus about today."

When Lullus arrived, Molly had just finished breakfast—or more precisely, she had stopped eating. Though usually blessed with a good appetite and never picky, Molly could not manage to finish the bread and butter on her tray. It wasn't just that the butter was quite rancid. The bread itself, though fairly fresh, had a musty taste to it and there had been some dark specks in it that Molly hoped were seeds. She had not been raised to throw away good bread and butter, but she simply couldn't manage more than a few bites. Henna fussed about her lack of appetite and letting food go to waste, but did not seem inclined to finish the bread her mistress had left on the tray.

Lullus' proposal to continue the tour of the estate was therefore very welcome. Molly dismissed Henna to go feed the unwanted bread to the chickens, and she and the steward proceeded to the disused great hall. Molly realized she was bursting with curiosity.

Lullus unbolted the great doors and led Molly in. It was difficult to see anything in the darkness until her eyes adjusted. A single column of light shone down from the smoke-hole in the middle of the roof. Lullus had left her with the candle and gone ahead inside, briskly proceeding from one window to the next opening the shutters. Shafts of light crisscrossed the darkness now, highlighting swirling particles of dust and defining the dark shapes of the furniture. Lullus' enormous leather shoes made a scuffing sound on the floor. The hall was long and wide, with a lofty ceiling and high-pitched roof: truly a hall of kingly proportions. It had been built by skilled carpenters and beautifully appointed with carved and painted details throughout. But the once-splendid hall was now a sad example of decay and neglect.

"Well, my lady," he said airily, "I suppose the King has left us enough to do in Lord Edwin's absence!"

Molly could not but agree. Looking around, her eye went from the wide, dark sooty stain on the ceiling above the hearth, down to the evenly spattered lines of bird droppings on the floor underneath every rafter. The floor was the least of their worries; but as for the soot, the entire thatch would probably have to be replaced.

As if reading her thoughts, Lullus anxiously remarked, "The hall itself is quite sound. No rot or anything of that sort. It's just not been used and kept up. I don't suppose it's seen much life since King Aethelbert's funeral." Lullus seemed unconscious of the irony. "The servants say that there hasn't been enough time or manpower to give the hall a good clean in a long time."

"Where in the world are we supposed to find staff?" Molly asked. "Getting this place back in shape will take more work than a housekeeper and a couple of maids could handle."

"Now that harvest is just about over," Lullus continued, "we can get some of the young folk from the farms to come in and get to work on these cobwebs and, er—stains," he said, motioning to the rafters.

Walking the length of the hall, Molly had been feeling of

the benches and peeking in the chests. None of the furniture seemed to wobble, but the yellowed tablecloths would have to be taken out and re-laundered before the household received any important visits. She opened a cupboard in one corner to be greeted by a flurry of moths. To her horror, she found that the cupboard contained embroidered hangings lying in a heap, and the moths had evidently been feasting on the coloured wool. Picking up one end, she pulled out a piece of the hanging. It was about five feet wide and very long. Lullus came over to investigate and began to help her disentangle it.

Only a few days before, Molly had helped her mother unpack and iron their own family's wall-hangings. They only came out on special occasions, and Molly had always thought it a shame that they spent most of their time at the bottom of a chest.

"No sense in leaving them out all year round. They'd only get sooty," her mother had replied. Molly had always been captivated by the rich colours, the figures of heroes and horses and fantastical designs, embroidered by her grandmother and great-grandmother years ago. But her mother valued them for a different reason: when the wall-hangings had been put in place around the walls of the hall, it was remarkable how they stifled noise. "The guests can make as much of a din as they like now," she had observed with satisfaction, "And I won't get a headache."

Molly looked up and saw Lullus studying the hem of the fabric. "I suppose these loops along the top edge would correspond to those little pegs at intervals up where the ceiling meets the wall," he said, sticking a finger through one of them.

They then proceeded to hang the loops on the pegs. Lullus was tall enough to reach the pegs, and Molly held the bundle of wall-hanging and fed him lengths of it as he progressed.

When they were finished, they saw that the linen backing was badly creased, but the woollen embroidery was still wonderfully vivid and unfaded. The moth damage only occurred in spots where the crumpled folds had been uppermost in the cupboard. Molly had great hopes that the other lengths, which had lain under this one, had escaped harm. She had a sudden vision of a royal hall alive with feasting, gleaming with candles, with beautiful hangings running the length of the walls, providing a bright backdrop for benches full of illustrious guests.

Looking again at the ruined wool stitching before her, she squared her shoulders and said, "I suppose I know now what Henna and I will be doing on the long winter evenings."

The bright colours of the embroidery were a sad contrast with the worn and chipping paint of the decorated wood columns and edging in the hall. Following the lines of carving with her eyes and fingers, Molly asked, "Are there any good painters in this area?"

"I don't know any by name, but there must be," Lullus said thoughtfully.

"We must get this decoration retouched," Molly explained. "Nothing so shabby as chipped paint in the King's hall!" *That is, besides a sooty ceiling, dusty benches, cobwebs in the rafters, and moth-eaten embroideries*, she thought ruefully. "And about these soot stains…," she said.

They discussed the possibility and priority of replacing the thatch as they folded all the tapestries neatly. Lullus then carried them for Molly to a tightly constructed chest which would keep them safe from further attack.

"What does this lead to?" asked Molly, walking to a large door with decorative forged hinges at one end of the hall.

"Oh! That's the royal quarters. Let me see if I have the key," Lullus began sorting through the keys on his ring. "Yes, here it is." He unlocked the door and lifted the latch. Molly cringed as the long-unopened hinges shrieked in protest.

Inside the door was only blackness. Molly peered in doubtfully. "Is there a window?" she asked.

"No," replied Lullus.

"Oh, security, of course." Molly found a candle and in a moment had it lit. Then, with some hesitation, she entered the royal bedchamber.

"Good gracious! This is worse than the hall!" she exclaimed, holding up the light to look around at the room. Dust and cobwebs covered every surface. The bare straw ticking on the bedstead showed several holes where it had been gnawed open to provide beds for many little sleepers. The woollen bedspread—once a showpiece of some noble lady's accomplishment in weaving and embroidery—was riddled with moth-holes. Only one square corner, the bottommost fold, was unscathed; but what good was a bedspread with only one usable corner? Molly picked up the folded coverlet. Perhaps some of it could be salvaged to repair the wall-hangings? The rest was fit only to be thrown away. In the corner there was a little loft for baggage and space for a servant to sleep. A dead bat lay on the steps up to this loft, as if guarding the way.

Lullus, who with Molly had been surveying the scene, suddenly began to sneeze. His sneezes were as large as the rest of him, and came out with such force that they stirred up still more dust. Molly began to sneeze as well, and without a word they both turned and fled the dreary place.

Chapter 8

"And this," Lullus said with a flourish as he opened the door, "is the kitchen." He had already shown Molly the stable-yard, smithy, henhouses, beehives, pig-sty, and storage barns. The gardener took her on a tour of his vegetable patch; he was particularly proud of his leeks, which grew row upon row, as straight as spears and spaced like well-trained warriors. There were onions, cabbages, and winter carrots as well.

Lullus took his opportunity to extricate her once the gardener moved on to turnips. Molly had waded through the mud, taking steps as large as she could to keep up with Lullus' long strides. By this time the cold rain had begun to penetrate her woollen cloak and hood. She had secret hopes that the kitchen would yield some sort of warming drink or snack.

But there was no one there. As she looked around, she could see the large stone bake-oven in the corner, and shelves of wooden trays and bowls. Some earthenware jugs were set higgledy-piggledy in a corner. Rows of crockery jars on a shelf contained herbs and seasonings. Next to the door was a bucket of questionable-looking water, and beside it another bucket of greasy rags. A partridge and a pheasant were lying on a table ready to be plucked; next to them was a bowl of flour and a baking dish. Molly's imagination immediately suggested the idea that this might be her evening meal, a steaming partridge and pheasant pie with golden crust and succulent filling. At least that was a promising prospect. There was a large hearth surrounded by blackened stones. Suspended over it was what had once been an elegant old wrought-iron cauldron chain, now charred and rusty. The cauldron itself sat on the sand next to the hearth, empty. The hearth-fire had nearly gone out. Perhaps at last feeling the chill, Lullus puffed at it with the bellows. The ash blew aside revealing a few lingering red coals underneath.

At once they heard a splash outside, as if someone had flung liquid from a bucket. Then they heard a shrill voice calling, "Get back to the kitchen, Bunny, and get to work," followed by irritable mumblings and mutterings. The source of the shrill voice proved to be an old woman in a cook's apron, who called at the top of her lungs from the door, "And bring another armful of wood while you're about it!" She then stopped short as she noticed her two visitors.

Lullus greeted her. "This, Lady Molgifu, is Eng, the cook," he said. Eng set down her bucket and bowed, and her hard mouth twisted into a simper. Molly felt the woman's sharp eyes scrutinizing her.

"There's also a cook's boy called Cnapa somewhere about."

Just then the little kitchen-maid, looking even more sickly and pale than she had the evening before, came in with two armfuls of damp firewood. She tripped on the bucket Eng had left and her armful of wood scattered everywhere. Eng turned around and began to unleash a string of curses before checking herself.

"And the wood's wet and all," she finished, in a tone of disgust. "Can't get decent help these days," she turned back to Lullus, with a wistful and self-pitying whine.

Bunny recovered herself and began collecting up the wood as unobtrusively as she knew how.

"I was wondering if you might give us a tour of the stores," prompted Lullus. "Lady Molgifu will need to take stock and receive the keys."

"As you wish," said Eng, torn evidently between the desire to appear obliging and the desire to express her resentment at having to relinquish a privilege she never had any right to claim. She waved a grubby hand at a door behind them, and preceded them into the storage room with a jingle of keys. Here Molly was shown locked chests of flour and meal, the salt store, the butter barrel, the honey crock, bins of onions and garlic, hams and cheeses hanging from the rafters along with some salt beef, bacon and mutton, and the half-cellar where the root vegetables were stored. It is difficult to take stock of supplies when you have no basis of comparison. Molly felt quite self-conscious with Lullus watching expectantly and Eng regarding her as an interloper as she examined all the foodstuffs. It did not help that Molly found mouse droppings in the flour right off. *That explains this morning's bread*, she thought, and felt a little sick.

Salt was low; honey was low; the cheeses and hams looked fresh and wholesome; the salt beef and three flitches of smoked bacon had just been delivered. The onions and garlic hung in heavy braids from the rafters, but the carrots and turnips in the root cellar were few and shrivelled.

"The famine," Eng shrugged. At least there seemed an endless supply of dried beans and peas.

Molly was shown the brewing shed adjacent to the kitchen. One vat of ale was still brewing, while someone had been engaged recently in filling casks from another with the finished product. However, the overwhelming aroma that greeted Molly on entering was that of apples being fermented into cider. A wizened little man was running here and there making various adjustments and arrangements as his helper, a younger man, operated the apple press. When he looked up and saw Molly and Lullus, he promptly wiped his hands on his apron and hurried over. Again, Lullus made the introductions.

"Beorelf, this is Lady Molgifu, Lord Edwin's new bride. Lady Molgifu, this is Beorelf, our brewer."

Molly looked at the beaming face of the little man. It seemed all of a piece with the work she had found him engaged in: his cheeks were as round and red as apples. His eyes twinkled out from under very bushy eyebrows. At the mention of the recent marriage his eyebrows went not up, but sideways, and his face broke into a friendly smile.

"May I make bold to wish you joy," he said. "And there is my son Beorcol, at the apple-press." Beorcol doffed his cap, then carried on with his work.

"We've got some glorious apples this year," Beorelf said, his eyes taking on a faraway gleam. "Best cider in a decade, it'll be."

He showed her the cider-making equipment and the bushels of apples still awaiting their ennoblement. Here, thought Molly, is a good old-fashioned Saxon craftsman, in love with his craft. Beorelf was only too glad to have an audience for his favourite subject and continued chattering. Molly, however, began to look curiously around the shed. Beorelf's innate sense of order had provided a rack for the drinking horns and shelves for cups. There were not even as many cups on the shelf as Molly's family possessed, and the horns arranged neatly on the rack looked worn and in need of replacement. Beorelf followed her gaze, seizing on a new point of departure.

"Yes, my lady, you see what a sad state our cups and horns are in. It's all very well me brewing up the ale and the cider, but if we don't even have vessels enough to drink it from …."

He showed her that some of the horns were deeply cracked and would leak if used. Molly began to hand the unusable horns to Eng, who had to open her apron to take the load.

"Take those to the refuse pit, Eng," said Molly. "We shall have to order up some new horns."

"That should not be difficult," said Lullus. "I'll put the word out."

"Is there any wine here?" asked Molly, looking around the shed. "Not that I foresee any need for it at present, but it may be as well to get a few casks in to have on hand."

"We get that from the wine-merchants, usually," said Beorelf. "We don't make it ourselves. But at the moment we only have one little cask there in the corner" (he motioned with his hand) "and that we keep around for medicinal use."

"Oh yes?" smiled Molly.

"But as no one has been ill and needed it, it's still full," Beorelf continued gravely. "Our usual procedure in the absence of wine-merchants is to send up to the monast'ry, and they can sell us a few of their casks. If you wish I can do that, my lady."

"Yes, do," said Molly, conferring with Lullus about arranging for payment. "Best to order a half-dozen at once, if we can get them. I suppose it will keep here just as well as at the monastery until it is needed."

At the end of this voyage of discovery, they returned to the kitchen. Lullus reminded Eng that it was time to hand over the keys. Eng began to fidget with her belt. The keys were tied to her belt by a greasy bit of black string which she found impossible to untie.

"I'll keep them safe for you, my lady," she said. "No need

for you to worry about keys. Whenever you need anything unlocked, just ask, and I'll unlock it for you."

"I don't think you understand," said Molly, surprised. "The keys are now my responsibility. The stores will remain unlocked during the day for cooking, but it's my duty to see to the security of all our supplies."

"You mean you don't trust me?" Eng's voice quavered.

Less and less, thought Molly, but she said, "It's not a question of whether I trust you. The King trusts me, and it's my duty to keep the keys to his stores now that I am here."

"If that's how it's going to be," said Eng, and with a slight bow, she turned to leave.

"Eng, the keys!" exclaimed Molly. Eng turned to face her new mistress, ill-disguised fury in her glinting little eyes. "And one more thing. You are not to leave until dismissed." Over Eng's indignant protests, Molly finally took out her knife and cut the string. The pleasure she had anticipated in putting them in her belt-bag was allayed by the fact that the keys themselves were sticky and grimy from long contact with their previous keeper.

"All right. Go about your duties, please," Molly felt she could not send the cook away fast enough.

She went to find some vinegar to clean off the keys. As she passed the kitchen worktable, she saw that the pheasant and partridge were gone. Molly took this as a silent declaration of war.

Chapter 9

The rain had subsided during the night, leaving behind dense banks of mist and muddy roads. As they set out, Edwin was conscious of a murmuring among Edmund's men that stopped abruptly if he happened to turn around. Again he felt the anger rise within him as he thought of Maca and Aeddi. He had been avoiding riding abreast of his brother because he felt that his critical comments would be worse than all.

But try as he might to keep Stig at a sedate medium gait, eventually they ended up side by side. Silence reigned for some time; then, true to his nature, Edmund had to say something.

"Rough night, little brother," he said, rather than asked.

Edwin answered with a grunt.

"By the time we're back, they'll have tried and hanged the fool and forgotten all about it," he said in what passed for a soothing tone.

Edwin tried to keep his eyes and concentration on the scenery. Despite the mist, the russet golds and reds and browns of the trees in their autumn garb seemed to glow; with a different atmosphere and quality of light the colours themselves seemed changed. Some people complained that such overcast days were gloomy; but they had a timeless feeling that gave Edwin a secret delight.

In the distance he could hear three or four of the men who had less poetry in their souls disputing on the respective values of Mercian and West Saxon pennies. No man seemed to know, but they all agreed that what they had to watch out for was the false coins from the Danish territories, which were underweight.

They travelled light, so they made good time on the road north. Following the Roman road to Buckingham, they met a merchant at Oxford who had chanced to travel part of the way south from Warwick with one of the great lords attending the council.

"Which lord?" asked Edmund brusquely.

"Wulfsige."

"Lord Wulfsige, who is he?" Edmund turned to Osgar.

Osgar replied, speaking with a smile to the merchant, "He is a kinsman of St Wigstan, and therefore in one of the royal lines of Mercia."

"Are you Mercian yourself?" Edwin asked the man. He had been trying to place the merchant's speech, which seemed to incline in different directions with every phrase.

"Sort of. Well, you know how it is—a Mercian merchant meets a West Saxon girl—they marry, settle on the frontier, have a son, and their son never knows what to say when someone asks," the man replied. Edwin nodded appreciatively.

Edmund ploughed forward, "Did this Lord Wulfsige say anything more about the council? Is King Ceolwulf there already?"

The man shook his head. "I know the king was in a big battle up on the Welsh borders a few weeks ago. The word is he was wounded. I suppose if all the great men of Mercia are at this council he will be right in the middle of it; he's no keener than anybody else to have the Danes back on our side of the border. But Lord Wulfsige's people said nothing of it." The merchant grinned. "I wasn't exactly riding bridle to bridle with Lord Wulfsige. I did see him up at the head of the company, all glittering in his finery, rings on his hands and gold and silver on his weapons, looking fit to be a king himself. I drove my cart at the back behind his baggage wagon. I mainly talked to his falconer, who was riding in the wagon with his hawks in cages and so forth. He sat on the back of the wagon and talked to me, then the wagon driver would come swap places with him, so it was those two I got my news from." He cocked his head on one side like a bird and said slowly, "You haven't run across any Danes in your travels, I suppose?"

"Danes?" The men of Wessex echoed in feigned surprise. "No, we haven't. Why?"

"They say that a renegade band of Danes split off from Guthrum after Cirencester. A chieftain called Orm—they say he headed north, greedy for plunder."

Edwin wanted to know how far north he had been traced. At the same time, Edmund was asking how many men Orm had with him. Their informant looked from one brother to the other and confessed that he did not have a sure answer for either. "At least twoscore men he had with him, they say, mounted on such ponies as they could steal from the country round about. But as to where they went, no one knows and no one's seen them since they turned north. It's thought they took Foss Way up to Nottingham or even York, but that's just speculation."

"Let's hope it's not wishful thinking." Edmund's voice was grim. "Well, thank you." Soon the merchant's way diverged from theirs: he went southwest while they pressed on to the northeast.

As they rode deeper into Mercia, Edwin realized that they had not seen a ruined cottage for miles. The sight of desolation had become so commonplace to them that a peaceful land had a look of almost eerie tidiness. The faces of the Mercian farmers looked rosy and content—a change from the lean faces and hollow-eyed stares of the war-torn population in the south. Edwin was struck by a pang of pity for his homeland. After all the harrying, burning, and occupation of the Vikings, he had almost come to expect the scars of ruin in every landscape: ruined houses, a timber church with its door hanging loose on one hinge, graves in little churchyards that were not yet covered with grass. One settlement might be spared; another, strategically located, might have been occupied, all its provisions eaten and its livestock taken by the raiders. Still another, suspected of harbouring resistance, might have been burned to the ground and its inhabitants slain or taken as slaves. Having lived through a year and more of such fears and realities, West Saxon faces had an uneasy look, as if to say, 'we survived—but will they be back? We are still alive—but will we eat this winter?' And beneath all, there was an enmity between those who had resisted the Danes and those who, for motives of survival or greed, had abetted the occupying heathen army. The peace of the Mercian countryside left Edwin feeling unsettled.

◆

They approached Buckingham from the west, where the Roman way intersected with a well-travelled road leading through the small settlement of Tingewick. Here they stopped to confer about what to do. It was soon decided that Osgar should ride ahead with Edmund's standard-bearer and the King's tokens. Alfred's standard and Edmund's flapped side by side in the breeze as the two emissaries rode off at a canter. The waiting afforded the rest of the party a chance to dismount. The horses were unbridled and set to graze along the roadside. Bread appeared from saddle-bags everywhere and men sat in little groups to talk and eat.

At length Osgar and his companion returned with assurances that the West Saxon contingent would be welcome at the hall of Aethelwulf, a distant relative of Alfred's wife, who was the lord of Buckingham.

Edmund, Edwin and Osgar rode at the head of the company. There was a sturdy timber bridge over the river Ouse and they crossed it two and two, hooves clattering on the planks. Then they were in Buckingham, which was situated in a bend in the river. Houses and workshops clustered around the river's banks, and there was a wide expanse of grassy common land where sheep grazed. From here the path led up to higher ground where the hall of Lord Aethelwulf stood overlooking the surrounding area.

Aethelwulf's hall was large and long, and the number of outbuildings surrounding it, like slaves around a great lord, reinforced the air of importance it held in the landscape. Just beyond, like a faithful retainer hovering at his lord's elbow, stood the monastery. The hall was surrounded by a sturdily-built wood palisade with a wide double gate and watchtower. A guard spotted their standard from a distance and blew a horn, and the gates were opened.

Passing through the gate, they saw a well-dressed figure approaching, surrounded by servants and about a half-dozen dogs of all shapes and sizes.

"Welcome, men of Wessex!" said their host. "I am Aethelwulf, lord of Buckingham." Lord Aethelwulf was a broad-shouldered, handsome man a little past middle age; his curly hair was greying at the temples, and his beard was streaked, badger-like, with silver.

"Apparently something of a local potentate," Edmund observed under his breath.

Osgar took the role of introducing their party. With less ceremony, the dogs trotted round and got acquainted with Fram. The top dog in Buckingham was a saucy little creature with a curling tail and pricked ears, and his second-in-command was a lanky fellow of Fram's size and build. Aethelwulf called the pack to heel and sent them away with a servant clad in a sheepskin jacket. "You must forgive a childless man for choosing such hearth-companions," he smiled after the wagging tails, with the complacent air of one who feels no need for forgiveness. Calling his steward, Lord Aethelwulf instructed him to make their foreign guests comfortable in one of the guest houses. They were to dine that night in company with the entire council, for all had now arrived.

Aethelwulf's hall was imposing in appearance, with large, heavy timbering. Carved monster-heads in bright colours grinned from the ends of the roof-beams. This hall was built on the modern plan with an upper story over part of its length and a set of stairs coming down the outside wall.

Edwin, Edmund and Osgar were allocated one of the guest houses. Owing to the large numbers of guests and servants, most of Edmund's and Osgar's men had to pitch tents along the outer wall, but the Mercians did their best to make them comfortable in every way.

The guest house was a simple rectangular building with a single room. It had a window, a smoke-hole and a brazier, one big bed and one narrow. Edwin, being the youngest, willingly took the small bed. By now he was familiar enough with

Osgar's snores and Edmund's sprawling to have no desire to share a bed, however warm, with either, if he could choose a cold bed without them.

"I wonder that Lord Aethelwulf did not make place for us in his hall," grumbled Edmund, throwing his satchel of gear down on the bed.

"It's not surprising to me," said Edwin. "Did you see how many people were already here?"

"He also has to make room for his nephew, Ealdorman Aethelred, who has come from Gloucester with two or three dozen men," said Osgar.

"Yes, I suppose you're right," Edmund paused with one boot in his hand. "I think there is another ealdorman here as well, and he brought his lady and whole train of womenfolk."

Osgar stretched out on his half of the bed and fluffed a pillow under his head. "Well, you fellows know that I love a crowd. The more the merrier, say I. But this way we can keep our own counsel without being overheard on all sides."

They soon found that even the kingly proportions of Aethelwulf's hall were not large enough to contain all the worthies that had flocked to the meeting. When they had had a chance to get familiar with their surroundings, they found that there were almost as many guests at the monastery as at the hall; at least one important nobleman with his household, as well as two bishops, neither of whom would have come unattended.

At dinner, the style and scale of entertaining offered by this kinsman of Alfred's wife spoke well of Mercia. Edmund, Edwin and Osgar were seated at the high table along with their host and his nephew Ealdorman Aethelred. The latter's industrious steward, like an older shadow of his young master, came twice during the meal and hovered over Aethelred's shoulder on some errand of business. On the other side of Aethelwulf was Ealdorman Beornoth, a man in his late forties with a receding chin and a paunch.

The roasted fowl, the bread and butter, the legs of mutton, the ham, the stewed leeks and the sweet-meats had all had their moment of glory, and wine and ale had flowed in seemingly limitless abundance. As they ate, Edwin let his eyes wander around the hall. Lord Aethelwulf was certainly not stingy in the matter of candles, and by their light Edwin saw weapons and other paraphernalia arranged on the walls as decoration. Behind the high seat was a row of shields hung alternately with standing spears. Along the other walls there were two short embroidered wall-hangings depicting some scenes with which Edwin was unfamiliar, and, at the other side, more shields. There were two upright posts set in the floor that had held the warp-beam of a loom; these appeared to be long neglected, and Edwin wondered if there had ever been a lady of the house.

Certainly not for some time—to judge by the way Ealdorman Beornoth's wife had taken over the duties of hostess. She was much younger than her husband, with a pert and knowing expression on her pretty face. She and her maids flirted with all the lords as they refilled drinking horns. Edwin saw the lady approach Lord Aethelwulf with a pitcher of ale and close her hand around his as he held up his horn to her. The look they exchanged was unmistakable. Edwin's glance darted to Beornoth, but he was looking down, dabbing with his napkin at a stain down the front of his tunic. Even his own brother Edmund seemed unable to resist flirting with the maid serving his drink. Down by the lower tables, Aethelwulf's housekeeper turned to refill her serving-jug. As she did so she levelled a venomous look at the fine lady that had usurped her ceremonial role, relegating her to quenching the inexhaustible thirst of the visiting men-at-arms.

Dinner conversation at the lower tables revolved around wenches, weapons, ale, and gripes about the latrine. At the high table the men were taken up with the two absorbing topics of the moment: the departure of Guthrum and the death of King Ceolwulf in battle with the Welsh. Edwin and Edmund exchanged glances. Had the physician told his tale to the Mercian lords? How did the king really meet his fate? Edmund pressed for a blow-by-blow account of the battle and the Mercian king's death.

All the Mercians at the high table, it turned out, had been in the battle. Ealdorman Aethelred, who was only eighteen, described the progress of the battle with enthusiasm; after all, he had come away unscathed and his side had won. The chief casualty of the battle opened the kingship to the ealdormen of the several competing royal families, all of which were represented at the Buckingham council. Now that Ceolwulf was dead, this council that had gathered to confer on what to do about the Danes had become a council to elect a new king for the Mercian people.

"And King Ceolwulf?" Edmund persisted. "Was he slain on the battlefield?"

"No," said Lord Aethelwulf. "He was wounded in the chest and leg, and died of his wounds a few days later. Ealdorman Beornoth could tell you more," he said. "He attended the king in his final hours. I started back here when news reached us that Guthrum was on the move."

All eyes turned to Ealdorman Beornoth. Beornoth made a strange sound in his throat and the flickering light of a table candle caught beads of sweat starting on his forehead. "Yes," he said hoarsely, "I—er, I did attend the king in his final hours.

His wounds were grievous." Then he directed his attention resolutely to his drinking-horn, and would say no more.

"The loss is still fresh," said Aethelwulf apologetically. "Beornoth was closest to the king these past few years."

The conversation flagged for a while after this. By the time they arrived at the poached pears and cream, however, Aethelwulf had hit upon another topic, his plans for developing his estate.

"I am going to build some larger barns on the east side of the river," he said, "and I am going to put in a mill which should prove very profitable. Did you know I could make as much in a year running a mill as I make on all my farms put together?"

"A mill?" his nephew interjected. "Have you found a spot, then?"

"Right there at the south bend in the river," Aethelwulf replied.

"Oh, uncle, not that old plan. Are you still harping on that little spot? You'll never be able to buy it!"

"Nonsense. Everyone has a price; if I keep at it, eventually I shall get my way."

Throughout the feast Edwin, Edmund and Osgar were treated with assiduous (or, Edwin felt, officious) courtesy: the best cuts of meat, and wine from the host's own casks. Osgar actually preferred wine, but when Aethelred called for a horn of his uncle's ale instead, Edwin and Edmund felt free to do so as well. Beornoth seemed to answer Aethelwulf's every wish as a commentator on the food. He traced the progress of every joint roasting over the fire before them; he dabbed his bread in the stewed leeks to absorb every drop of sauce. Osgar entered into their conversation, but sometimes tried to involve himself in what was going on at the other end of the table where Ealdorman Aethelred held sway. Though seated next to his uncle he largely ignored him when the talk turned to the delights of the table. He seemed glad to have found an attentive audience for his plans to restore Mercia's reputation for culture and trade. He questioned Osgar and the others about conditions in Wessex, the king and his family, and the aftermath of the recent Viking invasions. Edmund was close to poking Osgar in the ribs or stepping on his toe a few times when his elder colleague seemed about to be too chatty about troop numbers or the king's provisional locations for his plan of defensive forts.

"My dear Edmund," said Osgar later when they were in private. "Even under the influence of our host's excellent wine, I would reveal nothing to our Mercian friends that they could not find out for themselves."

"Don't you think you are overestimating the goodwill in this place? Or underestimating our need to keep our bargaining position strong?"

"No, I don't think so," said Osgar in measured tones, so different from his expansive manner at table. "In order to get a little information it is sometimes necessary to give a little. I wanted to know where Aethelred stood with regard to London. Did you not notice me drawing him out on that subject?"

"Yes, and I daresay even Aethelwulf and Beornoth took the trouble to listen then," Edmund conceded.

Chapter 10

Molly was standing next to an open window, spindle in hand, wishing there was some pressing matter to take her away from the enormous pile of wool which Henna had helpfully combed and laid ready for her, when Lullus entered with one of the guardsmen.

"My lady, there is a problem in the guardhouse," Lullus began.

Guardhouse? Be careful what you wish for, Molly thought to herself. For all its monotony, at least spinning was something she knew how to handle. She laid her spindle on top of the wool and invited the young guardsman to speak.

"My lady," said the guardsman, his forehead puckered in worry, "When Lullus went to meet Lord Edwin for the wedding, he took two of our number with him. One of them was our leader. He set another of us over the rest until he got back."

"Well?"

"This fellow, our provisional leader, is down with a fever, and my lord isn't back yet with our regular leader, and the fellows are starting to disagree about who should be in charge."

Molly went with Lullus and the young guardsman to the guardhouse, the dragon-gabled timber building next to the

Roman road which they had passed when they first arrived at the King's estate. The guardhouse had a tower next to it which rose just above the level of the treetops to give a commanding view of the countryside, southeast down to the Minster as well as northwest toward the Rings.

The house was sparsely furnished with long benches along the walls that also served as bunks. There was an iron brazier instead of a hearth; shields and spears of the battered but serviceable variety hung on the walls. Across one end of the structure, where a civilian house would have sleeping quarters, was the jail cell, its identity announced by the heavy bolted door.

Molly enquired as to the usual routine. She was completely unprepared for such a question as she was faced with and unfamiliar with the management of a guardhouse. Her father's household was never conducted on such a scale as this. If only she could ask his advice!

But she could not. Any knowledge she could garner would perhaps help in her decision, and would in any case buy her a little time. It seemed there were eight guards in all, including the two that went with Lord Edwin and the one that was at home with the fever. Four were on duty at any given time. The leader managed the rotation, trained the men, gave orders for patrols and served as the contact with the King's hall. Reserves could be called upon when needed.

Molly looked at the faces of the five guardsmen, whose eyes were all trained on her. They were sitting meekly enough on their benches waiting for her decision. What in the world could she do? How was she to choose a new leader from this group of men? Would they really abide by the decision of one who knew as little about them as anyone possibly could?

She found that two of the men were the most senior, and

it was between these two that the disputes had begun to arise.

She asked them both to stand up, and they did so. One was tall and lean, with a handsome and boyish appearance; he gave Molly a little wink. The other man was heavyset and bald. He had sharp eyes, but the crow's-feet that lined his face gave it a friendly look. First Molly asked them some questions about their duties, which both answered satisfactorily. Both seemed to have reasonably good eyesight and handled a spear and shield well. When she had run out of things to ask and felt at a complete loss, Molly remembered an anecdote her father had told many years before. As a young man he had seen a lord inspect his retainers, and found that one had failed to polish the back of his belt buckle. "It doesn't show," had been the hapless retainer's excuse. "Do you wipe your arse after you go to the latrine?" the lord had growled. When the retainer answered in the affirmative, his master said, "Why? It doesn't show!"

Molly was not about to ask these men to show her the backs of their belt buckles. But surely it would not be out of place to inspect their personal gear? She asked them to present their seaxes for inspection. The bald guardsman pulled his out of the sheath and offered Molly the handle. She took it to the doorway and looked closely at the blade and handle in the daylight. The blade was clean and bright with no grime in the crevices, and it was sharp. She handed it back to the guardsman with a nod. The tall guardsman pulled his seax with a flourish and held it out before Molly. Again she took the knife to the doorway for a closer look. Though similar in craftsmanship and value to the other seax, this one was less carefully kept. She saw sticky matter and crumbs in the place where the bone handle joined the iron blade. The blade was sharp at the point, but the rest of the cutting edge alternated sharp and dull. There was even a trace of rust near the handle.

"Thank you," said Molly, returning the man's seax. "You are both skilful and knowledgeable guardsmen who can serve the King's estate with honour. Today I choose you," said Molly, motioning to the bald man, "to take the place of your leader in his absence. Take as good care of your men as you have of your weapon, and you will be able to make a good report on my lord's return."

◆

In Winchester, the King's steward knocked on the door to his daytime apartment. Alfred was sitting with his advisors at a large table, numerous maps and charters spread before him. "Yes?" he said, raising his head.

"Sir," said the man. "It's about the killing that took place the other night. The one Wimborne man killing the other. A man-at-arms has come forward, saying he has evidence about the prisoner."

"What is this evidence?" asked the King. "Let's hear him."

The man-at-arms was ushered in. He was a tall, burly young man who looked equal to the task of keeping order in a jail. Nevertheless, he stood sheepishly, awed by the company in which he found himself.

"My steward tells me you have evidence about the killing?" the King asked.

"My lord the King, yes, sir, I do. I was the one standing guard over the prisoner all last night, sir. And this prisoner, he had a bad night of it. Tossing and turning on the straw, like. Then he starts to moaning, and then he says a few words. He says, 'Can't stop me. Got to do it now. Aetheling,' or something like that."

Alfred looked at him narrowly. "'Or something like that'? How close are your words to those the man actually uttered?"

The man exhaled and was silent for a moment, staring at nothing in particular as he considered the question. Then he raised his head and met the King's eye. "As close as may be, I am sure of it. I remember the first words; they was very distinct. The last word was less clear, but it sounded like 'aetheling'."

"Thank you," said the King. "You may be called at the prisoner's trial."

At this both the man-at-arms and the steward left the room. Silence reigned for a few moments. Finally a retainer said, "That doesn't sound like an ale-quarrel to me." This remark met with general agreement.

Another man spoke up. "This mention of an aetheling, a prince. You don't suppose he could have been after young Prince Edward?"

"Could he have known that the child would be here at court?"

"There is no way the man could even have known he would be coming to Winchester," said the King. "If you remember, as far as he or anyone knew at the time, he was merely attending a wedding-feast for a few days."

"So this was a crime of opportunity?" asked one advisor.

"Obviously. And this fellow Maca tried to stop him, it appears."

Another man spoke up. "But where does this mention of the prince come in, then?"

"The witness said he wasn't *quite* sure the man said 'aetheling.'"

"But he was intent on murder—that much is proven by the event."

"And the mention of having to do 'it'—whatever 'it' was—

'now'—that suggests that he was seizing the chance at some sort of assassination."

Alfred's advisors exchanged glances. A retainer addressed Alfred: "Are you thinking what we're thinking?"

"I expect so," said the King. "Whether it is part of a wider plot I am not sure, but I suspect the guard probably did hear the prisoner speak of an 'aetheling'. And that prince is none other than my late brother's son Aethelwold."

"So the man was intending to assassinate—you, my lord the King?" his chaplain asked.

"I think it most likely. He thought he saw his chance to kill me so that Aethelwold could take over. Since it was a crime of opportunity, I cannot conclude that Aethelwold actually ordered such an attempt. It will be our business in the coming days to interrogate the prisoner and find this out. At least we must ascertain how widespread this support for Aethelwold is around the vicinity of Wimborne. I don't want any nests of insurrection in Wessex, especially so close to the coast. We might as well invite the Danes to come back and make slaves of us all."

At this he turned to his chaplain, who was responsible for taking notes. "Send out a summons for my nephews Aethelwold and Aethelhelm to come and take up residence here with me at Winchester without delay. I want them where I can keep my eye on them, the young adders. Make the invitation sound neutrally cordial, of course," he added, "but nevertheless not open to demur. And alert the palace guard also to be especially vigilant with Aethelflaed and young Edward. We don't want to make any mistakes in interpreting the ramblings of a sleeping murderer."

Another thought seemed to have crossed the mind of one of the advisors.

"Do you think, sir, that this means your officers at Wimborne will be in danger?"

The King considered this for a moment. "It's a distinct possibility," he said at last. "If there is a plot, anyone who represents me may be seen as a target. Get Hana in here. We do not want the plotters to seize an opportunity to proclaim my nephew king."

◆

As they walked back from the guardhouse, Lullus said, "My lady, I almost forgot. I've put together a crew of young people from the farms around the estate. They are going to come tomorrow to clean the hall."

This had been one of Molly's first official orders to Lullus. The estate could not be properly run without a functioning hall. Molly had already been running over her mental list of what needed to be done. She had assembled as many rags and buckets as she could find around the household and even set aside some long poles which she thought might be convenient for reaching the cobwebs.

The collection of youths who arrived as a cleaning crew were a pleasant surprise: Molly was delighted with their willingness. Having given each one a task, she went around making sure that everyone had enough cleaning supplies and no one ran into difficulties.

After they were finished, she gave them their wages and a hearty lunch of pease pottage with bread and butter. Molly had to exercise her authority with Eng, who had been very grudging about the sausage and ham, which Molly considered an essential part of the soup. In the end she could understand Eng's reluctance; she was astonished at the volume of food they were able to put away. They headed back to their homes together in a noisy gaggle that afternoon, and Molly returned to the hall to survey the final result. If one didn't focus on details like the soot stain on the ceiling or the chipping paint, it now actually looked quite good. *Yes, I could feel at home here*, thought Molly. *My new home.* The gloomy mood that accompanied her first impression of the place was completely dispelled. With the grime and cobwebs removed the old woodwork glowed, its quality and solidity giving a reassuring appearance to the hall. It now looked almost welcoming. Molly was now more eager than ever to find a painter to touch up that trim work.

<h1 style="text-align:center">Chapter 11</h1>

The day after their arrival, everyone in Buckingham was up early. Tension and uncertainty hung in the air. Since the council of war had become a council to decide the kingship, the question in everyone's mind was no longer 'what will the king do?' but instead, 'who will be our king?' For a few, the question was 'will I be chosen?'

Men began to move restlessly in the direction of the abbey as the bells rang for Tierce.

"Good grief, what is that smell?" exclaimed Edmund as they came out of the hall. When they had walked a little farther, they saw workmen digging a new latrine. The outhouse had been laid on its side. Men were busy with iron-edged wooden spades digging a new hole and filling the old with dirt from the new. Another man had a brush and a bucket of whitewash and was painting wide brush strokes over the inside of the latrine.

"I suppose Lord Aethelwulf wants to make a good impression as a host," said Osgar.

"Or he suddenly realized the demands that were going to be placed on his facilities," said Edmund, as they passed.

The men of Wessex were escorted to the church by young Aethelred, who kept looking over his shoulder as they walked

83

the short distance down the hill to the abbey. It seemed his industrious steward was late for his duties. They squeezed their way into the little nave, which was already crowded with high and mighty visitors.

After the office had been sung, the nobles all filed into the guest-hall of the abbey, which was set up for the meeting with four long tables arranged in a square. The guest-hall was less grand than Aethelwulf's hall but probably built by the same craftsmen; the carving on the posts and furnishings was better for being less ostentatious in style. The walls were freshly whitewashed, so with candles the room was relatively bright. The room was decorated, somewhat incongruously, with hunting trophies of wolf, deer and boar skulls—perhaps souvenirs retained by Abbot Aethelhun from his former, secular existence.

Edwin and Edmund were introduced to all the most prominent men in Mercia. It looked like a royal council, to be sure, with so many lordly men gathered together, their colourful clothing and shining ornaments concentrated together like gems on a reliquary. Only—for the time being, anyway—there was no king.

The Abbot took on the duty of introductions. "This, Ealdorman, is Bishop Deorlaf of Hereford," he said. The first thing Edwin noticed about the Bishop was his eyebrows. They were so bushy that they seemed an extension of the grizzled grey tufts of hair over either ear. His head was a shiny bald dome. Keen, sharp grey eyes glinted underneath the eyebrows. The rest of him was small and wizened. Edwin had known a schoolmaster that reminded him of Deorlaf once: prickly as a hedgehog, a fearless advocate if he was on your side or an implacable enemy otherwise. The Bishop acknowledged Edmund and the others with a nod.

They were introduced next to Bishop Waerferth of Worcester, and there could not have been a greater contrast between these two Mercian prelates. Waerferth was a young man for his office, forty at best. He had a tall, powerful frame but went about with a habitual stoop, as if in apology for his size. Or perhaps, thought Edwin, from long hours of study: he had the look of a scholar about him. In any case, his eyes were bright with intelligence and a hint of merriment.

Edwin was given a place to stand behind Edmund, who had taken care to wear his very finest finery. In Edmund's case this ran to a very finely-woven wool tunic trimmed with a patterned silk braid around the neck, sleeves and hem. He wore a new pair of trousers in a dark woven pattern and matching leg-wraps. A round silver pin fastened his cloak at the shoulder, and a gold ring given to him by King Alfred glinted on his finger. Never let it be said that the Danes had taken all the pride of Wessex away with them! His moustache seemed particularly flamboyant today, the points extending outward past the curve of his cheek where Edwin could see it move when Edmund spoke.

Next to him was Osgar leaning on one elbow. Rounding the corner to the left was their host Lord Aethelwulf and his nephew, Ealdorman Aethelred. The contrast between the two was more striking in daylight with uncle and nephew sitting side by side. The older man had an air of casual confidence. The younger looked like a bored young soldier; his expression was serious but his face was thin and unformed.

Round the corner across from the Wessex party Abbot Aethelhun sat between Lord Aethelwulf and Ealdorman Beornoth. This was the man who had been so emotional about King Ceolwulf's death when they were at dinner the night before. Now his posture suggested a sort of blustery bravado.

Then Bishop Waerferth and Bishop Deorlaf were squeezed in at the corner.

To Edmund's right was Lord Wulfsige. This was the nobleman they had heard about on the road from the Mercian merchant, and now here he was in the flesh. He was splendidly, one might even say excessively, adorned: he wore a silk tunic embroidered with gold thread around the collar and cuffs, and his hands dripped with rings. He had dark hair, worn rather longer than was fashionable in Wessex, and a put-upon air. His pointed beard made his narrow face look even longer.

A gruff old nobleman named Aethelferth sat next to him. He was apologizing to Bishop Deorlaf for the absence of his son, who was unable to attend for a reason Edwin could not hear over the general din of voices.

Bishop Deorlaf, who as senior cleric had been given the task of leading the meeting by the consensus of all, called the men to order by rapping the edge of his writing tablet sharply on the table.

"In these troubled times," he began, "we find ourselves without a king." Deorlaf began to speak of the glory-days of Offa, when the Mercian king was the only Saxon leader the great Charles of Francia considered an equal.

"Now our homeland has sunk by degrees to the level of a Danish dependency. And why? Because of this unseemly squabbling amongst those who should be leaders of men!" Deorlaf's eyes blazed beneath his brows, and he looked at each of the men in turn. Some returned his glare with confidence, while others looked offended or averted their eyes. Edwin noticed that Deorlaf reserved his sharpest look for Beornoth. Beornoth spoke.

"It is time, reverend bishop, to return to the rightful line of good King Burgred. As his only surviving kinsman, I am naturally the legitimate choice as Mercia's king."

Before Beornoth had finished speaking, others had begun to shout him down.

"My son, you are indeed Burgred's kinsman, but only a distant one," said Deorlaf, having silenced the hecklers with a wave of his gnarled hand.

"That is true, reverend bishop, but I am his only surviving kinsman here in Mercia."

The others who had been heckling him before, Edwin noticed, were all of the party of Wulfsige.

Wulfsige himself now joined in: "And where were you when your kinsman Burgred needed you most? When Guthrum ran him out of Mercia? And in whose service have you since distinguished yourself as the chief toady and turncoat of the land?"

Deorlaf, it seemed to Edwin, was not as hasty in calling Wulfsige to order after this outburst as he had been with Beornoth. But perhaps this was only Edwin's imagination, as Deorlaf did indeed signal Wulfsige to hold his peace. The bishop spoke.

"Indeed, my son, your claim to leadership must be accompanied by a clarification of these facts."

"I fought valiantly in support of my royal cousin," protested Beornoth unconvincingly, "until we realized our cause was lost. When I heard that Burgred had abdicated and fled to Rome, I decided to regroup and wait for another convenient opportunity."

This was the wrong choice of words, bringing shouts of derision from his opponents again. A chaotic chorus of voices began their accusations of treachery.

"I did indeed serve in the court of King Ceolwulf," began Beornoth, "but my reasons for doing so are not as these men claim. I felt it was my duty to my royal cousin and to my homeland to put myself in a position to influence the new king for good."

"Your place was by the side of King Burgred!" someone at the back shouted.

"How could I help Burgred more than by watching over Ceolwulf's every move?" cried Beornoth.

This suggestion that Beornoth had accepted an influential post in the regime of his cousin's usurper for the deposed king's benefit was greeted with hoots and howls. Again Deorlaf silenced the hecklers.

"Are you suggesting that all the time you served King Ceolwulf, you were acting as a spy?"

"Reverend bishop, I do not say that I was acting as a spy, exactly. Only that I took it upon myself to keep watch for an opportunity for Burgred to return in conquest."

Waerferth leaned over and said to Deorlaf, "*Nemo potest duobus dominis servire.*"

Edmund turned to Edwin with a questioning look. "No one can serve two masters," Edwin whispered. "From the Gospel of St Matthew—" but his brother had already turned back to the table.

Bishop Deorlaf, whose knowledge of Latin was wideranging and minute when it came to deeds and charters but not up to comprehending a Scriptural quotation sprung on him without warning, looked blank and murmured, "Hmm, yes." Aloud, Deorlaf said, "Very well, Ealdorman Beornoth. Perhaps you have some plans for the defence of our country? How much support can you command?"

"As you know, reverend bishop, I have extensive holdings to the west of Lichfield," Beornoth began, but was interrupted by Wulfsige again.

"Everyone knows about your estates, but have you got fighting men? Yes, you're rich. Were you planning to buy a foreign army or just bribe our enemies out of your own coffers when they come calling?"

"And where are your fighting men, Wulfsige?" Beornoth shot back, seizing on a point he felt was no more to his adversary's advantage than his.

"I have a small corps of dedicated followers," said the latter with dignity. "And owing to my position as the grandson of King Wigmund and nephew of the blessed St Wigstan" (here he crossed himself and everyone else was obliged to do so as well), "I have but to send word, and men will flock to my name and cause."

Beornoth said nothing, perhaps not as certain as he might wish that men would flock to his name and cause.

"Now then, Ealdorman," prompted Deorlaf, "Could you outline to us your plans for our country's defence?"

"I would concentrate our forces in the east, to defend against the Danes," said Beornoth, as if the idea had just occurred to him.

"And what about the Welsh threat in the west?"

All eyes turned to young Ealdorman Aethelred, who had spoken for the first time. He directed a keen but impersonal gaze on Beornoth. The question hung in the air.

"Of course some of our forces would be stationed in the west," said Beornoth quickly.

"Where?" asked Aethelred.

"Where?"

"Yes, where? My estates are all around Gloucester, but the Welsh threat extends especially to Hereford, Worcester, and up to Shrewsbury. I can field a force to ward off Danes coming in through the estuary and up the Severn, or Welshmen from the western frontier, but have you a plan for defending Hereford and Worcester?"

At this the two bishops pricked their ears; Deorlaf's seat was in Hereford, and Waerferth's in Worcester. But Beornoth's plans seemed rather insubstantial. Judging by the bishops' faces, Edwin thought Beornoth's chances of becoming king of Mercia were already on the wane. No one could expect to be chosen without their support. And it seemed that by posing this seemingly innocent and quite relevant question, Aethelred might have dispensed with one of his rivals quite easily.

But Wulfsige was not ready to concede. And it seemed that Deorlaf was not yet ready to let young Aethelred's contingent commandeer the attention of those assembled.

"Wulfsige, your claims to the throne derive from your grandfather, you say." The bishop gave Wulfsige an opening.

Wulfsige spoke eloquently, and as long as he might with interruptions from the followers of his rivals. The gist of his argument, as far as Edwin could make out, was that he should be king because it was his destiny.

The West Saxons had agreed ahead of time that Osgar, as the senior nobleman of their party, should be the first to speak and explain King Alfred's reasons for sending them.

Bishop Deorlaf nodded to Osgar and he began.

"Honoured friends of Mercia, we bring you greetings from King Alfred and the West Saxon people. We have come to you on this occasion to rejoice in the departure of our mutual foe, Guthrum the Dane, from these lands."

In Wessex, this beginning would have called forth cheers and foot-stamping. At a table with Mercian worthies, however, Osgar's words merited only silence. As he looked at their faces they looked back with reserved expectation.

"Ahem. Moreover, had he known of the death of King

Ceolwulf, our King would have considered it appropriate to send a group of his representatives to your deliberations regarding the kingship, considering his threefold interest in the matter."

Aethelferth, the old ealdorman, spoke up. "Threefold?"

"Yes," said Osgar, who was relieved that at least one of the Mercians was actually paying attention. "First, our King is related by ties of marriage to the Mercian royal house. His sister, as you know, was good King Burgred's wife." Osgar then reminded them that Alfred's own wife was the daughter of a Mercian ealdorman.

"Of course we all remember Ealdorman Mucel," said Wulfsige. "A fine man—a brave warrior and a wise counsellor."

"His daughter is also a wise and intelligent woman, and naturally takes an eager interest in the land of her birth. She also sends greetings to all her kin and friends here."

Aethelferth spoke again. "The attention and, indeed, affection of the royal house of the West Saxons is welcome. We send our cordial greetings back with you to Alfred and Ealhswith."

"My sons, you have come from King Alfred," said Deorlaf. "Though you have come with a large retinue, by your own account you come in peace. What have you been charged to accomplish?"

"I will offer no reproof that no one in Mercia saw fit to invite Wessex to the table here today, in view of our interests," Osgar smiled disarmingly. "We are here not in support of a particular party, but to underscore our King's desire for good relations with our neighbours. He also wishes to extend his assurances of military support to Saxon West Mercia."

"That is, on the surface, a generous offer," said Wulfsige. "But how are we to know it is not merely a pretence to seize control?" He had begun calmly, but the last words were carried by emotion and his Mercian dialect to an almost hysterical note.

Mildness and good humour were the weapons with which Osgar had customarily kept friends from coming to blows, and he employed them here with assurance. "If my royal master had intended to take Mercia for his own, I assure you he would be here now himself at the head of a mighty army of warriors, instead of sending—" he motioned to himself with an amused smile, which was answered by a few little smiles around the table. However, Wulfsige remained unmoved.

At this point voices were heard in the courtyard outside and all heads turned to the sound of the heavy iron-bound door being opened. A pale servant came in and, looking around in an agitated manner, hurried to Ealdorman Aethelred's side. He whispered something in his lord's ear.

Aethelred stiffened. "Reverend bishops and honoured guests," he said. "I must ask you to adjourn this council for the day, or at least excuse me from it. My missing steward has been found dead at the edge of the forest, killed by a wolf!"

Chapter 12

Ashudder went through all the assembly as they heard this news. There was not a man among them that had not seen first-hand the ravages of a wolf attack or heard from a kinsman a horrifying account of dismembered limbs, spilled entrails, animal jaws red with human gore. Aethelred rose from his seat and followed the distraught retainer out of the hall.

Upon the tragic announcement, the council quickly dispersed. Aethelred and his uncle went to retrieve the body, the bishops went to ground somewhere in the abbey, Wulfsige excused himself to see to his hawks, and old Aethelferth said something huffy to the effect that choosing a new king was a tolerably important business and what were men doing here today scampering around after fools of retainers who went fooling around with wolves and were foolish enough to go and get themselves killed.

"Well, I suppose that's it for today, little brother," said Edmund, turning as he got up. To Osgar, he said, "I was going to follow you up by handing out the King's gifts, but now they'll just have to wait." Osgar shrugged ruefully. "Come, my friends," he said, laying a hand on each of the brothers' shoulders, "All this trouble, you know, makes me terribly thirsty." As they headed for the door, Osgar invited Aethelferth to join them, and the old Mercian brightened.

Neither Edmund nor Edwin felt like spending the entire afternoon at the mead-bench, however, so after a friendly horn of ale had been passed around, Edwin excused himself to go look at the horses and Edmund said he would have a quick lie-down in their quarters.

A nap didn't sound too bad to Edwin either after a couple of long days in the saddle, but he had not checked on the horses since the night before. More to the point, he had not checked on Bert, and there was really no telling what the well-meaning but hapless lad might be up to.

Edwin ended up spending longer in the stable than he intended. Edmund's groom met Edwin with a baleful eye and Bert met him with a sore ear. It seemed Bert had given a bucket of cold water to a hot horse and nearly sent it into colic. One of the other grooms had kicked the bucket over before the horse had drunk too much, and Bert had been charged with walking the horse most of the night until the crisis was averted. Stig and old Red seemed none the worse for wear, however, after their journey, so when he had seen them happily turned out with the rest, Edwin sauntered back to their quarters, thinking perhaps he should also lie down for a little while before dinner.

He crossed the yard and lifted the latch on the door. As he did so, he thought he heard his brother's voice. He took a step in the door, stumbling as he did so over a broom and a pile of folded linens. Before he could stop himself he was flat on his face. His attempt to gather his wits was impeded by shrieks coming from under the covers of the big bed and his brother's voice in a low growl in his ear, "Do you mind?" Before Edwin knew it, the maid had darted past him, grabbing up the broom and linens as she went, and pausing only to wrap her head-cloth around her dishevelled hair before the door slammed shut, leaving the brothers alone together.

Edwin was stunned. There was no other interpretation he could put on what he had just seen. And yet, why should he be shocked? He was no child; he knew what went on in the world. But somehow he had never imagined his elder brother as that kind of man.

In the meantime, Edmund observed the look of undisguised astonishment on his brother's face with disgust.

He instantly went on the attack, as he always did when he felt in need of defence. "So you have become my nursemaid now? Did you come back here just to spy on me?"

Edwin vigorously denied having wished to spy on his brother. "Believe me, there are some things I don't want to know."

But this remark, intended to convey a lack of inquisitiveness into Edmund's private concerns, only served to increase his irritation.

"I don't need you as my confessor, and I don't need you passing judgement on me as if you were some kind of saint! If you can't understand what it is like for a man in my situation you really ought to have become a priest or a blasted monk."

Edwin was so offended by this tirade that he was about to turn away and leave; but something in Edmund's words had caught him. He wheeled around to face Edmund.

"What do you mean, 'a man in my situation'?"

But Edmund had suddenly clammed up. "Nothing," he said, turning away.

Now Edwin knew there was something on his brother's mind. He stood still, waiting.

"Look, if you must know," said Edmund, his broad back now heaving with the effort of steadying his voice, "Eadburg is dying." Then the words came tumbling out. "She has a cancer of the womb. We've taken her to every herbalist, learned physician, and wise woman in the country, but they've run out of treatments. They say now it's only a matter of months."

"Brother, I don't know what to say."

Edmund's attempt at a wry smile looked more like a grimace of pain. "She's been through torments. And all the old biddies hinting that it's about time we produced an heir. It's been a couple of years now since she's been well enough to—share her bed. Well, she finally just said that if I needed a woman, I should look elsewhere."

Strangely, Edwin found that he could imagine the scene. The marriage between his brother and Eadburg had been a strategic one encouraged by both families; it was no love match. And Eadburg had never been a particularly gracious woman; ill-natured and shrewish were more the adjectives that came to mind. Was her disagreeable personality due to the constant pain of her illness? Or was it just her nature? In any case, Edwin could well envision her giving her husband this kind of licence. But knowing Eadburg, it seemed to him less likely to be the misguided generosity of a dying wife, and instead a gesture of masochistic spite.

Edmund, however, reading his brother's silence as still deeper moral horror, snapped back into his self-defensive posture.

"Look, I don't know why I'm telling you all this," he grunted. "We didn't tell you because we didn't want the news to overshadow the wedding, of course." And with a cynical shrug, he added, "Sorry to expose you to the seamier side of married life."

What was there left for Edwin to say? Every expression of sympathy he could think of seemed equally hollow and weak. In the end he simply put his hand on Edmund's shoulder.

◆

When the horn was blown for dinner in Aethelwulf's hall Edwin was surprised that so much time had passed. He—and, he imagined, his brother also—welcomed the chance to mix with other company and pretend that nothing had happened. At dinner all the talk was of the terrible accident. Since word had spread of the retainer Helmstan's death, there was considerable pressure on Lord Aethelwulf for a wolf-hunt to be mounted as quickly as possible. And the nobles were not averse to the idea; besides the practical necessity of dealing with a man-eating wolf, they relished an opportunity to get out away from the council table for a day.

When bedtime came, however, Edwin found that he could not get his brother's situation out of his head. He went out to get a breath of fresh air, and saw the lights in the abbey chapel.

All he wanted was a chance to compose the roiling cauldron of emotions in his heart: anger at Edmund, the horror and sadness of Eadburg's terminal illness, disgust at himself for being so naive. But as he entered the chapel he saw that it was already occupied by a lone monk washing the body of a dead man in preparation for burial. It was, in fact, the man who had been found that morning.

The corpse was laid out on a long wooden table and had been covered with a cloth to await the coffin that was being made. As he knelt to pray, Edwin saw the elderly monk washing the exposed parts of the dead body. Edwin only managed to get through one *Ure faeder* before the monk and his silent work absorbed his attention entirely.

The monk was trying to turn the body onto its side slightly so as to clean the back, but his strength was unequal to the task. Edwin rose.

"Brother, may I give you a hand?" he called out. In the silent chapel with its high stone walls his voice sounded unnaturally loud, although he had not meant to shout. The monk, who had been absorbed in his work, gave a violent start. Recovering himself, he peered vaguely into the darkness of the nave. Edwin walked towards the monk into the light of his candle.

"Bless my soul!" cried the monk as he caught sight of Edwin. "I didn't see you there. A little short-sighted, I am, I fear. No idea you were even there. Quiet as a mouse. Suppose you came in for a little peace and quiet yourself. And here I was with this poor fellow." He patted the corpse's hand.

"It looks as though you could use a little help," said Edwin.

"Well, as a matter of fact I was finding it a bit hard going," the monk replied. "There aren't that many of us left now, you see, and none of us are what you might call able-bodied youths." He tittered a little at the expense of his equally aged brethren and then returned to the point. "If you could just hold the fellow's shoulder up, so, then I can get in here and clean his back and slip this shroud under. But perhaps you'd rather not?"

The monk's friendly eyes squinted at Edwin, trying to see whether his face registered any hesitation in touching the body. But Edwin had already forced himself to put his hand on the cold, inert shoulder and turn the body so that its back was exposed.

"Who was he?" Edwin asked, mainly to make conversation.

"Oh, terrible tragedy, terrible, terrible," the monk replied obliquely, shaking his head. "Such a waste. Why, this was

Lord Aethelred's very own steward. He was found outside the enclosure this morning. He must have been out all the night. And the wolves got him. Just look."

As he said this he motioned with his washcloth at the pale corpse. He had been a tall man, and handsome, when the blood still flowed in his veins. Even in death, he had a well-proportioned, handsome face. But more likely to be noticed now was the alabaster cast of his body which had been drained of blood, and the well-defined imprints of animal teeth like dotted purple lines here and there in his skin. No flesh had been torn loose on his arms or legs, which were still stiff and slightly bent, but his throat was completely bitten away. From where he stood holding the body by its shoulder so that it lay on its side, he could see a jagged void under the man's beard where once his neck had been.

The monk had finished his washing and had stretched the shroud out on the table. Edwin helped him lower the body back into place on it. As he did so, one of the hands suddenly swung loose from the elbow at an unexpected angle.

"He's starting to loosen up. That's good," said the monk. "Then we can lay him out properly."

"Hmm," was Edwin's only reply. He felt the elbow; it was as stiff as ever. The stiffness was the same in the shoulder and wrist. The fingers were beginning to loosen, that was true. But as he felt the arm, he found that the bones below the elbow were broken. Edwin put the hand back into its original position, elbow bent over the stomach. When Helmstan's body stiffened, this was how he had lain. Something had yanked hard enough on his rigid arm to break the bones.

"Do you often have trouble with wolves up here?" Edwin asked.

"Now and then," the monk nodded. "Not lately, but I

certainly remember one or two attacks in my time."

"I don't suppose anyone knows what this man was doing outside the enclosure at night, do they?"

"Well, the fellow was last seen going to the latrine. But the latrine's right there by the hall, so why he was found outside the enclosure by the edge of the wood is a mystery to me." The monk shook his head sadly.

◆

It had been a while since Edwin had had one of his nightmares. Awake, Edwin had little or no problem shelving away the scenes burned into his mind in the terrible years of war. He imagined writing them on the page of a book, then closing the book forcefully and shoving it back on the shelf.

At night this bit of mental trickery was no help at all. Confused visions of terror gripped him, bringing back all the gory scenes of battle without any of the relieving memories of comradeship or the zest of adventure that had seen him through.

Edwin had had his bedroll brought into the hall with the men; he did not fancy sleeping in quarters with his brother so soon after what had passed between them. Coming into the hall, he picked his way through the sleepers to his own place. On finally lying down, tired and careworn, Edwin felt sure of finally getting some rest. But his overwrought mind determined otherwise. Tonight it was the beasts of the battlefield that haunted him. The carrion crows that pecked out the eyes of the slain, their disgusting beaks dripping with jelly, the wolves that came sniffing around hungering for the meat of freshly slaughtered men. He could see them now as they attacked any exposed flesh, biting and tearing until their maws were red with blood—Danish or Saxon tasted all the same to them.

And that memory he had tried so hard for so long to bury, the memory of the wolves in a tug-of-war over a man's dismembered arm, now came popping up again, and the arm in the dream was his own arm. He pulled and pulled to get it away from the tearing teeth, and woke up screaming.

One of the men bunking nearby was tugging at his arm trying to wake him up.

"Easy there, friend," said a kindly voice in the dark. "You must have been dreaming. Wake up and calm yourself."

Slowly Edwin's senses returned to him. He could feel his heart pounding in his chest and he was bathed in a cold sweat. He forced himself to breathe more slowly. From somewhere, someone had procured him a cup of something – water it turned out to be – and Edwin drank it by the hearth, staring at the glowing embers.

Wolves. It was the sight of the mauling victim in the chapel that had set it off this time. There was a strangeness in comparing the man laid out on the chapel table and the memories of slain warriors in his dream. One so pale and peaceful, the others so bloody and disordered. The strange feeling outlasted the cup of water and accompanied him back to bed, where he finally fell into a heavy and dreamless slumber.

When Edwin awoke, he realized that he knew what he had felt as strange about the body in the chapel. The bite-marks he had seen on the man's arms and legs—the clear, neat imprints of a canine bite—were all wrong.

Chapter 13

What, then, did this mean? If this was not a wolf attack, the only other conclusion was murder. If he was murdered by men, or a man, the guilty one must have wanted his death to be passed off as an accident and took considerable pains to make it look that way. Questions were already crowding Edwin's mind. Who were these people? What secret grievance did they have against this man? What means did they use to disfigure the body? And what should Edwin do about it?

It was this last question that stopped him in his tracks. At home he would have known exactly what to do and how to go about it. At home he was Lord Edwin, reeve of Wimborne. He had the right and the duty to take the necessary steps. But here in Mercia? First of all, the entire situation would be like sticking one's hand in a hornet's nest. Any of these people could be guilty; any one of the great and powerful lords of Mercia might be behind the death, or ready to protect the perpetrator. That, in turn, might throw the negotiations entirely off balance. And that would be in direct contravention of his mission. Ha! But this was assuming that anyone would even listen to him or believe his testimony that the body showed signs of human violence. Never had Edwin been so acutely aware of his insignificance.

The first person to try to convince, of course, was Edmund.

Edmund seemed to have spent the night saving up abuse to hurl at Edwin. "Fine that you have decided to join us again! I had no idea where you were all night long. For all I knew you were out getting eaten by a wolf. Or maybe you decided to desert us and go over to the Mercians. Do you think that the King's interests are best served by letting the Mercians witness the total dissolution of our mission here? I won't have anyone in my party shirking his responsibilities."

"Your party?" Edwin rejoined, before he could stop himself.

"Yes, my party, and don't forget it. From now on you follow my orders and see that you keep your mind on why we are here in the first place."

Where was your mind yesterday afternoon, brother? thought Edwin, but aloud he said, "Edmund, I have to talk to you."

"No, you don't. I already know what you're going to say, and the subject is closed."

"It's about—" but Edmund, having now worked himself into a fury, came and towered over Edwin.

"Didn't I just tell you to shut up?" he roared, his face too close to Edwin's. "Do I need to send you out to dig latrines until you learn to follow orders?"

"It's about a killing." Edwin could never out-shout his brother, but at the quiet words Edmund went silent.

"I saw the body of Aethelred's steward, the one who was supposed to have been killed by a wolf. I think he shows signs of being murdered instead."

"What? How? They all said he was killed by a wolf. What are you talking about?" Once he had his brother's attention, Edwin began to explain to him the events of the night before and the reasons for his suspicions.

"What I saw were neat, even tooth-marks—"

"Of a wolf?"

"Yes, a wolf, or perhaps a large dog—"

"Well, there you go then. Couldn't have been a man, unless he was a werewolf." Edmund let out a disturbingly realistic howl.

"Will you please listen! A wolf attacking a man doesn't get his mouth round the limb, bite down and let go, leaving an impression of each individual tooth. He doesn't let go until he pulls out a chunk of flesh."

"And what you saw were tooth marks with no actual bites taken out?"

"Well, a little tearing here and there, but mostly just punctures. Hardly any blood at all. Only the throat was completely ripped out."

"What did that, if not a wolf?"

"I don't know how it was done. But in the corner of the ragged throat wound I saw a clean knife cut."

Edmund sat down and cracked his knuckles, looking pensive.

"Edmund, what should we do?"

"Hm. I don't know. Trouble is, we are just guests here, and strangers, without any jurisdiction, and I don't want to get involved in anything that's going to compromise our mission."

"Agreed. But we have to report it. Since the man was Aethelred's steward, I suppose we report the matter to Aethelred."

Edmund turned and looked Edwin in the eye. "Are you sure of what you saw? Sure enough to report it as a crime?"

"Yes, I am sure of what I saw." Edwin paused. Was he? Was lack of sleep causing his nightmares to bleed into a real memory, to contaminate reality with fantasy? "Even so," he added, "I would appreciate a chance to look again, in daylight, with witnesses. But I believe they are going to bury him today."

"He's over at the abbey church?"

"Yes."

Edmund twisted his moustache thoughtfully. "Then I suppose we'll need to talk to Abbot Aethelhun," he said. "If he allows the examination, we can see what there is to see and tell Aethelred about it. Then it will be his problem."

They sought out Aethelhun after Prime, when the sun was beginning to provide the light they would need for their errand. The Abbot was a broad-shouldered middle-aged man who looked like he would have been more at home with a sword in his belt. He was very concerned when he heard what they wanted, and seemed entirely surprised by the notion that the steward had been murdered.

"Then why the big wolf-hunt tomorrow?" he asked.

"Father Abbot, we believe that the murder was made to look like a wolf attack in order to divert suspicion from the killer. It was only when I saw the body being prepared for burial that I spotted certain signs of foul play. What we ask is that you allow us to view the body once more, in daylight, with witnesses, and point out these signs to you. For now we do not want this request to go any further than ourselves and your chosen witnesses. We do not know who is responsible, but until the killer is identified and brought to justice we are all potentially in danger."

Abbot Aethelhun nodded. "I suppose we had better get this taken care of as soon as may be. I will call my prior and together we will open the coffin and view these signs you speak of. Then we may discuss what should happen next. If there is a delay in the burial, there will have to be explanations."

Not long afterward the four men found themselves standing around the coffin in the little stone church, with shafts of sunlight from the small, high stone windows casting long beams of light across the nave. Abbot Aethelhun himself pried open the lid of the coffin. Fortunately the weather and the church were cool, so no cloud of noxious vapours assaulted them as the lid came off. There lay the bloodless corpse, decently shrouded, with his arms lying by his sides and his beard carefully combed to cover the gaping void of his throat. His skin had a greenish pallor in daylight that made him look, as it were, even deader than he had by warm candlelight the night before. With a reluctant Edmund to help pulling the shroud aside, Edwin carefully pointed out the marks and explained to the abbot and prior why these were not what they appeared to be. Absorbed in his brother's explanations, Edmund almost forgot his unsavoury task as assistant.

"See," said Edwin, pointing to the bite-marks at random places on the man's arms and legs. "Wolves do not bite this way. Imagine what a wolf would have to do to make a mark like this. He would have to take hold of the flesh with his teeth"— here Edwin clenched his own teeth in spite of himself— "and then, without taking away any flesh, let go again. The wolves that I have seen will bite down all the way; they either bite out a chunk or they pull and tear, but either way they do not leave neat little tooth-marks all over a man's arms and legs."

Abbot Aethelhun was nodding. The prior looked a little pale and was gripping a piece of stonework behind him.

Aethelhun, brows knitted, asked, "So how were these marks made?"

"There you have me. They are wolf tooth-marks, but how they were made I have no idea. I have to suppose they were made after the man's death. The clean marks and the absence of torn skin on his forearms, which he would have held up to defend himself, suggest he put up no resistance."

Edwin then had Edmund hold the beard aside while he showed them the throat.

"The throat was torn away, as you see," he said, "but if you look way up in the corner of the wound, up by where the jawbone meets up with the ear, there is a clear knife-cut."

Abbot Aethelhun leaned in for a closer look. The prior swayed, and Edmund was just in time to catch him before his head hit the stone floor. Aethelhun helped prop him up and called another brother to tend him while they arranged the body decently again.

Abbot Aethelhun asked, "So how do you imagine the man was killed? Was his throat cut, then?"

"Yes," Edwin replied. I think his throat was cut with a knife—presumably from behind. That was his death. Then, for whatever reason, the killer saw fit to make his deed look like a wolf attack, and desecrated the body in this gruesome fashion."

A new point struck Edmund. "Why make it look like a wolf attack? Why not just bury him in a shallow grave in the woods, and let him simply 'disappear'?"

"I don't know," sighed Edwin. "There must have been a reason. You both, I presume, agree that these signs I have shown you indicate foul play?"

They both nodded.

"So there must have been a reason. But as yet I have no idea what. Have you anything to suggest, Father Abbot?"

Abbot Aethelhun shook his head. The prior was just beginning to revive and take notice of the conversation again.

Edmund said, "Who would want this man dead?"

"You've asked the two questions we have no way of answering right now," said Edwin. "Who did it, and why in this way? I suppose the next step is to report the matter to

Aethelred, Helmstan's lord."

"Supposing he did it?" said Edmund.

"Murder his own steward? Seems rather improbable."

"Well, he could have had his henchmen do it. He wouldn't have had to slit the man's throat himself."

"But this man was Aethelred's henchman, if you want to call him that."

Edwin glanced at Abbot Aethelhun, who was beginning to look a little lost.

"Father Abbot, do you know of any reason why Aethelred, or anyone, should want this man dead?"

Abbot Aethelhun shrugged. "No, I really don't," he said, musing. "But I am not really the proper person to ask. He was in Lord Aethelred's service, and Lord Aethelred doesn't come here to Buckingham often, since his lands are out west towards Gloucester. If someone bore him ill will, it would probably have been among Aethelred's household, wouldn't it?"

Just then the door opened. It was Aethelred. He had come to pray over his slain attendant, only to find the coffin open and strangers crowding around the body.

"What's going on here?" he demanded.

Edwin, feeling that he was the one who owed an explanation, stepped forward; but before he could speak, the Abbot began, "Cousin, these men have some dreadful news which they came to discuss with me. I am glad you are come, because it concerns you as well."

Edwin and Edmund exchanged glances as if to say, "Cousin?"

Ealdorman Aethelred approached the coffin and looked at the dead man, while the Abbot told him about the suspicions of foul play.

"I had no idea," he murmured to himself, lifting the shroud

to follow a chain of bite-marks that started high on the shoulder and petered out as they reached the forearm. Then he looked up. The others were leaning in, watching intently in spite of themselves.

"Oh, I see," Aethelred bristled, "you wanted to see if the wounds began to ooze blood when I touched him. You think I killed my own man? Aethelhun, do you? Am I some kind of werewolf that could do this to a man?"

Abbot Aethelhun said, "My lord, I beg your pardon. Will you listen to what these men of Wessex have discovered?"

"Tell me," Aethelred said, and Edwin then explained for a third time his observations and conclusions.

"And we are still mystified as to why he was killed and why the deed was concealed this way," Edwin finished.

Aethelred chewed his lip.

"The last time I saw him was two nights ago, after supper," he said. "We were in the upper room of my uncle's hall, as we had some matters to discuss. Helmstan came with more mead, and I had sent for some sealing wax, and he stayed for a while to answer some questions I had for him. At some point he excused himself and went out again. I don't remember why. He never came back, and soon afterward the rest of us went to bed."

"Did he seem worried about anything?"

"Not that I noticed, but I can't say I was paying much attention."

"Did he have any enemies?"

"No, not to my knowledge."

Edmund spoke up. "What about his kin? He wasn't involved in any feuds?"

"Not that I know of," said Aethelred. "Surely he would have told me if he'd been involved in anything of that nature."

He began abruptly pacing the floor at the head of the coffin.

"It's just so unaccountable. This was a good man. A really good man. He was competent and well-liked. No problems, at least not that he ever mentioned, and not a troublemaker among his companions."

"Perhaps we are ignoring the most obvious solution after all. Lord Aethelred, was he carrying coins, or anything valuable?" asked Edwin. "Abbot Aethelhun, do you still have his personal effects?"

"Well, his clothing was torn to shreds, of course," replied the Abbot. "There wasn't much of it left. Nothing but his personal ornaments. We were able to save his cloak, and his belt was intact." As he said this, the Abbot led them to a small storeroom elsewhere in the abbey precincts. He brought out a nondescript bundle and suggested that they go outside where the light was better. Edwin was eager to look at the clothing, but had to wait until the practical Abbot had a table set up in the grass by the outer wall.

Helmstan's cloak was of an excellent patterned weave, a good weight but well-draping. Close inspection showed slight wear on the corners and some breakdown of the threads around the places the cloak-pin customarily pierced to hold it in place. The part around the neck was soaked and stiff with blood, and there were also spatters.

"Where is the brooch?" asked Edwin.

The Abbot shrugged. "It was not found with the cloak."

Edwin went through the rest of Helmstan's belongings on the table: his tunic, shirt and trousers, badly torn and stained as if a bucket of blood had been flung at them. Large blood stains showed around the neck and down the front of the shirt and tunic. The others shifted uncomfortably on their feet as Edwin spread the pieces of clothing out one by one and studied the stains like a heathen reading omens in an animal's entrails. Edwin looked closely at the shoes and leg-wraps, but could discern no clues. There was a good leather belt with a fair-quality bronze buckle. The other end of the belt was supposed to have a matching bronze strap-end mount riveted onto it; but only one sharp corner remained, in its rivet, the broken surface jagged and bright.

Edwin tried another angle.

"Lord Aethelred, does the location where the body was found mean anything to you? Outside the enclosure, at the edge of the wood. You didn't send him on any errands?"

"No. To be honest, I have the impression that when I saw him last, he was going out to the latrine." He shrugged. "But that would have been close to the hall. How or why he would then leave the enclosure and wander about at the edge of the woods, I've no idea."

At this point some monks showed their faces at the door and signalled to the Abbot that they were about to start ringing the bell for Tierce. Abbot Aethelhun started in surprise to find that so much time had passed. He got Lord Aethelred's permission to close the coffin and proceed with the burial later that day as planned.

"Since he was my man, I am responsible for seeing that he gets justice," Aethelred said. This satisfied Edwin that he had convinced at least two Mercian witnesses—or three, if one could count the prior.

As he and Edmund strolled back to their lodgings, the latter began, 'Well, this is a fine mess you've got us into. What's next?"

Annoyed, Edwin shot back, "How should I know?"

"I don't mean what are you going to get us into next. I

mean what do we do next?"

"Ah. Hm. I've just been thinking of that." Edwin lapsed into silence.

"Well?"

"Well, what do you think of what Aethelred told us?"

"What I think," said Edmund, "is that there are too many cousins, uncles, nephews and grandsons in this hole." He kicked a pebble spitefully.

"I noticed that too. But think how an outsider would feel in Wessex. It's no different with us, it's just not the families we're used to dealing with."

"But for all we know, they could be covering up for each other and we'd never get to the bottom of it. I mean, you pick a random abbot and a random dead man's lord, and they happen to be cousins! They are just going to close ranks."

"They were not random, as well you know. This is Lord Aethelwulf's estate. It's only natural that if a man gets killed around here he's going to be connected in some way to Lord Aethelwulf's household. It's just as natural that the abbot of the local monastery is going to be some distant relation."

"Fine. Where does that get us?"

"Nowhere, I was just making a point. And as we know, cousins always stick together, right? Like in Wessex, where Aetheling Aethelwold is always looking out for the best interests of his uncle Alfred and his children?"

"Point taken. So what do we do now to get this mess cleaned up and get back home?"

"The young ealdorman is going to make enquiries among his household and see if he can find out anything about the man's movements. For now he and the abbot and the prior have promised not to tell anyone about the death being suspicious. I'm just afraid that if we let it be generally known, the killer will slip away. Later they can come out as witnesses when there is someone to accuse."

"So we can put this behind us and let Aethelred make his enquiries."

Edwin was silent. He couldn't help but think that investigating the crime would be too much for one eighteen-year-old, even if he was an ealdorman.

Edmund read his thoughts. "Great. Mercia's king is dead and Guthrum's hordes are just over the border, and you want us all to drop everything and go looking for someone who might have killed somebody's steward? That's fine. I'll just send the Danes a message to put off their attack till next summer."

"No, you are expected at the council-table and we don't want Osgar to have to carry the banner of the West Saxons on his own. I won't be missed. I will nose around the neighbourhood and see what I can find out, then join you in time for supper."

Chapter 14

They buried Helmstan that afternoon under a clouded sky. Dead leaves carried along by a cold, sighing wind came to rest in the open grave as the prayers were spoken over the coffin. In the end there was no one there but the Abbot, an old woman whom Edwin took to be Helmstan's mother, and two other men. Edwin stood at a respectful distance. Ealdorman Aethelred ducked out of the council to stand at the graveside, observing the solemnities very correctly. When the last prayers had been spoken and Aethelred had circulated among the mourners, nearly all the small party quickly dispersed. The only mourner still lingering was one of Aethelred's retainers.

This retainer was a bony, narrow man, balding, with a large Adam's apple and a wispy beard. His face was lined with sorrow and sleeplessness, and he carried a soggy handkerchief. He had, nevertheless, an upright posture and a wary look in his red-rimmed eyes. Hoping for some information, Edwin edged closer and introduced himself.

"My condolences."

The man nodded jerkily and looked away.

"I'm part of the delegation from Wessex, and just wanted to pay my respects. I hope I'm not intruding."

The man shook his head and in a barely audible, husky

voice, replied, "No." Then after a pause, he said something that sounded like "Much appreciated."

"Were you a kinsman of Helmstan's?" Edwin asked.

The man cleared his throat and looked up into the trees as if trying to control his tears. "No, we worked together for the young Ealdorman. My name is Garmund."

"Were you old friends?"

"It's been five or six years. And as for knowing him, I don't suppose anyone knew him better. He was my protégé; I taught him everything I knew. I'm getting older, you see, and my eyesight's not what it was. My lord liked to have a younger man about to help me with my duties."

"News of his death must have been a terrible shock."

"News! I was the one who brought the news! I was the one who—who found him." He pursed his lips together in an effort to control his grief. Edwin began to make some sympathetic comment.

Suddenly Garmund's Adam's apple wobbled and his eyes narrowed. "And I'll tell you something, my lord. Someone is going to pay for this!"

Edwin stared in surprise. "Pay? For Helmstan's death?" Had Aethelred's enquiries already given this Garmund the idea that the death was suspicious?

"Yes, someone will pay, I'll see to that. To die in such a way! Helmstan didn't deserve such a fate."

Still unsure of what Garmund meant and how much he knew, Edwin probed, "But surely you cannot try a wolf in a court of law?"

"No, but who allowed the wolves to come so close to Buckingham? Answer me that. And who lured Helmstan out of the enclosure so that he was at their mercy? You mark my words, someone will pay for his death." With these bitter words Garmund stalked off, leaving Edwin looking after him in surprise.

After the encounter with Garmund, Edwin sauntered down the hill to the houses clustered by the riverside. He had no particular aim in mind and just felt like seeing the settlement. As he walked through the street, he knew he was being watched from windows and doorways, but no one called out to try and sell him anything. He heard the sound of wood being chopped somewhere close by, and the bleat of a goat; but other than that the houses were unusually quiet.

At length he reached the riverbank. There was another timber bridge to the south, besides the western bridge they had crossed on their way in. Edwin did not cross the bridge, but continued along the bank. A few paces on he came to a very large willow tree, its last leaves clinging to the branches like bright yellow streamers. A man was squatting against the trunk of the tree with a fishing line.

Edwin squatted down also and watched the river for a while.

When he had remained silent for the proper amount of time, he ventured to ask, "Are they biting today?"

"Eh? Oh, well, not as well as they do in summertime. One or two more, and that's my supper taken care of," the man said, motioning to the fishing basket by his side.

Edwin remained looking at the water. He let a leaf fall from his fingers and watched the water carry it away. He waited.

"You're not from these parts, are you, er—m'lord?" said the old man at last, with a sidelong glance at Edwin's clothing.

"No indeed. My brother and I came up from Wessex for the council."

"Ah. Now, I could tell you wasn't from here by your funny way o' talking. Begging your pardon, like." He flashed a grin.

Edwin answered with a smile. "Not so many wolves down in my country as there are here, I reckon." He didn't really know if this were strictly true, but it was the only bait he could come up with for his own fishing line.

"Well, that was a terrible fate for the young feller. And there was something uncanny about it." The man turned and put his finger on the side of his nose. Lowering his voice, he said, "That's what folk round here are saying. Something uncanny. And there's folk as had a sheep stolen in the dead of night, and on the last full moon somebody out there past where this feller was killed, seen a hairy figure like a man, hiding in the trees." He stared at Edwin in a meaningful manner.

The way the man spoke made the hairs on Edwin's arms stand up, but on reflection he concluded that this was due more to the way the words were delivered rather than their substance. There had been a death that caught the local imagination. Some farmer had lost a sheep, and somebody saw—or thought he saw—a figure in the woods by the light of the moon. Fearing that the man might carry on with more tales unless diverted, Edwin said, "You've lived here all your life, then?"

"Man and boy, these fifty-seven winters," he replied. "This'll be my fifty-eighth, if I'm spared." He pulled in his line, found that the worm had drowned, and replaced it with another from a crock. "Time was, when I was a lad, that I even had the care of their young lordships from time to time."

"You mean—"

"The brothers, Aethelheard and Aethelwulf." He jerked his thumb toward the hall.

"Aethelheard—that would have been young Aethelred's father?"

The man nodded. "'Hardy' we called him back then. Hardy

and Wulfie."

"Were they far apart in age?"

"No, no more'n a year or two. Never a moment's rest, chasing after those boys. Young Lord Aethelwulf wanted to be just like his older brother. Always wanted to best him in everything. Why, I remember a time when Wulfie stretched a piece of string right across the path through the wood where they were to have a foot-race. Hardy could scarcely believe it when he landed face-down in the bracken and his younger brother won. Always up to tricks, those two." The man smiled at the reminiscence.

Edwin was poised to take his leave, but the man kept talking.

"Funny how things turn out. Starting out you would say Hardy had it all. The rank, the wealth, a fine lady for a wife, then a son. Vast estates," the man gestured broadly. "Wulfie did his best to follow. He married but his wife died giving birth, and the child died with her. So he had nothing and his brother had everything."

"Well, not exactly nothing," Edwin observed. "He seems to be doing well enough himself here in Buckingham."

"Oh, true enough, m'lord," agreed the man. "I'm just looking at it from his eyes, you know. But see the way things turn out," he continued. "Now Hardy is gone, and Wulfie is still around. That's the thing about life. You never know, you just never know." As he was saying this there was a little jerk on his fishing line, and he lifted out a fish just big enough to be worth eating. With practiced fingers he took it off the hook and popped it in his basket. Then, with a "Well, g'day to you," he picked up his fishing gear and started back to the village.

◆

Dinner could not come soon enough for either of the brothers after the elder had spent a dull afternoon at the negotiating table with the different claimants to the Mercian throne, and the younger had spent his time in more rustic company. They were placed, along with Osgar, in a reasonably good spot near the end of the head table. Unfortunately, it was the opposite end of the table from Lord Aethelred, so there was no chance of a tête-à-tête with him during supper. The dogs were luckier. Most of Lord Aethelwulf's dogs were sitting at his feet, apart from the large one, and he was just handing a piece of meat to one of them when Fram came to greet his canine table-companions. They indulged in a lively tug-of-war over a bone until Edwin called Fram to order with a curt whistle and gesture. Fram came to lie down at Edwin's feet and was edibly rewarded for his obedience.

As the first courses were served, Osgar exclaimed over the Mercian dishes he had not tasted in so long.

"Of course," said Aethelwulf. "I take great pride in my reputation as a host, and we would not want you to go home with a poor opinion of our hospitality. We in Mercia, of course, have a reputation to uphold. The sauce—" he passed a small bowl with a ladle to his guests, "—is a speciality of my cook's. He calls it his secret sauce, because he will not share the recipe."

Edwin could feel the bench wiggle as Edmund's feet began to tap impatiently. Luckily Aethelwulf was sitting in a chair and could neither feel the bench shaking nor hear the quiet tapping of Edmund's soft leather shoes.

Then Aethelwulf turned to his guests. "And what do you think of our ham this evening? No hams quite as fine as Buckinghamshire hams. It's the beech-mast, we say. It gives our hams the best flavour of any—not to slight your Wessex hams, which I am sure are good, of course, but our Buckinghamshire hams are renowned." Edwin thought to himself that if they had arrived at the stage of a feast when conversation devolved into a drunken ramble, they might as well give up now.

Osgar, diplomatic even when plastered, took up the subject of hams as seriously as it was offered. "We did certainly appreciate the distinctive flavour, though I would have put it down to the skill of your preparation rather than mere beech-mast. Where we come from, you know, is more beef country."

"Yes, of course," assented Aethelwulf complacently.

Edmund sighed and scratched his forehead.

"Speaking of our two lands," said Osgar, taking Edmund's hint, "It is true that Wessex and Mercia have been good neighbours for many years, so naturally when King Alfred heard of Guthrum's departure, he wished to assure himself of the well-being of our neighbours to the north." *Good neighbours for many years?* thought Edwin. *Well, a diplomat might say that, but not under oath.*

But this speech seemed acceptable to Aethelwulf, and he and his nephew exchanged a pleased glance.

"And now we have Guthrum moving his army north out of Cirencester," added Osgar.

"Yes, north and east," Aethelred added. "My uncle has men tracking them to ensure that they cross dutifully into the Danish territory without stopping in western Mercia on the way."

"Which is why our king thought it best to ensure that our Saxon neighbours had no such trouble during our mutual enemy's retreat," Osgar said smoothly. What Osgar did not say was just as plain to the uncle and nephew, Edwin thought, as what he did say. Help might be available from Wessex, but no Danish alliances would be tolerated.

"I wonder," said Aethelwulf, and paused. He chose his words carefully; there was no sign of the wine-soaked rambling about hams now. "What overall strategy your king intends to employ to contend with the Danish threat now that the immediate peril is past?"

"I am not sure exactly what you mean," said Osgar.

"One can fight the Danes when they attack. One can pay the Danes to go away. Has your master any further ideas?"

The West Saxons had perhaps expected the Mercians' response to their presence to combine suspicion with a plea for assistance. In this conversation, however, the shoe seemed to be on the other foot. Did Aethelwulf presume to advise and instruct the King of the West Saxons?

Edmund said gruffly, "We are not entirely sure the peril is past. That is why we intend to keep our eye on Guthrum's movements. Paying off the Vikings is a delaying tactic our King has used only as a last resort when he had need of time to gather forces. Is it a tactic you would use to defend Mercia?"

"I think I speak for my uncle as well as myself when I say that we would also see Danegeld payment as a last resort," said the young Mercian ealdorman.

Was it Edwin's imagination, or had there been a tension created and resolved between the uncle and the nephew as this question was asked? Aethelwulf's eyes had been fixed on Aethelred as he spoke, in a look both inscrutable and intense. Aethelred looked up and the expression dissolved into a grave nod of assent.

"I believe we have the forces—and what's more, the will—to resist an attacking Danish foe up to a point," said Aethelred. "With my uncle's forces in the east and my stronghold in the west, we can mount a defence on a certain scale on either side of the country. However," he paused, and continued with a little smile, eyeing the West Saxons, "knowing we have an ally to the south might make all the difference."

The conversation throughout the rest of the meal revolved around the wolf-hunt that had been planned for the following day. The men of Wessex took their leave from the dinner-table promptly when the last toast had been drunk, stating their desire to get a good night's rest in preparation for the next day's sport. When the door of their guest quarters had been bolted for the night, however, they resumed their talk. It seemed that a great deal turned on which of the ealdormen would be able to garner the most support both in the east, where the threat of Viking attack was the greatest, and in the west, where people were more concerned about the Welsh.

"Our host, Aethelwulf, certainly knows how to live like a king," said Osgar. He unbuckled his belt with a sigh of relief.

"He certainly does!" exclaimed Edmund. "Too bad the kid, his nephew, is the ealdorman. Aethelred should be glad his uncle is putting him forward so royally."

Osgar's laughing eyes turned serious as he mused on Aethelred's qualifications. "He is young," he conceded, "perhaps too young. His uncle holds lands here in the east, and he himself holds power in the west, so with his uncle's help he *might* be able to keep both sides of the country united under his leadership. But without his uncle I doubt that he would account for much."

"What about Beornoth, the relative of the deposed king, and Wulfsige, the nephew of the saint?" Edwin asked.

"Beornoth," Osgar said, "is rich, and has what some might consider a right to the throne as the only surviving kinsman of King Burgred. But he is soft on defence. He is a talker. His opponents are right in saying he thinks riches are equivalent to leadership."

Edmund nodded. "You have lands, estates, farms, all occupied by men sworn to fight with you against an enemy threat. But if they have no confidence in your leadership, if you're seen as a vacillator—as you say, 'soft'—they might as easily stay home and surrender, hoping the enemy will take their possessions but not their lives. Which is probably what would happen anyway under Beornoth. He would buy off the Vikings again and again, rather than put together a plan and an army."

"Soft, and no charisma," Osgar concurred.

What was left unsaid, out of deference for their hosts, was that perhaps the Mercians were accustomed to this kind of leadership after King Ceolwulf's Danish-approved rule. However, another Ceolwulf was exactly what they were determined to prevent.

"Well, unlike Beornoth, Wulfsige certainly has charisma," remarked Edmund, who was reclining on the bed. "He's got buckets of it. I'm told the people up here can't get enough of him."

"Yes, and he seems to enjoy the wholehearted favour of Bishop Deorlaf," noted Osgar. "It can't hurt to have a bishop behind you, if you want to be king."

Edwin shrugged. "All right, suppose we disregard Beornoth. That leaves us with Wulfsige and Aethelred. Which one would make the better ally for Wessex and King Alfred?"

"You do ask the hard ones, little brother. Well, young Aethelred has some points in his favour. He's distantly related to Alfred's wife; the kinship ties may prove helpful. Then he seems fairly organized too, and with his uncle would be able to put up a fighting force to face Guthrum."

"Wulfsige might be able to command more numbers,"

said Osgar, who had taken off his shoes to ease his gouty feet. "And he's certainly more mature, seasoned. Aethelred is still young—very young."

"But in general," said Edwin, "Wulfsige seems more the type for noble gestures and heroic acts than as a king for daily use."

Osgar smiled. "I like that. A king for daily use. No, he's certainly not that. But of course, we are in Mercia, land of legend. He seems to fit the mould! I have a notion that the council will swing in his favour. By the end of this, we will probably be making our treaties with King Wulfsige. Now, friends, what do you make of this incident with the steward and the wolves? Most unfortunate." And then it was Osgar's turn to listen as the brothers told him of their suspicions.

Chapter 15

On the day of the wolf hunt, Aethelwulf's hall was abuzz with activity even before the first light of dawn. Horses were being groomed and saddled, dogs were barking excitedly, and men were crisscrossing the yard busy with preparations. Edmund liked nothing better than a hunt of any kind, but had never hunted wolf. Neither had Edwin, but he was intrigued by their reputed cunning and thought it might prove to be a most interesting day. Edwin suspected that the Mercian lords had only invited him because of Fram, who had some wolfhound in him; his big, tough appearance had caught the eye of Wulfsige's hound-master. Edwin had warned him that Fram was not trained for wolves, but with the hound-master's urging his hosts had been insistent.

When the hunting party were assembled, they rode out of the enclosure to meet the gamekeeper and his party of local farmers armed with nets. The gamekeeper, Cynric, looked crestfallen, Edwin thought. He marshalled his farmers and dogs with resignation, leading the way to a place in the forest where the baits had been set out and the dogs were to be put on the scent.

It was, in fact, a beautiful day for a hunt. The sun was shining through the thinning canopy and the forest floor looked as if it were littered with gold. The birds stopped singing as the hunting party approached, but their music was replaced by that of happy hounds and ringing harness. The scent led the dogs deeper into the forest, then around the edges of a meadow, then once again into the heart of the wood. As they approached a stream there was some confusion about the trail, then the hounds picked it up and were off again. Most of the horses splashed through, as it was shallow, but Stig took one look at the sparkling ribbon of water and balked.

"Oh, no you don't, you scoundrel," growled Edwin under his breath. "As if you'd never seen a stream before."

He dug his heels into Stig's sides and Stig realized he had no choice but to go forward. He took a few steps, looked again at the strange barrier, and took a sudden long leap, scrambling up the other side through the mud. This so impressed the party behind them that the next horse unexpectedly tried to follow his lead. This horse landed with a splash midstream, then galloped out and ran into Stig's tail on the other side. Its rider was unseated by this manoeuvre and had to climb back into the saddle.

After a while, the trail widened again and riders were able to ride two and three abreast. Edwin saw he was near Aethelred and rode up alongside. He made some remark about the hunt.

"It's remarkable you and your brother decided to come along at all, since we know the culprit walks on two legs rather than four," Aethelred replied dryly.

"Well, my dog was invited," said Edwin, "and I felt I had better tag along as chaperon."

Aethelred laughed. "Where's your other companion? Lord Osgar?" he asked.

"Lord Osgar begged to be excused owing to his gout," Edwin explained. "He said, however, that he would be happy to eat whatever we kill."

"Hmm, yes. You are probably wanting to know the results of my enquiries among my people," Aethelred ventured cautiously. "No one in my company saw Helmstan after he left the upper room that evening. No one knows of any enemies who would want to take his life in particular, though his family has been involved in a long-running feud with some other family about—well, who knows? If you get far enough into one, it hardly matters anymore what it's about. I didn't know about it until I asked the men. Helmstan never mentioned it to me."

"Where's Helmstan's home, then?"

"Here, actually."

They rode on for a space.

"It's so unfortunate," Aethelred said suddenly. "Cynric is just devastated. He holds himself responsible for the death of his half-brother, and it's likely he will take the blame legally as well."

Edwin stared.

"Half-brother? Do you mean Helmstan was the gamekeeper's half-brother?"

"Yes, indeed," said Aethelred. "Helmstan actually owned a bit of land around here. He was the prosperous one of the family."

Edwin shook his head. This was something. If Aethelred's word could be trusted, then his whole household could be ruled out, and the murderer must be sought among Helmstan's local ties. Could he trust Aethelred? He wanted to. He wanted something to go on, and he had next to nothing unless he took Aethelred's information at face value.

"So what are the legal implications for Cynric?" asked Edwin.

"Well, he will likely be charged with negligence for allowing a wolf to get so close to my uncle's enclosure," said Aethelred. "He will lose his place as gamekeeper and probably have to pay a fine. Since he's also, to the best of my knowledge, Helmstan's next-of-kin, he will inherit Helmstan's land, but he'll probably have to sell it to pay the fine. Or rather, my uncle will consider it forfeited and take it in lieu of the fine."

"So either way, he's lost a half-brother, the family land, and his place as gamekeeper," concluded Edwin. "I suppose having lost everything clears him of suspicion, at least. I mean, he had nothing to gain by killing his half-brother and making it look like a wolf attack."

"Certainly not," Aethelred looked back at him and smiled, then spotted some of his uncle's men overtaking them. Aethelred spurred his horse forward, then said casually as he moved away, "I hope this trail does lead to the culprit. I'd like to look that man-killer in the eye and strike him down myself."

By midday the hunters had reached the heart of the forest. A massive outcropping of rock jutted out over the forest floor, creating an overhang. Here the trackers found signs of wolf habitation and the hounds ran frantically back and forth as they discovered divergent trails away from the den. Aethelwulf suggested that they split into groups, each with a group of dogs following one of the trails. Edwin ended up in the group with Aethelwulf and some of his men and a few local farmers; Aethelred took some of his uncle's other retainers and went with Beornoth. Edmund and Wulfsige were in the third group with Cynric and the rest of the local men. Edwin wished he had had a chance to relay to Edmund what he had found out about the two half-brothers, and urge Edmund to try and find out more; but that was impossible. Perhaps Edmund would find out from Cynric about the family relationship and the feud independently. More likely, though, Edwin thought, Edmund would return from the hunt with Cynric's best tips on tracking wolves and breeding wolf-hounds.

It turned out that several of the farmers had been on a wolf-hunt before. Aethelwulf was in a talkative mood and got the men to explain a little of their technique—so Edwin realized that he, instead of his brother, was going to be the recipient of much wolf-lore and very little pertinent information. Aethelwulf asked Edwin about his dog, and about hunting in Wessex, as the dogs continued eagerly following their trail through woods and clearings.

Just when Edwin thought they would never see any action, they heard a horn off to the north. One of the farmers said there would be a path farther up that would lead them in the right direction, so the party sent an answering horn-call. The expectation that one of the parties had met with their quarry infused the group's flagging spirits with a new burst of good cheer. The men began to talk amongst themselves and Edwin wondered aloud whether the wolf would be killed by the time the parties met up.

"It might have just been a sighting," said Aethelwulf. "On the other hand—well, I'm glad your brother and Wulfsige are there with Cynric. Our faith in our gamekeeper has been shaken of late."

"Is he not very experienced, then?" asked Edwin innocently. He hoped to hear more but did not wish to appear over-curious to someone who did not know the true cause of Helmstan's death.

Aethelwulf shook his head.

" I suppose it comes down to laziness. You see how easily we were able to track the wolf down when we came out here. I suppose I shall have to find a new gamekeeper now."

"Does he have family in the area?"

Aethelwulf hesitated a moment, then said, "Yes, he has relatives around here. I suppose he can go back to them. His father was a small-time thegn or rich yeoman. His mother was nothing much."

"How did Cynric come to be gamekeeper?" Edwin asked.

"That you'd have to ask my steward. I was in the west at the time, fighting Welshmen."

Conversation was suspended as their path led them over some rough ground. They had to cross what Edwin assumed was the same stream again, but this time Stig was too tired to make a fuss about it. At last, with the sun glinting low through the trees, they began to hear excited voices—human and canine—and hallooed their greetings.

The dogs joyfully rejoined their fellows, and the men hurried to the hunters crouching together in a tight knot in a clearing. Edmund stood up, his face as excited as a boy's.

"We got her, little brother! We got her. Come see."

Edwin, Aethelwulf and the others hurried and bent over the dead wolf, a spear still jutting from its side. "Here, you, help me pull my spear out of the wolf's heart," said Wulfsige to Cynric.

As the gamekeeper obeyed, he said almost to himself, "Not too large, but she gave us a fight to the last."

If Edwin had not known the grief behind his words, it would have sounded like the epitaph of a respected quarry at the end of a good day's hunting.

When all the back-slapping and tale-swapping had begun to abate, Edwin asked Edmund if they had heard anything from Aethelred's party.

"No, I thought they were off on the other side of you," Edmund said, surprised. "If you remember, we followed the north-bound scent, you went east, and Aethelred's party went sort of south-east. So you haven't heard anything from them, either?"

"Not a thing," said Edwin.

Someone suggested they might have given up and gone back to the hall.

"And miss the fun? I've never known my nephew to give up on a hunt!" said Aethelwulf.

They began to look around.

"It will be dark soon, and we need to be starting back. Perhaps as we retrace our steps back to Buckingham we can blow our horns at intervals and eventually meet up with them," said Edmund.

"Splendid idea. I know my nephew will want to hear the good news that the beast was killed."

Even the most seasoned hunting horses were reluctant to carry the freshly killed wolf, so Cynric and the farmers found a long branch and tied the dead wolf to it and two men carried it between them. The party then made their way at a peaceful walk through the lengthening shadows back the way they came.

Edmund and Edwin took turns blowing their horns every mile or so, and the entire party would stop to listen for a reply. For the first few miles, there was nothing but an unsettling silence. Then, finally, when the brothers had nearly lost hope of hearing a reply to their horn-calls, there was a faint echo of a horn in the distance to the east. Edmund blasted off a new call. A reply came, but distant and unsteady, as if the man blowing it was unfamiliar with the technique. Aethelwulf's brow clouded.

"That's not my nephew," he said.

They sent most of the men and dogs and the wolf back to

the estate, and hurried in the direction of the horn-call.

It seemed an age, but within minutes they had found Aethelred's party in the fading light. Aethelred was on the ground with Beornoth and the other men stooped over him. The horses stood nearby.

"He fell from his horse," said one of the retainers in a louder voice than was necessary.

Aethelwulf stammered, "Is he…?"

The man went on, "I'm sorry, my lord. It happened so sudden."

Edwin was on the ground searching for Aethelred's pulse and breathing. "He's alive," was his contribution.

Someone finally managed to make a light and they could see blood streaming down Aethelred's forehead. Edwin felt his head and found a large gash, but no soft spots or fractures. He got his water-flask out and washed the wound, and Aethelred stirred.

"What happened?" the injured man murmured.

"You fell from your horse, my lord," replied the loud-voiced retainer in a tone as if falling from a horse made a man deaf.

"Yes, the saddle just slipped from under me," Aethelred recalled. He tried to sit up, then groaned and lay back on the leaves.

"Are you hurt anywhere else besides your head?" asked Edwin.

"Um, I'm not sure. Let me see."

A moment later Aethelred said that his ankle was throbbing.

"Which one?"

"Left."

Edwin felt the ankle through Aethelred's boot. It seemed to be swelling.

"We'll have to get the boot off," he said. "If it's too tight we can cut it."

"Go ahead," said the wounded ealdorman, and he braced himself as Edwin and one of the other men gently pulled it off. There were no broken bones, but it was a bad sprain.

Aethelwulf asked, "How did it happen?"

"We were going down an incline, and the horse lost its footing. The young ealdorman tumbled down, and the animal fell sideways onto his foot," replied one of his companions.

"Aethelred must have hit his head on a rock and blacked out," said Edmund.

"Yes, and just then we heard your horn," the retainer replied.

Aethelred, who had been handed Edmund's flask of wine, raised himself to an elbow and took a sip. The men helped Edwin bandage Aethelred's forehead and one found a strong forked stick for a crutch.

"So did you get a wolf?" Aethelred asked at last.

This was greeted with relieved laughter. Edmund told how they had tracked the wolf down and how she had almost bit Wulfsige in the arm as he plunged his spear in her side.

"Well, well," he mused. "So you did manage to track one down. Any sign of a pack, or of a he-wolf?" asked Aethelred. The answer was negative.

"As far as Cynric can tell from tracks and droppings and so forth, and based on what the dogs could find, she might have been the last one."

"The last wolf of Buckingham," Aethelred smiled in the growing darkness. "Still, we would do well to return to my uncle's estate and relish our victory from within the walls of the enclosure, eh?"

Aethelred said he thought he could move, if only someone would help him onto his horse. There was the problem of reattaching the saddle. Edwin, since he was still kneeling on the ground next to the ealdorman, volunteered his horse; Stig was not only tired and quiet now, but also saddled and ready. He borrowed some rope from one of the farmers and went to tie Aethelred's saddle back on his horse. He passed the rope round and round over the saddle's seat and under the horse's body until it felt secure, and mounted. Aethelred felt light-headed after mounting, so one of the farmers got on behind him to hold him up. So the hunting party, now more relieved than triumphant, made their way back to Aethelwulf's hall.

◆

Edwin had promised to return the farmer's rope the next day, so he went to the stable at first light to retrieve it. It was hung up neatly on the rack with Aethelred's saddle and the broken girth waiting to be taken away for repair. Edwin felt oddly curious when he saw the broken girth. He had heard of girths breaking, but it had never happened to him; the sturdiest leather was always used for the straps, and his father had taught him to always, always check his girth before mounting. "Your life can depend on it," he said.

The leather was fairly new, thick, strong and butter-soft, the kind made from well-fed and unblemished cattle, which few but ealdormen could afford. Edwin examined the broken ends. The fine strap leather had broken in a straight line below the fastening, not at a buckle-hole or worn section. The torn fibres of the leather formed a short fringe at close inspection; quite normal. Edwin turned the strap over to the rough side, and his eyes caught something odd. Instead of the fine fringe of fibres where the leather gave way, on the back the broken end showed a rough line as if the leather had been abraded instead of pulling apart. This side would have been against the horse's soft coat, not exposed to any abrasive surface, so that made no sense. Then, suddenly, it did. Someone had weakened the strap, probably with a file, so that at some point it would give way to the strain and cause an accident. Could this strap be evidence of a crime?

Edwin was alone, so he quickly coiled the strap and hid it under his tunic. Then he took the farmer's rope and left. He would have to think this over as he went. The farm was a couple of miles' ride in the pale autumn morning. How pleasant it was to saunter out on old Red, thought Edwin, who had given Stig the day off. Riding on Red today was better for thinking, anyway. He considered his discovery about the strap. It was on Aethelred's personal saddle, which only he used, so whoever sabotaged it wanted Aethelred to meet with an accident.

"Who would want to harm Aethelred?" was his next consideration. Certainly any of his political rivals here could be considered suspect. Any of them, or their servants, could have come into the stable at any time and tampered with the strap. Both Wulfsige and Beornoth were out on the hunt yesterday. Or Aethelred could have tampered with the strap to deflect suspicion from himself, if he were guilty of Helmstan's slaying. His discovery really got him no farther than he was before, it seemed, since he already knew that someone at the meeting was a murderer. He wondered which of them might be next to suffer some sort of 'accident.'

With a sudden pang of doubt, he pulled out the strap and examined the broken end again. He was afraid that he was jumping to conclusions. What would Edmund say this time? Was it only his own fevered imagination that saw evidence of sabotage in this broken piece of leather?

But as he looked, he saw the same signs as before, still telling him the same tale. He could imagine some man secretly slipping a file under the strap. It could be done without anyone noticing. It would have to have been done after the saddle was already on the horse, or it would have been noticed when the girth was first tightened. Anytime between morning and evening, then. And anyone could have done it. It would be impossible to search the lords, and futile to try and search underlings for a file. By now it would have been quietly returned to whatever tool box it had been taken from.

Back at the hall, he showed Edmund what he had found. Edmund's face was grim.

"We had better talk to Aethelred about this," he said.

Chapter 16

"My lady, Father Ingeld to see you." Henna ushered the priest into the hall where Eng had interrupted Molly's efforts at planning the week's meals.

"Please, my lady," Eng was able to swap curses for courtesy when she pleased. "The market only comes round once a season. Might I have a day's holiday to go, a week from today?"

Molly, impatient, glanced at the waiting priest. "Very well," she said.

"Then," said Eng, her eyes taking on a bright glint, "you had better let me have the keys the night before, so I can get breakfast early before leaving."

"All right. You may go now, Eng. We had better work on meal planning together later." Dismissing her was a relief. "Ah, Father Ingeld," said Molly, smiling him a welcome. She motioned him to a bench.

The priest of Wimborne was not a tall man, nor particularly young. He had broad shoulders and short legs and a bit of a paunch. The hair that grew over his ears was iron-grey and curly, and in his younger years it must have been darker and covered more of his head than it did now. He had kindly eyes under his bushy eyebrows.

"I'm so glad you came today," Molly said. "I did want to

meet you before Sunday. And to tell you the truth, if you had not come we would have had to call for you."

"Oh yes?" the priest's eyes registered concern.

"Nothing acute, I assure you," said Molly quickly. "Just a matter of our having eaten some bread from unwholesome flour. But where are my manners?" She quickly got up and poured him a cup of cider from the pitcher on the side table.

"Ah," said Ingeld appreciatively as he tasted the brew. "Beorelf has surpassed himself again." He drained the cup. "I needed that." Molly brought the pitcher to the table where they were sitting and poured him another. "I was up all night with a sick baby," he said in explanation.

"Yours?"

"No, I'm not married. This was a new baby at one of the farms on the edge of the downs. They were afraid it might die and I had to hurry out there for the baptism."

"Will the child make it?" Molly asked.

"It's got a chance, I believe. If the parents will take my advice."

"Which is?"

"Nothing too complicated. Fewer amulets, more blankets."

"Have they enough firewood?" asked Molly.

"They certainly have gathering rights, so they should be able to get it. It's a matter of the husband finding the time to gather it since the wife must stay indoors with the baby."

Molly nodded.

"Now, Lady Molgifu, what was this problem with the bad bread?"

"It seems of little significance compared to the life of a new-born child. But the day after my first meal here I made an inspection of our stores. I found—er—signs of mice in the flour used to make our bread. I must assume we have all ingested this unwholesome bread."

"By signs of mice I assume you mean droppings. And now you need to know what to do. Is it a very large amount of flour?"

"The bin is about half-full, so yes."

"Were the droppings mixed through or only on the surface?"

"Pretty well-distributed through the top few inches, but I believe the rest was untouched."

"I suppose you got rid of the unwholesome portion?"

"Yes, over the protests of our cook, who wanted to just sift them out."

"Famine does that to people," said Ingeld. "Well, that's good. I can bless the rest of the flour but you have to keep the vermin from getting back in. As for penance, it seems rather to defeat the object if I put you on a bread and water diet for eating unwholesome bread."

Molly nodded slowly. She had been expecting, and dreading, this part.

"The penalty is intended as a curb to negligence and gluttony. As far as I can tell you have not been guilty of either in this accidental consumption of unwholesome bread. I will impose no fast on your household, but I will require all the flour to be thoroughly sifted and the bin cleaned before any more bread is made in this hall. Any bread that is already made must be thrown out. You may feed it to the chickens but you may not distribute it to slaves or the poor."

Molly would never have dreamed of such a thing anyway, but she was in any case overcome with relief not to be faced with a penitential fast.

Molly soon adjusted to the weekly rounds of the estate, though her responsibilities constantly confronted her with the depth of her inexperience. She longed for Edwin's return—and readily admitted to herself that it was not just as a husband and companion, but as a friend that she missed him. Lullus was helpful but unfailingly deferential. Henna had her quiet way of offering advice, but her conversation was always familiar, domestic, feminine. Molly therefore came to appreciate her passing visits with Father Ingeld. He spent a great deal of time out and about among his flock, and when his errands took him past the hall he never failed to stop in for a moment or two.

One quiet afternoon a few days later he dropped by again. Molly rose as he entered the hall. "Why, Father," she said, gratefully setting aside her spindle and wool, "How good to see you today."

"I can't stop for long," said the priest as Molly moved to the side table where the cider-jug stood. "I just came to bring you something."

He indicated the covered basket he was carrying on his arm.

Molly took the basket, puzzled, and opened the lid. A furry little face surmounted by two large ears popped out.

"A kitten! How lovely!" she exclaimed, scooping him up as he pawed the air and mewed in protest. His grey-striped fur was losing the baby kitten's downy softness as his sleek top coat was growing in.

"I figured he would be the most practical solution to your mouse problem," said Ingeld. "His mother is a famous mouser down our way. I waited to make sure he had started to follow her career. See his ears?"

"It's impossible to miss them."

"You can always tell a good mouser by his big ears. I trust he'll do well for you."

Sebbi had risen from his lounging posture and was

watching the new creature intently. Molly lowered the kitten down to Sebbi's eye level. The animals leaned forward to sniff noses, and the kitten gave Sebbi's nose a lick. Sebbi snorted and turned away to observe at a short distance.

"I think he's just what we needed," Molly beamed. "Thank you. What shall I name him?"

"Well, he was born right after St Swithun's day. You remember that big thunderstorm? No, of course, you weren't here during the summer."

"Swithun sounds like a fine name for this little fellow. Thanks again."

"Well, I must be getting on," said Ingeld, rising and gathering his belongings. "I am going to call on little Eadgyth today," he said. Seeing Molly's quizzical look, he said, "The sick baby."

"Oh!" Molly exclaimed, springing up in sudden recollection. "I've got something for you, too."

From a chest she pulled out a folded piece of woollen cloth.

"You mentioned they needed blankets. Here's something just big enough, if you think they can use it."

"This is almost as soft as that kitten," said Ingeld, feeling the cloth between his fingers.

"Yes, it was—shall we say—rescued from the corner of an otherwise unusable blanket we found in the King's quarters. They don't need to know that, of course, but I've put a bit of a hem around the edges and the mother can embroider it more if she likes." Ingeld went on his way rejoicing, and Molly picked up Swithun and went to show him to Henna.

Swithun, in his own way, made his mark on the household. He soon had the measure of Eng, and after suffering a few swipes from her broom, learned when to slip into the larder and when to hang back. Around the hall and outbuildings, he walked with a proprietorial air, tail held high with its tip curled into a questioning crook. He learned when the cows were milked and knew which dairy-maid would treat him to a little taste from her pail. Most importantly, he found out where the mice lived. Sebbi followed his little friend faithfully, and was frequently permitted to share in the spoils, though the mouse that would have fed young Swithun twice over was swallowed by Sebbi in one gulp. Swithun's devoted and generous side, however, was reserved for Molly. To her he presented the best of his catches. His mistress soon learned, on opening her door in the morning, to step aside so as to avoid treading on some small defunct creature laid out on the threshold of her quarters. Usually it was a mouse; sometimes a vole; once, a young rat almost as big as Swithun himself. The reward he received was a dish of cream and a nap near the hearth in the hall, in the corner by the window where Molly and Henna usually sat in the gloom of late afternoon to do their spinning.

Chapter 17

"So you really believe I am in danger? That someone is trying to kill me, or put me out of the running?" Aethelred adjusted the bedclothes and sat up carefully to spare his ankle. "Until yesterday I would not have believed it, but now, I suppose—"

The brothers had come for a private audience with the young ealdorman, who was confined to his bed with his injuries. His uncle had given him the best guest-house, which was larger, more decorated, and closer to the main hall than that occupied by the West Saxons. At Edwin's request, Aethelred had dismissed all his men, closed the window-shutter and bolted the door while they talked.

"This man—whoever he is—seems to be a very subtle assassin," said Edmund. "First there was the faked wolf-attack. Now the simulated hunting accident. If I were you," he said, poking his finger absently in some cold porridge at Aethelred's bedside, "I'd watch out for poison."

"You will need a couple of trusted men-at-arms to guard you at all times," Edwin advised. "And I do mean *all* times."

"Even when I go to the latrine?"

"Yes. They must not let you out of their sight. And yes, as my brother says, take care about your food."

"A diet of boiled eggs it is, then," said Aethelred.

"Eh?"

"Well, you can't tamper with the inside of a boiled egg," Aethelred grinned. Then, turning serious, he said, "I'll keep mum about my hunting accident not being accidental, but I don't see any further point in keeping the truth about Helmstan's death a secret. People are talking anyway since I started asking all those questions. Don't you think it would be better to put everyone on their guard?"

Edmund was against it, saying that it could compromise the council. Edwin said it would make it harder to catch the killer out. "Though then again," he reasoned, "there would be more eyes watching for suspicious actions and circumstances."

"I couldn't agree more. I will go ahead and make the facts public," Aethelred concluded. Edmund scowled at Edwin.

"Speaking of eyes watching for suspects," said Aethelred, "I won't be able to do that for the next few days. Ealdorman Edmund, I won't impose on you," he said, reading Edmund's face. "But Lord Osgar has told me something of your antecedents, Lord Edwin, how you have helped King Alfred by investigating some of his cases for him. Would you—could you—consider looking into this matter a little more until I am up and about again? I can't just let this matter drop; I owe it to Helmstan."

"Certainly," said Edwin.

"Just so you understand," Edmund cut in, "that he is doing this as a favour and not as a token of our premature support for any of the parties here. We can't just—"

"Purely as a personal favour," Aethelred nodded at Edwin, and Edwin nodded back.

It was not hard to locate Aethelwulf's steward, but

impossible to find a time when he was not busy. He was a stocky, round-headed man with ruddy cheeks; Edwin remembered him as the man who had blown the horn to summon help for Aethelred in the wolf-hunt. He was the sort of servant who seemed to always have his mind halfway on the next task. At the moment he was in the storeroom taking stock of the candle supply. The long candles he piled neatly on one side; the ones that were burned down to stubs he tossed into a pile beside an iron pot. A scrawny servant or slave of indeterminate age was squatting by the bucket with a little knife, cutting out the wicks and putting the wax into the pot. The helper sneezed wetly and wiped his nose on his sleeve.

"Yeah, too bad what's happened to Cynric," Putta said when Edwin introduced himself. "Known him for years. It'll be tough to replace him. Still, the company you keep…"

"What do you mean by that?" Edwin asked, surprised.

"Well, he's been friends with the local poacher since they were boys. No telling what them two get up to when they're together."

"Do you think Cynric has been cheating his master by allowing his friend to hunt on Aethelwulf's land?"

Putta tossed another few stubs into the bucket and shrugged. "I'm not making any accusations," he said. "I never knew for sure of any poaching on my lord's land, or I would have told him. Things being as they are I kept my own counsel about it all. Cynric, as a gamekeeper, he's all right—keeps the hounds in trim and knows the woods. My lord could do a lot worse. That friend of his, though, he's probably mixed up in it somehow. If he gets accused in this, it'll be the end of the road for him. He's what you might call one of our usual suspects."

He said this, Edwin thought, with some relish, as if it were a matter of local pride for a district to have men who were often accused of crime and never convicted.

"Mind you," Putta went on speculatively, "you wouldn't go wrong, my lord, to talk to Lord Wulfsige's falconer."

"Does he know Cynric's friend?"

"No, but my friend here saw him, the falconer I mean, sneaking through the wicket-gate on the night before Helmstan was found dead. Didn't you?" he said, elbowing his companion. The latter nodded, his stringy hair swinging on either side of his head. "Now, my lord, I'll lay you any odds you like that Wulfsige's man will be lying. You just ask him and see. I wouldn't trust him farther than I could throw him. Any odds you like."

Remarkable, Edwin thought, how rivalries between lords carried through to their household staff. He thanked them and resolved to track down Wulfsige in his lair as soon as he could.

◆

"Did you hear about the big blow-up between Aethelwulf and Beornoth?" Edmund said. He had seen Edwin walking around the enclosure before breakfast and strode over to catch up.

"I thought there was a bit of an atmosphere this morning. What was it—Lady Hereburg?"

"What's she got to do with it?"

"Oh, come on. You've seen how she and Aethelwulf make eyes at each other."

"Have to admit I missed that one, little brother," said Edmund, "though she's a good-looking woman and a trifle too young for old Beornoth."

They had reached the place along the wall where Edmund's men had their tents. The tents were deserted except for one man on guard duty squatting by a low fire polishing weapons. Seeing Edmund, he rose to attention.

"Godhelm took the men out for exercises, sir," he reported.

"Fine," said Edmund. "Carry on."

Edmund continued along the line of tents conducting an impromptu inspection, then the brothers proceeded through the gate. They saw, in the distance, Edmund's chief retainer, who was at this time leading the men in relay races on the green.

"What I was trying to tell you," said Edmund, "was that Aethelwulf and Beornoth had some kind of parting of the ways. I don't know what it was about, but I doubt if it was the woman. She and her maids are still in the women's quarters over there, but I hear Beornoth left the hall after dinner in high dudgeon and spent last night at the abbey."

"Hmm. Do you suppose it will affect the deliberations of the council? I mean, Aethelwulf wasn't supporting Beornoth anyway. Was the blow-up with Ealdorman Aethelred as well?"

"As far as I know, Aethelred is completely indifferent. I don't think he takes Beornoth all that seriously."

"But Aethelwulf does, apparently."

"Well, evidently they were thrown together a good deal on the recent Welsh campaign. I suppose they are, or were, friends."

They were watching the foot-races as they spoke. Then Godhelm had the men all sit, red-cheeked and panting, on the grass.

"Wrestling," he barked. "You and you. Strip down and wait for my word."

The two men, who had shed their tunics before the races, now peeled off their damp linen shirts and faced off in their breeches.

"Now!" said Godhelm, and the two warriors soon enclosed one another in a painful and warlike embrace. Urged on by the shouts of their comrades they gripped and grappled until finally one had the other face down with his knee in his opponent's back.

"That will do," said Godhelm. He then gave them a brief exposition on wrestling techniques before choosing another pair of opponents. They reminded Edwin of the gripping beasts that craftsmen fashioned in wood and metal. As they watched they saw another group of warriors strolling out onto the green, yawning and scratching, driven, it seemed, by their captain.

"Aethelwulf's men, it looks like," said Edwin. "I think your men woke them up."

A flicker of gratification showed on Edmund's face.

"You have to keep 'em busy or they get lazy," he said.

As they stood talking they heard a scream from the direction of the abbey. After a shocked second the brothers heard people running in the direction from which it had come and they followed as well. In his room in the abbey's guest quarters, they found Beornoth, white as a ghost, staring transfixed at a pillow hung in a noose over his bed. The spell was broken as people began to come in, and he tried to find speech.

"Wha-wha-what's the meaning of this?" he quivered. "Who did this?"

Someone practical had already brought a ladder to reach the high beam to which the rope was tied, and cut it down. Everyone burst into excited speculation about what it could mean and who might have done it. Edwin sidled up to the rope and pillow and looked them over. The pillow was from Beornoth's own bed; the rope was just an ordinary rope from the stables, to which anyone might have access at virtually any time of day. He was sure that, when asked, no one would have seen anyone doing anything suspicious.

Within a brief time Beornoth had regained his composure somewhat; he laughed the incident off as a prank and the crowd began to disperse. It didn't feel like a prank to Edwin, however, and he wandered away so deep in thought that he was scarcely aware of his dog, or his brother, at his side. They ended up in the graveyard on the other side of the abbey. Passing the mound of freshly turned earth that marked Helmstan's grave, they made their way to a private corner of the enclosure which was partly shielded from view by a tall standing cross more than a hundred years old. There, in the shelter of a yew-tree, they felt sufficiently removed from listening ears.

"Strange things going on in Buckingham," said Edmund, breaking the silence.

"I can't make heads or tails of it," Edwin agreed. "Why was Aethelred's steward killed? Why did someone try to harm Aethelred?"

"Come to that, why is someone threatening Beornoth?"

"You thought that too. Yes, if someone hangs a noose in an ealdorman's bedchamber at a council of state, that's not a prank." Edwin began to pace in very small circles. "Surely it's the same man. It had to be someone who had come to the council, at least in the cases of Aethelred and Beornoth; no ordinary folk would have either the motive or the means to threaten both men."

"Then who's left? The bishops?"

Edwin stopped pacing and considered. "Doubtful. But then again…a bishop isn't necessarily a saint. Bishop Deorlaf does seem dreadfully keen to get Wulfsige chosen as King of Mercia. Bishop Waerferth doesn't seem the type to engage in a violent plot, but who really knows the heart of man?"

"They would have no opportunity at all," added Edmund, ever practical. "Well, perhaps for the noose and pillow prank—er, threat, but not for Helmstan's killing, and they didn't go on the wolf-hunt either. So they're out."

"Well, let's just say they are unlikely but will bear watching," Edwin qualified. "They could be involved without being on the spot when the deed was done. How about Aethelwulf?"

"He has no need to harm his own nephew. If he sticks to Aethelred, and Aethelred becomes king, Aethelwulf could end up being the power behind the throne. That way he could keep up his lavish lifestyle and have all the women he likes."

"All I noticed was some flirtation with Beornoth's wife," said Edwin. "But that might add another more personal reason to get Beornoth out of the way—besides the political motive to clear the way for his nephew." He thought this over. "But how a noose and pillow would do that is beyond me. And it happened *after* Beornoth fell out with Aethelwulf and decamped to the abbey. Nor can I see any connection with the attack on Aethelred."

Edmund laughed. "Aethelred doesn't need to worry about old Beornoth. If I were Aethelred—or his uncle wanting to intervene for him—it's Wulfsige's popularity I'd worry about."

"True enough! Then there's Wulfsige himself. Both Aethelred and Beornoth stand in the way of his ambitions. And let's not forget, someone was out to get Aethelred. Look here, do you suppose Wulfsige was behind that?"

"Perhaps," Edmund reflected. "Wulfsige might be trying to clear his path of rivals."

"He certainly had the motive and he was close by at the time of all the events."

"It doesn't explain Helmstan's murder, though. Wulfsige

has been staying at the Abbey the whole time, so he wasn't anywhere near Helmstan," objected Edmund.

"Well," Edwin pondered, "even if he was not personally in striking distance of Helmstan, he has some very loyal men who will probably do anything for him."

"That's what's wrong with all these suspects. None of them actually have to be in the right place at the right time. They all have servants, retainers, underlings they can get to do the deeds."

"Not always as easy as you make it sound," Edwin remarked, thinking of how hard it was to get his young groom Bert to follow the simplest instructions. "But I take your point. In Wulfsige's case, though, he was on the hunt, so he could have sabotaged the saddle, and since he's staying at the abbey he would certainly have had opportunity to put up that noose and pillow in Beornoth's quarters when Beornoth was staying there last night."

"You are making him sound like a serious suspect," Edmund said.

Edwin shrugged. "The only thing that sits ill with me is the underhanded way the crimes were committed. Wulfsige is a man who wears his heart on his sleeve. He seems always more interested in getting credit for his involvement in something than hiding it."

"All right. I suppose he's another one to watch closely," grumbled Edmund.

Then another thought caused Edwin's brow to furrow. "Listen, suppose different men were responsible for the different acts? Suppose Beornoth was responsible for Helmstan's death and the sabotage of Aethelred's saddle, and Aethelred then threatened Beornoth with the noose?"

"Or Wulfsige," said Edmund. "Remember, he could easily

have done the noose." Edmund shifted and made to leave. "I'm going for a drink," he said. "They'll be setting up tables for dinner soon and all your maybes and what-ifs are driving me out of my mind."

Edwin shook his head. His brother was right; he was driving himself out of his mind as well. He stroked Fram's ears absentmindedly as he continued thinking for a moment over all the possibilities. Then Fram's tail began to wag and he looked at Edwin, then at the gate. "You hounds have it easy," Edwin smiled as he took the hint. "All you have to do is put your nose to the ground and follow the trail."

It was not until after dinner that Edwin was able to speak to Ealdorman Beornoth alone. Beornoth had taken leave of the abbey and had crossed the yard back to Aethelwulf's hall with his servants and belongings, so apparently either his disagreement with Aethelwulf was resolved, or he found the prospect of further anonymous threats at the abbey even less palatable than forgiving his friend for whatever slight he might have suffered. It was good for all concerned that the rift was healed; the tension between Beornoth and Aethelwulf had only added further to the atmosphere of distrust and uneasiness at the council. Edwin had caught sight of Abbot Aethelhun earlier in the day and had noticed the man's broad, easy-going features were contracted with strain. No wonder— he was hosting two kingly rivals under his not terribly wide roof, and one of those rivals had fallen out with the Abbot's cousin, who was also his noble patron.

Edwin wanted to find out more about the threat from Beornoth without appearing unduly inquisitive. The consciousness of his position as a guest and a foreigner dogged him; if he came to be regarded as a spy or even just a busybody, it might endanger the mission for his whole party. At the same time, dangerous things were happening and no one else at the council seemed to want to get to the bottom of it all. The Mercian rivals were content to blame one another or settle for an obvious solution regardless of whether or not it was actually correct.

When Edwin got into conversation with Beornoth, then, he tried not to lead with the theme of nooses and pillows. Instead, he asked conversationally if the ealdorman had ever been to Buckingham before. It was a short step from there to asking about Beornoth's own estates, which Edwin had learned long ago was an excellent tongue-loosener for the high-born. Beornoth was, Edwin found, very rich indeed—even more so than Edwin had imagined—with far-flung estates mostly in the north of Mercia.

"Fine country up there, you know," Beornoth's chest swelled with pride as he spoke. "Fine for rye and turnips, and the hunting's pretty good too."

"What do you hunt?"

"Oh, boar—deer—we do some hawking also," Beornoth said. "Wolves, of course, have to be kept in check."

"Speaking of wolves," said Edwin, who felt that the door had been flung wide for him, "I hear that you were in the west fighting a Welsh wolf not too long ago."

"Welsh wolf? Oh, yes," replied Beornoth. "Rhodri Mawr, that's very apt. Terrible. If it's not the Vikings, it's the Welsh. I don't know what he was after, but he was a most unreliable ally."

"I'm sure King Ceolwulf would not have disagreed with your estimation! It's not a king's reliable allies that cause his death."

These words seemed to strike Beornoth forcibly. He looked keenly at Edwin for a moment before saying, "His death was a great shock, especially as he left the succession in such disarray."

"You feel he should have made it clear that you were next in line?"

"I? Well, yes, if he had done that it might have been different. But now—" (he gave a little sigh) "now I suppose I shall withdraw my claim and put my support behind one or other of my rivals."

So Beornoth was withdrawing his claim to the throne! He was frightened of something, but what or who could it be? Edwin ventured, "I suppose it must have been one of your rivals that left the threat in your bedchamber today."

"What? No! That was merely a practical joke, I assure you." Beornoth licked his dry lips. "Now, if you'll excuse me, I must go and see how my wife is doing."

◆

Edwin decided it was high time to ask Wulfsige if he knew anything about the incident with Beornoth's pillow. Wulfsige's party were housed at the abbey; for a small establishment it had decent guest quarters. He made for the long thatch-roofed building at the edge of the abbey precincts. Edwin recognized Wulfsige's lodgings chiefly by the cages of hunting hawks arranged outside the door. They were being tended by a grizzled old man and a boy.

Approaching a servant leaning against the wall by the door, he asked for Lord Wulfsige.

The man looked him insolently up and down. There was no mistaking the silver inlay on Edwin's sword-hilt or the deep-dyed quality of his cloak, but the man was unmoved. "Who wants to know?"

"Lord Edwin of the West Saxons."

The man pulled his knife out of its sheath and felt the edge, then slowly and deliberately picked his teeth with it. Examining the point and wiping off the residue, imaginary or otherwise, he said " 'Scuse me," and turned and went inside.

After a short wait, the man returned. "He'll see you," he said, waving Edwin in. Edwin reflected that he was better off not having a servant at all than one who picked his teeth at visitors.

Inside, Wulfsige was sitting on a carved chair surrounded by several of his warriors, a small lapdog, and a great many boxes and chests. The man evidently did not believe in travelling light.

"Ah," Wulfsige stretched out his hand in welcome. "Lord—er—Edmund, is it?"

"Edwin," said the visitor, "Ealdorman Edmund is my brother."

"Ah yes. Of Wessex. But where is the rest of your deputation?" Wulfsige looked over Edwin's shoulder.

"I am not here on an official visit, you understand," said Edwin. "Although Ealdorman Edmund and Lord Osgar would be honoured to make you such a visit soon." Wulfsige looked gratified. "No, my lord, I am here purely in a private capacity. I wonder if you heard of the disturbance that occurred here at the abbey earlier in the day?"

"Disturbance? No—what do you mean?" Wulfsige raised one eyebrow, but showed no other sign of concern.

"And your men—they also heard nothing?" The retainers shook their heads.

Then one man from the far corner of the room piped up, "I heard something when I was out checking on the horses."

"Silence!" Wulfsige snapped. "Now, Lord Edwin, why are

you really here? What was this disturbance, and why are you so clearly wanting to blame my household for it?"

"I assure you, it is not a question of blame. There was an incident in Beornoth's quarters—"

"So you immediately thought that I was responsible. Well, what else can we expect? I know that you and your Wessex busybodies are here to make sure I am edged out of the kingship that is rightfully mine in favour of the young upstart Aethelred or that pig at the trough, Beornoth."

For a moment, Edwin was speechless. "Look," he finally said. "I simply came here to ask if anyone had seen anything that would help our host, Lord Aethelwulf, determine who threatened Lord Beornoth. I did not come here with notions about who is guilty. As far as I can tell, anyone could have done it. If you prefer by your hostile words to bring suspicion upon yourself, where none had been before, that is certainly your prerogative—but it will not help your cause." At this, trembling with anger, Edwin turned on his heel and made for the door.

As his hand reached for the latch, Wulfsige's voice called out, "Wait."

Edwin turned around.

"Perhaps I spoke hastily," Wulfsige laughed. "I am rather precipitate at times. Please do not take offense. Won't you come and make yourself comfortable?"

He motioned toward a chair which was immediately vacated by the senior retainer who had been sitting in it. Edwin sat down.

"Now, what ill has befallen Lord Beornoth?"

"He received a threat, an anonymous threat. At least, that is how he understood it and I see no other way of interpreting it."

"And this threat, was it a threat of physical harm, or…"

"It was the pillow from his bed strung up in a noose and hanging from a rafter in his quarters."

Wulfsige clapped his hands. "Excuse me. Perhaps I should not regard this incident as an occasion for mirth," the Mercian said. "But by my sainted uncle, I can hardly help myself!" At this he threw back his head and laughed, and his retainers saw fit to laugh with him.

As the noise died away Wulfsige finally noticed that Edwin did not share the joke. "I say, you West Saxons are a dour lot," he remarked. "Pranks are supposed to be funny."

"This was no prank, I am certain," said Edwin. "There is evidence—growing evidence—that there is an assassin amongst us who wishes to kill or frighten off the candidates for the kingship. Aethelred's fall during the wolf-hunt was no accident." He looked closely at Wulfsige as he said this, but Wulfsige's face registered only surprise.

"An assassin! That means I could be next."

"Indeed. So the purpose for my visit to you today is twofold. I wanted to know if anyone in your party had seen suspicious activity around Beornoth's quarters earlier today, and to warn you to be on your guard."

It couldn't hurt to ask Wulfsige about the night of Helmstan's death, Edwin thought. There was the danger, though, that a badly-phrased question might send Wulfsige back into another pout.

"By the way," he paused, hand on the door-frame. "I was hoping I could ask you about what happened before the wolf-hunt. For instance, if any of your men knew Helmstan—"

"Who's that?" Wulfsige stared at him blankly.

"The man who was killed. Aethelred's retainer."

"Ah, I see. Poor man. No, we were at the abbey getting

settled, and didn't stir abroad until the next morning when the council met."

On his way out, Edwin noticed the old falconer and the boy cutting up meat for their charges. He loitered to watch.

"What an expensive pastime hawking is," Edwin remarked. "At least if you keep your birds year round."

The old man shrugged. "That it is, my lord; you should know, I suppose. But there's nothing like it."

"That is true," Edwin conceded. "For two minds so different as that of man and bird to work together. It's almost like having wings ourselves." Edwin peered into the cages made from slats of wood. Wulfsige seemed to be a sort of collector, with all sorts of hawks and falcons in cages neatly arranged from large to small. The proud birds with their sharp eyes took him in as he passed, but they had sized him up and looked away again long before he was finished admiring them. Slightly apart from the others was a large cage of new wood with wide slats and narrow gaps between. Edwin peered through the gaps and saw that the cage was occupied. The bird inside was pure white with a black-and-white speckled back.

"What is this one?" Edwin asked, pointing to the cage. "I've never seen anything like it."

The falconer replied, "It's a kind of, er, goshawk, my lord. Commoner up here than where you come from." Edwin saw him exchange a look with his young helper.

"He's beautiful. Can you take him out and show him to me?"

The man scratched the back of his neck and shook his head regretfully. "I'm sorry, my lord, but she's still in training. A young 'un, she can't be trusted yet to stay on my glove."

"Well, she's very handsome, anyway. Perhaps sometime I can watch you train her. Do you ever go into Lord Aethelwulf's enclosure to train, by the way?"

"The enclosure? No," the man replied in some surprise. "We've been going out to the green, or into the fields over the river. You need wide open spaces," he said, as if explaining to a small child, "to train hawks and falcons."

"I understand that. But as you were going in and out of Aethelwulf's enclosure on the night the steward Helmstan was killed, I wondered if—"

"Who told you that?" The man's eyes were now wary.

"Well, did you see anything? A man has been accused in his death, and I am charged with finding out the circumstances."

"I did nothing but tend to my own business," the falconer said, folding his arms. "Which is what every man ought to do."

"You must have gone to speak to someone inside the enclosure. What was your errand? Perhaps the person you went to speak to might have seen something."

The falconer took up the piece of meat and began cutting again.

"Killing Helmstan—was that the business you were attending to that night?"

"No! I didn't even know the man. I tell you I was attending to my lord's—to my own business. I didn't see no wolf, nor no killing, and I have nothing more to tell you." He punctuated this assertion with a hard whack of his knife on the cutting board, and a little piece of meat went flying. The boy fetched it and put it back in the bucket with the rest. Edwin took his leave, having found out less than he wished but more than the falconer had intended to disclose.

◆

"Well, little brother, we West Saxons certainly know how to

conduct a smooth diplomatic mission," Edmund said that evening in their quarters. They had just endured a dinner in which even the atmosphere could be cut with a knife. "Tell everyone at a meeting deadlocked by fierce rivalries that one of them is a killer out to get the rest."

"Yes, now that everyone knows about the assassin it has rather put a damper on dinner conversation," reflected Osgar.

"Sorry, I should have kept my mouth shut. Then the dinner conversation could flow uninterrupted until everyone was dead." Edwin had been bursting to tell them about his interview with Wulfsige and the strange encounter with his falconer, about the fact that the falconer had been inside the enclosure on the night of Helmstan's death on some mysterious business for Wulfsige, and the fact that Wulfsige had somehow got his hands on an Icelandic gyrfalcon but his falconer wanted Edwin to believe it was a common goshawk; but now there was no point. Would then even listen?

Edwin was in no mood even for Osgar this evening. He would sleep in the hall again. His mind revolted against his every attempt to find a way through the maze of circumstances and possibilities. He wanted to be home, he wanted to be with Molly. He was desperately afraid he would forget her lovely, cheerful face, that it would be lost to him amid these new faces in Mercia that he was utterly unable to read.

◆

Deep in the night, Edwin was awakened suddenly by a punch in the stomach. In an instant he was on his feet in a crouching attack position, his seax at the ready, every sense awakened. But the hall was full of the sound of sleeping men; there was no attacker to confront. The only light was the faint red glow of the coals on the hearth, the remains of the fire that had been allowed to die down, and all it revealed were the lumpish contours of sleeping men. Edwin peered into the darkness and saw nothing moving. He could still feel the impact on his stomach, but it certainly wasn't the hardest punch he'd ever taken.

Then, from a few yards away, he heard a strange growl and a scuffling. It took his dazed mind a moment to place the sound. It was the growl of a cat that had caught its prey. He rubbed his stomach. The cat, prowling the hall, had launched itself off his body in pursuit of some creature. From the sound of it (he heard a squeak), it was a mouse. His own breathing sounded louder than the snores of the warriors.

Trembling, he sheathed his seax and lay back down in his place. He tried to force his mind to focus on something, anything, to calm his pounding heart and racing mind. The cat. By the sound of it the cat had caught the mouse; he could hear the crunching as it devoured the hapless rodent. And warrior though he was, the sound made his stomach turn over; he covered his ears and hummed a repetitive little tune to drown it out. He finally managed to slow his breathing by starting on an idea for a new riddle; but it was still some time before his mind was calm enough to allow sleep to take over again.

Chapter 18

In the meantime, mindful of the King's instructions, Edwin sought an audience with the two Mercian bishops. It was Deorlaf who received him first. The bishop was sitting at a table in the abbey's guest-hall with an ink-stained young monk, acting as his amanuensis, and a tidy stack of parchments.

"Yes?" drawled Deorlaf, not looking up.

"My lord bishop," began Edwin. "I am charged with the pleasant task of bringing you the personal greetings of my king, Alfred of the West Saxons."

"Oh yes?" Deorlaf looked at him appraisingly. "You are—" he paused in thought. "No, it's gone. One of those Wessex visitors."

Edwin reintroduced himself and also named his companions. Only Edmund was with him, and that under protest. Edwin was glad the bishop could not guess what his brother had said to the prospect of a private audience with him.

"I was personally charged by my lord King Alfred to convey his friendship to the Mercian bishops and his deep respect for their reputation of holiness and learning." The ink-stained amanuensis flicked a startled glance at his bishop, then at Edwin, but was concentrating on his letters by the time

Edwin looked at him again.

"I see." Deorlaf's words left a chill in the air. Was the bishop, Edwin wondered, one of those men who became colder the more polite one tried to be? Edwin let the silence hang a bit. He looked around the room. The animal skulls and weapons had been taken down from the walls, probably because Deorlaf had disapproved of those as well.

"Lord Edwin," said the bishop, "do sit down. You and, of course, Ealdorman Edmund. I will be perfectly frank with you. I have nothing against your king, but your presence here in Mercia at this time was not my choice. I have reached an age at which I have little patience for foreign kings and their attempts at statecraft. What does your royal master really mean by sending you here to meddle in concerns outside of Wessex?"

"You can easily understand that we in Wessex have an interest in our northern neighbours, especially since our recent victory over Guthrum," Edmund said.

"Yes, you've mentioned that *several* times since your arrival," said Deorlaf dryly.

"However, that was not the aim of our visit to you today," Edwin took back the reins. "King Alfred has a great desire to augment learning and renew the church in Wessex since the depredations we have suffered at the hands of heathen men. I will not conceal from you that we stand in great need of learned churchmen and teachers who can re-establish scholarship in our land. King Alfred also asked me to enquire what books might be available for immediate purchase, and what volumes he might commission to be copied and sent to Winchester at a later time."

Edwin knew without looking that his brother's eyes were already glazed over, and it was only a matter of time until he started tapping his foot.

Deorlaf raised his shaggy eyebrows. He said slowly, "I am an old man and cannot leave my see to traipse up and down the land at every king's pleasure. Moreover, I work with a small staff and cannot readily let any of them leave their duties for long spaces of time."

With an effort, Edwin concealed his frustration. He knew Alfred had set his heart on this part of the embassy to Mercia. What would be his disappointment if Edwin came home empty-handed?

"However, I will review my library and see whether I can find any extraneous copies to sell your royal master for an appropriate consideration. And I can provide a list of books from which copies can be ordered. Our establishments here are always grateful to receive additional funds—as you say, after the depredations of heathen men. I may find something to help him out. A reading man, is he?"

"King Alfred has not, alas, had as much leisure to devote to reading and writing as he would wish," Edwin replied. "I believe that he is now learning Saxon letters when the pressure of his duties permits. At other times he has someone read to him. I assure you, nothing would please him more than to learn Latin as well."

"Unusual," Deorlaf murmured, "not to say eccentric."

These sentiments exactly paralleled Edmund's own, though his personal loyalty to his King prevented him from voicing his thoughts in Deorlaf's acid tones. Edwin, in the meantime, was beginning to feel that approaching Bishop Deorlaf on the side of scholarship had not been the straight road to his enthusiasm. So he reiterated his assurances that he had come authorized and enabled by the King to make immediate purchases of books, which ended the interview on a satisfactory note.

But Edwin, of course, was far from satisfied. He saw himself returning to the King empty-handed, without a single book or promise of scholarly help for the West Saxons, his whole mission a failure.

Edmund flatly refused to go with Edwin to talk to Bishop Waerferth, and Edwin could hardly blame him.

"If only you'd come to me first," smiled Waerferth when Edwin explained his errand and told something of Bishop Deorlaf's response. "My episcopal colleague is something of an elder statesman here in Mercia and as such you did right to address your request to him. But really, Deorlaf's gifts lie in administration rather than in scholarship."

Waerferth was enthusiastic when Edwin mentioned an official visit to Winchester to instruct the king and encourage the West Saxon bishops.

"I know my uncle wouldn't miss it," said Edwin, catching a little of Waerferth's spark.

"Your uncle?"

"Yes, the Bishop of Sherborne," explained Edwin. After that there was no stopping them; it was a mercy indeed that Edmund had not come along, for his own sake and for that of his bookworm of a younger brother. When the Vespers bell signalled an end to their cordial conference, Edwin glowed with relief that, at least in regard to this meeting with Waerferth, he could give the King a good report.

When Edwin returned from the abbey, there was a great commotion outside Aethelwulf's hall. A crowd—in fact, an angry mob—was advancing toward the door, and to Edwin's surprise he saw that they were dragging the gamekeeper Cynric with them. Edwin followed, wondering what it was all about.

Cynric was admitted to the hall with a half-dozen or so of the most articulate of his accusers; Edwin slipped in and took his place beside Edmund.

Aethelwulf strode up to the dais and sat down in his high seat at a stately and unhurried pace. He waited until a silence had fallen and then gave permission for one of the men to speak. Edwin recognized the man with a start. It was Garmund, the grief-stricken retainer who had been at Helmstan's funeral.

"My lord Aethelwulf," Garmund said, "we have brought Cynric here to you to keep under guard until the court-day arrives. He is a murderer!"

"A murderer?" Aethelwulf repeated in surprise. "This is a serious charge."

"Just a moment, Uncle," said Aethelred, who was recovered enough from his injuries now to sit in hall. "This man bringing the accusation is my retainer. Garmund, what is the meaning of this?"

Before the man could reply, Aethelwulf said gruffly, "And the man being accused is my gamekeeper." Turning to Garmund, Aethelwulf demanded, "I suppose you have proof?"

All the men began shouting and gesticulating at once. Edwin looked at Cynric. He was standing, strangely passive, hanging his head. One of the men came forward with a coarse cloth sack.

"Have a look at this here, my lord," he said, "and I think you'll have all the proof you need." He reached into the sack and pulled out a bundle of clothes. He held the linen shirt, spattered with red, for everyone to see.

"Well, gamekeeper?" asked Aethelwulf. "What is your explanation?"

In a sullen voice Cynric replied, "It's my clothes from the

wolf-hunt, my lord. I hadn't got round to washing them yet. Who said you could go through my laundry?"

Then the retainer Garmund said, "That's not the only proof. Look here." And he delved his hand into the sack and pulled out a small object that gleamed of metal in the firelight.

"What's this?" asked Aethelred, taking the object. "A cloak-pin?"

"It belonged to Helmstan, the dead man," said the accuser. "Ask anyone. Ask his brother."

These last words were spat out in a deliberate provocation. Cynric bristled at the insult, then the fire seemed to go out of his eyes again.

"It's his," he sighed.

Aethelred looked at the brooch, then it was shown round to various others who had known Helmstan. All attested that they had seen it fastening his cloak at the shoulder.

"Now," Aethelwulf leaned forward and addressed Garmund, "Where was it found?"

"In the toe of an old sock stuffed down in his chest," the man said.

"Where was the chest?"

"In his house, my lord."

"So, gamekeeper," said Aethelwulf. "What have you to say to this?"

"I didn't put it there, my lord," said Cynric. "I had no idea that it was there."

"But your chest was locked with your key?"

"No, my lord."

"No? What, you left your possessions unlocked and freely available to thieves?"

"Normally the chest is locked, my lord," said Cynric, "but the padlock was old. I was having trouble with it so I took it to be repaired."

"Leaving your possessions unlocked?"

"I had no choice, my lord. Besides, I don't have that much a thief would want."

"Well, how do you think your brother's brooch got into your chest?"

Cynric looked at the ground and said quietly, "I don't know."

At this point the proceedings were interrupted by Garmund suffering a coughing fit. Old Ealdorman Aethelferth took the opportunity to speak up and protest that the accusations and interrogations were not being carried out in accordance with the established laws and procedures.

"Ealdorman, is this my hall or your own?" Aethelwulf's voice was even sharper than when he had been questioning Cynric.

Aethelferth replied with such gravity, and what is more, in such legal detail, that the accusers had simmered down by the time he had finished. It was then agreed that Cynric should be put in close hold until a proper hearing could be held.

Edwin was glad that the impromptu trial was broken up. He knew little of the differences in Mercian and West Saxon laws, but the way Aethelwulf had presided over the mob as if it were a valid court was surely as irregular here as it would have been at home. Moreover, Cynric's demeanour during the entire episode had been most strange. He seemed—Edwin groped for the right way to describe it in his mind—defeated. As if the trial had already been held, and Cynric condemned, and the fact of his guilt or innocence had been deemed irrelevant.

The retainers hustled the crowd out of the hall, and two armed men escorted Cynric to a place where he could be locked up. Edwin's eyes followed them, and he made a mental note of where the guard-house was situated. There was something about Cynric's indifference before his accusers that bothered Edwin; and certainly the discovery of the cloak-pin in Cynric's unlocked chest required explanation.

Ealdorman Aethelred and his uncle remained together on the dais, speaking in low but insistent tones. As the noise of the crowd died away, Edwin caught the words, "put me in an embarrassing situation with your…!" He couldn't tell which one of them had said it.

◆

The West Saxons were invited to talk with Aethelwulf and Aethelred that evening before dinner began. The older man welcomed them courteously to the high table. Ealdorman Aethelred had wine poured for them. The guests sipped politely as they waited for their hosts to open the conversation.

With a good-natured chuckle, Aethelwulf turned to the brothers. "I am sorry for our little disturbance this afternoon. It seems our national crisis has intruded upon a little local drama."

"You may call it a little local drama," said Aethelred wryly, "but in Helmstan I have lost a trusted steward, counsellor and friend. And you, uncle, may be in danger of losing an excellent gamekeeper."

"Don't worry about me," said Aethelwulf. "I have a wealth of skilled men to draw on. But what is awkward is the legal situation."

"You see," Aethelred turned to the men of Wessex. "Ordinarily Helmstan's next-of-kin would prosecute his killer. That would be Cynric, his half-brother. But now Cynric has been accused of the crime—and by my own retainer, no less. Which puts both my uncle and me in a difficult position. I cannot put any weight behind a prosecution of my uncle's people. My uncle cannot appear to be egging my people on to prosecute his own. However, the law demands that someone answer my retainer's accusation of my uncle's gamekeeper. It would be hard to think of anyone here in the district who would want to get involved in this. Too much local feeling, too many conflicting loyalties."

This open discussion of the Helmstan murder and its legal complications by uncle and nephew gave Edwin the feeling that they were leading up to something.

"I wonder," Aethelwulf began, "whether anyone in your party would be willing to act as advocate for the gamekeeper Cynric. Purely to see that the legal niceties were observed. You need not go out of your way. If we can get this little business taken care of, it would clear the air for our more weighty considerations at the council."

Edmund had already drawn back and the points of his moustache were poised to register refusal. Aethelwulf quickly added, "We wouldn't dream of asking an ealdorman, of course, but perhaps someone more junior…"

"I can't spare anybody," said Edmund shortly. "Besides, I didn't bring anyone of sufficient standing to counter an Ealdorman's retainer."

Osgar shook his head. "Alas, I am in the same position as my noble colleague. Only men-at-arms and body servants; no one suitable."

Edwin was staring straight ahead. He felt, rather than saw, the eyes of the others turn to him. At once he felt the heavy-hearted sensation he got when he knew he had been manoeuvred into accepting an ogre of a task and, in good conscience, had to accept it.

"I think he's innocent," Edwin said.

"What?" Edmund and Aethelwulf exclaimed at once.

"Are you really willing to take on this matter for us?" There was gratitude in Aethelred's voice.

Shooting a glance at his brother, whose grey eyes were fixed on him, Edwin said, "I could talk to him. At least find out some details and see what his story is. It's only a continuation of the help I was already giving Ealdorman Aethelred." He added pointedly, "I'm sure this small service for our King's kin-by-marriage would not be any impediment to the rest of our party." Edmund was stiff and did not meet Edwin's eye. Too bad for him, Edwin thought. There were some things his older brother had power to command, and some things he did not. This was one instance in which submission to Edmund's wishes would please no one but Edmund, so Edwin let him pout.

"Well, well, that's settled then. Our next court date is Wednesday week—see what you can do by then, ah, Edwin." Aethelwulf's eyes looked past him to where the cooks had been grilling fish on the central hearth and now were putting them on a platter. "Ah! Here comes the first course." In the meantime, the rest of the company had arrived in the hall and taken their seats at the tables. Aethelwulf addressed himself to them in the magnanimous way that had now become familiar to his guests: "Friends, I want you to enjoy yourselves. Eat and drink your fill!"

Chapter 19

Early the next morning Edwin went to the guard-house and asked to see the prisoner.

"What do you want—er, certainly, my lord," said the guard, correcting his address as he recognized Edwin as "one of the West Saxon lordships."

"Hey, Cynric, you have a visitor," he said, opening the cell door with a clank and rattle of iron keys. The man handed Edwin a candle in an earthenware holder. The cell was furnished with a rough old bench and a slop-bucket, nothing more. A tiny triangle of light shone through the gable window high above. Cynric sat on the bench, his head drooping. When Edwin came in he did not look up. There was no space on either side of the bench for Edwin to sit down, so he placed the candle on the floor and leaned against the wall. The candle cast weird shadows on the room and on their faces. Edwin was just thinking of how to open the conversation when Cynric spoke.

"I suppose Lord Aethelwulf sent you to take a statement," he said flatly. Which showed his ignorance of criminal matters. To take a statement Edwin would have had to bring a second man as witness.

"No, Lord Aethelwulf did not send me. I'm a king's reeve

from Wessex. I sometimes have to deal with difficult legal cases. I don't know if I can help, but I'd like to if I can. Will you talk to me?"

Cynric shrugged.

"Why not. But I don't know what there is to tell."

"You can start by telling me about your brother Helmstan," said Edwin.

For a few moments Cynric was silent. Edwin shifted his weight from one foot to the other. At length, as he was about to take his leave, Cynric began talking.

"I suppose you know we were really half-brothers, sons of the same father but different mothers. No two sons of the same mother could have loved each other better, though. My father was almost a thegn—well, his father had just been an ambitious farmer—and by the time my father came of age he was able to take arms and serve as a thegn. He married a thegn's daughter and that was Helmstan's mother."

"I see."

"When he was small she ran off with somebody. My father had to get a nursemaid to look after the little fellow. He must have been about two or three years old at the time. Well, with the two of them together in one hall, and she was pretty, one thing led to another and he married her and that was my mother. Not such a fine lady as Helmstan's mother but a better woman. So you see, we was raised as brothers. Helmstan was hers before I was, if you see what I mean. Helmstan took service with Lord Aethelred's father and I don't believe either he or Lord Aethelred ever has had any cause to complain from that day to—" He suddenly stopped.

"Do you," Edwin said softly, "remember anything unusual about that day?"

"No, my lord. Since Helmstan was in Lord Aethelred's

service we didn't see each other much. I had my duties out in the forest and he had his in and around the hall. He sent word when Aethelred's party arrived to say he'd come and visit when he could get away."

"Did he come to see you?"

Cynric passed a hand over his face. "Never got the chance."

"Someone said your family was involved in a feud," said Edwin.

"Feud? Well, if you'd call it that. Those Ceaddings live across the river from us. I guess in my granddad's time one of them did something to one of us, and ever since they've been out to get us and we've done our best to make their lives unpleasant whenever they do. There's been no killings, though, in a good fifteen or twenty year."

"Was Helmstan involved?"

"Same as any of us. I think he sort of disliked feuding, though, and was that glad to go with Lord Aethelred to Gloucester to get away from it."

"Do you suspect any of the Ceaddings?" asked Edwin.

"Hard to say," replied Cynric. "A feigned wolf attack—not really their style. I mean, they'd want to take credit, wouldn't they? And when I think what was done to my brother—" Cynric buried his face in his hands.

"But don't you want your brother to be avenged?" countered Edwin in his most encouraging tone. "Surely you want to defend yourself against these charges that have been brought against you?"

Cynric shrugged. This was maddening.

"Or are the charges justified?"

"No!" Cynric shouted.

"Then why the hesitation, man? You are acting as if you had already been tried and convicted. Do you want to be hanged?"

"Of course not," Cynric sighed, "but I don't exactly have a choice in the matter, do I?"

"Yes, or why do you think I am here talking to you?" Edwin said, kicking the slop bucket. Fortunately it was empty. "If you didn't hide that brooch in your chest, who did?"

"Could have been anyone," replied Cynric, returning to his tragic indifference.

"No, it couldn't," said Edwin, swallowing his frustration. "It could only have been someone who was there at the time and who wanted to get you in trouble. Now, who could it have been?"

"I don't know. Nobody much comes out my way. Does it really matter if I am going to be hanged anyway?"

"So that's it," said Edwin. "You think there's no hope. Ealdorman Aethelred seems a reasonable young man. I'm sure Lord Aethelwulf just wants to get to the bottom of it. And don't forget, any man may call witnesses to swear oaths on his behalf."

"And who's going to swear for me, eh? Everyone around here's ready to string me up on the nearest oak bough."

"Don't you have anyone? A kinsman who will swear an oath as to your innocence?"

Cynric shook his head sadly. "Maybe I could find one or two. But the other side.... You saw that mob." He waved his hand in despair.

"Any friends you can rely on? Come on, Cynric, give me something to start with."

"I have a mate who lives out in the woods. We were lads together. But he's no good to you; he's been in some trouble, and his oath would be invalid."

"Well, if we can't swear your innocence," said Edwin, returning to his previous line of thought, "we'll just have to find out who's guilty and lodge a counter-accusation. Cynric, please. Is there anything you remember about the last few days? Anything?"

"Everything's been out of order the past few days. We had the wolf-hunt, of course."

"Who arranged that with you?" Edwin interjected.

"Oh, Lord Aethelwulf sent Putta out to command me to be there with dogs and all, first thing the next morning. Why, I had to scramble to lay out my baits that very evening before dark. I could barely see what I was doing by the time I got back."

"Do you think anyone could have got into your house while you were away with the hunt?"

"Well, I didn't find a trail of blood when I came home."

"Eh?"

"My dog. He would have seen to any thief, wouldn't he?"

"Could a thief sneak through a window while the dog was on the other side of the house?"

"You haven't been to my house. It's got a fence all the way round, and the dog runs free inside the fence. Then if he got past my dog, he'd have Mother to contend with."

Edwin had to concede that it was very hard to imagine anyone getting past a guard dog and the gamekeeper's mother. He turned the problem over in his mind, this way and that. No one had come for a visit who might have slipped the brooch into the chest? Had the chest itself ever been outside his house? Had no one given Cynric an object that might have had the brooch hidden in it, which Cynric then put into the chest? Cynric shook his head at every possibility.

Edwin promised to see what he could find out in the short time allotted, and also to try and drum up some supporters who would swear to Cynric's innocence. He hoped that he sounded more optimistic than he was.

The next day was a Sunday, and the business of the council was suspended. Rain streamed down from the eaves of Aethelwulf's hall. After church there was nothing to do but file back to the hall and try to find some way to pass the time.

Edmund, chin in hand, played a table game with Osgar. Aethelwulf sat in his high seat paring his nails meticulously with a small knife. Beornoth was sitting near Aethelwulf staring blankly into a horn of ale. Edwin, as was his habit when at a loose end, poked aimlessly at the fire.

It made things worse to know that he was mostly to blame for the mood of gloom and distrust that had settled on the meeting. Since it had become generally known that Helmstan was murdered, men were eyeing one another with baleful glances and taking their seaxes with them to bed. But could Edwin have suppressed the information? Could he have concealed from Ealdorman Aethelred that his life was in danger, or allow Cynric to be hanged without attempting to prove his innocence? He still felt no closer to finding out who was responsible for the killing, the sabotage, and the planted evidence. And then there was the strange threat to Ealdorman Beornoth, assuming he had not done it himself for some sort of effect.

Edwin let his mind wander along this possibility, all the while turning over half-burnt logs and glowing coals. It seemed preposterous. It was more likely that someone had done it to frighten him into withdrawing himself from consideration as king. Yes—that made sense. There was a sudden shower of sparks as Edwin flipped a log over. But who would do this? Surely only Wulfsige or Aethelred, his rivals. One of them must be the unseen hand behind all this devilry. He remembered that there had been a wolf's skull among the trophies hanging on the wall in the abbey's guest-hall. Now the hunting trophies had all been removed. Anyone staying at the abbey would then have been able to use the wolf's skull to inflict the bite-marks on poor Helmstan's body. Wulfsige's falconer and his boy could have taken the body out of Aethelwulf's enclosure and mutilated it with the wolf's skull. If that was their errand, no wonder they refused to speak of it! But why would Wulfsige, or his falconer for that matter, want to kill Helmstan? They probably had never met him before this council.

It looked—reluctantly Edwin admitted it to himself—as if Aethelred was more likely to be at the back of it all. After all, he could just as easily have sent a servant to Beornoth's quarters as Wulfsige could. But then, would Aethelred have had his own man killed? That seemed improbable. And why a pillow in a noose to threaten Beornoth? That was another imponderable. A pillow because of Beornoth's perceived softness? But a noose had only one meaning and that was the execution of a criminal. Who was the criminal? What was the crime? And how was one to find the answers?

Edwin's chain of thought was broken by the sound of his brother's voice raised in an oath as Osgar made a masterful move on the board. Edwin could tell who was winning at the game merely by how Osgar's beard pointed forward in complacency, as Edmund's face contorted with frustration. He hoped he was not showing it as openly, but Edwin was no stranger to frustration himself at the moment. While this had been going on, a harpist had been practicing on a bench at the far end of the hall. After at least his twentieth failed attempt to play a certain musical phrase correctly, interspersed with endless tuning in the upper registers, Aethelwulf testily ordered the harpist to begone from his sight and go and practice somewhere more amenable such as the cow-shed or the bottom of the well.

Chapter 20

Molly looked forward to her first Sunday service at Wimborne Minster with eager curiosity, though she was a little daunted by the prospect as well. It was a large stone church, so different from the cosy little timber chapel of her father's estate. The old King, Alfred's older brother who had died eight years ago, was buried there, so Molly prepared a wreath of yew and holly and some candles to pay proper respect at his tomb. It was odd to walk at the head of the people from the estate, with Lullus and Henna following, along with Beorelf and his son, the gardener, Bunny, and a few others.

They arrived to the pealing of the bell. Molly was wearing her wine-red gown and light blue cloak with woven trim, pinned with her round silver brooch. Her linen headdress was white and crisp. She found the church already full of people. As she entered, all the long, gaunt faces turned in hostile appraisal. To them she was a stranger and scarcely more than a girl, small and insignificant in the tall rounded arch of the doorway. She smiled at the people and got glares in response; others averted their eyes.

"Where is King Aethelred's tomb?" Molly whispered to Lullus.

He motioned to a porticus off to the side, and she laid the wreath and prayed for a few moments at the tomb of the dead king before the service began.

◆

Early the next morning Molly decided to take a walk before breakfast. Whether she was hoping to find the kitchen deserted and help herself to a snack was a question on which she did not care to reflect. She tried not to hear the echoes of her mother's voice even now: 'Eating in between meals is sinful gluttony.' Snacking featured prominently in nine out of ten of Molly's confessions.

As she neared the kitchen, however, she heard whispered voices and instinctively hung back. As she peeked round the corner, she caught a glimpse of Cnapa loading something into a cart. It looked like one of the sides of beef that had been delivered to the estate the preceding week, closely wrapped, with salt crystals glistening on the surface of the cloth. From where she was looking, the end of the cart was partly visible and seemed to be loaded with cuts of beef, ropes of sausage, and assorted crocks and sacks—all items that Molly recognized from the estate's own storerooms. With a sinking feeling she remembered the eager gleam in the cook's eye as she asked for the keys. Now it was all too clear why Eng had asked for a holiday at the market.

Cnapa was covering the load with a sheet when she heard Eng's voice from somewhere out of sight, "That's it, I think it's all we'd better take this time. We'll leave after I get breakfast, so have the oxen in the yoke by then." Molly then heard what sounded like pans clanking and darted back behind the wall just in time to avoid Cnapa lumbering away toward the cowshed.

Molly did not allow herself a moment to ponder the scene she had just witnessed until she got back to her quarters, which she did with haste. Had appearances deceived her, or were Eng and Cnapa really taking—that is, stealing—food from the estate to sell at the market?

She could confront her; but she had the feeling that if Eng were up to no good, she would probably deny everything with a plausible story and simply take more pains to conceal what she was doing from then on. She must ask Lullus. Could she send anyone to spy on the pair? But she knew hardly anyone yet, certainly no one she could trust. If it transpired that the sale of supplies had been authorized by Lullus, they were doing innocent estate business. But if it was as she suspected, she must find out what was going on. The danger of her position chilled her. If Eng was discovered in a crime of this magnitude, she could lose her freedom, even her life. So could Cnapa, and Molly did not know what he might be capable of, or what he might do at Eng's bidding, to any unprotected witness of their crime.

As Molly thought this over she was going through her things looking for her riding dress. She almost jumped out of her skin when Henna came in and asked, "What are you looking for, my lady?"

"Oh, Henna, it's you," Molly sighed with relief. "Quick, my riding dress. Where is it?"

Henna extended her arm, showing the dress along with the other clean laundry she had brought in from the line. "Henna, would you see if Lullus is around? And get a message to the stables to get some horses saddled—quietly? Then come right back here and I'll tell you what is going on."

When Henna returned, Molly filled her in on what she

had seen and what it might signify.

"I am going to confer with Lullus to find out what they are up to," said Molly in an undertone. "If they are on legitimate business, I will have a fine time at the market and come home. If they are up to what I think they are, they must be stopped."

Henna wanted to come too, but Molly shook her head. "I need you here, Henna. After everyone has gone, you can go to the kitchen. I believe they will leave Bunny there with the chores. Just see that she stays here and doesn't try to get word to Eng. I don't think she'll try, but we can't be sure. I hope… Oh, I hope I'm wrong and this day will end with me feeling foolish. I don't like to have suspicions of people. But I just can't let this go. If it is—*theft*—" (she lowered her voice still further for this word) "we have to deal with it, don't we?"

It was very hard for Molly to eat her breakfast and give the appearance of calm she so wished to convey. Presently there was a knock at the door, and Henna admitted Lullus. The honest man was surprised at Molly's question and the circumstances that had given rise to it.

"No, my lady. No order has been given to sell any of the supplies. Whatever Eng and Cnapa are intending to do, it certainly is not under my authorization. Shall I go and demand an explanation from her?"

Molly eagerly dissuaded him. "Lullus, I am afraid that if you confront her now, she will tell some believable tale and will only take more care from now on. We need someone she does not know very well to follow after her and find out for certain whether she is selling the goods. We cannot confront her until we are certain."

"I suppose that would mean waiting to see what she does with the money," reasoned Lullus, beginning to get into the spirit.

"I have sent for the groom. Perhaps he can get close enough—I don't know how crowded this market is—to see what's going on and report back to us without being caught, I think. Then you and he can be witnesses, should it come to that."

"Are you going too, then?" he asked in some surprise.

"Well, yes, I thought I might," Molly said. "That is, with you and the groom as escorts it would be all right, wouldn't it?"

When, with careful watchfulness, she was satisfied that Eng and Cnapa and the laden ox-cart were far enough down the muddy path to the main road, she and Lullus made for the stables. There she found the groom waiting for her; he had saddled the horses with admirable discretion. Old Winebald the head groom was having a lie-in, as was his custom, till sometime in mid-morning. (There was no one in those parts who could doctor a sick or lame horse better than Winebald, but he was also a drunkard.) The under-groom, the man who really kept the stable going, had only been told that Lady Molgifu was riding out this morning with the steward and required his attendance.

Lullus needed someone strong to help him if Cnapa proved troublesome. "And you can leave your duties for a few hours to accompany me to the market?" The groom nodded and helped Molly onto Stapa before mounting his pony.

There was but one road to the market and their job was to hang back, just close enough to keep the ox-cart in view. As they went on, market-goers laden with baskets and barrows began to join the road at every junction until the road was dotted with animals, carts and foot-travellers and they felt almost inconspicuous. Evidently the same effect was enjoyed by Eng and Cnapa; their manner became less furtive as they began to be surrounded by others on the road. A few times

Molly did have a fright when one of them turned around and seemed to look straight at her. Molly was glad she had remembered what her mother always told her: "Take your hooded cloak whenever you go out: you never know when it might rain." It wasn't raining, but a hood did serve to obscure her face and headdress. Her main concern was to make sure the groom knew what they were about. She had told him enough to make him understand that they were on no ordinary outing and it was of the utmost importance to remain inconspicuous.

They continued on the road with woods on either side of them for some time; then, all of a sudden, there were no more trees and they found themselves on a patch of barren moorland, the edge of the district and an intersection with another well-travelled old track. Booths and tents, the cries of merchants hawking their wares and wafts of food-smells mixed with those of newly-tanned leather and fresh wool cloth declared that this was the meeting-place where the market was being held. It seemed a casual affair, with just locals milling about. It was not one of those crowded once-a-year markets with the foreign traders and the holiday atmosphere. Terrified of being spotted, Molly quickly dismounted and tried to keep the tents and booths between her and Eng's cart.

There were numerous carts and wheelbarrows being pushed into position opposite the tents and, as Molly watched, the market-goers flocked to them. She told the groom to go closer and see what happened to the wares on Eng's cart, as he might be called as a witness later. He nodded solemnly and fixed his gaze keenly on the cart.

Eng did most of the bargaining. "I'd hate to be the one trying to get a better price out of her," thought Molly. All the while, Cnapa cut saleable pieces off the side of beef and unloaded the goods that had been purchased. Some buyers bartered, but Eng seemed to prefer coin. It was also Eng who kept the purse. It was suspended on a string from her belt, and it grew heavier and heavier as the morning wore on, until her rope belt was pulled down into a deep V.

It was when most of the wares had been sold, and Molly, absorbed with watching, was quite sure they had come from the estate, that she and Lullus received the fright of their lives. A man came up behind them and said sharply, "Say now, who may you be?"

Chapter 21

Molly started violently and turned around. When she did so, the man stepped back and began to beg her pardon immediately. "I didn't know you was quality. Only you was standing behind my booth, see, and I was worried you might be spies."

"Spies!" exclaimed Molly with a pang of disappointment at being found out. Determined to play it out to the end, she quickly assumed an indignant expression and replied, "The idea! I am Lady Molgifu of Wimborne, and this is my steward Lullus."

"Pleased to make your acquaintance, my lady," said the man with deference. My name's Ead and this here is my pie booth. Won't you come set yourself down and take a rest. Try one of my pies. I've got apple here, and this 'un's custard, and here we have our pork pies, very popular they are."

He showed Molly to a bench at the back of his booth and cut her samples of all his pies. From this vantage point she could watch the market without being seen, while the groom edged closer to Eng's cart and Lullus, conspicuous by his size, remained outside with the horses.

Summoning her courage, Molly asked why he thought they would have been spies.

"Oh, you don't know the people round here. See that tent over yonder?" he said, pointing. "Well, that's the tent of old Sicel son of Sicel. He's been trying to get my recipes for years. You wouldn't believe the things he's tried. Rotten to the core, he is."

"So you come to this market quite often?" asked Molly.

"Every month unless the weather gets too bad in winter. Hot pies sell pretty well on a December day. Last winter, I heard that Sicel stretched his pork pies with sawdust. Sawdust, and rat's meat! I had to stretch mine too—food was scarce—but I used nice clean roasted acorns all ground up. Mix it up with a bit of suet and you don't taste it. Or rather just a nice nutty taste. No rats nor sawdust in my sweet tasty pies."

Molly jumped at the chance to break in before the list of Sicel son of Sicel's culinary crimes got any longer.

"Have you seen that woman—the one with the cart third from the left—here before, then?"

Ead glanced in the direction she indicated.

"What, Eng? Yes, prosperous widow woman with a big farm somewhere west of here. The big fellow's her son. One of yours, I think, or used to be; she worked at the estate till she got her own place. She's not here every time, maybe four times a year. Shall I call her over here for you? She's always got top notch wares. Meat, bacon, sausage, meal, honey, vegetables, fruits sometimes, even some spices now and again. 'Eng,' I tell her, 'Your wares is fit for the lordships.' That's what I always say because it's such fine stuff. Let me hail her over here and maybe you can place an order."

Molly hastily declined his offer, asking instead to purchase some of his pies. His face brightened and Molly was relieved to see that it turned his mind entirely from the subject of Eng and her wares. It was clear from what Ead said that Eng had established a false identity to explain her being in possession of so much quality merchandise. She had included enough truth in it—her real name and a connection to Wimborne—to get by any breezy contact with anyone from the estate that happened to attend this out-of-the-way gathering. Under close scrutiny her story would not hold water, but Molly supposed there had been no one up to now who had been in a position to level such scrutiny. She watched Eng and Cnapa as they re-yoked the oxen and pulled back towards the road. The groom sidled back to the pie booth with admirable discretion.

Now was the time to think and act quickly. Molly ordered the groom to follow the pair inconspicuously on foot. Molly and Lullus would make their way with the horses once Eng and Cnapa were well out of sight. In the meantime Molly had all her pies packed up.

They started back homeward, and had been proceeding at a leisurely pace for about an hour, when the groom reappeared at Molly's side, winded but eager. At Molly's encouragement he began to tell them his news.

"There's a little track off into the woods about a half a mile up ahead," he began, when he had caught his breath somewhat. "So small you'd hardly notice. The man stayed with the cart while the cook went into the woods. At first I thought she was on a call of nature"—he averted his eyes a moment in embarrassment—"but I followed her anyway. You, er, have to make sure. Sure enough, she goes a ways back in the woods to an old fallen-down hut, one of those sunken-floor things. Then she takes the purse of money off her belt, looks all around, and—"

Here he was interrupted by Molly, who demanded, alarmed, "She didn't see you!"

"No, my lady," the groom smiled. "I crouched low behind a

tree and stayed still as a mouse. She took the purse of money, as I was telling you, and hid it under some timbers of that ruined hut. Then she went back to the cart and they went on their way."

Molly and Lullus exchanged glances.

"Can you show us exactly where to find this hut?" Lullus asked.

The groom nodded.

"And it's certain that Eng and Cnapa are gone back home?" Molly added.

"Yes, my lady," the groom replied. "That is, they continued down the road towards home, as content as you please."

"So I suppose the coast is clear. Lead on, then," said Molly, as the groom climbed on his pony.

The groom had no trouble in finding the hut and Eng's hoard again. Further investigation revealed a mighty stash of coins, most of the smallest values but adding up to a considerable amount. Presumably, all of this was embezzled from the estate's stores by Eng over many months or years. Molly saw Lullus' face grow more solemn than she had yet known it as he contemplated the scale and seriousness of her crime. He made sure the groom could serve as a witness to the discovery of the money, then he loaded it onto his horse to be counted back at Wimborne.

"You go home ahead of us. Try and overtake the ox-cart if you can so as to get to the guard-house ahead of Eng and Cnapa. Here's a token," Lullus said, handing the groom his ring, "Don't lose it! Give the guards my order to seize them when they return."

The groom nodded and Molly silently prayed that he would not fail.

Chapter 22

When Edwin next went to visit Cynric, the prisoner asked him to ascertain that his mother was doing all right. She lived with him in his little cottage at the edge of the wood east of the settlement. He rode out directly, taking old Red this time as the distance was not great. Coming in sight of the cottage he smelled the heartening smell of wood smoke, and his approach was announced by a chorus of hounds. A particularly fierce-looking mastiff was patrolling the chest-high wattle fence that surrounded the house and yard, which had the late-season remains of a little vegetable garden at one end.

Edwin stopped several feet from the gate, where the mastiff was jumping and growling and barking. Presently the door opened and an old woman appeared, the one who had attended Helmstan's funeral. She was not tall, but strongly-built and dressed for work. Her face, now careworn, had probably been quite pretty in her youth. She called the mastiff to order and, once quiet again prevailed, asked in guarded tones who Edwin was.

Dismounting, he introduced himself and gave her the latest news of Cynric. The woman, whose name was Thryth, opened the gate and invited him in.

The house was small but neatly kept. Cynric's gamekeeper paraphernalia was arranged along the wall, with leashes and nets hanging on pegs and an assortment of spears and arrows and a bow leaned in the corner. The window was open and Edwin could see a shed and some pens behind the house. Tails wagged over the top of the wattle fences: these were the kennels. Cynric's mother motioned Edwin to a seat and served him ale in a wooden mug.

"First of all, I must offer my condolences on the loss of your elder son," he said.

"Thank you, my lord," she said, and they solemnly drank a draught together in Helmstan's honour. She dabbed her eye with the corner of her headdress. After he had finished his ale, she offered him another mug but he declined.

"I have come also because I need to know more about Cynric, the house, and how Helmstan's brooch might have got into Cynric's chest without his knowing about it."

"I've turned that question over and over in my mind and can't make anything of it. But," she turned her face to look full in Edwin's eyes, "my son Cynric is not guilty. He is not a thief, and he is not his brother's killer."

Edwin stood up and paced back and forth across the clean-swept earthen floor along the hearth-stones. The fire was low, but he instinctively held in his cloak as he crossed the narrow space between the bench and the hearth, to keep the hem from getting singed. On the other side of the house, close to the curtain that partitioned the sleeping quarters, was an old wooden chest bound with straps of blackened iron, but fitted with a shiny new iron padlock.

"Is this the chest where Helmstan's cloak-pin was found?"

"Yes," said Thryth. "That's the new lock—wasn't finished at the time, of course."

"Who knew that the chest was unlocked?" asked Edwin.

"Everyone, I suppose. It wasn't a secret. Poor Cynric, he doesn't have anything worth stealing but the clothes on his back."

"Who kept the key to the chest?"

"Well, Cynric did, but he handed it in with the old lock in hopes that the smith would be able to repair it after all. When he couldn't, he re-forged it to fit the new lock."

"How about his gear?" Edwin indicated the hunting equipment.

"Most of that comes with the post," she said. "And of course, the hounds are his lordship's."

"If you don't mind my asking, how did you come to live here? Wasn't your husband a thegn?"

"Ah," said the woman, sitting down again. "Now, my husband was almost a thegn. He had some land and he served as a man-at-arms for a while. He was up-and-coming when he married his first wife, Helmstan's real mother that was. She brought more money to the match, but then you know, she left and took a goodly bit with her when she went. They had to go to law to get a settlement for Helmstan, so he had some money. At least enough to try and keep up with what his father had reached. Then along I came, and that was about the time of the payment to the Danes, and we lost some cattle to the murrain—and so on and so forth," Thryth smiled gamely. My husband left a lot of debts and we had to sell the farm. Helmstan kept us going once he took service with the Ealdorman. Then Cynric got this post as gamekeeper. And he's a good one, too. What wolves there were ... Well, he took care of most of them as soon as he came to the post."

She went behind the curtain and brought out a large wolf pelt.

"The rest were sold but we got to keep this one." She showed Edwin a large gash in the skin that had been neatly mended. "That was the brute's death, but the damage meant it wouldn't bring a good price so Lord Aethelwulf didn't want it."

"Were you surprised to hear that Helmstan had been mauled?"

"Now you're going to get me started again," she said, turning her head away. After a moment she apologized and said, "Yes. Cynric had told me he thought the wolf problem was pretty much taken care of. 'More game for his lordship, and safety for the flocks and herds now,' he told me. Helmstan sent word that he'd come and see us when he could, but he can't have been on the way to see us when he was struck down way over there, could he?"

The question did not seem to call for a reply, so Edwin gave none. Instead his mind went back to pondering the problem of where the body was found.

"And if that wasn't bad enough, that retainer of Lord Aethelwulf's came here and told us to get up a wolf-hunt, as if he didn't know of all the wolves Cynric had killed."

"Did he, then?"

"Why, he was the one that came to collect the pelts each time. Putta, his name is. And I was in a state, trying to get things together, and Cynric had to go out and see to the hounds and set out the baits for the morrow."

"Was this retainer in the house with you?"

"Yes, I was busy so I paid him little notice. He hung round till Cynric told him everything was in order."

"Was this retainer your only visitor between the time Helmstan died and the day Cynric was accused?"

Thryth thought for a moment.

"Yes." Then, "That is to say, apart from my god-daughter and her little one."

"Your god-daughter?" asked Edwin.

"Yes, the daughter of a friend of mine. I look after her little girl, just three years old, on wash-days. She wandered into the fire once when her mother wasn't looking and was very badly burned. So now she's asked me to watch her on those days."

Edwin was thinking hard. If he could rule out Cynric and his mother, the only people who could have hidden the cloak-pin in the chest were this woman, her child, and the retainer. Surely the woman could have no occasion to commit a gruesome murder and hide the victim's brooch in a dear friend's house. The idea was preposterous. Could she have obtained the pin in some way, innocently perhaps, from the murderer? But then she would have no reason to hide it in Cynric's chest. The child, though. Children have a knack of finding small objects and they are equally good at hiding them. Could the child have found the brooch somewhere and put it in the chest as a game? The only other possibility, if Thryth's account was to be believed, was the retainer. Again, why? It seemed improbable that the man would have hidden the cloak-pin on his lord's order. Why would Lord Aethelwulf, after all, want to cast suspicion on his own gamekeeper? Why, for that matter, would he want to kill his nephew's retainer? It made no sense at all. And yet, the brooch had been found in Cynric's chest. As much as it might seem like witchcraft it was, Edwin sensed, a human hand that was responsible.

Edwin had been silent a long time, pacing and thinking. Evidently Thryth was accustomed to silent men; she went about her business with wordless efficiency, sweeping the floor, preparing food for the hounds, and finally, wiping her hands on her apron, settling onto a stool in the corner with a basket of wool and her spindle.

"This retainer," said Edwin suddenly. Thryth caught her spindle and looked up. "He didn't have a grudge against your family, I suppose?"

Thryth shook her head slowly and set the spindle spinning again. "Though he's an ill-favoured fellow," she said. "Always finding fault."

"He's not, by any chance, a friend of the Ceaddings?"

"The Ceaddings?" said Thryth in surprise. "You don't think they are behind all this?"

"I don't know," Edwin admitted. "Your son thinks not, but I wanted to ask anyway. What property do you have left? What have you got to live on?"

"The only thing we have left is that little meadow by the river and the fishing rights that go with it," said Thryth. "Helmstan held onto it because it was his father's dying wish. Now I suppose it goes to Cynric, and he will have to sell it to pay the fines for his conviction."

Edwin wanted to say something debonair like "Never fear, that won't be necessary," but one has to be confident to be debonair.

"I wonder if Lord Aethelwulf still wants it," she mused. "He offered to buy it before, several years ago when the Danes came. Anybody but those Ceaddings."

She picked up the pelt and went to put it back. "Oh!" she exclaimed.

"What is it?"

"Buntel was here that day too. He came by to ask if I'd wash his shirt—he usually does his own, but—"

"Buntel? Who is he?"

"He and Cynric have been friends since they were lads."

"Where is he now? I should like to talk to him. If nothing

else, we'll need him as a witness."

Thryth was back behind the curtain and her voice was muffled. "He—er—he comes and goes," she called. Then, returning, she said, "We never know when we'll get to see him. Likely he won't be back anytime soon."

"Is he a peddler?"

Thryth smiled briefly and shook her head. "He comes and goes, that's all."

Edwin waited for a moment, to see if she would say anything more, but she did not. It was most strange that Cynric's mother had suddenly locked up her hoard of words as tight as the new padlock on her son's storage chest.

Presently Edwin stood to take his leave. Thryth gave him a basket of food to take to Cynric.

"This should hold him a few days. Bread, cheese, apples, some dried meat. Sorry there's no butter, but we haven't any more. Tell Cynric the hounds are thriving."

Edwin agreed to do this.

"And, my lord," she said, "Thank you."

Edwin left Cynric's house with a little more appreciation for him. Despite the exasperating reticence of mother and son, Edwin had respect for people who did their work diligently and well. And if Cynric were condemned for his brother's murder, what would become of Thryth? Perhaps she would be all right. She was not too old to marry some well-off widowed farmer, for instance, or become a waiting-woman for a great lady. That would keep her well in body; but what about her spirit? She would still be a widow who had lost both sons in the worst possible circumstances. The best that could be hoped for—which Edwin hoped and prayed he could accomplish— was to save the one son she had left.

Chapter 23

After Molly left to follow Eng to the market on her suspicious errand, Henna said a prayer for her safety and went to follow her mistress's orders. Arriving in the kitchen, she found the fire nearly out and Bunny peeling turnips in a disconsolate manner. It seemed to her that the kitchen-maid was close to tears.

Almost without a thought Henna added a log and stoked the fire, then pulled up a stool next to Bunny and started peeling. A sympathetic remark about there being too many turnips for one body to peel brought a torrent of weeping.

"There's always too much. Eng don't do none of it. She says that's what they have me there for, and of course Cnapa doesn't either, it being woman's work. But's it's always so many and it's never done quick enough, seems I can't do anything right," she wailed. "And that's why they never let me go to market. 'Stay and tend the fire,' says Cnapa. 'We don't need you. You just stay here and mind all these turnips is peeled ere we get back,' that's what Eng says."

"Do they go to market often, then?" asked Henna sympathetically.

"Three or four times a year. And they could at least bring me something back, but Cnapa says that Eng won't let him."

"Does Cnapa have something for barter?"

"Not by himself, but he helps Eng load the goods and then he gets a share of the takings."

"I see," said Henna. How long would Bunny go on in this informative vein before Henna's questions put her on her guard?

"Eng must be a hardworking woman," Henna shook her head in amazement, "to be able to work her own farm for trade while keeping up with the royal hall as well."

"Oh, no, Henna, she doesn't have a farm of her own. That would never do!" Bunny hacked vengefully at the turnip she was holding. "She is far too busy trading for the King, isn't she? She takes the goods to market and then sends the money to the King. She's allowed to keep some, but mostly she sends it to the King."

"Well, now! That is a position of importance for a cook. I suppose the King came and saw how responsible she was, and added that to her duties?"

"I don't know, actually. The King hasn't ever been here since I came. I never asked Eng how she came to be trading for the King. She just said it was very important work and I mustn't talk about it, because of the danger of robbers, you know. But since you belong to the estate now, I can tell you. She's got nothing to fear from you."

Henna laughed at the very thought. "But you never get to help out at market, and share in the earnings?"

"No," said Bunny, tossing another peeled turnip into the pot. Chickens were pecking at the peels that fell on the dirt floor at her feet.

"Let's see," said Henna, looking around her, "if we catch the peels in this bucket rather than letting them fall, we can take them out and use them as fodder for the animals. Then they won't go to waste."

"I never thought of that," said Bunny.

For a little while the women went on peeling in silence. Henna was trying to think of a way to re-open the subject of Eng's market activities, but she soon found that Bunny had her mind on other matters.

Bunny sighed. "He says someday he will have enough money for us to get married, but when?"

"Cnapa—is he your sweetheart, then?"

"Yes," said Bunny. "I suppose it's all right to tell." She gave Henna a sidelong glance.

There were only two turnips left now, and each woman took one.

"I will speak to my lady, if I may, about your situation," said Henna. "She may find a way for you to marry sooner, or something—if you continue your good work here in the kitchen." Henna hoped that was not too much of a lie; neither Bunny's kitchen skills nor Cnapa's future looked very promising. She was relieved beyond measure that at least Bunny did not seem to be implicated in the thefts. If she received any of the takings, she would be liable to the same punishment. She helped Bunny stoke up the fire and showed her a better way of arranging the wood, then went back to her quarters to finish her duties and await Molly's return.

As Eng and Cnapa passed the guard-house on their way back to the King's hall, the guards suddenly called for them to halt and surrounded the empty ox-cart. Eng insisted it must be some mistake—she was the cook and must get back to her kitchen—the guards had no right—she would speak to the King about it. The guards were unmoved. Eng then tried pity: how could they do this to a helpless old woman? When guards on either side tried to lead her into the guardhouse, she then shouted, "It's because of that little strumpet who came here calling herself our new lady, isn't it? Don't listen to her! You know me, I'm one of you! When the rightful heir of Wessex comes to take possession of his home, she and all her ilk will be swept away! You'll see!"

The new interim leader of the guards did not hesitate. "Take her and lock her up!" he directed.

Eng, her arms in the firm grip of two guards, turned on them and said portentously, "A curse be on you!" The sound of her vituperations faded as the heavy door closed with a thud.

In the meantime, Cnapa decided to take to his heels. He was long-legged, but heavy; having spent more time hanging round the kitchen than competing in foot races, he was quickly run down by a fleet young guard, who tackled him and brought him face-down in the road. The leader of the guards was close behind, and sat on him with all his weight while the other bound his hands behind his back. He had blubbered out a full confession before they got back to the guard-house.

Chapter 24

The West Saxons were invited by Abbot Aethelhun to dine in the abbey's guest-hall that evening. It had doubtless cost the Abbot some headaches to determine the proper seating arrangements for two bishops, a possible future king, and a party of distinguished foreign guests including one ealdorman and two lords. He arrived at an alternating arrangement of secular and clergy with Bishop Deorlaf, as the senior thegn of God, in the high seat. Edwin was sorry he did not get to sit next to Bishop Waerferth. He was between Abbot Aethelhun and Lord Wulfsige, so instead of a pleasurable evening talking of books and ideas with Waerferth, he would have the opportunity to plumb the depths of Wulfsige's soul while drinking toasts with the Abbot.

"Edwin! I'll be stuck next to that younger bishop," said Edmund, clutching his brother's arm and speaking in an undertone, "so the dinner is going to be dull as ditch-water. See what you can get out of Wulfsige, especially about his plans for dealing with the Welsh."

Edwin nodded. The horn sounded for dinner, and they all took their seats on the benches. The dinner itself was, as Osgar described it later, 'a pretty decent nosebag for an abbey of that size.' What it lacked in meat—there was only roast goose and some cold ham for the high table—it made up for in its barley bread and butter and its stewed leeks. For most of the first course little was said on Edwin's end of the table, though Abbot Aethelhun did his hearty best to make small talk. Lord Wulfsige appeared to be in an ill humour, and looked at Edwin with a faint sneer.

"You," he said, and it was surprising how much loathing he could put into one syllable. "You practically accused me of threatening Beornoth, and then you turned around and accused my falconer of murder?"

"Ealdorman Aethelred has asked me to try to find the truth about the death of his steward. Finding things out requires asking questions. I don't know who is guilty of Helmstan's death."

"So you try to make an innocent man look guilty?"

"No," Edwin retorted. "Someone else has done that already. Lord Aethelwulf's gamekeeper Cynric is languishing in jail because someone made him look guilty with false evidence."

"That is nothing to do with me or my falconer."

"I had no way of knowing that unless I asked. But the truth is, your falconer has been less than forthcoming about what he was doing the night Helmstan was killed. I think he and his young helper were in Lord Aethelwulf's enclosure that night. Whether they are guilty in some way, I don't know. They certainly act guilty. But even if their errand was entirely innocent, I think they might have seen something, heard something that could help me find out the identity of the true killer."

"I don't care what you think," said Wulfsige coldly.

"Lord Wulfsige, do you know what your falconer was doing that night? Was he on an errand for you?"

Wulfsige went white. "I tell you, that is none of your

concern!" After that he stubbornly refused to look at Edwin or turn in his direction. The Abbot, who felt that an awkwardness had occurred between his two dinner guests but could not hear what had been said, tried his best to radiate an atmosphere of bonhomie. Edwin took pity on him and laughed at his moderately funny anecdotes. So Edwin passed an entire course of the dinner getting a chill from one side and hectic warmth from the other.

Eventually, however, Wulfsige could not avoid asking for the butter; so as Edwin passed it he said by way of a peace-offering, "Sir, I have never heard the story of your illustrious relative, the saint. Would you recount it to me?"

Wulfsige seemed to struggle for a moment between dudgeon and vanity; but soon enough the latter won out and he began in his deep, sonorous voice to tell the story. Conversation at the other end of the table also trailed off as they heard a tale being told. The nobleman held everyone's attention through the account of the battle, but when he arrived at the part where the martyr's relics were found to effect miraculous healings after his death, Edwin fervently hoped his brother would keep his foot-tapping under control. Edmund's interest in any story, sung or spoken, was in direct correlation to the number and duration of its battle scenes.

Edmund and Osgar were counting on Edwin to sound Wulfsige out in the matter of the kingship and possible treaties with the West Saxons, in spite of his avowed hostility to their embassy. To Edwin's surprise, when he made overtures on the topic, Wulfsige's response was quite civil.

"Yes, I suppose that's the only thing I agree with Aethelwulf about," he said, taking a morsel of roast goose and drawing patterns with it in the sauce. Before he had finished chewing, he went on, "Mercia for the Mercians. The Danes must either be eradicated or brought into subjection. We must expel this heathen presence that has compromised our greatness and our standing with God."

"But many of the Danes in eastern Mercia are settling down to farm," said Edwin. "Surely you would not advocate the wholesale slaughter of families living in peace."

Wulfsige fidgeted with his finger-rings. "They cannot be trusted. They would as soon join a raiding-party from their country and slaughter their Saxon neighbours, given the chance."

"Have there been such incidents up here?" asked Edwin.

"No," Wulfsige conceded, "but that, I am sure, was because they saw themselves as being ruled by the Danes. They had no complaints while Ceolwulf was king, because they knew that it was really their countryman Guthrum who was in charge."

"Don't you think farmers, Saxon or Dane, just want peace, stability, the rule of law?"

"Who knows what the bumpkins want?" asked Wulfsige. "But having Danes settled in the country is a liability."

"The way our King sees it," said Edwin, "the main thing is to keep raiders from coming over the sea. Whether that means more coastal defences or even Saxon ships to meet them in the water, I don't know."

"It's all very easy for your King to pursue such kind-hearted policies," said Wulfsige, brushing aside the years of conflict between Wessex and the Danes, the miles of unprotected coastline in Alfred's kingdom, and the famine, underpopulation, and disease that inevitably followed the repeated raids.

"Kind-hearted? I would call it even-handed to raise armies against attacking raiders but leave peaceful farmers to keep the land under cultivation." Remembering his instructions to ask about the Welsh, Edwin began, "Tell me, what would you do about—"

"What one *should* do," said Wulfsige, "what I *shall* do as king, when I have gathered a large enough army, is to sweep eastward across Mercia and cleanse our land of the Danish pestilence. Believe me, they would hop into their ships and sail back where they came from, if they were given a reason! If they saw the whole land they laid claim to, and everything in it, laid waste by fire and sword! It would not take long for me to share out the reconquered territories with my men and get it resettled," he waved his hand at the simplicity of it, "then perhaps your King would come begging for my help instead of so condescendingly offering his."

Edwin concluded that it was not worthwhile asking Wulfsige what he would do about the Welsh.

◆

In the evening, while the candles were still lit but men had begun to concentrate more on their ale than on one another, Edwin pulled out his wax tablet and began to make little notes to try and make sense of all the things that had been going on. He decided to list the events in the order of the time they must have happened:

> Helmstan killed by man: False wolf-bites added later
> Wulfsige's falconer: what is he hiding?
> Aethelred's saddle sabotaged
> Beornoth threatened: noose & pillow
> Cynric accused: brooch in chest
> Where is Cynric's friend?

Looking at the list he had just made, Edwin realized that there was an important question he had failed to answer. Where was Helmstan actually killed? Had he been lured outside the enclosure? If so, by whom and on what pretext? Or—Edwin's mind tested the other possibility—could Helmstan have been killed somewhere inside the enclosure and taken outside to the place where he was found? Wouldn't he have left a trail of blood? There would have been a lot of blood. The mutilation would only have been possible outside the enclosure, and more than likely was done at the spot where he was found. Inside the palisade somebody would have seen or heard something, even at night. It would have taken too long to finish that gruesome work without being discovered.

He was still puzzling over the list at bedtime, when they returned to their quarters after bidding their host good night.

"Well, little brother," sighed Edmund, "I think I have the easier task negotiating with the Mercians. You've picked yourself quite a problem."

"I'm afraid I have to agree with you. I am certain Cynric is innocent, but who could be guilty? Right now I've only got three suspects for the planting of Helmstan's brooch in Cynric's chest, and one of them is three years old."

"They start 'em young these days."

"If the little girl had the brooch and dropped it in Cynric's chest, where did she get it? I have it on good authority that her father is the local bronzesmith. The brooch might have been brought to his workshop by the killer to be sold and melted down or altered in some way. The little girl finds it and starts playing with it, takes it with her to Cynric's house on her mother's wash-day, and drops it in the chest. Does that sound plausible?"

Edmund shrugged his assent.

"Then I will have to interview the family and see if they know anything about the brooch. If the father remembers who brought the brooch to his workshop, we might have the matter solved right there."

"You're such an optimist. What if no one wants to talk to you? What if the bronzesmith is in league with a band of thieves who kill men for their bronze ornaments?"

Edmund was in a flippant mood; but he had nearly made an important point, which Edwin pounced on.

"What if the bronzesmith himself is guilty? The brooch being dropped in the chest by his little daughter would be a complete coincidence."

"Either way, it would make the gamekeeper innocent," said Edmund, "which ought to make you happy."

"If only I could prove it."

Edwin shook his head to dislodge the doubts that crowded into his mind. The only thing to do would be to interview the family and see what there was to find out.

Edwin asked Lord Aethelwulf if he could look at the cloak-pin, and Aethelwulf fetched it from his chamber. Edwin held it close to the light and turned it over in his fingers. It was just an ordinary bronze brooch with a mediocre design of two facing beasts, well-polished and functional: the sort of thing a practical man of Helmstan's type would wear. He probably bought it as a set from the bronzesmith with a matching belt buckle and strap-end. Then Edwin remembered that there had been no strap-end on Helmstan's belt, just the holes where it had been riveted into the leather and one sharp triangular corner that had remained when the rest broke off.

Edwin went outside. Helmstan had last been seen in the upper room of the hall. No one had seen him downstairs in the hall after dinnertime. Some witnesses had thought that he went out to the latrine, as it had not been closed for repairs until past midnight; so he must have come down the outside stairs. What happened then?

Edwin went up the stairs, and then started back down them, scrutinizing each step as he did so, and looking out over what was visible of the yard from the steps. To his left he could see the roof of the latrine and the trampled square of earth where it had previously stood; to his right the eaves of the roof, the firewood stacked under the eaves. Farther beyond the latrine was a pigpen, a sheep-pen and a smokehouse, then the gate. All the inhabited outbuildings were on the other side of the hall. No human eye must have seen Helmstan come down the steps to the latrine. No human eye but that of his killer. Edwin shivered.

At the foot of the steps Edwin began scanning the ground. He kicked his feet through the dead leaves that had accumulated around the steps. He walked around the latrine several times, examining the wood, then went inside and did the same. What was he looking for? He could not have said. Just some sign that Helmstan had been there.

Footprints were everywhere; it had rained off and on since Helmstan's death, so there was really no point in trying to trace his foot-marks now. Just then he heard the door open at the top of the steps; someone came out onto the wooden landing and Edwin ducked under the steps into the shadows against the wall of the hall, next to the stacked firewood. Above him he heard a woman's voice, and then a man's. There was a quiet feminine giggle, then the door closed and a man's steps came thumping down the plank stairs. To Edwin's surprise it was Aethelwulf who emerged heading for the latrine. Edwin stayed concealed till he saw him come from the outhouse and go on his way around the corner of the hall and out of sight.

He had been crouching and resting his right hand on one of the diagonal wooden supports under the stairs. He now pushed himself to a stooping position to come out, and as he did so he gasped in pain. His hand was sliced open crossways across the palm and fingers, and blood was oozing out of the jagged cuts. Quickly he wrapped a handkerchief around his hand. What had he cut his hand on? A big splinter? He got back under the steps and squinted at the wooden support, feeling gingerly up and down the wood. Then his fingers found what his eyes had missed in the shadows: a broken piece of metal that had become lodged in the join between two planks. He wiggled it carefully out of the wood and brought it into the light. It was a strap-end—small, made of bronze, crudely decorated but well-polished, with one corner broken forcibly off leaving a jagged sharp edge. It only wanted verifying side by side with Helmstan's belt, but here at last was proof that he had finally found the dead man's trail.

Chapter 25

On Tuesday morning, the new applicant for cook was waiting in the hall with Lullus when Molly came in. She was tailed by Henna, who was bursting with curiosity. The applicant was about Molly's own height, but probably twice her age. Her heavyset, bosomy frame was clad in a clean dress of homespun which Molly's quick eye observed had been patched by an expert hand in a couple of places. The cook's hair was caught up in a clean linen kerchief; she held a basket in one hand and an apron over her arm.

Molly introduced herself. "I am Lady Molgifu. Are you here about the position as cook?"

The woman bowed. "Yes, my lady. My name is Winfred."

Her voice was rough as a crow's, and her accent broad, but her mannish features were friendly and she smiled as she spoke, showing a gap between her front teeth.

"Welcome, Winfred. Have you any experience cooking on this scale before?"

Molly knew the answers to most of the questions she intended to ask, having had prior information from Lullus, but she had learned from her father to let people explain themselves—it was often quite instructive. It seemed Winfred was a widow, the second wife of a farmer with one grown son from his first marriage. She herself had borne him no children, so the farm had gone to the son and his wife. She was not made to feel unwelcome, but, as she said, "They'll be happier running the farm without me hanging around always. I'm able-bodied, and like to keep busy."

With this, she opened the basket and brought out three loaves of bread, handing them to Molly.

"By your leave, ma'am, these are loaves I just baked this morning. By way of a recommendation."

Molly could feel that the loaves were still just warm. She broke one in four and handed out portions to all. Though not up to her mother's standard, it was the best bread she'd had in a week, and she wanted to envelop the woman in a tearful embrace of gratitude.

Instead, she said briskly, "Very good. Have you equal skill with meats, vegetables, and sweets?"

Winfred grinned. "I've experience enough, but no samples."

Molly laughed at this, and suddenly the ice was broken.

Winfred continued, "What I always prided myself on was my roasts. I can do a pretty good roast of beef or pork, though I say so myself. Say, let me just be clear," Winfred said, shifting her weight to the other foot. "I'm a good cook, if I do say so, but a plain one. I can cook for a big company, but nothing fancy. What you'll want when you can find one is one of those trained cooks from Winchester or London. I'll be glad to serve you as long as there's none to be found."

"That's understood, and your bread speaks for you that you'll do well for us at present," Molly smiled. "Perhaps we might go ahead and see the kitchen," she proposed, rising. "I'm afraid we only have one helper for you at the moment, but then we aren't planning any major feasts."

Winfred tied on her apron as she followed Molly to the

kitchen. When they got there, Bunny was looking as frightened as ever, but at least appeared respectable. This time Molly was the one to give the kitchen tour to the newcomer. She saw Winfred's quick and professional appraisal of the hearth, worktable, stores, and implements. She proposed a trial period of two weeks, to which Winfred agreed. Molly was overcome with relief at the prospect of an intelligent human being in the kitchen, and real food for supper. Feeling more confident, then, she decided to recruit Winfred in her effort to restore the normal life of the hall.

"Meals have not been served in the hall for some time, and I would like that to change," said Molly.

"What? No meals in hall? Where've folks been eating then?" asked Winfred.

"My maid Henna was told to fetch a tray from the kitchen," said Molly. Winfred made a sound of impatient incredulity.

"I know. I don't know where everyone else eats. But we must get some work done on the hall first."

◆

The next thing Molly intended to do was to call on the housekeeper of Wimborne, who was said to be bedridden as a result of a long-standing illness. "Hence the cobwebs in the hall," she reasoned.

She took along a fresh loaf of Winfred's bread, some apples, and, out of the goodness of her generous heart, the last of the pies she had bought at the market. Every time she had asked the dour gardener how his wife was doing, she had received a noncommittal shrug. The poor woman must, Molly reasoned, be very bad off indeed.

Having got directions, she and Henna set off on a fine

autumn day, making their way down a winding, wooded lane to a neat little cottage with a high-sloped roof of thatch. The windows were closed but smoke was rising from the roof-vent; at least someone was home. In any case, Molly knew she had found the right place because there was no mistaking the straight, regular rows of leeks in the garden by the door. They stood there like sentinels, saluting her and Henna as they walked up and knocked.

"Who is it?" a female voice called.

The two visitors identified themselves, and were admitted into what would probably be a pleasant home, if it were not so neglected. Molly could hardly make out anything at all till her eyes adjusted to the gloom. The air was close in the cottage, and at first the smell of wood smoke predominated. A tall, stout woman with a pale face welcomed them and introduced herself as Cuthburga. She procured stools for them, then said breathlessly, "You must excuse me but I simply have to lie down. I get so fatigued with this illness. It makes me quite light-headed to stand up for any length of time."

At this she lay back down on the bed where she had evidently been reposing before they arrived, propped up with pillows. There were all sorts of small pots, bowls, bottles, and boxes on a little table beside her bed. She saw Molly's eyes turned in that direction.

"Yes, it is difficult being an invalid. I am used to being active, and it is a great trial to have to rest and take medicines all day long." She sighed heavily.

"If I may ask," said Molly, "what is the nature of your terrible illness?"

"The healers do not know. They simply don't know. They have tried everything on me. At first they thought it might be the flying venom. That's when everyone else had it. But that passed, and I was still ill. I began to get elf-shot here–" she indicated her lower back with a grimace, "–which hasn't ever gone away no matter what the treatment."

She went into quite a detailed recital of the different diagnoses and the widely varying treatments that had been prescribed.

"Then one physician asked if I might have had some kind of spell cast on me, if I had any enemies. And then I thought: Aha! I know who's to blame for *that*."

She gave Molly and Henna a knowing look that left them none the wiser.

"So I've stayed right away since then and kept on with the elf-shot treatments, and, though I haven't got any worse, I am still no better." Another sigh.

Henna spoke up.

"You think a witch has cast a spell on you?"

"And why not?" returned Cuthburga. "Would you put it past her? And right after she and I had had the most dreadful row that ever two grown women could have. Witch or no witch, I never want to see her again."

"Who?" Molly and Henna both asked.

"Why, that dreadful cook Eng," replied Cuthburga. She gave a little shiver. "Just talking about her gives me a chill. I am not going back to the hall ever again. I haven't told my husband, mind you," she said in a confidential tone. "I don't want him to even look at her in a strange questioning way, or she might do for him too."

Molly and Henna exchanged glances.

"I suppose we have good news for you then," Molly smiled. "Eng was, er, dismissed, so she is no longer the cook at the royal hall."

"I hope you got a *man* to take her place," said Cuthburga.

"No, unfortunately we couldn't find a skilled male cook on short notice," said Molly. Cuthburga's face fell. "Our new cook is named Winfred. She comes from an outlying farm. She's a widow without children, not too old, and we've brought you some of her bread and some other things. Here."

Molly handed Cuthburga the basket, and Henna put the bag of apples next to it.

"Why thank you, my lady, much obliged. That smells nice. I don't get up to do much baking as you might imagine. My husband has to make do with a porridge or a pottage most nights, something I can fix up and stir around from time to time on a low fire. So kind, very thoughtful."

Cuthburga's toes started to fidget on the bed.

"I'll just get up and see if I can get you two a cup of cider, shall I? You must be thirsty after your walk from the hall. That's it. Easy does it."

And with remarkable quickness she made her way out of bed and over to a barrel in the corner. She dipped out two cups of cider and handed them to her visitors. She dipped out one for herself and set it on the table with all the medicines. Absentmindedly she began picking up odds and ends and tidying them away. Then she came back and drained her cup.

"I declare, this is a good year for cider, is it not? How is old Beorelf these days? Still brewing enough for an entire king's company?"

Molly replied that he did indeed stay busy at his craft and had said the same thing about it being a good year for cider.

"Well, well! I suppose the maids kept the hall and your quarters decent for you, did they?"

"Maids?" Molly asked in surprise. "There has been no one. Henna here has tended to our quarters, and our new steward Lullus got together a cleaning party from among the young people a few days ago to get the hall back in order."

"Back in order?" It was Cuthburga's turn to sound incredulous. "But yes, I remember now. One of the maids left to get married and the other one just left. Well, we'll soon see about that."

"Er, will we?"

"Why yes, I think I could just come out in the next few days and see how it goes. You know, ease back into things?"

Molly had come to visit an old ailing servant, and was on the point of finding a replacement for her. And now this old, ailing servant was on her feet serving them a second cup of cider. Nothing at Wimborne seemed to go the way Molly expected.

Chapter 26

Once resolved, Edwin would have gone the very next day to see the bronzesmith and his family, but the king's business intervened. When, two days later, he had a chance to find the bronzesmith's workshop in the cluster of houses downhill from the abbey, he ended up wishing he hadn't bothered.

A young woman in an apron answered Edwin's knock and ushered him into the workshop, which was also the couple's home. She said that her husband was just out back and would be in shortly. Edwin sat down on a bench, opened his belt-bag, and took out the brooch and broken strap-mount. As he fingered them he looked around. The workshop had a large, wide shuttered window to let in the light. At this window was a workbench with a great many tools in a wooden rack—cutters and nippers, chisels and hammers, and all kinds of files.

The woman broke into Edwin's reverie with the question, "Come for a repair, my lord?" She motioned to the bronze pieces in Edwin's hand.

Just then a little girl appeared from behind the partition separating the sleeping quarters from the rest of the house. She announced, "I'm awake!"

"Excuse me," said the bronzesmith's wife and went to tend

to her daughter. "Now then, I don't know what's keeping my husband, but perhaps you can just tell me what you had in mind?"

Now it was Edwin's turn to catch her off guard.

"You are acquainted with Cynric the gamekeeper and his mother?"

"Yes," said the woman in mild surprise.

"My name is Edwin of Wimborne. I am helping Cynric with his legal case."

"Very sad," she said. "Thryth is completely devastated, though she doesn't let it show."

"And she looks after your daughter on wash-days," Edwin smiled as the little girl came up and hugged her mother's skirt. Edwin noticed that the child, though pretty and relatively clean, had a bad burn scar on one side of her face.

"I wonder if you have seen these before," he said, handing her the brooch and strap-mount. As he did so, he made sure the girl could see the pieces. Her eyes registered interest but no recognition. The bronzesmith's wife examined them with an appraising eye.

"Not my husband's work," she said. "My husband does his interlace so—" she held up a newly-made brooch next to Helmstan's, "and his beasts so—," the woman showed him some competent pieces with somewhat crude decoration: if the figures were supposed to be beasts, Edwin was indebted to the woman for pointing it out. The fastening-pins also looked different even to Edwin's untrained eye. "And this mount— why, it's definitely in need of repair. It looks like it got caught on something and ripped loose with mighty force. Was it a horse? If you still have the other piece, I'm sure we can repair it, though if the strap's broken you will have to get a saddler to put it back on."

As she was saying this, the little girl peeked out from behind her mother's apron and grinned at Edwin. He gave her a quick conspiratorial wink. Turning back to the child's mother, Edwin said that he did not know how it had got broken. A sudden thought crossed the woman's mind.

"This isn't—*the* brooch, is it?"

"Yes, it is," Edwin admitted, and the woman crossed herself. Just then a shadow appeared in the doorway and the bronzesmith came in. His wife turned to him.

"Look, dear, this is Lord Edwin of, I forget, the one who is helping Cynric."

The man crossed the room in three long paces to stand by his wife.

"See, look at this brooch," she said, handing him the piece.

"It's none of mine," he said dismissively. "Looks like Tamworth work, or Gloucester. Does it need a repair?" he asked, turning it over to look for damage.

"It's the brooch found in Cynric's chest. Helmstan's brooch," said the woman with emphasis. "My lord wants to know if we seen it before."

"He does, eh?" said the bronzesmith, a growl creeping into his words. "Well, his lordship can go to the devil." The bronzesmith punctuated this statement by flinging the brooch and strap-mount across the room. "Do you realize why he's here? He wants to find someone else to accuse so he can get Cynric out of trouble! He's not even one of ours, he's a West Saxon! We don't need to have any dealings with him."

The woman's eyes showed suspicion when she looked again at Edwin.

"Look, I only want information. If you know anything that can help Cynric—" Edwin knew that this appeal was pointless, but he made it anyway.

"No, you look, my foreign lord," said the bronzesmith, shaking his finger in Edwin's face. "You'll get out of my shop and you'll leave me and my family alone!"

"Very well," said Edwin quietly, meeting the bronzesmith's irate glare with his cold grey eyes. "But I hope you find your friends more willing in your hour of need."

Edwin was spared the indignity of having to scramble for the brooch and strap mount because the little girl had found them and sneaked under Edwin's cloak to silently press them into his hand. It was the hand with the cut, but Edwin was grateful all the same. Edwin turned and left to the sounds of husband and wife quarrelling behind him.

Returning to his quarters, Edwin steeled himself for his next interview. He could not appear as an innocuous customer when he went to the Ceaddings. Over the handsome new tunic belt Molly had given him he buckled on his thin seax belt, which held his ell-long seax in its tooled leather sheath. And as always he slipped his short knife, the one he'd been given as a boy, into his boot. He wondered what Molly could be doing now. Certainly something more pleasant, he hoped, than the errand he had before him. He knew it was never wise to get involved in other people's quarrels, but today he was going to. He had to. He called Fram to heel and went out to the stable-yard, where Bert was leading Stig out saddled and bridled for the errand.

Riding in the direction he had been advised, he soon came to the homestead of Cenred, the head of the clan. It was a ramshackle dwelling which was too large for a cottage but would have been considered too cramped for a thegn's household. Edwin heard the intermittent sounds of wood being chopped. As he approached, the sounds stopped and a raw-boned young man stepped forward from behind the hall, axe in hand.

"Stop right there, stranger," he said. "Who are you and where do you think you are going?" As he spoke he adjusted his grip on the axe-handle in a significant manner.

"I've come to speak to Cenred," said Edwin. He tried to keep his voice even and neutral. "My name is Lord Edwin. I have a legal matter to discuss."

The young man sneered in answer and, swiping the axe at a passing chicken, stalked off into the house. Edwin could hear him call "Father!" and the door closed.

Presently the door opened again and a grizzled old man came out.

"What do you want?" he demanded.

Edwin spoke from the saddle. "I presume you are Cenred. I wish to talk with you on a legal matter."

"We don't have anything to do with their lordships," said Cenred, and made to shut the door.

"The law is everyone's business," said Edwin. "And if you don't talk to me about the night Helmstan was killed, you may find that the law has a lot to do with you."

At the name of Helmstan the man's wary, animal-like eyes narrowed and fixed on Edwin.

"Very well," he said, "You may come in and talk. Most of the law is just talk anyway. But mind you leave your weapons by the door."

"Not a bit of it," said Edwin. "I received a most unfriendly welcome from your son, though I have come on peaceful terms and offered no threats. My weapons and my dog come with me."

"Suit yourself," the man mumbled as he disappeared into the house.

With some misgivings, Edwin dismounted and gave Stig's

reins to a younger brother who had come out of the woodwork. This one had an avaricious gleam in his eye and apparently was hoping to profit by a willing show of hospitality.

Inside the house, Cenred motioned Edwin to a bench. An old woman was stirring something in a pot on the hearth. Clouds of steam arose, filling the hall with the smell of boiled cabbage. A younger woman was peeling onions. An infant's shrill cry rang out from behind the curtain stretched across one end of the house. The younger woman threw down her knife with an oath and shuffled back to quiet the child.

"You are one of Lord Aethelwulf's men?" asked Cenred.

"No," replied Edwin. "I am assisting the court at Buckingham where Cynric has been accused."

Cenred could surely tell that he was a stranger to the area; but Edwin wanted to appear as neutral and official as possible. Cenred's suspicion, however, was relentless.

"Are you one of Cynric's kin?" he asked, examining Edwin's face closely. Edwin was glad to be able to deny this. He countered, "What is your opinion of Helmstan and Cynric?"

The man raised his head and spat into the fire.

"Helmstan was always too good for his company. Cynric is a son of a slut."

"I'm told that your kin and theirs have a long-standing dispute."

"That's no secret."

"Do you have any unaddressed grievances at present?"

"No," said Cenred, and grinned.

"Does Cynric have any grievances against you?"

"I don't know or care. Helmstan's dead and that's nothing to me. If Cynric gets the rope, maybe us Ceaddings will get some peace for once."

"Isn't there some question of fishing rights?"

"What's that to you?" Cenred growled.

"If Helmstan is dead and Cynric is condemned, you have no one to oppose you in claiming them for yourself."

"Isn't that something." Cenred squinted stubbornly at the fire.

"Do you know—have you heard—anything about the night of Helmstan's death?"

"Like did I hear a wolf howl?" Cenred let out an obscene chuckle.

"Well?"

"What do you think?"

"Or about Helmstan's brooch being found in Cynric's chest? Did you see anyone or hear anyone going out there on that day?"

"We ain't on visiting terms. If we came calling he'd have the dogs out. Same welcome as we'd give him. And we ain't ones to keep up with every little scrap of gossip in the district."

Edwin found this highly unlikely. He looked at the old woman, who had tended her cooking-pot, swept the hearth and spun several ells of yarn, all staying carefully within earshot as they talked.

"Were you the one who told Garmund to look in Cynric's chest for that brooch?" It was a guess, but from Cenred's reaction Edwin knew he was right.

"We may know something or we may not," Cenred mumbled, covering his surprise. "Depends on what it's worth to you."

The man was playing him, or trying to. An appeal to honour or duty would only call forth more derision. Edwin stood up.

"If you know anything that might be of relevance in the case pending in the court of Buckingham regarding the death of Helmstan and the accusation against Cynric, I summon you to appear and bear faithful witness!" He thought he could hear Cenred sniggering as he closed the door. Well, there was only one way to get the truth out of that sort of wretch, but he did not bring any extra men to help hold him down for it.

Out in the yard, he reclaimed Stig from the avaricious boy. Horse and trappings appeared intact, so he felt around in his belt-bag for something to offer the child. He pulled out a stump of beeswax candle about the length of a man's thumb. The boy took the candle eagerly but as Edwin mounted, he said, "What is this, anyway? Swindler! Swindler!"

The boy ran after him shouting some way down the track toward the main road. Finally Edwin stopped and turned to the boy.

"It's a candle," he said. "Have you never wanted to see in the dark?" Edwin asked. The boy, half impressed and half still mistrusting, turned back toward home rolling the candle between his fingers all the while. Edwin shook his head. A nice bit of candle poorer, and not a scrap of information to show for it.

Chapter 27

Having made a good start getting the hall in order, Molly was eager to see more of her new district. It was time to pay a ceremonial call on the abbey of Wimborne adjacent to the Minster. This was barely three miles from the King's hall, but as it looked like rain, Molly decided to go on horseback, accompanied by Henna and the groom.

The bracing autumn breeze and the rhythmic crunch of rustling leaves as they proceeded were invigorating after hours spent indoors. She raised her head and took in gulps of the fresh air blowing across the downs, and was glad Stapa was so tame as to continue quietly on his way when she had to drop the reins and re-pin her headdress, which the wind had caught and pulled loose. They soon spotted the tall stone Minster and the cluster of abbey buildings around it. There were some houses outside the abbey gate, and farther out some farmers' cottages surrounded by fields and meadows leading down to the river.

Molly sent the groom ahead to announce their arrival, so when the lady and her maid arrived at the Minster, the abbess and prioress were there to greet them. Abbess Eormengyth, a tall pigeon-breasted woman with aristocratic manners, received Molly with all the appropriate etiquette. She was,

Molly had been informed, related to the royal family.

Molly was ushered into the Abbess's room, a sparsely decorated but spacious chamber on the Minster side of the dormitories. The breeze had become gusty, so Eormengyth ordered the window-shutter closed and candles lit. She pulled her cloak about her and re-pinned it with a large and splendid gilt brooch. Molly, in her simple woollen riding habit, felt underdressed.

"Lady Molgifu," began the abbess, in a bellowing tone that almost caused Molly to start. Molly suddenly pitied the young novices who heard that voice when caught in some misdemeanour. "That's a rather unusual name."

"Yes, it is unusual," agreed Molly. Why did everyone always have to say something about her name?

"But of course it is probably a family name," said the abbess. "Not much you could have done about it. Well, I suppose you want the usual talk and tour." And before Molly could reply, Abbess Eormengyth launched in.

"We may as well start at the beginning. My royal cousin Aethelbald granted me this abbey twenty years ago in the early part of his reign. He was, of course, the second eldest half-brother of our present king," she said. "Before your time, I should think. Since then it has been my aim to rule this house in a manner fitting to the memory of our revered founder St Cuthburga."

"What..." Molly began.

"What that entails is that in contrast to some houses these days, here at Wimborne our vows to leave the world behind for the life of the cloister are *very* strictly observed. No nun is ever permitted to stray outside the bounds of the abbey."

"Don't you sometimes have errands outside the cloister? The abbey lands, and so forth?" Molly ventured to ask, as the abbess had finally stopped for a breath.

"We are in fact a double house with a small number of monks. They are housed in a facility on the other side of the Minster where we have contact only as necessitated by common abbey concerns. Their vows permit them to go out on abbey business on behalf of their sisters."

Molly nodded, as an actual reply seemed unnecessary. The abbess then abruptly returned to her first interrogation about Molly's own family.

"And your parents?" she said. "Whose kin are they?"

Molly obligingly began to outline her family connections. She had got as far as her father's name when the abbess interjected, "Sigebert. I see. You must be related to Ealdorman Sigefrith of Wilton."

"No, actually..."

"Ah! I remember him well. Is Sigefrith still in good health? No, I suppose he's long dead. But do you get up to Wilton very often to see the rest of your family?"

Molly said no, she had never been to Wilton. This seemed to surprise the abbess.

"In fact," Molly said with some exasperation, "My father's family doesn't come from anywhere near Wilton. My father is a thegn from a place near Warminster. Lord Edwin's father, Ealdorman Edgar, had an estate adjacent to my father's. Lord Edwin's late mother was the sister of the present Bishop of Sherborne."

For the first time Abbess Eormengyth seemed to pay attention. "Ealdorman, bishop! Why, Lady Molgifu, you do seem to have enjoyed singular good fortune."

A hot retort was on Molly's lips but she checked herself. What would that accomplish? Pretending to misunderstand, then, Molly replied, "Yes, my lord Edwin has been greatly favoured by the King in being chosen as reeve of Wimborne. I assure you that he feels the honour keenly. But no one is quite so capable and knowledgeable as Lord Edwin when it comes to the law."

"Good, good," said the Abbess, without seeming to hear. "And how are you finding the King's hall?"

Molly briefly described the work they had been doing to spruce the place up. "And just yesterday I engaged a painter to retouch the décor, and then I believe it will be back to its former glory," she finished.

"A painter? Who?" the Abbess demanded.

"A jack-of-all-trades who came and offered his services. He calls himself Handy Henc."

"Handy Henc? Has he shown his face around these parts again?" The Abbess' bosom began to quiver and heave like a custard taken too soon out of the oven, and her ruddy face took on a deeper hue. It did not take her long to burst out in peals of violent laughter, punctuate by snorts. "Don't tell me you hired Handy Henc! You poor little dear! Why, the man's legendary around here. *If* he turns up, which is not guaranteed to happen, he leaves a path of destruction in his wake." She caught her breath and wiped her eyes. "We have a good workman here who will paint your woodwork for you most satisfactorily. Just let me know and I will send him up to you."

"Thank you," said Molly faintly, as embarrassment at being laughed at gave way to a sense of dread about what disaster she might just have unleashed on the royal hall. Seeking an opportunity to move things along, she rose from her seat. "Weren't you going to favour me with a tour of your abbey precincts?"

As they walked, the Abbess waxed verbose on the early style of the arches, the Minster's glass windows, its fine relics, and plans for improving the abbey's aging timber buildings. Molly, in the meantime, was considering and reconsidering how to end the visit in a way that would reflect credit on herself, Edwin, and the estate. It was not until they reached the end of the walkway, however, that she had an idea.

"We have a small scriptorium here," the abbess waved her hand towards a room where several nuns were bent over manuscript pages. Molly stood a few moments to admire their methodical work before being led outside. She was so taken up with her idea that she completely missed what the abbess was saying.

"…the nuns actually danced on her grave! And this is where it happened, but I don't ever allow it to be discussed in this house, of course," she finished with a severe look and tone. "Nuns were much more licentious in those times."

Molly immediately put on a serious look and nodded her assent, wondering with regret what saucy story she had just missed. She had come prepared to give a gift of money to Wimborne Abbey. However, her reception by the abbess had left her feeling less than charitable. This was what she had been mulling over as the abbess chattered on about carved stonework and novices and the days of the illustrious Cuthburga. Her intention to give a gift did not waver; but she now saw that her gift, to reflect credit on the king's estate, must do more to bind the estate and abbey together than the proverbial purse of gold might do.

"Reverend abbess," said Molly, when she got the chance. "The time has come for me to take my leave. Before I go I wish to speak to you about a gift I would like to bestow on this venerable abbey."

The Abbess stopped short, full of attention.

"A gift?" she echoed, and it was amusing to Molly to see

the abbess' features rearrange themselves.

"Yes, I would like to give a gift of money, to be used for the benefit of the abbey and Minster, for whatever use is deemed most fitting."

The Abbess murmured something that contained the words "delighted" and "so generous."

"There is only one thing I would ask," continued Molly. "I ask that you find one of your number who is a good teacher of letters, to give me reading lessons."

The abbess' face registered surprise, mingled perhaps with some relief.

"Certainly, my dear," she nearly beamed. "I will make arrangements at once. When would you care to begin?"

Molly named a date the following week. She followed the abbess back into her room, where the prioress took a note of the amount of the gift for the purpose of the charter.

"We will have it drawn up and ready for you to sign next week during chapter," she said. Two nuns had been ushered into the room, and it was clear that the Abbess' attention had moved on to her next order of business. As Molly took her leave, the Abbess briefly glanced up, then called after her.

"Lovely to have met you, ah, Lady Mildgyth. Do give my kindest regards to Sigefrith next time you are in Wilton."

As Molly and her attendants started home, they felt the first drops of rain on their faces. The sky was beginning to darken, but the rain had not started in earnest. They proceeded at a brisk pace back to the estate with little conversation. This gave Molly the opportunity to think back over the visit.

She found herself smiling at the Abbess' peculiarities. Nevertheless, her overwhelming feeling after the visit was one of embarrassment. If she was honest, she had been taken aback by her ungracious reception. While Henna was saying how well it had gone and how pleased the abbey would be with her gift, Molly considered that she had pledged a high price for such a fleeting moment of notice from Abbess Eormengyth. Truly, Molly upbraided herself, I have been the centre of attention for months, as the bride-to-be in my own small circle at home, at the wedding itself, and to a degree at the King's hall as the reeve's new lady. But at the abbey a bride of Christ had no need to pay court to a worldly bride, and if the daughter of a country thegn chooses to throw her money around in a good cause, should a king's cousin be impressed?

Molly concluded, however, that she was right to have given the money but to have asked for reading lessons in return. For one thing, she really wanted to learn how to read, and had never had a chance to learn. Edwin came from a bookish family, at least on his mother's side, and she knew he would like it if she could read more than just a few letters, and write as well. Here, her thoughts began to wander more in the direction of Edwin. Then she remembered that Handy Henc might already have started his work back at the hall, and felt a little queasy.

◆

For Edwin, the day was taken up with fruitless searching for the mysterious Buntel—who some said was a poacher and not worth his lordship's trouble. He had even heard whispers of a quarrel between Helmstan and Buntel. And he continued his quest to find anyone else willing to witness for Cynric. At last, Edwin was forced to admit defeat and turn Stig homeward.

Edwin groaned softly as he lowered himself onto the bench beside Osgar and Edmund.

"You look done in, little brother," said the latter.

"I am," Edwin said, burying his face in his folded his arms on the table.

"Any success?"

Edwin looked up. "Frankly, no. Most of the people I talked to thought he was guilty. Why? No reason, but it was probably so because everyone else was talking of it. A handful said he was a decent bloke, so far as they knew, and promised not to swear against him. But swearing an oath on his behalf? No thanks, not this time."

"Doesn't the fellow have any friends—any kinsmen?"

"I located three cousins and a friend who did undertake to swear the oath, but you can't expect to win a murder case on the oaths of four ceorls. We've got to come up with at least as many more, or his head's in the noose for certain."

"Edwin," said Edmund, as a servant handed them a much-needed horn of ale, "Are you certain of your case? I mean, this Cynric seems on closer inspection to be somewhat of a clot. Maybe he's guilty, maybe he isn't. But you know what we have been sent here to do. Is it really worth putting all that in danger for the sake of this fellow who has nothing to do with us? Can't we let the Mercians handle it?"

"I agree," said Osgar, leaning in and joining the conversation. "He doesn't even seem to command that much loyalty or affection amongst his own people."

"All the more reason, then, for me to help him," said Edwin, hoping that if he left Edmund and Osgar out of it they might be mollified. "I can't just stand by and let an innocent man be hanged."

"And now we're back to the question of guilt or innocence," said Edmund with a touch of exasperation.

"It's not a question. I know he's innocent." Edwin folded his arms.

"But my dear boy—my dear fellow," said Osgar, "I don't know how you can explain the fact that the dead man's brooch was found in the gamekeeper's chest, in his house."

"Have all your years and experience taught you nothing about human nature?" Edwin asked. "Edmund, I concede the point that Cynric is a clot. But we all saw how he worked on the day of the wolf-hunt. He knows his trade. He's not stupid, and hiding proof of his guilt in his own unlocked chest? There's no other word for that than stupid. He could have hidden it anywhere: buried it in the woods or thrown it in the river, and no one would have been the wiser. No, that brooch was put in his chest by some other hand."

"Whose?" Edmund grunted.

"That is the question. If I knew the answer we could lodge a counter-accusation. But Cynric, though he doesn't have many friends, also doesn't seem to have enemies. Well, not conniving ones like that, anyway."

"Oh yes, you've looked into that feud they were in," said Edmund. "What did you find out?"

Edwin made an expression of disgust.

"A local family called the Ceaddings. They regard being in a feud as a sort of distinction. Believe me, it is their only distinction."

"In a way," said Osgar, "they are the natural suspects, if they are Helmstan's and Cynric's only enemies."

"True," said Edmund.

"Yes, well, it's possible," said Edwin, "but somehow it just doesn't feel like the sort of thing they would do. The Ceaddings are the sort of people who would steal your cattle or cut your fishing lines. They aren't the sort of people to come up with a grand *plot*—do you know what I mean?"

Chapter 28

When Molly returned home from her visit to Wimborne Abbey there could be no doubt that Handy Henc was at work, because she found his hand-cart blocking the main doors to the King's hall. The nondescript contents of the cart were covered with an old scrap of cowhide.

Molly squeezed past the cart and went inside. When her eyes had adjusted to the gloom, she saw the man himself singing gleefully at the far end as he plied his paintbrush. The wet bristles made gliding, slapping sounds in the silence in between verses of his song.

It was not the song, however—crude as it might have been—that made the colour drain from Molly's face, which had a moment earlier been flushed from her ride in the chilly October air. It was the sight of the hall. The pillars which Handy Henc had been engaged to paint were solid oak beams carved with intertwining ribbons and creatures by a masterful hand of some two generations past. These designs had been picked out with equal skill in contrasting paint colours so that each detail could be seen and admired. The remnants of these colours still remained, and Henc had assured Lullus and Molly that he could match them.

What greeted Molly's eye when she came in the hall was

something quite different than she had imagined. Instead of using a different colour for each motif, Henc had painted each pillar a different solid colour. With the one closest to the door, he had evidently run out of the reddish-brown he had been using about halfway up, and had continued higher up in a sort of greenish-yellow which had bled and dripped onto the darker paint below. The floor was spattered and smeared with pigments. Clapping her hands to her head in dismay, Molly shouted, "Stop!"

Before he knew what was happening, Handy Henc was bundled out of the hall and sent away, bag and baggage. Lullus, who was just returning from an outlying farm, heard the commotion and came to the hall to see what was going on. He stopped short, gazing at Henc's handiwork in silent amazement.

"Lullus," said Molly, who had buried her face in her hands, "Please send a message to the Abbey that we would be interested in the services of their painter."

The painter from the abbey arrived the next day. He was a small, wiry lay-brother who smiled wanly when Molly showed him the pillars. Fortunately Henc had not managed to ruin them all; one was untouched and still retained the original, faded colours. The painter said that he would scrub off the new paint and use the untouched pillar as his colour guide for the rest. It would take many days, however, to undo one morning of Henc's mischief.

◆

The days seemed to fly by, and before Molly knew it, the time had arrived for her first writing lesson. She first attended chapter in the monastery of Wimborne, where her donation was made official by virtue of a charter being drawn up. She was surprised at how small the strip of parchment was with its tiny, even letters in black ink. With trembling fingers she had grasped the quill and put a cross next to the place the Prioress had indicated.

Now her writing lessons were to begin. Following the nuns out of chapter, she wondered which one had been assigned as her teacher. She was conducted along the timber-columned cloister walk to the door of the scriptorium. Three of the nuns entered, and the novice who had accompanied Molly took her leave at the door.

The scriptorium was a small room with high shuttered windows which on fine days would let the light in sideways across the six wooden desks. In one corner there was an old table against the wall with a stack of uncut parchment and some other supplies: goose quills, little pots of ink. A box of candles. Then a shelf with several books from which the nuns made copies on commission. Unfinished work was left on the desks for the sisters to return to each day.

Looking round at the desks, writing materials, and women in sombre nun's dresses, she felt like backing right out the door. This was not her world; she felt like an intruder. But then one of the nuns turned and smiled, and beckoned her in.

The nun was a small, spare, freckled girl of about Molly's own age. She reminded Molly of her sister-in-law Wynnie, and she warmed to the young nun instantly.

First the nun, whose name was Sister Rowena, asked Molly if she could read runes.

"Of course," was Molly's reply.

"Well then, you will have no trouble learning the Roman letters. There is really no more mystery to it than that. The only challenge will come in learning how to handle ink and parchment, but we needn't start in on that just yet."

At this she produced a wax tablet like Edwin carried, and Molly started with recognition and a sudden pang of loneliness.

"You have seen one of these?" Sister Rowena asked.

"Yes, my husband uses one."

Sister Rowena opened the tablet so that the halves were lying flat on the table. Then she began to look around the table for a stylus. Finding none on the table, she ducked her head down to search the floor. Molly looked as well, but saw only a smoothly-swept stone-paved floor without even enough space in between the stones to admit a fallen blade of grass. As Rowena raised her head again, a pin in her dark grey veil scraped against the edge of the table. "Oh!" she exclaimed with a shake of her head, pulling a stylus out from a fold of the coarse linen beside her left temple. "So that's where that stylus got to!" She handed it to Molly. It was a simple bronze stylus, not a gold one such as the king had given Edwin. "I'm forever losing my pins and substituting whatever I can find in their place. It's a wonder my veil doesn't just fly off!" Rowena laughed. This was answered by an austere "Ahem!" from one of the other desks.

Chastened, Rowena said in a lowered voice, "Now, let's see your runes."

Molly took the stylus in her hand. It was thinner than a spindle but not as thin as a needle, and her fingers felt clumsy. On the rare occasions she had felt the need to carve runes she had scratched them in wood with the tip of her knife. Nevertheless, Molly began to write the runes in the soft beeswax. When she got about halfway she found she had run out of space on both sides of the tablet.

"Never mind," Sister Rowena smiled. "It takes practice to

write small letters."

She rubbed out Molly's runes from the beeswax with her thumb. "Now let's try Roman," she said. "I'll write a letter and then you copy it as many times as you can."

In this way, gradually, they got through the whole alphabet. By the end Molly's hand was aching but her heart was light. Writing letters was fun!

"Here is something I made for you," said Sister Rowena as the bell began to ring for Sext. She handed Molly a tiny roll of parchment. "See, it has all the letters we practiced today. Don't get it wet or the ink may wash off. Practice writing them whenever you can. Every day would be best. Then next week we'll see where we are."

"But how do I practice them?" asked Molly.

"Silly me, you don't have a wax tablet of your own, do you? Take this one on loan," said Sister Rowena rapidly as she hurried away with the other nuns. "And don't forget to close the door behind you!"

Molly unrolled the parchment and looked at it. The letters were neat and even, sharply defined in black against the white sheepskin. One edge of the parchment was neatly cut and the other was irregular: it was a scrap trimmed off the edge of the skin when a page was made for a manuscript. Still, to Molly it was beautiful. It looked like a line right out of a book.

◆

Back at the hall she sat by the window and opened the wax tablet to start practicing her letters. With supreme concentration she had got to *h*, her letters getting smaller and more confident as she went. Then the silence was broken by a discreet cough. She looked up and saw Lullus advancing toward the table.

"My lady?"

"Yes, Lullus, what is it?"

"Perhaps Winfred could help you sort out the autumn gifts for the estate families," he said. "About this time of year they expect a cheese, or some bread, or a sack of some provision at each of the farms." It took her only a moment to close the wax tablet over the stylus and parchment strip and put it away: duty was calling.

"Certainly. Can you tell us how many gifts we need to prepare?"

"Yes. We ought to make them fairly generous, since the feast isn't done anymore."

"Feast?"

"Yes, there used to be an autumn feast for all the estate families held here at the hall. It hasn't been done, I don't believe, since the king died."

Molly was silent for a moment.

"It's been a hard couple of years, with the famine and all," she finally said. "But we certainly have more than enough provisions at the moment, even taking into account what Eng embezzled. Surely we could manage a modest autumn feast for principal farmers, retainers, and staff. Simple food, nothing elaborate, but plenty of it."

"Instead of the gifts?"

"We can hardly deny them their gifts! They might be counting on them. We'll hand them out at the feast. How do you think that would be received?" Lullus was surprised, but agreed that it would go over well.

Winfred had caught Molly's enthusiasm. "We could brew up some ale and serve bread and sausages, and fried onions. That would be cheap and easy, and at the same time put everyone in a right good humour. And I've got a couple of nephews that can come and help out for the day if you need them."

"Good. Lullus, you and I must talk about a day, and Winfred, you can have a look at our provisions and let me know how much you think we can afford to serve."

Molly left the kitchen humming to herself, delighted at the prospect of the feast—and of a cook she could really work with. She had been anxious about never having held a feast on her own before. An autumn feast for the estate families would serve her well as a practice event. Unlikely as it was, she knew she could be called upon to entertain royal guests at any time.

◆

When the harvest feast was over Molly was exhausted but satisfied. Most of all she had enjoyed meeting the people connected with the estate. She had faces, personalities, conversations to associate with what had been mere farm and field names. Especially heart-warming was their evident pleasure in the renewal of this old custom of the estate. Father Ingeld came to bless the food and represent the Minster, as the abbey's nuns were under strict vows and even the monks did not venture out on mere social occasions.

At first, it is true, the gathering had been awkward and stiff. Four dozen pairs of eyes stared balefully at her as she invited them to take their places at the tables. Molly did not have a prepared speech—and if she had, the stares would have robbed her of it before she opened her mouth. She merely said—

"I'd like to welcome you all to the King's hall. I suppose you have happy memories of your feasts here under the old king. Now that the Danes are gone and the harvests are in, let's join together to make some new happy memories. Because of your hard work on the land, we will all eat well this winter. And tonight you may all eat well, and drink deeply! But not too deeply, mind; you will have your autumn gifts to carry back home as you go." At this she smiled nervously and sat down, and the feast began.

The sausage and beans with barley bread was served with a dish of turnips and buttered carrots. Bunny, in a rare departure from her usual reticence, said she never wanted to set eyes on another carrot as long as she lived, considering the bushels she had had to scrub and chop for this feast.

Molly's role was to preside at the high table, which gave her an excellent vantage point for people-watching. Down at the low end the cow man was the only one who would talk to the shepherd, who was a slave. Both were wearing their only clothes, evidently not washed; but their hands and faces at least were clean, and they drank deeply of Beorelf's cider as they talked and ate. Molly knew they had left boys to look after their charges and would have to leave early to relieve the lads before they fell asleep.

She saw the gardener talking earnestly to the bee man, his hands measuring the width of something and making a straight-down motion. The bee man nodded absently. Then the gardener's hands made a gathering motion. "I don't believe it," thought Molly. "He is telling the fellow how he spaces and hills up his leeks. He can think of nothing else!"

Breaking into her reverie, Father Ingeld said, "You look as if you're finally settling in."

Molly agreed. "Yes—well, at least I will feel that way after tonight, now that I've met everyone. Then when Lord Edwin returns it will be the same process all over again, I suppose."

"Well, you will have done the hard part for him, if I may say so."

"Oh, I don't know about that. He has to collect their taxes and adjudicate their disputes." Molly shuddered at the very thought of it.

"Even taxes and adjudication are sorely lacking around here, I can tell you. You're needed—both of you. You're a sign that normal life has resumed."

Laughing, Molly said, "I appreciate that." She paused. "I've been thinking about my new mill—that was my morning-gift, you know—and how many bits and pieces have to come together in the right way to make it all work. There's the water, and the wheel, and the axle, and the mill-stones, and so forth. If any of these are absent, or maladjusted, then ultimately there's no bread, which is the point of it all. We—" she motioned around the hall, "—are all like parts of the mill. Mind you, I don't know which parts would correspond to which people, but we all need each other to be able to work and live together properly." Then she looked at Ingeld with a worried frown. "Am I just talking nonsense?"

"Not at all, daughter," the priest chuckled.

Winfred's nephews came up behind Molly's chair lugging the first crate of gifts. Lullus wiped his mouth with a napkin and prepared to help his mistress in the distribution. Each person or household was called up in turn, from the least to the greatest, and received the seasonal perquisite which long tradition had entitled them to. Thanks to Lullus' minute knowledge of these matters, there were no mistakes. Some received wheels of cheese; others got fleeces, bound (this was Molly's touch) with pretty red string; pots of honey or sacks of meal that would feed a family through the season. No one went away empty-handed. The dour gathering had been transformed: the guests went away into the darkness with their loads and lanterns, singing.

Chapter 29

As the court date loomed, Edwin thought it best to consult the reigning authority on the proper procedures rather than endangering Cynric's case still farther by some technical misstep.

"Lord Edwin of Wimborne!" Aethelferth greeted him. "Aha. I thought it would be your elder brother acting for the accused."

Edwin explained that his brother was much engaged in the negotiations surrounding the kingship.

"The kingship, yes," echoed Aethelferth. "It ought to have been decided by now, of course. If it hadn't been for the wolf business, and of course this fellow Cynric."

"How do you think it will go—the kingship, I mean?" Edwin asked.

"Oh, it'll probably go with Wulfsige if the bish has his way." He made a sort of harrumphing sound that could have been disapproval or merely catarrh.

"You are an ealdorman. Why didn't you put yourself forward?"

"Too many marks against me, young man," he said. "I am from the same lineage as Aethelred, of course, but not so illustrious nor so—ahem!—well provided for. I have some good estates, but Aethelred and his uncle own half the kingdom between the two of them, you see."

Edwin nodded.

"And I remained in Mercia when King Burgred went into exile. Found it hard enough to get on with the man at home. Weeks and months on the road to Rome with him, imagine it! And at my age! So I stayed here and more or less ran things. Ceolwulf was not the fool some men say he was, but he was not brought up to run a country. He could fight, and he could talk. He talked Guthrum's axe right off his neck, so to speak, and before we knew it the Dane had put him in the top spot."

Edwin decided to try and take advantage of Aethelferth's talkative vein. He still wondered how all these Mercian bluebloods had managed to subordinate themselves to an upstart set over them by Danes.

"Did he reward his followers well?" he asked.

"At first he had plenty of Danish silver and captured lands to give out. So he got the sort of men who were after quick promotion."

"Did he eventually win over the old guard?"

"I suppose you think I am the prime representative of such a group," said Aethelferth gruffly, but eyeing Edwin with amusement.

"No!—that is—I just wondered if there had been any opposition to him from the royal families."

"Never mind, my boy. I'm old; I admit it. To answer your question, I daresay there were a few with us here in Buckingham that were not at all sorry to get the news of Ceolwulf's demise. But none of them singly was strong enough to topple him with Guthrum at his back. And of course they would never band together, even against him." He laughed at the thought.

"I thought Ceolwulf issued a new coinage," Edwin

remarked.

Aethelferth beamed with pleasure.

"Saw those, did you? My idea entirely. Our late king knew nothing of trade and cared even less. I got hold of some of Alfred's pennies and had our moneyers use 'em as an example."

"But to get back to Ceolwulf. Were you," Edwin said, feigning nonchalance, "around when he died?"

"No, they didn't need me out there fighting the Welsh. But I heard all about it. He wasn't killed outright in battle. Died of his wounds a couple of days later. They were all at his bedside—Beornoth, Wulfsige, Aethelwulf and Aethelred. Beornoth would know the gory details." Aethelferth harrumphed again. "He wept like a woman when the king breathed his last, they say."

Edwin asked Aethelferth about the Mercian procedure for oath-swearing.

"Not too different from your West Saxon procedure, I'll warrant. The accusers come forward with their witnesses. The accusation is stated and the witnesses swear by Almighty God that the accuser is telling the truth. You need at least two churchmen to administer the oaths."

"How are witnesses qualified as oath-worthy?" Edwin asked.

'Well, no prior convictions, of course," replied Aethelferth. "No men who have been frequently accused of wrongdoing. No slaves. If you use Welshmen, their oaths are worth half as much as a Saxon's. Not that Buckingham conceals too many Welshmen, ha, ha!"

'What is Cynric's wergild in Mercia?" Edwin asked. 'What is his life legally worth?"

"Two hundred shillings."

"The same as in Wessex, then. Good. That makes it easier

to know how many witnesses we will have to produce."

"But Helmstan was of a higher rank, don't forget. His wergild is six times as high."

"Twelve hundred shillings—yes, and frankly I've no idea how we are going to find the witnesses we need to swear to his innocence."

"Witnesses…you want him to swear the oath, then?" Aethelferth asked in surprise. "I thought he was guilty."

Edwin explained why he believed Cynric was innocent.

"Hmm, yes. Yes, I see your problem. What you need to do to cut off Garmund's accusation against Cynric, and the danger of his defeating your case, is to lodge a counter-accusation of your own against the fellow who actually did it."

"There's nothing I'd like better," Edwin swallowed his frustration, "but so far I have encountered only obstacles. At least three people could have put Helmstan's cloak-pin into Cynric's chest."

"Besides Cynric himself."

"Yes, but I've already explained that he would not have been so foolish as to do that when he could have thrown it in the river. One of the possible people is Putta, Lord Aethelwulf's steward. But he can account for his movements satisfactorily, and besides, has no motive. Then there is the bronzesmith's little girl. I don't think she put the pin in the chest, but even if she did, she must have picked it up somehow from the true killer. Then there's this dodgy friend of Cynric's that we can't seem to find. For my money, he seems the most likely right now." Edwin ran his fingers through his hair in exasperation. "There's also Wulfsige's falconer. I know he knows something about that night, and Wulfsige is protecting him."

"If you lodge your counter-accusation against the falconer, Wulfsige will have to let the truth come out," Aethelferth suggested.

"Yes, but what if he is not guilty? Wulfsige would surely sue me for false accusation. And even if I managed to get out of that, King Alfred would have my hide for endangering our embassy here."

"Well, I can't help you with the King of the West Saxons, my boy, but I'll do what I can to give you a hand with the case on Wednesday." Edwin was grateful that he had someone on his side, even if it was Aethelferth.

◆

It fell to Edmund to soothe Edwin's ragged nerves on Monday night, when Edwin had only one day left to prepare for the trial and still had no clear idea of who murdered Helmstan. With no credible suspect against which to lodge a counter-accusation, he would be entirely dependent on having enough witnesses to swear oaths that Cynric was telling the truth. Without the requisite number of witnesses, the case would be lost. If Garmund accused him of dereliction of duty, he could lose his livelihood. If he accused him of murder, and produced witnesses to back up his accusation, Cynric could lose his life. Or he could insist on his innocence—in which case he would have no choice but to undergo the ordeal, hoping for vindication. Edwin paced restlessly around the brazier in their guest quarters.

"No matter what, I've got to find out what Wulfsige's falconer knows. He was up to no good on the night Helmstan died, and Wulfsige knows it."

"On the other hand, it might have been something entirely innocent, and you'll have antagonized the possible next king of Mercia for no reason." Edmund lay on the big bed with his hands behind his head. Beside him, the sheets rose and fell over Osgar's chest as he slept the sleep of the just.

"I'm painfully aware of what's at stake here. But think about it: the falconer was within Aethelwulf's enclosure on the night, and as for how he might have done the mutilation, he had access to the wolf-skull that was hanging in the abbey guest hall."

"Which has since been taken down, never to be seen again," Edmund seemed to see his brother's point. "All right, go ahead and ask. What's the worst that could happen? We would probably win the war, anyway."

Edwin endeavoured to ignore this. Instead, he said, "I'd really like to be able to accuse Cenred. He is a scoundrel, and has surely been guilty of many crimes in the course of the feud. But I've no evidence that he had anything to do with Helmstan's death, and believe me, I've looked."

"Hm. Who else is there?"

"There's Putta, Lord Aethelwulf's chief servant. He knows Cynric—he hired him, in fact—but he didn't know Helmstan and had no reason to kill him. Not to mention that his helper, Bedwig, vouches for him staying put during the night, as do the other hall-servants who were sleeping in the same place."

"Do you suppose the accuser—Garmund—might be guilty? He might have had a quarrel with Helmstan and killed him, and invented this entire case to cover up his own deed."

"I suppose there could have been jealousy between the two men," said Edwin slowly, "which could have erupted into a killing. That's not a bad suggestion. It crossed my mind too. But against that we have the fact that Garmund was suffering from a bad cold in the head and had gone to bed early that night."

"Sneaked out?" Edmund suggested.

"He was sleeping in Ealdorman Aethelred's quarters—he would have had to get out unnoticed under the noses of all his other men, and they said he snored all night because of his cold."

Edmund sighed with discontent and shifted position. "Maybe you are going to have to admit defeat on this one, little brother. It doesn't look good. You don't have enough witnesses to defeat the accusation, do you?"

"No," Edwin said miserably. "I have looked—tried—asked—everywhere." He punched his fist into his palm. "If only I could find that friend of Cynric's! That poacher!"

"Why would he have killed Helmstan? And how would he have got into the enclosure?"

"I don't know," said Edwin, his shoulders drooping with exhaustion and discontent.

"Like I said," Edmund said soothingly, "it may just be time to give up. If you don't have the witnesses, you just don't. Maybe he really did do it. Most murders are simple, after all."

"But I'm sure he's innocent!" Edwin exclaimed.

Edmund was taking off his clothes and getting under the covers. He yawned, his mouth like a cavern overhung by a large moustache. "Go to bed," he said, and turned his back to Edwin with finality.

Yawning as well, Edwin found that for once, his brother had given him some good advice.

◆

It was never a good idea to pay a social call on a member of the Mercian nobility too early in the morning; but Edwin felt that if he did not, he might miss his chance—or lose his nerve. This time, Wulfsige did not offer him a chair. He finished getting dressed and sat down with his dog on his lap. His retainers ranged themselves around him.

Edwin did not waste time with pleasantries. "Lord Wulfsige, as you know, the trial of Cynric begins tomorrow. Since he is innocent of his brother's death, I have been trying to find out who is guilty. Your falconer was in the enclosure—"

"Enough!" Wulfsige interrupted. "You will leave my falconer alone. You should not have dared to come back here again with your groundless accusations!"

"I have made no accusations." Edwin stood his ground, his eyes boring into Wulfsige's. "But I do have a good reason to want to talk to your falconer. He was in Aethelwulf's enclosure at about the time the killing took place. This is a case of murder. If you won't let me find out his story now, I am going to be forced to summon him to testify tomorrow, in public, at the trial."

"Very well," Wulfsige suddenly gave way, to Edwin's surprise. To the retainer who picked his teeth with his knife, he said, "Bring Alf here. And all of you can leave."

When they were alone, Wulfsige turned to Edwin. "Do I have your word that what you hear here will never leave this chamber? That it will never become public?"

Edwin wondered what secrets were about to be revealed. "I cannot possibly say," he replied, "until I know what your falconer's testimony might be. But if I am satisfied that it is your private business and does not relate to the killing of Helmstan, it will not be mentioned during Cynric's trial."

"I suppose I cannot expect more," said Wulfsige ruefully, and they shook hands.

Alf the falconer came in and shut the door behind him.

"Alf, you have my permission to tell Lord Edwin the West Saxon about the errand you did for me on the night after we arrived here in Buckingham. He has promised to be discreet."

"Yes, my lord. We received word from a certain party—" his eyes questioned Wulfsige. Wulfsige nodded.

"That he had a certain rare bird for sale and did my lord want it. Turns out it was a gyrfalcon, and my lord has heard tell of them from nobles up north but neither of us has ever even seen one, much less got a chance to buy one."

Wulfsige chimed in. "I am a collector, Lord Edwin. If there is a hunting bird of a sort I do not have, I must possess it."

"So when you entered Lord Aethelwulf's enclosure, you were going to buy the gyrfalcon?" Edwin asked.

"Yes," said Alf.

"The nobleman had promised me the first chance at it. If I didn't meet his price, he said he would offer it elsewhere."

"How much did you pay?" Edwin had to know.

"Twelve mancuses of gold." When Edwin looked a little shocked, Wulfsige explained, "Do you know how rare these birds are? Not a single nobleman south of the Humber has one, that I know of. She was worth twice that to me."

"Who was this nobleman—name him!"

The falconer and his lord exchanged glances. "Ealdorman Aethelred."

Edwin, for a moment, was robbed of the power of speech. "I see," he replied, when he was sure he could keep the note of surprise out of his voice. "Did he tell you where he got the falcon?"

"No, we really don't know," Alf said.

"And you didn't care to ask." Edwin trailed off, wondering where Aethelred would have acquired a falcon that was only known to inhabit regions far to the north of Mercia. Then he thought of another question. "Did you have a lantern, or how did you see in the dark?"

"I had a lantern, and so did my guide, so I snuffed out my candle once I got inside, and lit it from his as I left again. And the moon shone clear when the clouds weren't over it, so I could see all right."

"Who let you in?"

"Aethelred sent somebody. An old fellow with white hair. He opened the wicket gate and let me in, then led me to the women's quarters. That's where the bird was being kept. He showed it me, and I gave it a good going over in the lantern-light, and then I agreed to the price. My lord had given me the money to hand over if I was satisfied with the bird. So that's what I did. I handed over the money and took the falcon in her crate back with me. The white-haired man shut the wicket gate behind me and that was that."

"Was anyone else about? Did you see or hear anything?"

"Nothing. There was nobody about—that's why we chose that time to meet. Animals were quiet in their pens. No light showing around the window-shutters of the hall. I think I did hear somebody go out to the privy. That's about it. Quiet time of night."

Edwin thanked them both for their help. "I am sorry to have caused you trouble, though if you had admitted your true errand at first, it would have saved a great deal of time. I wish you, Lord Wulfsige, much success with your beautiful new falcon—may she be worth every penny you paid."

As he walked away from the abbey, Edwin's relief at getting to the bottom of Wulfsige's secret gave way to the realization of how much he had depended on the falconer's testimony to clear up the mystery of Helmstan's death. Now he knew that Aethelred had been hiding this from him—what else might he be concealing as well? And there was only a day until Cynric went on trial for his life.

By the time he had taken the short walk back to Aethelwulf's enclosure, Edwin was so angry that he strode right up to Aethelred's quarters and pounded on the door. He heard the door being unbolted and it was opened just a crack. He saw Garmund's thin nose and watery eyes peering out at him.

"What do you want?" he asked.

"I want to speak to your master—now. Let me in." Edwin raised his voice hoping Aethelred would hear from inside. He heard muttering behind the door, and the white-haired servant came to the door.

"My lord is resting. I'm very sorry," the older servant shook his head.

"You must wake him. This concerns the trial tomorrow and I must speak with him immediately."

Then Edwin heard Aethelred's voice from inside the chamber, and the door opened. Aethelred was lying on the bed, fully dressed, but with his ankle resting on two pillows. Edwin was beginning to calm down—just enough to be able to conduct a proper interview.

"My lord, I have come into possession of information about the night of Helmstan's murder. Information that you appear to have kept from me."

Aethelred's face registered pure surprise. "I have kept nothing from you! What can you be speaking of?" and then, "Am I not the one who asked you to look into the matter on my behalf?"

The white-haired servant whispered something in his ear and his expression changed. He ordered, "Garmund, go and fetch my armourer."

When Garmund had gone, Aethelred admitted that he had sent Garmund away so that he would not become suspicious.

"So you found out about my little transaction with Wulfsige," he said sheepishly.

"What are you concealing about the night your steward was killed?"

"I didn't mean to conceal anything. It just slipped my mind." Aethelred felt of the bandage around his head. "I had spoken to Wulfsige, and had given my man here my instructions. Then I went about my business with my uncle and Helmstan that night and thought no more of it. When Helmstan turned up dead, it chased the matter clear out of my head."

So far, so plausible, Edwin had to admit. He probed further. "Where did you get the falcon, and why did you want to sell it?"

"It was a gift from my uncle when we got here. God only knows where he got the creature. It might have been Rhodri Mawr's, for all I know, taken as spoils from the Welsh. My uncle loves to give extravagant gifts. But I have all the hawks I need back in Gloucester, and that's where I left my falconer. I don't have anybody here to nursemaid a bird. I had heard Wulfsige was mad keen on hawks of all kinds, so I thought I'd try and make some money off it. I quoted him some ridiculous price, and to my surprise he accepted right away." For a moment, he shed his seriousness and flashed a youth's amused grin.

"What did you do when your uncle found out?"

"With all that has been going on, he hasn't noticed yet. I was hoping I could get back home without anything being said. Please don't mention it to him," Aethelred pleaded. "This is just the sort of thing he would get offended over, and I need his support right now."

"All right," Edwin said. "I suppose there's no need to mention it, since it has no bearing on Helmstan and Cynric."

"No, I don't think I even mentioned it to Helmstan—though I would have had to explain the money to him since he did my accounts."

"What would he have said to that?"

"I fancy we would have had a good laugh over it. Twelve gold mancuses! Wulfsige must be barmy. My man catches hawks in the woods every year for nothing and trains them up ready for the hunting season." Aethelred's face once again assumed its usual sober expression. "Ah well. I wish him joy of it."

Edwin turned to the white-haired servant. "I suppose your master has already asked, but did Helmstan say anything to you that was out of the ordinary?"

The man slowly shook his head. "I didn't see Helmstan at all after dinner. He went upstairs with my lord and his uncle to attend to their business, and I went about mine. When I'd seen this chamber set up for night-time and the bedclothes turned down and so forth, I went out to stay close by the wicket gate until the time we had agreed. I passed the time with the look-out and told him I was just waiting to let in a friend for a little drink. Sure enough, the knock came and I let in the other lordship's falconer. He came to the place we'd arranged and took a close squint at the bird, and I suppose he was satisfied because he handed the money over without a fuss. I counted it—twelve gold pieces right as can be. I nearly got light-headed at the sight of all that gold, and me the servant of an ealdorman. I lit his way back to the wicket-gate with the cage—it was covered, y'see, and you couldn't see what it was—and I says something like, 'You be careful with that keg and don't spill a drop, that's the best I ever brewed,' and the guard let him through, and that was the end of it for me. I went and bedded down in the stable, as I couldn't have anybody unbolting a door at that hour."

Edwin said, "Did you see or hear anything unusual as you crossed the enclosure? Was anybody else about?"

The man shook his head. "Nothing. All was still. The hall was shut up and dark, and I heard no one stirring."

"Not even someone in the latrine on a midnight call of nature?"

The man smiled. "Well, perhaps. I didn't take notice of that. But no real noises, that's what I meant."

"I shall have to speak to the guard to verify your story. Do you remember who it was?"

"No, it was too dark."

"Never mind. I'll find out. Thank you."

Edwin made the necessary enquiries. The guard in the watch-tower that night turned out to be Bedwig, Putta's weedy companion with the cold. He remembered waving the man with the keg through the wicket-gate at the beginning of the second watch. Did he know who the man was? Bedwig shook his head; but the fellow was known to the Ealdorman's servant, so he had to be all right. He knew the Ealdorman's servant by his white hair in the moonlight. Edwin thanked Bedwig and the man returned to his duties. They had been leaning on the wattle fence of the pigpen, and Edwin remained sitting there for some time, mulling over the possibilities and scratching the bristly backs of the pigs with a stick. Bedwig had opened the wicket-gate and confirmed the falconer's alibi; in doing so he had shut the door on Cynric's last possible avenue of escape.

◆

When the day arrived for the autumn law-courts to be held in Buckingham, everyone gathered at the meeting grounds. The assembled nobles of Mercia looked much as they had done at their first meeting, only more so: Wulfsige looked more annoyed and offended, Beornoth more sheepish, Aethelwulf more proprietorial. Wulfsige's annoyance was partly due to his being drawn into a local legal dispute. If this was not the day on which he would be proclaimed king, he would much rather have spent his time hunting or hawking. As it was, all his dogs, birds, and men were idle as he sat with the other lords to preside over the day. Wulfsige's sharpest complaints should have been directed at Aethelferth, who had insisted on all the lords being present. But Aethelferth was busy in pursuit of legal rectitude and indifferent to the inconvenience and disapprobation of others.

Cynric's passive demeanour had not altered in the days leading up to the trial. No matter what Edwin did or said, regardless of any helpful witness or positive development, the accused man remained stolidly pessimistic.

At least the weather was cooperative. By tradition, legal proceedings were always held in the open air. Some had pitched tents around the edge of the grounds to use as occasional retreats. Sometimes additional witnesses had to be summoned, and what was supposed to be a simple and expeditious process was often punctuated by unavoidable delays. Other legal business that had been reserved for the next regular meeting was brought forward, so the gathering soon swelled to much larger dimensions than would have been strictly necessary for Cynric's case alone.

Edwin looked across to where some men were setting up another tent. This one, evidently, was to be shared by the bishops, who were both watching the work. Deorlaf seemed as much in his element as Aethelferth; he had a bundle of rolled parchments under his arm probably waiting for signatures and seals. Waerferth listened politely, one thumb gently riffling the pages of a small book he had brought. Then Deorlaf asked Waerferth if he had brought his seal, and Waerferth took some time rummaging in his belt-bag before he located it. In the process he also found one and a half sticks of sealing wax, so his elder colleague nodded in satisfaction.

The horn was blown and the court fell silent. Cynric was brought forward, bound with a chain, and made to stand in the middle of the grounds where everyone could see him. Before Bishop Waerferth he swore that he was innocent both in deed and intent of the charge of which Garmund accused him. Garmund, who had accused Cynric originally of the theft of the cloak-pin, now formally accused him of the murder of Helmstan. Cynric's case could not have been on a more precarious footing. Helmstan was technically of the rank of thegn, and a man accused of killing a thegn had to bring a number of witnesses in his favour commensurate with a thegn's wergild, which was six times higher than that of Cynric.

Edwin thought of the six witnesses who, with great perseverance, he had managed to find: six honest local men who were now waiting in his tent at the edge of the grounds. If Cynric had only been accused of the theft of his brother's cloak-pin, these witnesses would easily have won Cynric's case. They would count for nothing to protect him from a charge of murder, however.

"Most likely," Edwin spoke to Cynric in an undertone, "your witnesses' oaths will stand, but will be inadequate to clear you entirely. Then you will be expected to pay compensation to make up for the rest."

"But—"

"I know. You're innocent. I believe it, and I won't give up

trying to find evidence to prove it."

"But I'll have to sell the spot by the river to get out of this," Cynric's voice was despondent.

"I can't imagine it will go that far. Before the sale is concluded, we'll get the charge dropped—"

"If it once goes up for sale, I'll never get it back. It's all we've got left from my father, you see. And it was to be a security in my mother's old age. I was going to build a mill. I'd make enough money to keep her comfortable and maybe even to—to—" The last word was so indistinct that Edwin leaned closer to hear. "To marry," came the shy admission.

Just then Garmund's witnesses came forward to swear their oaths. Cynric resumed his gloomy look as he outlined to Edwin who each man was as he came forward: "That one always jumps to the wrong conclusion. This one—he bears a grudge against me because of a girl."

Edwin raised his eyebrows.

"Different girl. It was a long time ago." A shadow of a smile showed briefly in the corners of Cynric's mouth. "He married the girl but still hates me. Now here comes one who's just a plain busybody. He always believes whatever he hears and considers it his bounden duty to do something about it. And this last one simply doesn't like my face and never has. Nothing you can do about that."

Edwin looked at the line of witnesses: some stubborn and resentful, others complacent and officious. The men stood, shoulder to shoulder, like a wall of lies. Edwin's witnesses would meet them with truth, swearing one by one that Cynric's oath was pure and without falsehood, and perhaps the gamekeeper would soon be free to pursue his modest dream.

Edwin motioned for his witnesses to be brought out. Bert, who had been on the lookout at the tent door, bounced in to summon them. Then a noise arose in the crowd of onlookers and three more figures stepped through to join the number of Cynric's accusers.

"Sorry we're late," said Cenred with a smirk. His eyes sought out Edwin's in defiance. "We are here to swear oaths against the accused."

The last light went out of Cynric's eyes. Cenred cackled in glee as Bishop Waerferth called him to take the oath. Fury surged up in Edwin's heart. He would not allow this wretch and his cronies to ruin a man who had lost so much already!

"You know what this means," said Edwin, not looking at Cynric. "Now there is no way to get you out of this by oaths or by paying fines. No way except the ordeal."

"God help me!" The words burst from Cynric's lips. It was the most emotion Edwin had ever seen in him.

"My lords," Garmund said in a shrill voice, "This man Cynric stands accused of murder. Not an accidental killing in the heat of a quarrel, not in defending himself against an attacker, but foul, sneaking, savage secret murder of a man who had drawn no weapon against him. I ask you to bear this in mind.

"Moreover, this murder was among the most treacherous known to mankind, the murder of his own father's son.

"Thirdly, this foul killing was not frankly confessed, but concealed; and not by burial in the earth, but by mutilation of the murdered man's body in the most gruesome and callous manner. Surely, as the blood of Abel cried out to God for vengeance, so does the blood of Helmstan. If this second Cain, this Cynric, will not confess his crime, let God reveal his guilt by the threefold ordeal!"

Sounds of assent rippled through the crowd. Edwin had said nothing to halt this tirade because there was nothing to say; he had no evidence, as yet, that would prove Cynric's innocence, and a man who maintained his innocence in the face of an accusation of secret murder was by definition subject to the threefold ordeal. Edwin looked at Cynric; the gamekeeper was staring at his toes.

"It is for you to determine," said Edwin, "whether the accused shall undergo the ordeal of the hot iron or of the hot water."

"It is my choice," said Garmund, "that the accused shall undergo the ordeal by—" here he paused and looked around, obviously for effect. Edwin's fist tightened; he yearned to wrap his fingers around Garmund's scrawny neck. "The hot iron," he announced.

◆

"Well, it could be worse," Edwin said to Cynric when he was returned to the guard-house.

"I don't see how," said Cynric.

"Only this. With the ordeal of the hot water, ordinarily you'd have to pick up a stone from a kettle of boiling water that's wrist-deep. With the threefold ordeal, the boiling water's up to your elbow. You have to feel around and pull that stone out and it really is three times as difficult when you have to plunge your arm in that deep."

"So? I've got to carry a red-hot iron for nine feet with my bare hand, and how is that any better?"

"Well, it's not a lot better, I grant you. But it does not expose as much of your skin to burning as the threefold ordeal of the hot water. And by the time you hold it, it's not exactly red-hot, though it is still quite hot. A distinction without a difference, perhaps, but it may mean slightly less pain."

"And I'm to walk nine feet? Who's to measure that, then? Garmund, I suppose!"

"No. The accuser chooses hot iron or hot water. You get to measure out nine feet by your own feet. The distance is measured out in advance and marked."

Cynric's face had taken on that blank look Edwin had come to recognize in him as loss of hope. He grasped Cynric by the shoulders and forced him to look in his eyes. "An innocent man will survive the ordeal," said Edwin. "He will be vindicated. I won't tell you that you have nothing to fear. It will be painful. But if you can bear the pain to a count of nine, the worst will be over. Can you keep your courage that long?"

Cynric hesitated, then nodded.

"Good man. When it is over, and you are vindicated," Edwin continued, "I say 'when' because I believe you are innocent—then no one will be able to accuse you of this crime again, because that would be to contradict the judgement of God Himself. I shall do my utmost to discover your brother's true murderer. If I can do it before the ordeal, you may be able to avoid it. Either way, your brother will have justice."

This last point seemed the most meaningful to Cynric, and he acknowledged it with a grateful nod.

"Are you sure your poacher friend isn't involved? I'd at least like to talk to him," Edwin urged.

Cynric shook his head resolutely.

"But they say he and your brother quarrelled."

Cynric picked at the sleeve of his tunic. "They say a lot of things."

"Is it true?"

"Helmstan said I ought to stay away from Buntel, that having him for a friend was—" Cynric's face twitched in a sort of fleeting smile, "bad for my career." He shrugged. "It's lonely working out in the woods. Buntel and me, we've been friends since we were so high. He turns up, we pass the time of day over a mug of ale, then he goes again. He don't get in my way, I don't get in his. Helmstan meant well, but he shouldn't have meddled."

Edwin said nothing. He knew all about older brothers who only had one's best interests at heart.

"I know it looks bad," Cynric said, "but trust me, he didn't do it. Trust me." He squinted up at the triangle of light far above from the window in the peak of the roof-gable. "Do they really expect this pain to make me tell them what they want to hear?" he asked.

"No," said Edwin. "They are not trying to torture the truth out of you. The point is to allow God to reveal the truth of a crime that is hidden from human eyes."

"How? Will God prevent me from feeling the pain?" Cynric studied his right hand doubtfully.

Edwin shook his head. "The proof is not in your ability to endure the pain of carrying a red-hot iron in your hand for nine paces. It will come three days later, when your bandaged hand is unwrapped and examined. If it's inflamed and festering, you are guilty. If your hand is healing, that shows God's protection of an innocent man."

"A man may have a lying tongue—or not—but his wounds tell the truth either way, I suppose," Cynric mused.

"True."

Edwin knew of several bald-faced liars who had been willing to confess their guilt rather than pay the painful price of the ordeal to maintain their false claims of innocence. Cynric had never, in Edwin's estimation, been a bald-faced liar. However, he was by no means a known quantity in terms of courage. Edwin had some uneasiness that if Cynric truly expected to be hanged regardless, he would choose to make a false confession and be done with it rather than go through the pain of the ordeal first. In the end, however, no one is in a hurry to die as long as there is the faintest glimmer of hope that it can be avoided; and Edwin took heart in the fact that he seemed to have given just that much confidence to the hapless gamekeeper. It was a matter of keeping his courage stoked now until the day arrived.

◆

It was about the tenth or eleventh time in the past hour that Fram had come and put his nose in Edwin's hand.

"All right, boy, I could use an airing myself," he said. Not really having any place in mind, Edwin found himself once out of the gate ambling toward the spot where Helmstan's body had been discovered. He wondered if there was anything to be seen; there was probably no sign left in the place where the body had lain, and so many feet had left their marks.

Once he came to the spot, however, he still felt a chill of disappointment. There was nothing to distinguish it besides the old stump that had been pointed out to him from a distance. Now Edwin had a closer look at the stump. It was a large old stump, overgrown with lichens and with an unevenly slanting cut surface where the axe had bitten. The wood was darkened with age, but Edwin saw some fresh knife-marks where something had been hacked or cut using the stump as its surface. The marks were just deep enough to have scored through to the raw, unweathered wood beneath.

Edwin was interrupted in his examination of the stump by Fram's whining, which was growing louder and more insistent. He had been nosing around casually in the leaves but was now digging with purpose. Edwin turned to see what he had found. Among the leaves and dirt he saw that Fram was pawing at a dirty piece of cord. Edwin took hold of the cord and pulled. It proved to be only two feet long, with a nondescript weight of filthy mess at the other end. It was no wonder the dog had found it; the smell of rotten meat was unmistakable. Some lure left by a hunter, most probably. Edwin eyed the object, about the size of Fram's head, slowly turning on its bit of cord before him. Then he caught sight of something like ivory amongst the dirt and mess.

He laid the object down and began poking and scraping with a stick. With a thrill of horror, he realized that the ivory was one of a row of wolflike teeth. He scraped dirt and leaves, and—probably—clotted blood until he exposed hair, short pendulous ears, and the place where the head had been severed from the body. He found that the cord had been wrapped with a slip-knot around the dog's snout. For some reason uncovering the dog's undamaged pinkish-brown nose was the most pitiful part of this unpleasant discovery.

Fram sat with a worried look on his hairy face. He had ceased whimpering when Edwin took charge of his find, but he was still looking on attentively.

"I know what you mean, old son," Edwin murmured. "We've seen this fellow before."

It was with a heavy heart that Edwin returned to Aethelwulf's hall to break the news of his favourite dog's death to his master. The usually self-possessed Aethelwulf sagged as Edwin told him of his gruesome find. "Who could have done this?" he exclaimed. "Poor old hound, that he suffered so at the hands of wicked men! You will find them, won't you, Edwin?" To Edwin's surprise, he asked for the head. When it was brought, wrapped in an old towel, Aethelwulf ordered a hole dug under the threshold of the hall. A small group stood around and watched as one of the hall servants buried it.

"Now he'll always be there to guard us," Aethelwulf said, thick-voiced, as he firmed the earth with his foot. Edwin said nothing; he was meditating on the fact that a severed dog's head, with a slip-knot around the jaws to make them bite, had been used to turn a murder into a wolf-attack.

Chapter 30

The bell tolled in the tower of the abbey church. Edwin stood outside, cloak wrapped tight against the wind, with Cynric and his mother. Despite the early hour, a crowd was gathering around the church door. Edwin had seen the monks and a lay brother carry in the brazier that was to heat the iron bar. Now they would be kindling the fire; when it was ready, Cynric and the others would be admitted.

Presently the door opened and a monk announced that all was in readiness.

Six men proceeded into the church: Cynric was accompanied by Edwin and one of Cynric's cousins. Garmund brought in Cenred, leering and smirking as usual, and the man who had found the brooch in Cynric's chest. Bishop Deorlaf and Bishop Waerferth were conversing in muted tones by the altar. Abbot Aethelhun met the men in the porch and directed them to come test the fire. Edwin just had time to lay a reassuring hand on Cynric's shoulder before walking with the others to the brazier set up in the centre of the narrow nave, halfway between the church door and the altar.

The lay brother whose task it was to tend the fire closed his bellows and stepped back. He had done his work well; the coals glowed red under the grey ash. Edwin and Cynric's cousin held their hands as close to the fire as they dared, then nodded to the lay brother.

Garmund stepped forward with his witnesses. He felt the fire with a show of meticulousness right above the coals, on the sides, and above the coals again. Cenred grabbed the bellows from the lay brother and was about to work up the fire, but Aethelhun appeared beside him with a restraining hand on his wrist. "If you find the fire insufficiently hot," the Abbot addressed Garmund, "you must say so, and we will attend to it."

"No," Garmund reversed course. "It's hot enough, I suppose."

Abbot Aethelhun asked them to take their places on either side of the aisle. During the little drama of the fire, Cynric had stripped down like a penitent to his white linen shirt and his steps had been measured and marked off.

"You have all fasted this night and withheld yourselves from women?" asked Bishop Waerferth. The men all nodded. Edwin's concentration slid away for a moment to Molly, so far from him, perhaps wondering why he had been gone so long. He returned to the present with a start as Bishop Waerferth began to move from one witness to the next, sprinkling each with rather cold holy water. Then he said, "You shall each kiss this Gospel-book and make the sign of the cross." He brought out a book the likes of which few of Edwin's generation had ever seen in Wessex. He hoisted the heavy codex so that both hands were holding it at the bottom and its jewelled front cover was presented to the witnesses. One by one they kissed the book and crossed themselves. Bishop Waerferth returned the book to the altar and gave a sign to Deorlaf. The lay brother ceased blowing the fire and laid a heavy iron bar about as thick as a man's thumb and an ell long across the coals.

Bishop Deorlaf then began the *Aduratio*, the first prayer of the service. Edwin had not heard Deorlaf's Latin before; the words *Deus omnipotens iudex iustus* lost, to his ear, some of their awful solemnity when spoken with the Bishop's Mercian intonation.

The old Bishop was certainly in no hurry, speaking each word with deliberation as the iron continued to heat up. Edwin, who could understand the words, at least had something to occupy his mind. To the others, he imagined, they must sound like a mysterious incantation, an interminable cataract of sounds.

When the last collect had been finished, and the lay brother had lifted the iron bar off the fire with a pair of tongs and set it ready at the marker where the ordeal was to begin, Waerferth said, "Let each one of you keep silence and pray that the truth shall be revealed."

Deorlaf, making the sign of the cross over the iron bar, concluded, "*Benedictio Dei Patris et Filii et Spiritus Sancti descendat super hoc ferrum ad discernendum iudicium Dei. Amen.*"

Cynric was, by now, bathed in sweat and Edwin could see the muscles of his legs flexing as he unsuccessfully tried to keep his knees from knocking together. Bishop Waerferth signalled that he should pick up the iron. Cynric gave a nervous, jerky nod and reached his hand out toward the bar. As he did so, a drop of sweat crawled down past the hairs on his arm and hit the iron. The sizzle of one drop of sweat was audible out of all proportion in the silence of the assembly. Abbot Aethelhun handed Cynric a towel. After he had dried his face and hands Cynric seemed to recover his courage somewhat. With an attitude of determination he picked up the bar, showing no discomfort other than a tightening of the lips.

Bishop Waerferth counted as Cynric, with purposeful but

not hasty movements, began to put one foot in front of the other.

"One…" Cynric passed Garmund, who opened one eye to glare at him.

"Two…three…" Cynric's steps passed his cousin, head bowed and lips moving.

"Four…five…" The sweat was streaming down Cynric's face and his breathing came in irregular gasps. He passed the other accusing witness.

"Six…seven…" Waerferth's voice was only a murmur, but they were all counting along.

"Eight…" Cynric had reached the place where Cenred and Edwin were standing opposite each other on either side of the aisle. Cenred's head was bowed in apparent reverence, but as Cynric passed Edwin heard him murmur a barely audible "Whoreson."

Cynric inhaled sharply. Edwin was afraid he was going to turn and hit Cenred a well-deserved blow with the hot iron. However, by a supreme effort, Cynric did not even turn his head.

"Nine." Cynric dropped the iron with a deafening clang. Edwin gasped for air; he realized he had been holding his breath all the time since Cynric had picked up the iron. The Abbot handed Cynric the towel again, and Cynric mopped his face with his left hand while an elderly monk began to wrap the ordeal hand with a long roll of clean bandage. Cynric's cousin brought his cloak and draped it over his shoulders. Then Deorlaf's secretary came with sealing wax and the bandage was sealed with the Bishop's seal in blood-red wax.

"In three days, we'll see whether the burns are healing or festering," announced Deorlaf, "and God's judgement on this case will be clear."

Cynric turned to Cenred, who was doing his best to slip out of the church with his companions. Cynric stepped in front of him, blocking his path.

"Insulting a man's kin is asking for trouble," he said.

"What are you talking about?"

"You know what you said, and I tell you again that you are asking for trouble."

"And you're the one who's going to dish it up?" Cenred leered, stepping up close to Cynric's face. "I suppose you'll do it single-handed!" Cenred knocked his hand hard against Cynric's bandage and walked away, laughing.

"Edwin," Edmund appeared at his brother's elbow as he came out of the church. He mumbled, "I did it. I—I went to confession."

"Good," said Edwin, who was watching Cenred swagger away into the distance.

"About—you know. I got forty days on bread and water."

"Forty days? You got off lightly. Seven years isn't unheard-of for adultery."

"Well, nothing actually happened, thanks to you. I gave a bunch of alms and swapped some days for singing psalms, so I've whittled it down to ten days that way. If we fast today and my men take it in turns, we can have this out of the way before the ordeal is over."

Edwin remembered what his uncle had taught him: sin was the soul's disease, and penance was like medicine. 'Did it help a sick man if someone else took his medicine?' the bishop would ask with a derisive smile. But Edmund could not understand this. For him, penance was a legal fine. God's law and his own conscience had testified against him in court, and the judgement was that he owed God this penance. To him, whether he paid in one type of coin or another, whether he paid all outright or passed the hat and remunerated his friends later, did not matter, as long as the fine was paid out. It was impossible to make him see otherwise. Tough luck on those beefy lads in his retinue who had counted on a good dinner tonight.

"Come on, then," Edwin said aloud. "Let's get started on those psalms." When they went in, all traces of the recent ordeal had been cleared away. They knelt right in front of the altar (for Edmund there was no such thing as looking for a quiet corner out in the porticus) and Edmund's deep voice mingled with Edwin's in the solemn music. As he sang, Edwin prayed: *Lord, have mercy on my brother. Christ, have mercy on Cynric. Lord, have mercy on me.*

Cynric, looking neither more nor less gloomy and taciturn after the three days' seclusion following his ordeal, was led out by two of the abbey's brothers. Edwin recognized one of them as the elderly near-sighted monk he had helped to prepare Helmstan's body for burial. When the witnesses had gathered round and Edwin had taken his place with Cynric's mother as near to him as possible, Bishop Deorlaf began to unwrap the bandage from Cynric's hand. Everyone held his breath: would Cynric's flesh be blistered and foul, or would the bandage fall from his hand to show clean, healing skin? Cynric's mouth was seen to twitch a little as he stood motionless with his hand outstretched. The old Bishop continued the unwrapping process with deliberate, orderly motions.

With a final flourish, Bishop Deorlaf caught up the last length of bandage as it slid from Cynric's hand. There was a collective gasp as the clergyman stepped back and held up Cynric's hand for all to see. It was pink and healing. Deorlaf pronounced a blessing over him and Cynric's mother ran to embrace him.

Seizing the moment, Edwin raised his voice and said, "Now we see that the gamekeeper Cynric has been accused falsely. I believe Helmstan was killed inside the palisade and his body taken out afterward as a subterfuge. I intend to look into this matter further and make a counter-accusation. The killer of Helmstan must be brought to justice."

Edwin had scarcely finished speaking when Cynric, his face bright and eager, took his hand and shook it nearly out of joint. "Thank you, my lord!" he exclaimed. "Thank you, thank you!" And with that, the gamekeeper hurried away with his mother trailing after.

◆

"Bringing Helmstan's killer to justice! That's Ealdorman Aethelred's job, not yours," Edmund reminded his brother earnestly when they were alone in their lodgings. "The gormless gamekeeper is vindicated; you did what you promised. You've no good reason to keep meddling in this affair."

"Meddling, you call it? A simple 'Well done, Edwin, for saving an innocent man' would have sufficed."

"It's really none of our business!" Edmund paced the floor in between Edwin and the door, effectively cutting off his means of escape from yet another dispute.

"It is our business," Edwin dug in. "I am convinced that there is something here that goes deeper than what we are seeing. There is some evil mind at work, ever trying to effect some end of his own."

"Tell me more. You know how I love ghost stories."

"Was Helmstan's killing the work of a ghost? The threat against Ealdorman Beornoth? Ealdorman Aethelred's accident on the day of the hunt? Or how about the deliberate attempt to frame Cynric? I don't think these are all coincidences, and they are certainly the work of a living man."

"All right, but I still don't see how getting entangled in a local matter can help our mission for the King," Edmund glared.

"Don't you see? This is—somehow—a play for the Mercian throne. I don't understand how yet. Why else would there have been attacks on two ealdormen already?"

"Helmstan was nobody. Why kill him?"

"That's the strangest thing of all," Edwin said, pensively. He stooped over his bed and began rearranging his baggage. "I don't understand it, unless it was a vendetta killing by the Ceaddings after all. But the brooch could only have been put in Cynric's chest by the actual killer in an attempt to draw off attention from Helmstan's death and make it seem a local matter."

"King Alfred said nothing in *my* instructions about getting involved in stuff like this."

Edwin turned around again and faced his brother. "We became involved as soon as we claimed a seat at the negotiating table. This has everything to do with who will succeed to the kingship, and if we don't find out who is behind it all, the West Saxons may end up supporting a murderer as king of the Mercians."

◆

Later, when Edwin was still fuming over the insolence of Cenred and the stubbornness of Edmund, Edmund appeared beside him in their lodgings and tapped him on the shoulder. "Come on, little brother! Get your kit and let's see what you're made of!"

Edwin assented willingly. Tomorrow would be soon enough to start gathering evidence and taking steps to pin down Helmstan's killer. In no time, Edwin had donned his battle-gear and was ready to vent his frustrations on the hulking form of his elder brother. They chose a corner of the green outside the enclosure where Edmund's men had exercised several times, and soon Edmund's men gathered to watch. The brothers wore their swords but started with shields and practice spears that were really just shafts without spearheads.

The power Edmund put behind his spear-thrusts, even without an iron point, could have given Edwin internal injuries; it was fortunate, then, that Edwin managed to evade or parry each one. Edwin got one squarely on Edmund's chest, causing him to cough, but he failed to press his advantage. Edmund caught his younger brother behind the knees and brought him down on his back, disarming his spear.

Unwilling to make the same mistake twice, Edwin quickly drew his sword as he scrambled to his feet and put Edmund on his guard before he could plant his huge foot on Edwin's chest and claim victory. Edmund drew his sword also and the brothers circled one another warily. They both remembered their father's instruction to watch one's opponent and be ready to counter his attack. The exertion had whetted the nerve of the two brothers to razor-keenness and their eyes held one another's gaze for a long moment as the retainers watched in breathless silence.

The two brothers also apparently had the same amount of patience with their father's advice, for at the same moment they both let out a terrible shout and fell on each other with a sudden clash of blades that made more than one of Edmund's warriors jump.

They fought on for longer than the usual set practice

imposed on bands of retainers—one moment Edmund gained the advantage, Edwin the next—until, despite the chill autumn air, the sweat was rolling down their faces and their breath was coming in hoarse gasps. Edmund's chief retainer Godhelm was beginning to wonder if he should step in and call a halt, at the risk of a reprimand from his very stubborn lord, when the sound of shouting and singing reached them. A crowd had gathered in the settlement not far away. By an unspoken mutual assent, the two brothers sheathed their swords and shook hands, pale and breathless.

"What's going on?" Edwin managed to say between gasps.

It seemed that Cynric was again on the receiving end of the fickle public mood. This time, however, instead of being accused of a crime, the gamekeeper was being carried on the shoulders of the people of Buckingham with cheers. Edwin, who had sat down in exhaustion on the grass, stood up again to see the spectacle. One of the shoulders bearing Cynric up was that of the truculent bronzesmith, and a pretty village girl walked significantly alongside. Cynric's face wore an expression of liveliness Edwin had never seen on it before, along with an enormous black eye and smears of blood about the nose.

One of the men sprinted over to find out what had happened. He quickly returned with the news: "Cenred of the Ceaddings was drinking in the settlement and Cynric called him out. I guess the fellow had insulted him or something. Cynric beat the living daylights out of the old sod, and now he's the hero of the hour!" Edwin sank back on the grass and indulged in a good, long laugh.

Somewhere, someone must hold the secret of how Helmstan met his fate. Somewhere out there was the mysterious poacher friend of Cynric's whose testimony at the trial might have saved him from the ordeal—or sent him to the gallows. Still he had not come forward, and Helmstan still lay in his grave unavenged.

Now that Cynric had been vindicated, Edwin could not let this question remain unanswered. He must find this man, who might be a witness or a perpetrator. He resolved to be out at first light to finally find out the truth.

◆

Aethelred awoke at the sound of his servant knocking on the door. The guard let him in and the old man shuffled to his lord's bedside. Aethelred sat up.

"What time is it?" he asked.

"Some time past sunrise, my lord," replied the old man. "I've brought you your breakfast. How are you feeling?"

"Better and better," said Aethelred, clearing a place on the table beside the bed. "I really feel I should be out and about."

"We'll see what the bonesetter says. You don't want to rush things, or you might do yourself another injury, and then where would you be?"

There was a cup of mead on the table, and Aethelred asked, "Did you bring me this?"

"No, my lord. I just brought you this Welsh ale here on the tray to wash down your bread and cheese. Here's some water for washing."

"Hmm," said Aethelred, looking doubtfully into the mead cup. He sniffed at it. "Hmm."

"You fancy mead rather than Welsh ale today, my lord?" asked the servant in surprise.

Aethelred set the cup down.

"Right now I fancy a wash," he said. After he had washed

his face, he poured the mead into the washbasin. "Empty that on your way out, if you please," he said. "And send a message to the West Saxon lords."

"Certainly, my lord," asked the servant, who found his master's actions increasingly puzzling.

Chapter 31

Edwin started out from Buckingham early that morning, with Fram trotting cheerily at Stig's heels. He took the road leading north and east out of the settlement and into the wilder country beyond. The river wound sluggishly to his right, lined with marsh and meadows on either side. The rising sun shone golden through the long grass. Three hundred years of Saxon habitation had pushed the forest back in many places to make room for farmland. The thatch-topped farmhouses Edwin could see here and there in the distance looked small and vulnerable. Just a few miles beyond the forest, Edwin knew, was Watling Street, the old Roman road that marked the frontier with eastern Mercia. There the Danes held sway. Somewhere in this wilderness he hoped to find Cynric's elusive friend and shine a light on all that remained dark in the strange matter of Helmstan's death.

As he rounded a curve he caught sight of a man leading a small ox-cart down the road. The man was wearing a drooping hood that cast his whole face in shadow; not even his nose stuck out. Edwin was about to turn around when he noticed the familiar colour of the man's trousers. This was one of the servants at the hall—or was it the abbey? He was sure he had seen those trousers somewhere recently. The man continued on, his cart laden with bundles of hay.

Edwin watched him. He didn't whistle as he walked. He did not look to the right or to the left. There was something in his walk that, if not furtive, spoke a desire of not being noticed.

As Edwin watched, the cart hit a rut in the track and tipped to the right. It lurched as if laden with something heavy and the man steadied it with all his strength. Edwin knew only too well how unwieldy a wooden cart could be; but this one only had a few bundles of hay in it. The man was not very careful with his burden, however. Some of the hay spilled out as he steadied the cart, and he did not gather them up, but chivvied the ox on its way.

"Careless slave," was what came to Edwin's mind at first; but the man was walking too fast to be that kind of lazy servant.

Edwin remained looking at the bundles of hay lying in the road until the man was out of sight. He remembered the man's nervous walk, the excessive lurching of the cart, and the man's indifference to the loss of some of his load. He decided to follow the man.

It was not hard to track him; what was more difficult was to remain at a distance so as not to be seen. Presently the man left the road and led the ox onto a path into the wood. Edwin was obliged to double back and leave Stig and Fram with a man and boy burning charcoal he had passed some quarter of a mile back. He then hurried to retrace his steps, which was made easier by the slow progress of the carter he was pursuing. Edwin had to be more careful as they got deeper into the forest, where autumn had laid a thick carpet of crackly dry leaves. He nearly lost him when the man walked right across a largish clearing in the forest where Edwin, for fear of detection, could not walk. He had to skirt the clearing, running in the shadow of the trees to keep up with the man. On several occasions, Edwin did have to duck into the bracken and brambles when a forest noise caused the man to look back.

They reached a narrow spot in the river which had been spanned by a new rough log bridge. With difficulty, the man got his cart across it. He gave a distinctive whistle and waited. Edwin, from a thick patch of bracken on the other side of the bridge, waited and watched as well. After a short time Edwin saw three men emerge from the trees. There was no mistaking their foreign hair styles and clothing, and the silver rings one of them was wearing on his arm: these were Danes.

Before Edwin had a chance to wonder how many Danes were there and why they were receiving small clandestine consignments of hay, the carter pushed the hay aside and the Danes leaned over to look into the cart. The Saxon produced a small object—a key, as it happened—and unlocked the chest which Edwin could now see had been concealed under the hay. The Saxon opened the chest and stepped back. Then the Dane with the arm-rings plunged his hands into the chest and brought up handfuls of silver coins. One of his henchmen smiled appreciatively, the other laughed. The Danish chief took a few of the coins in his hands and scrutinized them closely. Then he looked at the Saxon.

"Good," he said.

The Saxon put his hand on the chest of silver and said, "Another one of these after you help his lordship."

"When?" asked the chief.

"Listen for the church bell," said the Saxon.

The Danes looked at each other and Edwin could hear them discussing what this meant.

"The church bell," said the man in a louder voice, as if the Danes were hard of hearing. "The church bell. *BONG, BONG,*

BONG," he intoned. "Today."

Now the Danes seemed to comprehend.

Today! By the end of the day the Danish mercenaries would be coming to the aid of one of the lords now at Buckingham. Only that lord would be prepared. The rest of the luminaries of Mercia would be unarmed at court. This 'lordship' would be able to seize control and no one would be ready to stop him. As these thoughts raced through Edwin's mind, the hooded Saxon turned to leave. In his place of concealment, Edwin started in surprise. He recognized the face of the man who had delivered the silver to the Danes, and his mind whirled. Mercia seemed poised to exchange a Danish puppet for a Saxon traitor.

With the vital clue of the ox-cart man, he felt sure he could work out the truth about Helmstan's killing and who was behind all the things that had taken place since. But there were more pressing matters now. With an effort, Edwin took control of his thoughts. It was crucial that he should get back and warn the others of their danger. First, though, he needed to find out how large a force of Danes was gathered here.

He waited until the Danes had melted back into the forest on the other side of the bridge and the sounds of the ox-cart had receded into silence. Then silently he advanced toward the riverbank. He was reluctant to use the bridge to cross, as he could not see what was on the other side and it would leave him exposed. The river was too wide to jump and too deep to wade through; but a few yards farther on he saw a fallen log that spanned the two banks. Once across, he found that there was a farmstead on the other side of the bank. He remained within the trees and began to skirt the farm. It seemed an out-of-the-way place for gathering an army. And how many could this farm hold? That question was quickly answered. Over the next hillock Edwin could see the ruins of a burned farmhouse overlooking a large open field, certainly several hundred acres, and in it was a city of tents. It occupied no more than a third of the entire field, but that meant that there were at least fifty Vikings here.

Edwin's heart missed a beat or two as the danger suddenly hit him. Even with the West Saxon warriors thrown in, Buckingham could not hope to put up more than seventy-five men, of which perhaps only half were true warriors. There was no time to raise the fyrd of Buckinghamshire. Gathering a shire army would take at least four or five days under the best of circumstances.

Heart pounding, he retraced his steps. As he crossed the log it snapped; the crack of the rotten wood and the squashy sound of his foot on the mud sounded deafeningly loud in the empty forest. He waited for sounds that he had been detected, but when he heard nothing, he continued as silently as possible until he got to the main road. Then he broke into a run and, with considerable relief, reached the clearing where the man and boy were burning charcoal. Fram leapt up to greet him and Stig turned his head.

"Thank you," he said to the woodsman.

The man made no reply, but began walking around Edwin, looking him up and down. "By your leave," he murmured, and began picking dead leaves and twigs out of Edwin's cloak. He untied the handkerchief that had been around his face to shield it from the smoke and used it to brush him down. "Your nice clothes won't last if you treat them like that," he grunted.

"There's no time for this now," Edwin said impatiently. "I've just seen a Viking army across the river. You and your people are in grave danger. I've got to get back to Buckingham to warn them there."

"Were you seen?" the man asked.

"I don't think so."

"You can't be sure of that," the man said. "Come, get your horse and your hound and I'll show you another route back."

Chapter 32

Bert returned to the barn while the other stable hands were still at breakfast. He felt left out—the Mercian stable-boys showed little interest in being friendly, especially after an ill-judged remark about their accent sparked reprisals from the local lads. "Berrrrrt" they now insisted on calling him, mocking his West Saxon way of talking. He went and checked Red. He was fine—Bert had tended to him earlier and he needed nothing. The old gelding nickered a greeting, asking for and receiving a piece of bread that Bert had saved from his ration. Red had been turned out with the rest of the horses, but stayed by the fence waiting for the return of his friend Stig, whom Edwin had taken out at dawn.

Bert scarcely made any sound as he felt his way through the dark stable. As he felt the smooth-worn diagonal beams of the loft ladder, he suddenly froze. From somewhere up in the loft he heard a voice whispering.

"Quiet! I thought I heard something."

"Check and see what it was, then," said a second voice. There was a rustling of hay above and Bert quickly ducked into the deepest shadows against the wall. There was silence, except for Bert's breathing and heartbeat, which sounded deafening in his own ears.

"Nothing. Must have been a mouse," said the man, retreating again from the opening of the hayloft.

"Or old Helmstan's ghost," said the other.

"Shut up!"

"Well, you needn't get so bothered. His lordship ain't angry with us no more on *his* account. Only too bad your second try also came a cropper."

The man who had been speaking sneezed violently, causing a drowsy horse to raise its head. The sneeze was followed by some wet-sounding sniffles.

"I dunno," continued the gruffer voice. "He'll be stuck in bed a little longer, won't he? He might take a turn for the worse."

Bed? thought Bert. Second try? The man must be talking about Ealdorman Aethelred. It dawned on him that the terrible accident the man had suffered must have been deliberately caused by these men! Who were they, and why were they after the Ealdorman? In spite of the chill, a drop of cold sweat began to trickle slowly down Bert's back. The men had moved on to another subject.

"He screamed like a woman," the gruff man was saying. "Did you hear it?"

"I should think the whole of Bucks heard it," said the other man. "We aren't to finish him off, are we?"

Bert reasoned that they were now discussing Ealdorman Beornoth.

"No, just give him a little fright—so his lordship will be able to count on him in time of need." They laughed.

"That's done, then," said the gruff voice.

"Good and proper," sniffed the other. "What has he got on

the fellow?"

"I don't know, but it's something pretty good. His lordship was very insistent on the noose and pillow, so maybe that meant something to him."

"More likely he felt he needed to spell things out for you after—you know—Helmstan."

"Shut up!" the gruff man nearly shouted, and the sniffler tried to get him to be quiet.

"Don't try to shush me! You said there was no one about."

"But if you rouse the horses, someone will likely come out to check."

"Then I'll run a knife across your scrawny throat and we'll have some peace and quiet for sure."

"I don't know what you're so upset about," the sniffly man whined. "You'll still get your silver soon enough."

"Sure. We'll have to hope there's enough left over for us after his lordship has paid off the Danes."

"Danes?" The man seemed genuinely surprised.

"You didn't think he was going to assume the …er, control of the country by the force of his personal charm, did you? Danes. They don't fight for a lord or a land. They fight for the shiny stuff. His lordship has promised them silver, lots of it, to stay at his beck and call until needed."

Something in the words 'until needed' chilled Bert to the bone. But it was the cold hard coinage that had captured the gruff man's imagination.

"You've seen it?" he asked, with eagerness in his voice.

"Sure I've seen it," his companion replied. "Why do you think I was out with that ox-cart at the crack of dawn?"

"Well?"

"Now wait just a minute. Why should I tell you what I know? How do I know you're not going to sneak in behind my back?"

"What were you doing? Was it about the silver? Was it in the ox-cart?"

"I already said I'm not—"

"Is it in a chest, or sacks, or what?"

"What's your point?"

"My point is this," said the gruff man, speaking with particular emphasis. "It's a lot of silver, yeah? How far can *one* man get if he carries off a fully laden chest?"

"Not as far as two," said Sniffles, with a new appreciation for his comrade. "But won't we be giving up a good place with his lordship, or whatever he might soon become, if we run away?"

"That's slave talk," said the gruff man dismissively. "If it's as much as you say, we can live as kings. After all the special jobs we've done for his lordship, we're going to be awkward company for him. He'll probably want some new retainers that don't have a history like we do. Then you know for us it's—" He made the sound of slitting a throat. "Or we *could* go live on the border, get some fighting men and horses, and beat the Danes at their own game."

There was silence as the other man seemed to consider this.

"Yeah," he finally said, and began to chuckle. "So we need to come up with a plan for getting our hands on the silver and fading away quick."

"Yeah. A plan, yeah."

"Come on," the other said abruptly. "We've been gone too long. Let's meet later over a horn of ale and we'll talk more."

At this there was a rustling and creaking over Bert's head and two pairs of feet came down the ladder in the darkness, seemingly right in front of his face. Then they padded away to the door. Finally he ventured to breathe a sigh as he heard the door shut behind them. Bert slowly unfolded from his crouched position and grimaced as the pins and needles attacked his left foot.

He could hardly wait to get out of the barn and find Lord Edwin. As he stumbled towards the light of the hall, however, he realized that though he had heard some genuine villains discussing horrible crimes, he had no idea who they were or which 'lordship' they worked for. He only hoped Lord Edwin could sort it all out. An army of Danes was waiting nearby until needed—by someone!

◆

Lord Aethelred was still in bed when all the other men left for the court. It was quiet in his uncle's enclosure; only the ordinary sounds of daily work around the hall could be heard.

The latch slowly and silently began to lift on the door to the young ealdorman's chamber. It was dark inside with the window shut against the autumn winds. The only sound in the room was the slow, even breathing of the slumbering patient.

With furtive motions and footsteps as light as a cat's, a man entered the room and closed the door as silently as he had opened it. He approached the bed and stood motionless for some time, listening to Aethelred's breathing. Then he leapt heavily onto the bed, whisked Aethelred's pillow from under his head, and began to smother him with it.

But his erstwhile victim proved ready for him. Aethelred slid his head out from underneath the pillow and the weight of his assailant, and with a smooth quick action ran him through with the seax he had hidden under the bedclothes. A strangled death-rattle was the last sound the man made.

Aethelred got up, panting, and opened the window. The

light streamed across the disordered bed, the widening stains of crimson on the white linens, and over the lifeless body of Ealdorman Beornoth.

Attracted by the noise, servants came running to Aethelred's chamber. When three entered more or less at once, and were stricken with horror at the sight they found inside, Aethelred asked them to close the door and bolt it. He told them what had happened and swore them as witnesses, then ordered them to keep what they had seen in complete secrecy until they arrived at the court. "On pain of death," he said, and they could tell he meant it.

One of the servants, Aethelred's white-haired retainer, helped the ealdorman lay Beornoth out on the bed and cover his body with a sheet. Aethelred found a towel and water to clean off his seax and restore it to its sheath.

"We'll get the mess cleaned up later," said Aethelred, looking at the bed with distaste. "Bolt the door and set a guard. We need to report this to the assembly."

Chapter 33

Leaving his young helper to tend the fire, the woodsman led Edwin deeper into the woods past his charcoal-burning clearing, away from the main road, through brush and bracken and into the trees, until they reached a narrow track just large enough for them to walk single-file. Edwin bent low over Stig's neck to avoid being hit in the face by branches. They stopped from time to time to listen. Over the sounds of their own hearts they once heard the mutter of human voices and one brief metallic clink, as of a sword or knife clinking against a metal buckle. They hurried on in full knowledge that they were being tracked and that there was only a slim chance they would escape. Briefly, Edwin could see the river glistening through the trees before their path took them up onto rising ground. He longed to ask how far it was to the road, but silence was crucial. And, after all, he was at the man's mercy. If he were leading him into a trap there was nothing Edwin could do. Still, he reminded himself, he would already have been caught if the man had not offered to lead him through the woods.

Now, at last, Edwin was able to spot a road through the trees. Was this the Buckingham road at last? Just then the woodsman turned to him. With a quick gesture that seemed to point Edwin in an unexpected direction, he melted away back northwards into the wood. Edwin turned Stig in the direction indicated and urged him to a gallop.

At once, two Vikings leapt from their forest cover into his path, blocking his escape. With a snort of dismay, Stig half-reared and scrambled back on his hindquarters. More Danes emerged from the trees, silent and menacing as ghosts. Edwin's heart gave a sickening leap and he heard a rushing sound in his ears.

The Vikings were surrounding him on all sides. They poked their spears at him and he realized they wanted him to dismount. Reluctantly he did so, acknowledging to himself that all hope of pushing through the crowd and escaping at a mad gallop was vain anyway. He turned to Fram, who was waiting as if for orders. "Fram, go home!" Edwin said. Fram looked back in the direction of Buckingham, then back at Edwin with worried eyes. "Home!" Edwin repeated, pointing. Fram turned and began to amble off uncertainly down the way they had been going. A Dane sent an arrow after him, which missed; frightened, Fram broke into a lope, tail between his legs, and hurried on until he was out of view.

As Edwin slowly climbed down he could hear them discussing whether to kill him outright or take him prisoner. An ugly little man with a scar on his face divested Edwin of his seax and the smaller knife in his belt. Out of the corner of his eye he saw another Viking pass an appraising hand over Stig's red-brown body. Unfortunately Stig had never been a kicker or a biter.

Edwin wondered whether he should try to talk to the Vikings or keep his knowledge of Danish, such as it was, a secret. He saw the little man tap a larger companion, who was holding a large battle-axe, and decided that if he didn't try something it would soon be too late. In English, but choosing words similar to the Danish ones, he said, "Don't kill me! I am—er—Ealdorman Edmund of the West Saxons. Where is your chieftain?"

The warriors then spoke too rapidly for Edwin to catch more than a few words. It seemed opinions were divided on whether the prisoner would be better off with or without his head. Finally greed won out over blood-lust and the little man said to him, "Come."

Edwin had no choice but to comply, with a Viking on either side of him holding his arms in an iron grip. Up to now he had been living from one heartbeat to the next, without any thought but to his immediate actions. Now Edwin had a chance to think. Were these the Danish renegades that had broken off from Guthrum's retreating army?

Then the crowd parted and he saw a big Viking approach. He surmised that this must be the chieftain: his beard was neatly trimmed and he was wearing more silver arm-rings than the rest. He looked at Edwin with hard eyes.

"What have we here?" he asked the short man.

"We found him in the forest," the man said. "He says he's a jarl from the West Saxons."

He showed the chieftain Edwin's seax, the one with his father Edgar's name worked in gold in the iron blade, the one Edmund was mildly jealous of, and the chieftain felt the edge of it with his thumb. Approving, he buckled the scabbard around his own waist.

"Do you think he is a spy?" the man asked.

The chieftain turned to Edwin.

"How did you come here?" he asked in heavily accented Saxon.

Edwin shrugged helplessly and said that it was obviously not his lucky day.

"I was out with my falcon," he explained. "It's a young bird and, well, rather unreliable. It flew away out here, and—"

"Very unlucky," said the Viking chieftain as he exchanged amused glances with a couple of his men. Edwin heard someone explaining his predicament to a comrade, and some laughter.

"So your hawk flew away to this part of the wood?"

"Falcon," corrected Edwin fastidiously. "It was a falcon."

"Your falcon. As I say, unlucky for you, but perhaps a good omen for our little venture. My name is Orm. While you are here, jarl, let me show you to our hall. We would like for you to be our guest today."

He nodded to Edwin's captors, who dragged him into the camp and tied him to a tree. "Maybe his hawk will light on a branch and send him down a little message," the one said to the other.

Edwin found that sitting on damp ground, with legs sprawled out in front of him and roots intersecting with his seat bones, did not effectively distract him from the tightness of the ropes used around his upper body.

Tied to the same tree was the woodsman. "What are you doing here?" asked Edwin in consternation.

The woodsman looked just as surprised. "They headed us off somehow. They got me as soon as I doubled back into the forest." There was a pause. "You don't think I led you to 'em, do you?" When he got only silence in reply, he said, "Well, now you know different. I guess we're both done for now."

"Keep your wits about you," Edwin said. "You never know what might happen."

"Shut it!" their Danish guard growled, hitting his captives

on the tops of their heads with the flat of his sword. After this there was nothing to do but sit and fume in silence. It seemed like hours—though the sun had only changed its angle through the tree-tops a little—that their guard began to show signs of boredom and took up a new position leaning against a tree a few yards distant. That way he could keep an eye on the prisoners while watching what went on in the camp.

A chance remark by the Vikings had stuck in the woodsman's mind. "I didn't know you were an ealdorman," he said.

"I'm not," said Edwin in an undertone. "But my brother is. He's Edmund, I'm Edwin. Hoping to make myself more valuable as a hostage than as a corpse. Are you a farmer around here, then?"

"Me? No," the man smiled. "Buntel's my name. Since we're telling all our secrets, I'm a poacher by trade. Hard times."

"So you're the friend who couldn't swear an oath for Cynric," Edwin said.

"Yes, I'm 'a man oft accused.' Whatever goes wrong, I'm one of the men they suspect first. Since word got out that Cynric's brother was murdered, I've laid low out here."

"Did you do it?"

Buntel chuckled softly. "No, nor have I any notion who did. It's not been my habit to murder my friend's kin and men I don't have any quarrel with."

"I thought you did have a quarrel with Helmstan. He didn't approve of you."

"Oh, that. He did want the best for Cynric. He worried about him getting into trouble and losing his place. I suppose he had a point—about me, I mean. But it wasn't really a quarrel. We had words, and I told him to mind his own business. Afterwards I decided to make myself scarce for as long as the council was going on. When Helmstan went away again it would all blow over and things would get back to normal. No, I didn't kill him."

"Forgive me, but I had to ask." A breeze began to blow, rustling leaves overhead and sending some floating down onto the captives. Then the truth came to Edwin's mind as clearly as if someone had spoken it to his face. "Cynric!" he murmured to himself.

"Eh?" Buntel turned his head at the sound of his friend's name.

"At last, I'm beginning to understand. I wondered why he was so despairing when he knew all the time that he was innocent of his brother's death. He must have been shielding you."

"Me?" The poacher seemed incredulous. "You don't mean he thought I did it?"

"Well, you took a shirt stained with blood to Thryth to be cleaned."

"But I told her at the time—it was from a deer." He sighed. "Lord Aethelwulf's deer."

"I suppose he jumped to the worst conclusion because Helmstan died outside the enclosure," said Edwin. "Now I remember that when we learned Helmstan died inside the enclosure and was only taken out afterwards, it seemed to cheer him." Edwin was silent for a moment as the guard sauntered around the tree to check their ropes and scowl at them in a menacing manner. When he was out of earshot again, Buntel asked, "Well, who did kill him, then?"

"I didn't know who was behind that until this morning. My mistake was that I assumed that Helmstan was the intended target of the killing."

"You're saying he was killed by *mistake*?" These words came out as a barely suppressed yelp, and the Viking guard's eyes darted in their direction. The question hung in the air for agonizing moments until they were sure the guard's attention had strayed again.

"Yes, I'm afraid so. Like his master Ealdorman Aethelred, he was tall and thin. In the dark, from behind, coming from the upper room where Aethelred was known to be sitting, the assassin took him for Aethelred and cut his throat. He must have died instantly." Edwin hoped that this, at least, was a reassurance to Buntel.

"Well, who is this wretch? Name him! I will kill him with my bare hands!" growled the poacher, flexing in his ropes so vehemently that Edwin could feel them tighten and pull him harder against his side of the tree.

"It is either one or the other of Aethelwulf's two closest retainers—Putta or the other one."

"Bedwig," Buntel supplied the name.

"Of course, they were acting on the orders of their master. All this time, my brother and I have been sheltering in the hall of a man who would kill his own nephew for control of Mercia."

"Old Aethelwulf was behind all this?"

"Yes," said Edwin. "It was when I saw his servant—er, Bedwig—delivering a chest of silver to the Vikings here that it all fell into place. He set one of his men to kill Aethelred on the first night of the council, but in the darkness the man killed Helmstan instead. He must have done it in the latrine, where all the blood would go into the ground; the latrine was whitewashed and moved the very next morning. I can only imagine what Aethelwulf must have said when he found out they'd killed the wrong man. But he must have a deep well of schemes to draw from. Rather than just let Helmstan disappear, he had them take the body out to the wood and mutilate it to look as if wolves had attacked it." Edwin's stomach turned over as he remembered the buried dog's head. "He gave them his own dog to kill and use for making the tooth-marks. When I found the head later, his feigned grief was so convincing that we were all taken in. What a cold-blooded, lying son of the devil!"

"So why throw it all on Cynric?" Buntel asked.

"I think Aethelwulf must have had in mind some plan to gain control of a piece of land by the river, some spot owned by Helmstan and Cynric," said Edwin.

"Of course! I know the spot. Their old dad took us down there to fish when we were little."

"Aethelwulf used Helmstan's death to discredit Cynric and get hold of his inheritance. But in the meantime he had to try again to put his nephew out of the way. The accident during the wolf-hunt was deliberate sabotage. He must also have been behind Beornoth's noose and pillow, though I still don't understand the meaning of that. He must have some kind of weapon against Beornoth, something from his past that he can hold over him." Edwin fell silent, pondering. As Buntel knew nothing of the council and the intrigues of great men vying for the kingship, he was silent also. Soon Edwin began thinking aloud again. "The upshot was that Beornoth withdrew his claim to the throne. Everything Aethelwulf has done was in preparation for this day," said Edwin, rousing himself out of his reverie. "He has put everything in place, Danish mercenaries included, to seize control of western Mercia and he's going to do it today."

"So what do we do now?" Buntel asked.

"Try to reach my boot," said Edwin slowly.

"Why?"

"There is a little silver mouse in there with sharp teeth to gnaw through these ropes." Edwin did not want to call his knife by its proper name, because it was one of the English words he could be sure the Viking guard would recognize.

"Ah."

"If I can get my leg…turned…just so," Edwin said, "Perhaps you could reach it?"

At first it seemed as though their efforts would be in vain. Edwin felt as if his knee would come out of joint as he stretched his leg backward towards Buntel. The latter was trying to look casual as he stretched his hand toward Edwin's boot, the ropes cutting into his flesh as he did so. Many times they stretched, by mutual arrangement, to reach each other only to break off, exhausted, and having to rest their strained sinews before starting again. At last, by degrees, he noticed that they were getting closer. To add to the tension they had to do everything in the least obvious way so that the guard would not notice. He looked bored and did not keep his eye on the firmly-tied Saxon prisoners constantly, but every so often he would give them a long look or saunter over and check them more closely. They never knew when he would turn his eyes on them again. At last Edwin felt Buntel's fumbling fingers on his boot, and it was another maddening few tries before he could grasp the handle of the little knife.

The next question was what to do once they had the knife. Buntel could get his hands free, and the guard was unlikely to notice; but if he then cut the ropes holding them to the tree, it would be obvious immediately. If they made a sudden move to overpower the guard, as they could probably do, they would have the rest of the Vikings down on them in a heartbeat, as they were within view of the main company. The only option seemed to be to wait until dark, cut themselves free when the darkness would disguise the absence of ropes, and steal away. Edwin wondered if anyone had noticed his absence, or if Fram had really gone 'home' to Aethelwulf's hall.

Just then, faint on the breeze, came the sound of church bells. The Danes heard it too, and suddenly the camp was in turmoil. Above the hubbub Orm's voice shouted orders.

"What's going on now?" Buntel asked.

"They're all arming for battle," said Edwin, who had a better view from his part of the tree trunk. "The church bells were their signal."

The short, ugly man came and gave the guard some orders. The guard seemed to object, but the man's reply contained Orm's name, and the guard acquiesced with bad grace. He watched his comrades mount their horses and gallop away, heaving a wistful sigh as they disappeared from sight.

Edwin and Buntel were of one mind. Buntel quickly cut the ropes that bound them both to the tree.

With a shout the guard ran towards them, drawing his sword. Edwin sprang to his feet. His hands were still bound behind him, but he charged at the guard, ducking his head as the sword flashed past him, and levelling a savage kick that brought the guard to his knees. He continued kicking him in the stomach and head as the man grappled for his sword. He felt Buntel sawing at the ropes that held his hands and heard the Saxon poacher's frantic breathing.

All this had happened in a few seconds, and the noise had brought the other Dane running. Buntel was armed only with Edwin's boot-knife, and Edwin had nothing at all. He grabbed a heavy stick from the ground with which he hoped he might defend himself as he headed for the store of weapons in the tent next to Orm's. He had seen several of the Danes go into the tent and come out with blades and mail-coats. Now the short, ugly man came at him with a sword in one hand and a spear in the other. Edwin knew his type: the tough and dirty fighter who would stop at nothing. The hideous scar that left his face puckered and distorted was a witness to that.

He was ready when Edwin parried his attack with the stick and came at him again without hesitation. The stick was longer than the sword but was no defence against the spear. It was, however, the scarred man's excessive zeal for weapons that was his undoing. Edwin was hard pressed, parrying the man's sword blows with the stick while leaping and twisting to avoid stabs with the spear, when suddenly the tip of the spear lodged in a log. In the time it took for the man to shift his grip to pull it out, Edwin had taken hold of the shaft near the point and yanked it from his hand. As the man raised his sword to bring it down on Edwin, Edwin struck the man a blow on his breastbone with the butt of the spear-shaft that knocked him back and left him breathless. Before he could recover, Edwin had turned the spear around and plunged its gleaming iron head through the man's ribs and into the ground. The sword fell from the guard's hand and Edwin picked it up.

He looked up and saw Buntel still struggling with the other guard and ran to help. Somehow, armed only with Edwin's tiny boot-knife, he had kept from being killed by a Viking with a sword.

"Buntel!" he cried, tossing the poacher the spear as he did so. The guard hacked wildly at the spear's shaft as the two Saxons advanced on him. Then followed a frantic burst of swordplay with Edwin. The guard was taller but Edwin was lighter on his feet. Edwin got in some fierce blows, wounding the man superficially in both arms. Neither of them had a shield. Buntel was a couple of paces behind Edwin, holding the spear at the ready.

The blood on the Dane's arms only seemed to make him angrier. He redoubled his attack, forcing Edwin back farther into the trees. Edwin could feel branches and roots under his feet and was desperate not to trip. Then his free hand felt a tree branch behind him. He snapped it off and in one smooth motion, flogged the Viking in the face with it then cut him down with his sword.

"Quick, Buntel, the spear!" Edwin shouted, and Buntel finished the Viking off.

"There's not a moment to lose!" Edwin said, running back into the middle of the now-deserted Viking camp. "Get my horse!" he added, motioning to where Stig was tethered with the pack-horses. Orm had not ridden him to his assignation; evidently he did not want the fine bay stallion to be within the grasp of his Mercian ally.

Buckling the sword hastily about his waist, Edwin looked around. The Vikings had made their camp on the site of a Saxon farm. All the cattle had been driven into a muddy paddock and, judging by the refuse scattered around and piled by the pigpen, the farmer—if he were still alive—had a much smaller herd than he started with. The farm cottage itself was partly burned, its thatch showing signs of recent destruction. This was the reason the army had chosen to use tents rather than taking over the house. The door of the cottage was gone. Edwin looked in. Among the general ruin lighted by the holes in the roof his eye caught some movement. Was it his imagination, or had the movement come from the shadowy piles of mess around one of the supporting posts running from the floor to the roof-beams? He stepped closer, every muscle tensing. As he strained to make sense of the dark shapes outlined by strange shadows and slanting light, a sound like a muffled sob reached his ears. He realized with horror that there was a person in the house—a prisoner. He hurried forward to find a bedraggled and tear-stained woman tied to the post.

"I will not hurt you," said Edwin. "Let me untie you."

"You are a Saxon?" cried the woman when Edwin had untied the gag in her mouth. "What has happened?"

"The Danes are heading to Buckingham," Edwin explained rapidly. "They left two guards, but my friend and I escaped and killed them. Now we must follow."

Edwin took the woman by the shoulders and spoke urgently, because he was afraid she was close to fainting. "Do you have any other people here?"

"I—I don't know," stammered the woman. "My husband and sons. I am not sure. They may have killed them right away."

"I have seen no one, but I have not been searching."

"Grandmother is over there." She motioned to a heap of rags in the corner. "But she has not stirred today."

Edwin went over to the unconscious old woman and felt her pulse. It was slight, but at least it was there. Then he returned to the younger woman.

"Drink this," said Edwin, holding his skin bottle of water to her lips, "and listen to me. Find something around here to eat. Give your grandmother something to eat also and bundle her up for travel. Where is the nearest church?"

"In Winslow," she said.

"How far is that?"

"About five miles."

"Good. Take some bread and some water and blankets and load it on one of the Danes' pack-horses. Then load up your grandmother and head for Winslow. I don't know when the Danes will come back but when they do, you must be gone. Do you understand? Do not delay, but you must eat and drink first or you will not have the strength. All right?"

The woman nodded, her face pale and wan with deprivation, abuse and grief. He hoped she would be able to act on his instructions. He left the bottle with her.

"God be with you, then. I must go."

Emerging from the cottage he saw Buntel trying to keep Stig still while fastening the last buckles on the saddle. Edwin ran to the tents and rifled around for weapons. Of course the Viking army had been fully armed when they had departed. Nevertheless, Edwin managed to find some useful items here and there. In the supply tent next to Orm's tent he found several helmets. One of them fit—more or less—so he put it on, along with a mail-shirt that was slightly too large and with a hole on one side. He found a shield, and another spear for Buntel. By this time Stig was saddled and ready to go.

"Are you coming too?" Edwin asked, taking the reins.

"I'm not leaving you now," Buntel said. Edwin handed him the spear. "What's this for? I'm no warrior."

"You never know when you might need it," Edwin said.

"Can he take both of us?" Buntel motioned to Stig. Edwin looked over the saddle at the dull-eyed pack-horses tethered beyond. Not one of them had pricked its ears or shown any interest in the imminent departure. It would be hard to get an animal with that kind of attitude to keep up with Stig.

"He's going to have to." Edwin sprang into the saddle and pulled Buntel up behind him.

"Looks like they headed for the ford in the river," said Buntel. "They have no need to disguise their presence now, if they're headed for Buckingham."

Edwin conducted Stig onto the track that led to the ford and gave him a kick. It was less an order for Stig than a release; Buntel scrambled to grasp Edwin's middle as the horse nearly disappeared from underneath him. They splashed through the ford and charged back up the other side through the deep mud lately churned up by Orm's riders. From there the road was easy to follow, and Stig scarcely needed any direction from his rider. Once they passed a cart abandoned by its owner at the approach of the mercenaries. The ox, still yoked and harnessed, had wandered to the side of the road to graze. Stig galloped on, his breath coming in great jubilant snorts in time with the beats of his hooves and the working of his hindquarters.

"You all right?" Edwin shouted into the wind.

"Yeah," Buntel shouted back into Edwin's ear.

"We're in for a mess at Buckingham," Edwin continued. "Half a hundred Vikings can do a lot of damage. I only hope—"

"What?"

"I only hope my brother was ready," said Edwin, mostly to himself.

At Buckingham all was in uproar. The Vikings had come upon a large group of Saxon warriors—unarmed and holding a law-court. As arranged, they took their places behind Lord Aethelwulf and his Saxon retainers.

Chapter 34

Some hours before, Edmund had been surprised to see Fram whining next to the door of their quarters. He had seen Edwin leave. He stuck his head in the door and saw no signs of his brother having returned. Puzzled, he strode across the yard to the stables. No sign of Edwin or his flashy little horse in the stables or the paddocks. All the while, Fram followed with unwagging tail.

Just then, Bert came from the stables, breathing fast. "My lord!" he cried. "Oh, my lord, please excuse me, but I can't find Lord Edwin and there's something your lordships really must know!"

"Speak, then, boy," Edmund grunted.

Stifling his terror at having to address his master's exalted brother directly, he began to tell the tale of what he had overheard in the stable. As the story came tumbling out, Edmund's face darkened. He sent Bert back to the stables with a strict order not to tell anyone, and went swiftly to find his chief warrior.

"Get our men ready," Edmund ordered. "Full gear. And tell Lord Osgar I need to talk to him." The man nodded and hurried away to set things in motion.

So it was that when Orm's men rode onto the court grounds

fully armed, Edmund and his men were prepared.

Aethelwulf stood with his and Beornoth's men on one side of the field. Aethelred's men and those of the other Mercian noblemen, the West Saxons and the bishops, formed discrete groups around the other edges of the field, with the tents behind them, ready for another day of the shire court. When Orm and Sveinn rode up in full battle gear with their men and ranged themselves behind Aethelwulf, murmuring arose from the court and the groups began to close ranks.

Aethelwulf now addressed the assembly in his fine carrying voice.

"My countrymen," he cried, "Let us abandon these fruitless negotiations. Neither lineage nor wealth will save Mercia. We cannot live in the past. What the Mercians need now is strength!"

The court, shocked and nonplussed, was silent. Bishop Deorlaf hurried out to the centre of the assembly and held up his hands. Bishop Waerferth was with him.

"My lords… Lord Aethelwulf, what is the meaning of this? Do you mean to take the Mercian kingship by force, with these—" Deorlaf gestured to Orm's army, "—heathen hordes?"

"By force? I hope that some agreement can be reached," replied Aethelwulf. "When all of you realize that it is futile to resist. I am the only man in Mercia that can make her strong."

"And the end justifies the means?" Waerferth retorted. "We were met here to decide the kingship by law, according to proper custom. What you are doing is against the laws of man and of God!"

"Nonsense. I am negotiating. No sword has been unsheathed, no drop of blood spilled. Your other contenders have spoken of the forces they have to draw upon. I merely show mine here before you so that you know that for me it is not mere talk."

This provoked angry looks from Wulfsige's company.

"I presume you speak on behalf of your nephew?" asked Bishop Deorlaf. "After all, he is the ealdorman, not you."

Those closest in proximity to Aethelwulf saw his face tighten at these words, but he replied smoothly enough, "My nephew would offer his full support if he were well. Sadly, his condition after the hunting accident has left him unfit to carry on his duties at this time. Ealdorman Beornoth has also given me his full support..." Aethelwulf's eyes scanned the crowd on all sides, looking for his ally.

From the direction of Edmund's party a voice called out, "No!"

A warrior who had come unnoticed to stand beside the West Saxon ealdorman now removed his helmet. An audible gasp went up from the assembly as they recognized Ealdorman Aethelred.

"No, uncle, I do not consent to your actions here today. I consider your attempt to take my place in Mercia to be an act of hostility that erases your claim on the blood ties between us. I have taken my place beside my West-Saxon allies and have instructed my men to arm for battle."

"So be it!" shouted Aethelwulf, white with rage. "Then let the sword decide who will rule Mercia!"

At this he struck the shaft of his spear loudly against the rim of his shield and all his assembled men, Saxons and mercenaries, followed suit. The resounding crack frightened the birds from the trees at the edge of the field, and Edwin heard it over the pounding of Stig's hooves as he neared the settlement.

◆

When Edwin and Buntel arrived at Buckingham, the place was in chaos. The gate to Aethelwulf's enclosure was open and people were running this way and that.

"First, find Bert, my groom," Edwin said. "He's fourteen years old and has red hair. He may be in the stables." Buntel nodded, his eyes following Edwin's to the paddocks.

"Then check on the women. There is a noble lady with a retinue over there—" Edwin pointed to the women's quarters partially visible behind some other outbuildings.

"If they have no defender you and Bert must keep them safe. Shut and bolt the main gates. If anyone asks you, say it's on the order of the Ealdorman. Don't admit anyone unless they are in the company of Aethelred, Edmund, Osgar, or Wulfsige." Edwin had Buntel repeat these names back. "If the battle fares badly for us and the Danes seem to be prevailing late in the day, you may have to help the women escape. You would know a likely place and be able to hide them safely."

"What if they want to escape now?"

"I'll leave it to you, but I think there would be more danger if they leave the enclosure now. You've still got your spear? Good. Well, God be with you." Edwin clapped the poacher on the shoulder and was gone.

Buntel, reins in one hand and spear in the other, hurried toward the paddock with Stig, whose bright bay coat was lathered with sweat. Buntel had no trouble finding Bert, but a little in convincing him that he was a friend rather than a horse-thief.

"You there! What are you doing with my lord's horse?" Bert, who had been guarding old Red from possible theft during the confusion, accosted the poacher. This showed considerable spirit in view of their relative sizes.

"Easy now. Lord Edwin told me to bring the horse back

to you."

"How do I know you're telling the truth?" Bert squinted at Buntel in an attempt to look shrewd.

"If I was going to steal it, I'd hardly have brought it back to you, would I? I'd be miles down the road." And with this he pressed the reins into Bert's hand.

While Buntel relayed Edwin's instructions, Bert took off Stig's saddle and bridle and began to rub him down.

"What are you doing?" Buntel almost shouted. "We've got work to do!"

"I am doing my work."

"Do you know there's a battle going on out there, and your master is out there fighting an army of bloodthirsty Vikings?"

"And if he comes back and needs to ride away quick, he's got to have a fit horse, don't he? And not one that's lying on his back—" here he took a bucket of water and a bundle of hay out of an empty stall and handed it to Buntel—"dead of colic." Bert put Stig into the empty stall to cool off and Buntel saw him talking to a wizened old horseman. "That's the Ealdorman's head groom," Bert explained. "My lord's brother." He took back the hay and water bucket which Buntel was still holding and put them away. "Now I can go with you."

They hurried to the women's quarters where they found four men-at-arms before the door. Seeing them approach, the men-at-arms brandished their spears.

"Are the women safe?" asked Buntel.

"What business is it of yours?"

"I'm acting on the Ealdorman's instructions," said Buntel evenly. "Can one of them come to the door and assure me that all are safe within?"

One of the guards nodded to another and the latter knocked on the door. There was a brief exchange of words and the sound of the door being unbolted. A pale face surmounted by a headdress then peeked out.

"My lady, I am charged to ensure that all your party are safe," explained Buntel through the guard's spear-shafts.

"Yes, we are all safe," she replied.

She made to close the door, but Buntel spoke again, "How many of you are there?"

"Six," came the curt reply, then the door was bolted again. Buntel ascertained that the guards were from the noblewoman's own household.

"Our orders now are to bar the gate," Buntel announced.

"Fine with us," said the chief guardsman, and the menacing spears returned to the vertical. A burly man helped them close the heavy wooden gate to the enclosure; it groaned on its hinges and was reluctant to stay closed while the bar was lowered into position. Next to the gate was a watchtower reached by a ladder. Bert climbed the ladder, but when his head was even with the floor of the tower, he hesitated, then hastily climbed back down.

Reading his face, Buntel mounted the ladder and found a guardsman slumped on the floor with two arrows in his back. There was no pulse. He took firm hold of the body and lifted it over the parapet. With an effort he pushed it over the side, where it landed with a soft whump on the grassy earth below. Buntel climbed down again and asked the burly man who he belonged to.

"I'm Ealdorman Aethelred's blacksmith," the man replied. Buntel remembered Edwin's list of names and nodded approvingly.

"How's your eyesight?"

"Fine."

"Then stay up here and watch the battle. If time draws on

and it looks like the Danes are winning, alert the guards of the women's quarters to prepare for departure."

"Yes, sir." This was the first time Buntel had ever been so addressed.

"And watch yourself, mate," Buntel added. "Your predecessor at this post is down there with two arrows in him."

Having accomplished the tasks set for him, Buntel then looked around to see what next might need doing. "Come on," he said to Bert. "Let's check the hall."

The hall doors were unbolted and unguarded. A few domestics were cowering behind a table-board leaned sideways against its trestles along the wall. "Get up," said Buntel. "The main gates are bolted and we've set a lookout. Attend to your master's business." The servants emerged cautiously like animals from hiding.

"Where does this lead to?" asked Buntel, pointing to the stairs behind the high-seat.

"That's to the upper room," one of them managed to say.

"Is there a way out from there?"

"Yes, a-a-an outside stair."

"Bolt the doors, then, and don't admit anyone you don't know. I'll check upstairs." Buntel bounded up the stairs with Bert close behind.

In Lord Aethelwulf's upper room there was little to be seen. There was a table that had not been cleared away. Aethelwulf's bed was in an alcove with doors. Under the bed was a space for storage; it was empty. "Look," said Buntel to Bert, pointing to the cabinet doors. "The latch has been forced. Shame about the woodwork, too." He passed a reverent hand over the splintered carving. "Well, come on," he said, springing up and heading for the outside stairs.

They clattered down the stairs and past the latrine. On

the far side of the enclosure beyond the pigpen, they saw a man with a rope thrown over the palisade. He was calling to someone on the other side, but his words were drowned out by the noise of the restless animals. A cow had begun to bellow and set off a chorus of answers from chickens and sheep. Presently Bert and Buntel realized that there was a small but heavy iron-bound chest tied to one end of the rope. The man was trying to lift it and hold it while (it seemed) someone on the other side helped by pulling the rope. So far, the man had not noticed them. Buntel pulled Bert out of sight behind a cow-shed. Just then, the man glanced over his shoulder, his face contorted with anxiety.

"That's one of Aethelwulf's men," Bert said. Buntel made a sign for him to stay quiet.

"And there's another one on the other side of the wall. If we stop the one, we'll lose the other. I tell you what. You take this," Buntel shoved his spear in the boy's hand. "I'm going to make for the gate and get around on the outside. I'll take care of the accomplice and you hold the scrawny piece on this side. Don't let him get the chest over the wall."

"But—"

"But nothing. Forget what your mother told you about being careful with sharp things. Aim it at his heart, or his face. Don't let him grab it from you. If you have to, conk him on the head. Or—stick him. It's been that kind of a day." This last remark Buntel made to himself.

Bert nodded. His eyes were as wide as a hare's. Buntel made for the gate and watchtower. When he saw Buntel climbing the ladder to speak to the watchman, Bert emerged, trembling, from his place of concealment and strode towards the thief with spear in position.

"Stop!" he said. "Drop that box!"

The thief started violently and let go of the chest. There was an outraged shout from the other side where the accomplice had suddenly caught the full weight of the chest on his end of the rope.

Then the man raised his arms and said, "Quick! You need to catch that man on the other side! He's a thief and I was trying to stop him taking my lord's box of silver."

Bert blinked in surprise at this alternative version of events, but his instinct to follow orders prevailed and he kept the spear levelled at the man. "Walk," he said in his most serious tone.

The man on the other side of the wall, having discovered the way the wind was blowing, let go of the rope and made a run for it. The chest then fell down to the ground at Bert's feet and, doing credit to its skilful maker, did not burst open but merely landed on its face in the mud with a loud chink of its metallic contents.

"Move!" Bert repeated to the man, who had been distracted by this occurrence. The man wiped his nose on his sleeve and heeded Bert, or rather his spear, and they set off in the direction of the gate.

Buntel had just explained to the watchman why he needed the wicket-gate open when he saw his quarry let go of the rope and take to his heels. Though not built for speed, the man was running for his life, and would soon have been out of reach. Quicker than thought, Buntel snatched up the bow in the corner of the watchtower. Putting an arrow to the string, he took careful aim at the disappearing form of the thief. The arrow struck somewhere in the kidney region and the man fell. Buntel, descending from the ladder, found Bert with the other thief at spear-point. "You've fared better than your friend," Buntel grunted. "He's been detained by an arrow."

"Sir, I wish to report an attempted theft," the man, still

enamoured of his new story, addressed himself to Buntel. "Thankfully you seem to have killed the guilty man. Your underling here interrupted me in my efforts to recover the stolen box." The man smiled in what he probably imagined was an ingratiating manner.

Buntel answered by backhanding him across the mouth. "Shut your mouth if you've got nothing to say apart from lies. Your accomplice is alive and no doubt he'll tell us all about you." At this revelation the man's manner changed from confiding to abject. He fell to his knees and began to plead for his life on the basis of having been forced—no, deceived—into taking part in the theft. Buntel walked away in the midst of this recital to call a couple of the lady's guards to help secure the prisoners.

The chest of silver was stowed away quietly and safely, and the thief's arrow-wound attended to. "Will he survive?" asked Bert.

"He might," said the poacher. "But if this don't kill him, the hanging will."

Chapter 35

Leaving Buntel at the gate to the enclosure, Edwin dashed towards the field, spear at the ready, following the sounds of battle.

Aethelwulf, with all his warriors, was on his home turf; his ranks were further swelled by the Danish mercenaries and Beornoth's men. Against him were the combined forces of Aethelred, Edmund, Osgar and Wulfsige. These four had only brought smaller forces with them; Edmund's twenty men were joined by some thirty-odd of Aethelred's, and Osgar had just a handful. Wulfsige, though travelling with a large company, had only brought a dozen or so chosen warriors. Edwin took a deep breath, fixed his eye on his brother's standard, and rushed into the battle.

Fighting his way through, Edwin managed at last to reach Edmund's side.

"Well hello, little brother, where did you come from?" he said, neatly deflecting a blow from a large Dane and, in the same stroke, nearly severing the man's arm at the elbow.

"Finding out some vital information," replied Edwin, raising his voice above the Viking's anguished scream. "For instance, did you know that Lord Aethelwulf hired a renegade Viking and his followers to help him seize power?"

Edmund smirked beneath his helmet and the brothers fought on. In another part of the field, Wulfsige's banner was approaching that of Aethelwulf. Aethelwulf's shield-wall was still intact, and with a shout Wulfsige ordered his men to advance against it. They charged with all their might, and the clash that sounded when shields collided with shields was terrible to hear. Several of Aethelwulf's warriors faltered from the impact, and Wulfsige's men were quick to exploit these openings in the line. Soon Wulfsige's warriors had broken the shield-wall into disparate groups of three or four which they were able to fall on in equal numbers. Aethelwulf's warriors tried, as they fought, to regroup and position themselves around their lord, but it was the constant effort of Wulfsige's men to split them up and draw them away. Wulfsige, unmistakable in his helmet with its tall boar-bristle crest, soon pushed his way to stand face to face with Aethelwulf.

At length some of the Vikings noticed this frontal attack on their patron and crept around behind Wulfsige's company to attack their rear. So intent were they on their offensive against the standard of Aethelwulf that this attack from the rear found them almost entirely undefended; several brave men fell before a sufficient counterattack could be mustered.

Meanwhile, Edmund and Aethelred advanced together in natural coordination like a man's right and left hands. Both were tall enough to see over the heads of many of the other warriors and were constantly scanning the field as they fought to keep track of the progress of the battle. Edwin was amazed at how heartily Aethelred fought on his sprained ankle; he had been confined to bed only a few days before. He imagined Aethelred's head would begin to throb soon if it was not doing so already, and wondered how he would cope as the day wore on. Aethelred's closest retainer since the loss of Helmstan was sticking to his side like a limpet.

Edwin was not blessed with the advantage of height, and had to judge how the battle was going from the information of his ears as well as his eyes. Once he had adjusted to the din, a certain savage music began to emerge. The undertone was his own breathing and the pounding of his heart. Above this he could hear the men around him, the speed of their strokes and the impact of their blows. At the beginning of the battle the warriors were wary and keen. As the battle wore on they developed an almost workmanlike rhythm. But as the battle drew to its conclusion the sounds would grow more scattered and desperate. Edwin well remembered his father's warning many years ago.

With his grey eyes boring through his son's, Edgar had said, "Watch out for the later hours of a battle. Apart from the start of fighting, this is the deadliest time. Many are tired and no longer on their guard. Many are wounded but fight on. Your enemy is bitter and has tasted blood. He knows that one last rally means the difference between victory and death or slavery. Fortunately," Edgar had said, letting his gigantic hand fall heavily on his young son's shoulder, "so do you. So take advantage of your enemy's weakness as the battle wanes— don't be caught off guard and end up as one of the slain!"

These words had stuck in Edwin's mind now more than a decade and had kept him vigilant through many battles where he saw his young comrades fall.

At last it came to a bitter struggle between Aethelwulf and Wulfsige. Men who saw them fighting seemed to see a contest of wills between two futures for Mercia. Wulfsige's pride was matched by Aethelwulf's; lust for power they both had. Even their two hates battled in equal measure. Aethelwulf's was a cold, white hatred, Wulfsige's a bloody red passion.

While other warriors plied their shields and spears with an overwhelmingly defensive tendency, Wulfsige and Aethelwulf lashed out at one another with deadly abandon.

In the meantime, Edwin had fought his way to Orm's standard, flanked by some men of Aethelred's whom the ealdorman had assigned. Together with Aethelred and his main force, they mounted an all-out assault on the shield-wall where Orm was sheltered. The Danes in this part of the enemy line, seeing it subjected to a determined attack, moved along to a skirmish that looked more promising. This left only Orm's own retainers surrounding him.

The shield-wall bristled with spears, but Edwin urged the attacking warriors to lean in and attempt to push the defenders apart. One of the men had a battle-axe, which was invaluable in hacking into the shields and spear-shafts.

"Keep going, men! A few more blows and the egg is cracked!" Edwin shouted over his shoulder. Aethelred's warriors appreciated the encouragement so much that they redoubled their efforts, and soon Edwin was close enough to draw his sword.

"What—you?" Orm said in surprise as Edwin's eyes met his.

The fury of Aethelwulf and Wulfsige drew the attention of all in their immediate surroundings. The onlookers shouted along with every blow. The two combatants themselves were silent except for the grunts and growls that accompanied the strokes of their swords and the explosive punches with their domed shield-bosses. First Aethelwulf seemed to be winning: he came at Wulfsige with swift and savage swordplay, forcing him to retreat behind his shield. Then Wulfsige seemed to have a surge of energy and Aethelwulf, winded, was forced to parry Wulfsige's skilful stabs. At last Aethelwulf summoned a final fiendish desperation from within and ran his sword through Wulfsige's groin below the belt. Wulfsige fell and his warriors crowded in, desperate for vengeance.

"No, no, men!" rasped their lord. "Put a spear in my hand. God will not allow this murderer to rule the Mercians!" And with the final strength of his dying body he flung the spear at the gloating form of Aethelwulf.

Aethelwulf was wearing a red tunic under his mail-shirt, so his heart's blood did not begin to make an obvious stain around the spear-shaft until he had fallen to his knees. His face turned a terrible dusky purple and he fell lifeless to the ground.

The shouts of Aethelwulf's and Wulfsige's warriors as they fell on each other to avenge their lords was heard farther afield, where Aethelred and his men were pushing ever closer to the Viking chieftain Orm and his compatriot Sveinn. Ealdorman Aethelred was a match for Orm in height, but Orm was half again his weight. With Edmund's bulk on his side, though, and his burly Wessex warriors in a close shield-wall with Osgar and Aethelred's well-maintained force, they were an even match for the Danish invaders.

With a blood-curdling yell, Sveinn threw himself at Edmund. Edmund answered with an equally fearsome noise and met the Viking with full force. For a few minutes they exchanged clanging blows with sword and shield. They were so evenly matched that neither seemed to be able to gain the advantage. Then Sveinn, in one smooth motion covered by his shield, sheathed his sword and pulled out a battle-axe that was in his belt. Roaring all kinds of oaths in consternation, Edmund did his best to block the axe-blows that fell like thunderbolts from the Danish warrior's arm.

He saw the Viking's beard and moustache part to reveal

a line of white teeth in a savage, triumphant smile. This was Sveinn's mistake, for it kindled whatever was yet dormant of Edmund's fighting spirit. As the Viking raised the axe over his head to strike, perhaps, a death-blow, Edmund threw aside his splintered shield. Switching his sword to his left hand, with all his might he plunged it down the short sleeve of Sveinn's mail-coat and deep into his chest.

In eight years as a warrior Edwin had never seen anyone laugh in the heat of battle, but on that day he heard from his brother's mouth a ringing laugh of exultation. The moment was brief but seemed to give all the Saxons the courage to push on to victory. One of Edmund's retainers took a shield for his lord from one of the fallen, Edmund wiped his father's sword on the muddy grass, and they fought on.

Aethelred, in the meantime, had focused his energies on the Viking chieftain Orm. Aethelred's sword-strokes were fluid and precise, Orm's heavy but incessant. From the look of his leg-wraps, Edwin surmised that Aethelred had gone into battle with wooden splints on either side of his leg to protect the injured ankle. Somehow the Mercian ealdorman was managing to stay on his feet. He looked pale under his helmet but that was nothing unusual. Men in battle usually looked either very pale or very red in the face.

The ealdorman, despite his healing injuries, was quicker than the Viking. He constantly changed position, forcing his enemy to do the same.

"I like the way he fights," thought Edwin, who continued to repel the Danish mercenaries on Aethelred's right flank. Later, recalling the battle, Edwin had the impression of a series of fearsome faces, which might have been Saxon faces but for their outlandish hair and beards, and the foreign ornamentation of their clothes and weapons. Orm himself had white-blond hair and a reddish-brown beard. He had worn all his silver arm-rings into battle and they flashed from under the elbow-length sleeves of his mail-coat whenever he raised his arm. Some of the rings were made of stamped bands of silver, others were of tapering silver wires that wound around the Viking's massive arm almost as an evocation of his name.

Ealdorman Aethelred delivered a particularly well-aimed stroke at Orm, splintering one side of his shield and wounding him in the leg. Orm merely grunted, but a crimson stain soon appeared on his legging below the knee. Then, suddenly, Aethelred swayed and crumpled to the ground. With desperate cries his men surged forward around him. Edwin saw a trickle of blood running down his cheek.

"He's swooned. His head injury opened up. Get him out of here!" Edwin said to two of Aethelred's retainers. The men nodded and took hold of their unconscious lord. Edwin turned in time to see Orm about to fell him with his sword.

Edwin ducked and rolled, bouncing up with sword and shield at the ready, slightly to Orm's rear. Aethelred's remaining men adopted Edwin in their lord's absence and clustered around him to provide protection as he squared off with Orm.

"I should have finished you in the woods," the Viking growled as he rushed forward, his sword flashing dangerously close to Edwin's head.

Edwin could often do little more than keep himself alive as the Viking attacked, relentless as an angry bull. But Edwin had noticed that Orm, whenever he brought down his sword diagonally, jerked his shield up for a moment with his left hand. If he could use that unguarded moment to attack Orm's midsection, he might have a chance. He would have to position himself and time his blows perfectly, striking with deadly speed.

It was not easy to get in exactly the right position in front of Orm without putting himself within easy reach of Orm's sword-arm and almost certain death. This was his only hope of survival, however, so he readied himself for the proper moment. Deflecting with his shield, Edwin pulled back his sword arm, let out a tremendous yell, and then lunged, thrusting the blade with all his might into his enemy's unshielded abdomen.

Orm fell forward onto the sword, taking Edwin with him to the ground. Edwin was pinned underneath the dead or dying Viking. With an effort he commanded his hands to release his grip on the sword and shield, which he was still clutching. He pushed Orm's body over with his shield and managed to pull himself free. His whole front was stained with Orm's blood, and when he tried to pull the sword out it was too slippery. It had gone right through to the other side and was stuck fast in a bone. Then Edwin spied his father's seax at Orm's waist. The Viking had taken it from him when he was captured. "I'll take that back now," said Edwin to himself, unbuckling the belt.

As he did this, Orm opened his eyes and looked straight at Edwin.

Without a word, the Viking's massive hand grasped the hilt of the seax near the blade. Edwin already had a grip on the hilt and pulled with all his strength to get it free. The blade ran through Orm's fist, but little blood came. He had little left to shed. His grip, though, was still dangerous and his uncanny eyes followed Edwin with deliberate hatred. The hand moved now to grasp Edwin's hand, the hand that held the seax, and aim its pointed tip toward Edwin's face. Now four hands were in play, and it was a tribute to Orm's hideous strength that even now, within moments of dying and completely immobile except for his arms, he was still fighting hand-to-hand with Edwin, trying to take his Saxon enemy with him to the grave.

At last Edwin was able to position himself to wrench the seax from Orm. He levelled a stroke across Orm's throat that put an end to the matter. Buckling the seax-belt back around his own waist and picking up his shield, he scanned the field. Aethelred's warriors had kept Orm's men busy while Edwin fought him. Now two of them chanced to see their chieftain lying slain and Edwin standing over him. They shouted and began to make for Edwin. Edwin quickly grabbed a discarded spear and ran to meet them headlong. Aethelred's men joined him and it was not long before that entire band of Vikings was defeated.

By this point, their leaders fallen, the Viking mercenaries and Aethelwulf's men were only fighting to avoid capture. Some of Acthelwulf's men, indeed, had switched sides and were now fighting Danes with a vehemence fuelled by dread of judicial execution.

Edwin had made it thus far unharmed, with nothing but rope burns, scrapes and bruises to show for the exertions of the day. But now, as the shadows began to lengthen and the fury of the invaders gave way to despair, a last volley of arrows was loosed from the rear of the Viking lines. Edwin never heard the whistle of the shaft until it lodged itself in his upper arm.

This was the very moment that truce was called and the surviving handful of bloody, dog-tired Danes knelt in submission before the bloody, dog-tired victors. These survivors were taken prisoner, disarmed and tied with ropes to be taken to the guard-house. In due course they would be sold as slaves and the sale money shared out among the Saxons. In the meantime there were wounded men to be tended, dead to be buried, weapons and gear to be collected and shared out. The Vikings' horses also had to be confiscated and taken to pasture.

Accounts of the battle were flying around the countryside by dusk. There were rumours of hundreds of combatants; reports varied wildly regarding which noblemen had survived; and there was even a story about Danish werewolves having wiped out Buckingham.

Chapter 36

As the night passed, two well-muffled figures squatted near the fire, remaining motionless and silent for long stretches. Periodically one of them rose, made a round of the palisade, returned and poked the fire. The fire-poker was the only sign of any humanity in the dark form, which might otherwise have been the stump of a tree. The poker moved with precision, improving the fire; sometimes it turned a log; sometimes it seemed as if the poker were being used as a sword aggressively against the fire. But the result of the combat was not the death of the fire but its increase.

Edwin had learned from bitter experience not to go to bed the night after a battle. It was a choice he had to make between hellish nightmares and the maddening paranoia that kept him company on overnight guard duty. As anything was better than the nightmares, Edwin always volunteered for the night watch. With another warrior as a companion he could usually manage to discern the difference between enemies and shadows, a rustling leaf and a menacing spear-head.

Returning from another round, Edwin said, "Soon it will be dawn."

Buntel's head jerked up and he squinted at the horizon without a word. Had he been dozing? No matter. He was not officially on guard duty; he had merely volunteered to keep Edwin company. As an indistinct grey light crept over the eastern horizon, Buntel rose stiffly and made his way to the ladder leading to the watchtower, Edwin's lookout post of the night. He climbed the ladder and looked out at the country round about, its features slowly gaining clearer detail. He saw the fields and pastures, the huddle of cottages, some already showing signs of their inhabitants stirring abroad to tend livestock. The wood, the abbey, the assembly ground. As he turned, his eye halted on the mass-grave. Bodies had been stripped and lined out ready for burial, and a start had been made on a large trench at the edge of the wood for these heathen men who had met their fate far from home. Buntel climbed back down the ladder and returned to the glowing circle of light and warmth.

"At least it promises to be good weather today," said Edwin, scanning the sky.

"Only this morning," replied Buntel. "See them thin clouds away up there? You mark my words, the wind is going to pick up round about midday and blow in some rain clouds from the north-west."

Edwin looked at the sky again and was none the wiser. Then he looked at Buntel and saw a raindrop on his face. No; he shook his head to disperse the fog of a sleepless night. The man was weeping.

"Buntel, what is it?" he said, almost in an undertone, squatting beside him.

"You are a warrior," Buntel's husky voice emerged from the cloak into which he had retreated. "You were raised to it. I never seen such a slaughter of men as this."

"It's a terrible thing to see," agreed Edwin.

Evidently Buntel's mind had now gone back to their escape

from the Viking camp, for his next words were, "I never killed a man before."

Edwin walked around the fire and then squatted back down beside the poacher.

"It's hard—" he began.

"No," said Buntel emphatically. "No, that's just it. It wasn't hard, God help me. It was as easy as sticking a boar. Have I now the heart of a murderer, that I can take a man's life so easily?"

"If you are asking the question," replied Edwin, "you certainly do not have a murderer's heart."

"But I killed a man."

Edwin picked up a twig and began to trace patterns in the soft earth by his feet. The first rays of light were beginning to cast long shadows over Aethelwulf's enclosure.

"Your father taught you how to hunt, how to poach, and all the skills of a woodsman," he said. "My father taught me the law. I had to learn it off by heart or get a thrashing.

"It's good to know the law," he went on, "so you know the right thing to do when things go wrong. For instance, did you know that the law permits a man to fight, to kill, in defence of his lord? It is a merciful act, saving a life."

"But I'm a man oft accused," said Buntel. "No lord would want me to defend him."

"You defended me," said Edwin. "You don't have to be a lordless man any more if you don't want to."

The fire crackled softly, but Edwin could not see his companion's features in its flickering amber glow.

At last Buntel spoke. "All right," he said.

◆

So it was that Edwin made it through the first night without embarrassing himself. He was ashen-faced and barely functional, however, at the solemn mass of thanksgiving held at the abbey church the next morning. Bishop Waerferth preached an excellent sermon full of scriptural edification, but Edwin heard not a word; his eyes closed as he stood against the south wall under a window, and he slept like a baby.

In spite of the wounds and sore muscles—everyone moved a little stiffly, and Edwin was not the only one with his arm in a sling—men had begun to take stock of what had just happened, trying to make sense of it all and determine what was to be done next.

"Well, this clears the field of Mercian contenders pretty drastically," said Osgar, twiddling his toes in a basin of steaming water back at the hall. Rain had forced them all back indoors after the service. "Did I, or did I not, say that Wulfsige had a terminal case of heroics?"

"Unlike Beornoth," Edmund observed, tossing back a swallow of ale. "What did he expect to accomplish?"

"I think Aethelwulf must have put him up to it," said Edwin. "And I suppose we know now how King Ceolwulf was murdered, too."

"What?" Edmund and Osgar exclaimed together.

"Yes, I am sure now—seeing everything in the light of the noose and pillow—that Beornoth was behind Ceolwulf's death."

"How?" asked Edmund. "I never understood that noose and pillow thing, and why it seemed to scare him so."

"I didn't understand either until after the battle, when I found out about his attempt on Aethelred's life. Think about it: King Ceolwulf was in bed, wounded after the battle with Rhodri Mawr. Beornoth attended him. Ceolwulf was expected to recover, but instead he died. Suppose Beornoth did the same to him that he tried to do to Aethelred. Aethelred didn't take the drugged drink, so he was awake and able to defend himself. Ceolwulf wasn't so lucky."

"It's all surmise," said Osgar, "but I'll accept it as probable. How does the noose and pillow fit in?"

"That's surmise as well," Edwin admitted, "but if Beornoth did smother Ceolwulf with a pillow, and Aethelwulf knew about it, he could threaten Beornoth with exposure. Beornoth was guilty of murder—hence the noose."

"How could anybody prove that? You've admitted it's just a guess," Edmund tapped his foot impatiently.

"I don't see how Aethelwulf could prove it, but he somehow got Beornoth to believe that he could. Beornoth was already tortured by guilt. That put Beornoth entirely in Aethelwulf's power."

"I can see now that Aethelwulf's prime motivation was always to collect power to himself," Osgar mused.

"True. Aethelwulf must have concocted the plan to seize the kingdom as soon as Ceolwulf fell in battle. He got his friend Beornoth to attend to the invalid, and probably even told him how to do the murder. Then he used the threat of Guthrum's forces to convince everyone they needed to meet at Buckingham, close to the frontier, to make a show of strength while deciding the kingship."

"Supposedly Aethelwulf spent his time after the Welsh battle riding around the country gathering supplies. That's probably when he met up with Orm and Sveinn's band," said Osgar.

"When I saw that gyrfalcon and found out who had it first, I should have seen it all," said Edwin, chagrined. "The Danes must have obtained it in trade through their northern connections, and given it to Aethelwulf as an earnest of their contract with him."

"After all that, Aethelwulf was furious when Beornoth put himself forward on the first day of the council," said Edmund.

Osgar leaned back in his chair, causing its joints to creak in protest. "Beornoth started getting delusions of grandeur once King Ceolwulf was out of the way. He was, after all—as he liked to remind everyone—a kinsman of King Burgred, who was deposed by Ceolwulf."

"That was the point at which they had that falling-out!" recalled Edmund. "Yes. The noose and pillow came right after. It must have been a threat by Aethelwulf that he would expose Beornoth as a murderer if he did not withdraw."

"Why, then, would Beornoth try to kill the nephew? It seems to me that he would have done better to go after the uncle," Osgar said. His eyes were now closed and his fingers laced over his belly.

Edwin had found a fire-poker and was fiddling, one-handed, with a log that had only caught fire on one corner.

"He didn't dare. Guilt and fear are as strong as any prison," he said. "He was already guilty of murder. He had murdered his lord and king. Now Aethelwulf told him to do the same again to Aethelred, and the plan would be accomplished. Perhaps in his despair he felt one more crime would make no difference, since he was already guilty."

Edmund added, "Besides, Aethelwulf may have promised him a high position at his court."

"That was more than Putta and his little helper Bedwig could count on. Did I tell you? They made a full confession," said Edwin. "After they killed Helmstan in the dark, thinking he was Aethelred, their lord came up with the plan of mutilating the body to get Cynric in trouble."

"Couldn't he just dismiss Cynric if he didn't want him?"

"No, he wanted that bit of land by the river for his profitable milling enterprise, you remember? It belonged to Helmstan—and when Helmstan so unexpectedly met his death, Aethelwulf's rapacious brain quickly found a way to turn his underlings' mistake to his advantage. The land would go to Cynric, Helmstan's half-brother, and Cynric would be forced to sell the land to Aethelwulf to pay his legal fines if he was found guilty of negligence—or worse—in court."

"I suppose Putta and what's his name—the other one— were also responsible for the noose and pillow."

"And the sabotaged saddle, and the planted cloak-pin. But they had figured out that they would be a liability if Aethelwulf became king, so they tried to steal the second chest of silver he was saving for the Vikings and make their escape while the battle was going on. My men Buntel and Bert stopped them, however." Edwin could not keep the delight out of his voice.

"I can't imagine Aethelwulf would have kept those two, or Beornoth, close to him after he got what he wanted," Osgar said. "Why, he wouldn't feel safe in his bed!"

"I don't imagine he would have kept them around either, whatever he may have promised," said Edmund. "But we made a promise to our king, and this is how I think we should fulfil it."

And with that the West Saxons fell to discussing the kingship of Mercia.

◆

There were fewer faces than there had been around the council table the next day. The bishops were there: Deorlaf looking older and more shrunken; Waerferth looking haggard after the strains and exertions of recent days. Aethelferth was there with a bandage around his grizzled head. And Ealdorman Aethelred—to Edwin he seemed to have shed some of his youthful buoyancy, and become a little more grave.

"Men of the West Saxons," he said, "You have proven to be my truest friends in a moment when I should have been able to depend on a kinsman."

"We were very shocked by your uncle's betrayal," said Osgar with compassion.

"But I should not have been. He was always a greedy man. My father made sure I stayed out of his way as a child, so I wonder if he feared such a development."

"Be that as it may, Mercia still needs a king," Aethelferth interrupted his kinsman's introspection.

Bishop Deorlaf stirred.

"Your claim to the throne, my son, was strengthened when you had your uncle at your back. You had his forces to depend on to protect our land in the east and in the west."

"And now our land is in turmoil," said Aethelferth. "Beornoth is gone, and his great wealth will revert to the crown. Wulfsige is gone, and it will be difficult to get his followers to transfer their loyalties to one of his rivals."

Aethelred spoke. "I know that I will be able, in time, to earn the respect of Wulfsige's followers. Frankly, though, I will need support if I am to put up an adequate defence against the Danes. After all this time, and after what we have just been through, we could not face off an invading force alone."

He looked at Edmund with a question in his eyes.

Edmund said, "I think we are satisfied that our king would be pleased to have you as an ally. That is something King Alfred values greatly, and he has authorized us to assure you of his support."

"But, it has to be said, the West Saxons would also need to be assured of your support," said Osgar. "It is a well-known fact that—I beg your pardon—your rank is that of ealdorman, and you are slightly farther removed from the royal line than our own king's wife. Nor do we have certain knowledge of whether old King Burgred survives in exile in Rome. I don't know how your kingship would be received in Mercia, but there are those in Wessex that would be—er—*surprised* by your elevation to the kingship."

Despite Osgar's kindly tone, Aethelred looked a little affronted.

"He's right, of course," said Aethelferth. "You're in a quandary, my boy. No one more qualified to lead the Mercians, but you're just not at the head of the royal queue."

"Can we not come to some arrangement?" said Waerferth. "The historical precedent suggests—"

"There is one solution," Edmund was brusque enough to interrupt the bishop. "A partnership would be possible as long as there is no question of rivals in rank and succession. You could rule Mercia under Alfred's headship and be assured of full military cooperation as well as trade and monetary treaties that would be mutually beneficial."

"A new coinage!" exclaimed Aethelferth, his nostrils quivering like a horse scenting the race-course.

"It would give us better access to coastal ports and trade," said Bishop Deorlaf, almost reluctantly. "What would his title be?"

Several suggestions were made and rejected. Edwin felt his brother nudge him.

"How about 'Ealdorman of Mercia'?" he ventured.

"Hmm, yes, that might do," said Osgar. "'Ealdorman'—that is your rank, nothing controversial. 'Of Mercia.' No ordinary ealdorman, in other words, but a nobleman who rules an entire country. Sir, what do you think?"

All eyes turned toward Aethelred. He seemed to be weighing more than just the words of a title. Edwin knew that the young man was at a crossroads for himself and for his people. Aethelred had chafed under the Danish puppet-king Ceolwulf, but had not considered kingship a possibility for himself until Ceolwulf's death. He had evidently been prepared to abide by the decision of the council and either become Mercia's king or live under the rule of a King Beornoth or a King Wulfsige. His uncle had changed all that. If he listened to the men sitting around the table, he would have to give up the prospect of being King Aethelred of the Mercians. It was a humbling fact, a blow to his hopes. But his people would be assured of help and his desire of restoration in the land would have a chance to be realized.

What would it take to become king? Defiance of his councillors, affront to his allies—his only allies—and desperate attempts to gather forces against the Danes, the Welsh, and perhaps even the West Saxons. And all in the face of the uncertain loyalties of Beornoth's and Wulfsige's disappointed supporters. There was nothing ahead on that path but constant war, and he surely did not relish it. Gone would be any hope of restoring the glories of former days. His only concern would be power and how to hold onto it. He would become his uncle.

"Aethelred, Ealdorman of Mercia," he said aloud. "Yes."

◆

Before the end of the day, a delegation of important farmers had gathered at the law-court and were calling for Ealdorman Aethelred.

Aethelred was dressed in his best embroidered tunic, leg-wraps bound with mathematical exactness over his swollen ankle, and well-brushed cloak fastened with a glittering round silver brooch. On his finger was the gold ring King Alfred had sent for the occasion and Edmund lent him a supporting arm. He strode slowly out of the hall, through the yard, out the enclosure gate, and onto the trampled common where a law-court had so recently given way to bloody battle. At his back were Edwin and Osgar and all the warriors. Even Bert was permitted to stand with Edmund's men on the condition that his hair was combed and he kept quiet.

Aethelred's decision to remain an ealdorman under the overlordship of Alfred of the West Saxons came as a surprise to many of the men gathered there. Some greeted the news with dismay, but as Aethelred explained the reasons most of the doubt was dispelled from their faces. The end of the matter was sealed by a special service at the abbey and a feast for the principal people present.

Once the aftermath of the battle had been dealt with and the unprecedented rise of the young Ealdorman to the head of the kingdom was a settled fact, a flurry of official business followed. Bishop Deorlaf had been quick to present his stack of parchments (all extremely urgent) needing Aethelred's seal. Other petitioners thronged outside waiting for a brief moment with the Ealdorman—to take service with him, to beg redress for some wrong suffered under King Ceolwulf, or to ask some small favour.

Beornoth had been buried, and his lady came forth to ask permission to depart with her attendants to an estate farther north. This was attended with certain legal formalities, however, because as a murderer Beornoth's property was forfeit to the crown. His wife, Lady Hereburg, had to provide assurances that the estate at which she intended henceforth to reside was her property before her marriage and that she would not try to lay claim to any of Beornoth's extensive holdings.

"That should clip her wings a bit," said Aethelred when the lady had gone to supervise her packing. "I have the feeling that where she goes, mischief follows not far behind."

"Even without Beornoth's wealth she would be a profitable match for you, Ealdorman," said Bishop Deorlaf, whose mind ran along such lines. "She is still young enough for childbearing, and good-looking. You might keep her out of mischief, as you call it, that way."

"I think not," said Aethelred with a firmness that silenced even the bishop.

"Nevertheless," Deorlaf persisted after a pause, "a suitable marriage should not be far from your thoughts. You cannot expect to establish a royal house without begetting some children."

"All in good time, bishop," Aethelred said mildly.

Into the busy hall the West Saxons came to take their leave. Aethelred stood up from the table and came to shake their hands. "Please convey to King Alfred my most cordial, filial greetings. Lord Osgar, I may hope to see you again in Tamworth this spring, if your master is pleased to appoint you as his permanent liaison. And you all have the tokens you need? And your share of the battle spoils?" Edmund nodded, thanking Aethelred.

"Is there no other way I can show you my gratitude?" the young Ealdorman asked. He looked them in the eye—Osgar, Edmund, and Edwin—and seemed to mean what he said.

"I have one favour to ask of you, Ealdorman," Edwin spoke up unexpectedly.

"Tell me, Lord Edwin," said Aethelred. "What can I do

for you?"

Edwin nodded to Buntel. The craggy-faced poacher stepped forward to stand by the side of his new friend.

"This man is a ceorl of Buckingham. He is not beholden to any man and wishes to take service with me."

"Is this true?" Aethelred asked Buntel. Buntel nodded.

"Lord Edwin, I know this man," said Aethelred. "He's often been accused and has long been suspected of poaching in my uncle's forests."

"This he has admitted to me," said Edwin. "But he saved my life from the Danes and our fates have become intertwined."

"Very well then," said Aethelred. "He has my leave to enter your service and cross the frontiers of our land. Serve this man well, mind," said Aethelred to Buntel, "because I owe my life to him. Are you ready to swear?"

They crossed to the abbey, where Abbot Aethelhun was asked to assist. He came holding the abbey's reliquary, an elaborate small box in the shape of a house, bound with gold and set with gems. "This holds the relic of St Rumwold, our abbey's patron saint," he said. He asked Buntel and Edwin to put their hands on it.

Buntel repeated the oath at Aethelhun's prompting, "By the Lord, before whom these relics are holy, I will be loyal and true to Edwin, and love all that he loves, and hate all that he hates, subject to God's rights and the world's obligations; and never, willingly and intentionally, in word or deed, do anything against him; on condition that he keep me as I shall deserve, and carry out all that was our agreement, when I subjected myself to him and chose his favour."

Edwin's oath was the mirror-image of it, promising to provide for Buntel generously and treat him honourably.

What Buntel made of this was impossible to say, but Edwin

felt that he had grown an inch taller. Aethelred gave Buntel a horse fully fitted up, a stocky coal-black animal with kind and imperturbable eyes peeking out from a long wavy forelock. The brown leather saddle and bridle with brightly polished bronze and iron fittings stood out handsomely against his dark coat.

"What are you going to name him?" Edwin asked Buntel. Buntel shrugged.

"How about Raven?" suggested Bert, who had taken charge of the reins and was stroking the horse's soft nose.

"No," said Buntel, looking the horse in the face. "He's too friendly for a raven. And before you say it, he's too pretty for a crow. Blackbird's his name."

Aethelred smiled approvingly. "Now that I've given you means to fly from Mercia, Buntel," he said, "See that you don't meet up with any of my deer or boar on your way to the frontier."

The poacher bowed and replied, "No telling what we'll meet with, my lord. Doubtless I'll be so busy learning to ride this beast that I will miss my shot, in any case."

Chapter 37

Worthwhile as it had been, the autumn feast for estate folk had depleted the King's supply of sausages to a significant degree. Molly and Winfred planned a grand day of sausage-making as if it were a campaign of battle. When the hogs had been butchered, the seasonings gathered, and the casings scrubbed, it was time for the attack. The next day found Bunny in the kitchen with Winfred and a dozen buckets of those odd bits of pig that most people would not care to know about.

Winfred sorted and chopped the meat and fat while Bunny measured out the seasonings. Molly was not a squeamish person; indeed, she had a liking for the 'wobbly bits' that Edwin would usually throw to the dog. She had just dumped the seasonings in with the meat and she and Winfred had begun to mix it all together (the best way to mix it all was really to stick their arms in up to the elbows), when a breathless boy rushed into the kitchen and almost shouted,

"Lady Molgifu, the aethelings are coming today! There's a messenger just arrived in the hall from Prince Aethelwold."

He had blurted his message out in such a rush that Molly stared uncomprehending, her hands still kneading the meat.

"Aethelwold?" Winfred echoed.

"The old king's son!" the boy's whole frame writhed in exasperation. "He's travelling cross-country and will be stopping here at Wimborne to break his journey. He'll be here by Vespers!"

Molly suddenly became conscious of her sausage-covered arms and sausage-stained apron. Winfred began wiping her off with a washcloth as she attempted to preserve a calm and dignified demeanour. Inside, she was trembling. How was it that her father always managed to look so imperturbable, no matter what surprises sprang out at him? Nevertheless, her mind had begun the orderly planning of all that would be needed for this unexpected test of her managerial skills.

◆

In less time than it seemed to the anxious hostess, the hall was ready: resplendent in its old polished oak, carved and now properly painted pillars, tables set with clean white linen tablecloths, and the old embroidered wall-hanging on display (inconspicuously doubled up here and there to disguise the moth-eaten sections). Candles were set out on the tables and the fire in the long, stone-edged central hearth sizzled and popped as juices from the roasting meat dripped into it.

Right about sunset the aethelings and their followers arrived. Molly, in her best red gown and freshly ironed headdress, stood outside the door of the hall silently counting the group as they dismounted in the yard. At least two dozen! Through the windows, the wafted smell of the side of beef roasting over the hall-fire assured her that at least there would be enough food. Lullus and several other of the estate staff made up the greeting party. As she watched the visitors hand their horses off to the grooms, she felt her heart pounding.

She was suddenly aware that one of her garters was loose and as soon as she moved, her stocking would fall down to her ankle. She wished there was someone she could hide behind, someone to deflect attention from the mistakes she knew she would make. The worst of it was that she had no idea what to expect.

Out of the gathering group the two young princes approached, flanked by another almost as richly dressed. This third man, a few years older than the princes, came forward and identified himself as Goldwine, the royal chaplain. He then introduced Molly to the aethelings. Aethelwold, the elder, was tall and rangy in build with the nonchalant air often adopted by seventeen-year-olds. He and his younger brother, Aethelhelm, who was shorter and bulkier, were dressed in matching blue cloaks. As the wind caught the cloaks, they billowed out behind, revealing embroidered silk tunics of a scarlet so rich that they made Molly's new wool dress look drab by comparison.

The doors were thrown open for the aethelings to enter and Molly hurried away to check on the food. As she departed she heard Aethelwold's languid voice float after her, "Well, well, brother, back again to Wimborne."

"Yeah, what a dump."

Stopping by the kitchen, Molly found Winfred in full cry, bawling orders to her nephews and Bunny, and running dangerously in a thousand directions with a carving knife in one hand and a meat-fork in the other. When they saw Molly at the door they all halted in mid-air. Molly told Winfred that the guests had arrived and she would send word back when it was time to start serving. Quickly closing the door on the consternation that followed her announcement, she hurried to tell Cuthburga and the maids to light the candles and bring on the drinks.

There was a dissonant note in this harmonious whole, however. The drinking-horns Molly had ordered for the hall still had not arrived, and she had to find something to serve drinks to her royal guests. She could not use the rustic wooden cups and leather mugs normally reserved for the lower orders. Suddenly she remembered the pair of glass beakers her parents had given her as a wedding present. Surely it would not be inappropriate to use these family heirlooms to serve a king's sons in the royal hall? She went to her quarters and retrieved them. With somewhat more reluctance, she also took out the six silver cups Edwin had given her. The aethelings could be served in the glass beakers, and the highest-ranking of their followers could use the silver cups.

The glass beakers invited some comment at the beginning of the meal, with many of the aethelings' followers admiring their colour and transparency. "Like jewels you can drink from," she heard one hanger-on say breathlessly to another.

The guests took their seats and Father Ingeld invited the princes' chaplain, Goldwine, to bless the food. Goldwine motioned for silence and intoned a blessing in his most pretentious Latin, followed by an odd Amen that sounded like a question. Then Molly gave word for the bread to be brought.

All things considered, it was not a bad dinner she set out for her unexpected royal guests. Molly had worked hard to strike the right note: being no particular special day or occasion it was not exactly a feast, but it was a homecoming of sorts for two royal princes, even if they were just passing on their way with their retinue; offering them a worthy dinner was right and proper. Moreover, part of the food delivered by farmers as rent and tribute to the estate was theirs as members of the king's family, and they were entitled to consume it.

Besides the beef there were some geese and chickens, stew mainly for the lower tables, some dishes of vegetables, and as much bread as she and Winfred could make or buy in time. Molly reflected with contentment on the barrels of wine she had purchased from the Abbey and the gallons of cider and ale waiting in the brewing shed. Winfred had a nice warm apple and blackberry pudding for 'afters,' as she called it.

All eyes were on Aetheling Aethelwold as the first course was served. Customarily, in Molly's experience at least, the master of the feast would be served a choice joint of meat; he would take a portion for himself, then send the rest back as alms. Of course, everyone in the neighbourhood knew when a feast was being held, and the next morning it was the cook's duty to pass out bread, left-over meat and soup bones and uneaten sweetmeats to the poor who gathered eagerly at the door.

The poor in Molly's parents' neighbourhood were fortunate indeed that Molly's father Sigebert was a small, spare man with a kind heart; when presented with his first course, usually fowl of some kind, he would cut off a thigh and a drumstick from the whole bird and send the rest back. Following his example, his household and guests would be sure to leave some of every course on the serving-platters. Molly soon saw, however, that she had been guilty of making unjustified assumptions based on her limited experience.

Molly and Winfred had planned beef roast for the main course and spitted fowl, one per high-table guest, as a first course. With the main course in full view roasting over the central hearth-fire, Aethelwold declared he was positively starving and took two of the spitted fowls for his own portion. His brother and their close companions followed suit, which meant that the high table was short on its requisite number of spitted fowls. Molly wanted to sink through the floor in embarrassment. Lullus offered the last to Molly, but she encouraged him to split it with Father Ingeld instead. She was feeling too fluttered to eat anything substantial, and besides that, it was hard on Father Ingeld to invite him to a dinner and keep him on half-rations. He was no glutton, but she did not want it to seem as if the sole representative of the Minster was not being suitably honoured.

Molly was grateful that she was not obliged to sit and chat with the guests over dinner. It was as well, since she was a bundle of nerves, that the company kept her busy with the serving of drinks; a thirsty ride it must have been, judging from consumption at all the tables. Father Ingeld and Lullus took the burden of hospitable conversation upon them at the high table.

After the second course, when bread was being passed around again, Father Ingeld turned to Goldwine and asked him about how he had come to be the princes' chaplain. The younger prince, Aethelhelm, overheard the question and leaned in to give an answer: "My father was a very pious man. Always praying and confessing and whatnot, you know. So when he died he left in his will a pile of money so that we'd always have a chaplain about to mind us. Isn't that right, Goldy?" He nudged his father confessor and brayed with laughter. Goldwine smiled slightly and agreed that this was, in essence, the way it had turned out. Ingeld was thwarted in his further attempts to find out any news about church matters, however, by Goldwine's preference for discussing court gossip. Since neither Ingeld nor Lullus had any connections with the court, they let the conversation flow past them and ate their dinner in peace.

At length, as it always did, the topic of the Danes came up.

Lullus voiced his concern about the Irish slave trade which was becoming a profitable enterprise for Vikings sailing around the British Isles.

"Are you in need of more slaves here on the estate?" asked Aethelwold in a proprietorial way.

"No, not at present," said Lullus. "I was more concerned about the principle of buying Christians from pagans. Surely it would only encourage the Vikings?" Father Ingeld opened his mouth to speak, but Goldwine was there before him.

"The cheap Irish slaves brought over by our Woden-worshipping friends can be an excellent bargain."

"I don't think I could look a man in the eye, who had been a monk or a freeborn Christian man in his own country a month before, and call him a slave," said Ingeld. "Much less strike hands in bargain with the pagan who captured him."

"I don't see any problem trading and even forming alliances with the pagans, if it can be mutually profitable," said Goldwine.

"Forming alliances! Why, for the same silver they'd capture us and sell us to the Irish. You can't make alliances with cutthroats." Ingeld punctuated his words by banging the table with the butt of his knife.

"Well, think of this, then. Suppose there's some troublesome Saxon king that one needs out of the way. You could easily hire some Vikings to go and pay him a visit. No fuss, no muss, problem solved! And you've saved the lives of your own men who didn't have to go into battle themselves. Isn't that a most Christian thing to do, to save lives? But I'm being provocative, I see," he smiled, noting Ingeld's face. "Father, don't you think the Danes might sometimes be useful allies against a native foe?"

"Like sheep siding with wolves against other sheep,"

Ingeld replied shortly. He was angry with himself for being goaded into answering, and averted his eyes from Goldwine's deprecating smile.

Molly, meanwhile, was in a rhythm: go to casks, fill pitchers with mead and cider, make rounds of tables. Cuthburga did some of the serving while trying to supervise the maids, who had been made honorary kitchen staff for the evening.

As she was walking back to the table with more wine, she heard Aethelwold and his brother in an animated discussion about a horse race. The elder of the two princes gestured widely, and the edge of his sleeve caught the glass beaker full of wine. As Molly watched, the beaker wobbled, tipped over, and splashed its contents down the front of the clean white tablecloth. The beaker kept rolling; in fact, it rolled right off the edge of the table. It bounced off the dais and shattered into a thousand pieces on the broad, flat stones of the hearth with a tinkling crash that cut right through the din of men's voices.

Molly had never heard glass break before, and given the effect of the sound on her already ragged nerves, never hoped to again. The hall fell silent for one awful moment. Then Aetheling Aethelwold laughed heartily, and Molly recovered herself far enough to put on an unconcerned smile, and the feasters resumed their conversations. Aethelwold reached across the table to requisition his brother's cup. He drank its contents down in one gulp and, taking the pitcher from Molly's hand, poured himself another. Holding the glass up to the light, he said to his brother, "You must watch out with these elegant glass vessels. As you see, they have a tendency to break!"

With a mischievous sidelong glance at Aethelhelm, he held the full glass lightly by the rim, dangling it over the table. Aethelhelm, roused to action, leaped forward to prevent another catastrophe. His belt caught in the tablecloth and pulled it up with him, dashing the beaker from Aethelwold's hand and sending it hurtling down to meet the same fate as its partner, the painful sound of breaking glass mingling in Molly's ears with the clatter of wood, metal, and earthenware items as the tablecloth dumped its load onto the floor.

This time Molly just sighed. Bunny came in with a broom and dustpan, and she motioned her aside. "Try and save all the glass pieces you can," she instructed. "If I can find a glass-worker, the glass may perhaps be melted down and used again."

Aethelwold's voice rose above the general hum as he said, "What a nice little housekeeper she is. Oh dear, I hope they weren't too valuable. Here, Lady Molwhatsit," he fumbled in the bag at his belt and tossed her a purse of coins. "So sorry for your loss. We're a bit messy at table; did I forget to warn you?"

Much later—it seemed an age later, when long-suffering body-servants had heaved stumbling young princely retainers off the mead-benches long enough to convert the benches to beds, and Molly was supervising the last of the clean-up, someone behind her grabbed her arm.

"Hi there, lady." She felt—and smelled—Aethelwold's hot breath on her cheek. She froze. "My bed isn't made up right. You've got to come and fix it for me," he began to steer her toward the king's quarters where he and his brother were entitled to stay.

"Noble prince!" she said. Her voice came out as an unheroic squeak. She stiffened her body to resist being steered, and spoke up so that the conversation could be overheard. "I know your quarters are perfectly in order. I saw to it myself. If you have any further needs, I am sure your own servant can help you."

"Oh, no, he can't help me with these needs," Aethelwold continued in an undertone, and Molly turned her head away to avoid breathing his breath again. She looked around, but Winfred was not there; she would be out in the kitchen. Lullus had turned in for the night and was nowhere to be seen. Servants passed back and forth, but they were all the servants of the guests; and they were paying no attention to the drunken aetheling and his lady hostess. Aethelhelm, the younger aetheling, was snoring face-down on the table. Out of consideration to the old king's younger son, no one had taken down the high table yet. If the table disappeared from beneath his face, he would probably fall headfirst onto the floor.

"Come on," the drunken breath blew across her face again. His steps faltered, but his grip on her arm was firm. Molly really did not want to cause a scene, but soon she was going to have no choice but to scream and inflict bodily harm on the King's nephew.

They had nearly reached the dais—and behind the dais was the door to the king's quarters—and Molly's heart was pounding. She steeled herself to act.

"Sir, let me go," she said in a trembling voice.

"Go? No, no," said Aethelwold, turning to look at her with his head cocked on one side. "You're actually rather pretty just now." He pulled her closer. Molly could bear it no more. Quick as lightning she stamped hard on Aethelwold's toe and hit him as hard as she could with her knee. As he doubled over, he came face to face with Sebbi, who had been shadowing his mistress all the time. He was growling a steady, low, ominous growl, and he looked as Molly had never seen him look before. The hairs along his spine were standing on end. His teeth were bared in a monstrous, nightmare version of his usual canine grin. And those friendly hazel eyes had turned to cold yellow lights that were trained on Aethelwold in challenge. "Take one more step with my mistress," they seemed to say, "and I will bite your scrawny throat out of your worthless neck."

Molly felt the grip on her arm suddenly loosen. "Lady—I say—please call off your dog," Aethelwold gasped.

"Walk toward the door to your quarters," Molly commanded with a gesture of dismissal. "Sebbi, heel." His eyes still burning yellow, he watched the prince edge his way past him and close the door to the royal quarters with alacrity. The growl continued to rumble in his throat until Molly's breath became calmer and she turned to leave. Any disorder left in the hall now could be dealt with in the morning. Behind the bolted door of her own quarters, with her good dog, was where she wanted to be.

If Aethelwold remembered how he had finished the previous evening, he showed no sign. It seemed most likely to Molly that he had forgotten the entire incident; especially at breakfast when she saw him try to pat Sebbi on the head. He started back in surprise when Sebbi nearly took his hand off at the wrist.

When Molly came to make her rounds of the kitchen and brew-house, Winfred remarked that they were getting low on wine.

"What? How can that be?" asked Molly, remembering the six casks of wine from the abbey, and how much she'd had to pay for them. Had a couple of the casks been forgotten, mislaid in a corner somewhere?

But when she looked, she saw four empty casks, and the fifth was already half gone. It was a miracle any of the aethelings' party remembered their own names this morning! Since the aethelings had arrived, Molly felt as if she and the whole household had been riding a wagon drawn by a team of runaway horses. Now that she knew what they were capable of, she had to take the reins firmly in hand before they decided to bolt again. Molly called the hall servants and Lullus to a meeting, setting out new rules for serving guests with moderation. And she assigned Lullus to be in charge of cleaning up at the end of the night.

The royal party rode out to the Minster for the office of None, Molly and her household following on foot after them. As they filed into the church, Molly noticed with pleasure that her yew and holly wreath, still fairly fresh and hardly shedding any needles, had been left in place on the old King's tomb. A few little sprigs and branches had been brought by pious villagers and added to the display.

Aethelwold approached his father's tomb and turned to Father Ingeld. "You, priest, clear this rubbish. I want to pray." Ingeld handed the wreath and branches quickly to an acolyte, and the aethelings knelt. The whole party bowed their heads, but Molly caught Aethelhelm taking a quick backward glance. The church was full of curious locals, which seemed to please him.

After the service, the company proceeded slowly back to the King's hall, with Molly and her people following behind the aethelings as before. When word had spread that genuine aethelings were to be seen, dozens of people came to line the street and there were some cheers. The aethelings rode by talking amongst themselves.

In her belt-bag Molly still had the purse of coins Aethelwold had given her in compensation for the glass beakers. She had not looked at it until now. It was a fine purse of coins, almost the size of an apple; it had a satisfying heft in her palm, but the scores of little copper and silver coins did not make up anywhere near the value of antique glass heirlooms. It wouldn't even pay for the wine the aethelings and their followers had already drunk. The villagers turned their disappointed faces from the mounted party they had been watching recede slowly into the distance. *Why not?* thought Molly. She pulled open the drawstring and called out "Hurrah for King Alfred of the West Saxons!" This was met by some echoing hurrahs. She reached in the purse and flung the little coins in a wide arc. They scattered like a brief and glittering cloudburst. Cheers erupted from all of Wimborne as children—and a fair few adults—scrambled for a share of the King's bounty. Molly turned and blew them a kiss.

When they returned to the King's hall, they found a company of mounted warriors in full gear waiting outside to greet them. From her position behind the aethelings' company, Molly strained to see them. They had evidently made it past the guards without fighting, so Molly concluded that they must be friendly; she began to tremble, though, as she wondered why they were there. Was there bad news about Edwin?

The aethelings' party was brought up short by this unexpected circumstance, and testy words were exchanged. The company of warriors was headed by a short, stocky, rough-looking man who appeared to have combed his hair at the last minute. Molly could not hear everything, but did make out that the rough-looking man's name was Hana and that he had come from the King. Hana! He had been at the wedding. She would have to find out if he had news of Edwin. Hana was given an honourable welcome after presenting himself, his tokens, and his riders. He had come to escort the aethelings to Winchester; the party were to leave the following morning.

After dinner Molly retired to her quarters, relieved and satisfied. Despite double the number of guests in the hall, her new rules had ensured that the remaining wine lasted most of the way through the evening, and there was still plenty of cider and ale. The presence of the King's officers had also helped to dampen the spirit of unrestrained revelry.

At an opportune moment, Hana slipped out of the hall and sought out the reeve's quarters. He knocked on the door and Henna called suspiciously from within, "Who is it?"

Not until her mistress was satisfied that it was not a drunken retainer looking for the privy—or something—and had a firm hold on Sebbi's collar, did Henna unbolt the door.

"I've come on the King's business," explained Hana, when Molly had offered him a chair. "Tell me, my lady, about the goings-on at Wimborne since you arrived."

Briefly Molly told him what she thought his royal master might most want to know: the state of the farms, stock and stores, the appointment of a temporary captain of the guard, the feast given for the farmers according to ancient custom, and the arrest of Eng and Cnapa for embezzlement.

"Are they making trouble for you, my lady?"

"No, the guardsmen have given me no complaints. I'm only sorry that eating her own bread isn't part of Eng's punishment. But they don't have long to wait till our quarterly court."

Hana scratched his chin. "Theft from the royal estate. They'll be lucky if they get penal slavery. But speaking of judgements—you may not be aware, my lady, that the two guardsmen from the guardhouse here that Lord Edwin took with him are now dead."

Molly, horrified, cried, "Oh, Hana, was Lord Edwin—"

Hana shook his head. "It happened in Winchester, before they left for Mercia."

"Aha! Mercia," thought Molly. "So that is where he has been all this time!" Shaking off her desire to ask more about her husband for the time, she said aloud, "How did these two guardsmen meet their fate, then?"

"One murdered the other, and the murderer was executed.

But the reason I am telling you this is that some information passed to us by the condemned man before his death led us to suspect that Wimborne might be ripe for an insurrection."

"Insurrection!" echoed Molly. "Hana, you astonish me."

"After this information was obtained, the King called his nephews home to Winchester for—er—safety, and sent me out to locate and trail them."

"Didn't you attract attention with such a large contingent moving through the country?"

Hana smiled.

"I was alone until today. When the aethelings set their route to take in Wimborne I sent word back to Winchester. I suggested it would look well to send a sort of honour guard for the old king's sons while at the same time the boys themselves would not miss the significance of an honour guard showing up in the right place without their having called for it."

"Are they on such precarious terms with the King, then?"

Hana hemmed and hawed and said that he knew no harm of the aethelings themselves, but that the danger lay in disaffected and disloyal men about the country who might make these young, impressionable men the focus of their rebellion.

"So they did not come here on purpose to—"

"No, my lady."

Molly crossed herself.

"As I was saying, through this guardsman we traced certain veins of discontent, you might say, in this area. These have been dealt with one way or another. Part of my work was to go through the country and gauge the level of sympathy for the aethelings and whether it might prove dangerous. But as I did so a curious thing occurred. I found that somebody had been before me." He paused meaningfully.

"Who?" Molly, after hearing so many wonders, eagerly prepared herself for another.

"Why, your good self, to be sure," said Hana.

"What in the world do you mean?"

"As I rode about the countryside, listening here and listening there, this is what I heard. I heard of farmers weary from the famine who had got a penny or a shilling slipped in with their cheese or their fleeces from the estate. I heard of workmen hired and paid for repairs on the hall. I heard of a traditional autumn feast revived, prayers and donations given at the Minster, a high-handed dishonest servant punished, and even a sick baby with a new blanket that had royal symbols sewn across one edge." Molly blushed and was speechless.

He read her bewildered and embarrassed expression.

"No insurrection can succeed without popular support. If the people at large feel that they have a grievance, that they have not been treated in accordance with their rights and privileges, they will start to listen to rebellious talk. What you've done, my lady, just since you've been here, is to knock the pins right out from under those that might tempt them to rise up against the King."

"I had no idea—" Molly began.

"No, my lady, I imagine not; but anyway it's the truth. Well, I must excuse myself and get back to the men before I'm missed."

Chapter 38

When they finally rode through the gate and away from Buckingham, Edmund breathed a gusty sigh. "I was never so glad to leave a place in my life," he exclaimed.

"Look on the bright side," Osgar smiled. "Mercia now has one uncontested ruler and his strongest rivals have graciously withdrawn—forever."

"Not only that," said Edwin, moving Stig closer to the others. "This new ruler has acknowledged Alfred's overlordship. With Mercia at our backs, we now have the strength to withstand the Danes if they return."

"Potentially," Edmund conceded, jerking his horse's head away in time to prevent an altercation with Stig. Edwin, holding both reins in his good hand, put a little more space between them.

"Well," said Osgar, "I think the King will be pleased. All he had hoped for was an alliance, but we have got him an overlordship. Moreover, I think Aethelred will be staunch. And you seem to have made an episcopal ally as well, Lord Edwin."

Edmund had grumbled long and loudly when Bishop Waerferth's consignment of books for Alfred had been brought from the Abbey. It was a matter of a few little octavos and quartos that Waerferth happened to have with him on his travels stacked on top of one folio which Abbot Aethelhun had reverently left untouched for many years. Neatly bound up in waxed leather and string and sealed with the Bishop's seal, they made a most unobjectionable parcel, taking up no more space in the supply wagon than one crate of provisions that had already been used up. Edwin suspected that his brother's only reason to complain was that they represented a successful embassy for the King in which he had had no part.

"Do tell the King I have a few finer volumes I can send once I get back to my see," said Waerferth eagerly. "These are just what I could cobble together at the moment, and the manuscripts themselves have seen better days. As royal gifts they don't really look the part, but if it's the contents he's after, I trust King Alfred won't be disappointed. And after Easter I will send word about arrangements for a visit."

◆

Edwin and his companions arrived in Winchester on the afternoon of the following day and were closeted with King Alfred for some time, telling him the results of their embassy. News of the skirmish with Orm and his band had not reached the south, nor had news of Aethelwulf's treachery. Edwin explained the circumstances of Ealdorman Beornoth's death and shared his surmises regarding the death of King Ceolwulf. King Alfred shook his head in amazement. At the end of their conference he warmly expressed his approval of the outcome of their mission.

"I had no idea it would prove so dangerous," he said, "but the resolution of the conflict will be better, in the long run, for Mercia and for us. Yes, with a good ally to our north we will have a fighting chance against the next Danish attack. I've no doubt they will be back again before too long."

Osgar, Edmund and Edwin were then dismissed to freshen up for dinner. While they were washing off the dust of the road and digging through their baggage to find their least-wrinkled tunics, Hana arrived with the aethelings. Of course this led to a rearrangement of the seating plan, so the places at the high table the weary warriors had looked forward to were taken up by the King's nephews.

Edwin ended up next to Hana, who treated him to a detailed account of his corns and bunions. Edwin nodded politely. Hana did not suffer from corns and bunions; it was his coded method of telling his young comrade-in-arms that he had a confidential matter to discuss. To those at court who were not aware of what Hana did for the King, he was just a scruffy old retainer who constantly complained about his feet because he travelled a good deal. In fact he was constantly picking up intelligence and pulling aside one or the other of Alfred's inner circle to deliver it, prefaced by enough talk of corns and bunions to ward off any busybody seeking gossip.

Later, after dinner was finished and a singer had started a long legendary account, Edwin got up and made for the paddock, ostensibly to check on his horses. Stig was, of course, a joy to behold at any time of the day or night, and Edwin wanted to see how old Red had held up through the long southward journey, so it was a plausible pretext.

He was looking out over the backs of the horses, picked out like hills and valleys in the moonlight. Here a head was raised and lowered drowsily; there a drooping ear twitched. At length Edwin was able to discern the short back and rounded hindquarters of Stig, and beside him the high withers and sloping croup of Red. Remarkable how the two stuck together even in a herd of other horses. At length Edwin also spotted Blackbird standing diffidently nearby; his coat seemed to swallow up the moonlight rather than reflecting it.

Suddenly Edwin sensed a presence behind him and whirled around. "It's only me," the quiet voice of Hana emerged from the darkness. Then Hana stepped forward and took his place beside him and leaned his elbow on the top of the fence. He had allowed Edwin to feel his approach. If he wanted to, Hana could remain completely undetected.

After a brief silence Hana described his assignment to bring the aethelings back to Winchester, and his discoveries around Wimborne. He spoke of Molly in the most glowing terms Edwin had ever heard him speak of any woman; though Edwin reflected that he had hardly ever heard Hana speak of any woman. "You're onto a good thing there, my lord," he summed up. "Some fellows have all the luck. If I'd known a lass like her twenty years since…" Edwin looked at him, but his face was in shadow. Presently the old spy turned back towards the hall. "Well, that rest has done my corns a power of good," he said as he walked away. "Not to mention your bunions," smiled Edwin to himself. What Hana had done was to make Edwin's homesickness almost intolerable. He could leap on Stig's back right there and then, and gallop home to Wimborne as fast as his fast horse could carry him. He was just imagining slipping from Stig's back and falling exhausted but joyful into Molly's arms when he saw Buntel coming out of the hall. "My lord? Is that you?" the man called in the direction of the shadowy form by the paddock fence.

"Yes, Buntel?"

"My lord, the King's calling for you."

"Right you are." Edwin trotted back towards the shaft of golden light from the open door.

"He wants a riddle," Buntel said as Edwin came up to him and they passed back into the hall. Buntel said this with an apologetic little shrug, as if to say that kings did call for some odd things at times.

Edwin had his riddle ready, and what is more, he was pretty confident this time that it would keep the King busy for a while. Thus when the King called him forward and a hush fell over the company, Edwin spoke his riddle:

Grim and greedy the hungry one waits
at night for the hapless hall-dweller.
With fell talons he tears his prey,
Crushes his bones in a deadly bite.
The thegn's companions run and cower
Before the horror of the stealthy heath-stepper.
They will not band together
to slay this devourer with spears.
One by one he will take their lives
And creep back at dawn to his lair.
But these thegns are thieves,
And this Grendel is the hall's guardian.
How can this be?

The king was silent as he pondered this riddle. His lips moved as he took each phrase in its turn. He did not speak for so long that Edwin began to feel fidgety. Where was the knowing twinkle in the king's eye? Where was the triumphant glance about the room?

"I'm trying to tie it up with anything from your adventures in Mercia," said Alfred at last, "but nothing comes to mind. Do you fellows know the answer?" he addressed himself to Edmund and Osgar.

"Sir, he has told us nothing," Osgar said with a graceful gesture of helplessness.

"Let us think a while longer," said the King. "Just give me until the morning."

◆

Coming back from a foray into the town after breakfast to buy Molly a gift, Edwin was surprised to find the King silent and preoccupied. He supposed it to be some matter of state, but Alfred clapped him on the shoulder and said, "Edwin, this is a real puzzle. I have looked at your riddle backward and forward. I have tried a biblical interpretation to no avail. Nor do your monster-guardian and thief-thegns appear to be any sort of weapons or other common objects. If the solution is something obscure, I shall be angry with you. If it is something obvious and ordinary, I shall be angry with myself."

"Does this mean you give up?" grinned Edwin. "If you give up, then you know I win."

The King rubbed his forehead and, not meeting Edwin's eye, said, "You win."

"Well," said Edwin, stroking an aged old she-cat curled up in the autumn sun; she warbled a faint feline protest at being disturbed. "Every hall should have such a grim guardian as long as there are thieving little hall-mice to be caught," he said.

A smile slowly spread across Alfred's face as he went back over the words of Edwin's riddle in light of the solution.

"Very good, very good," the King laughed softly to himself. He pressed a purse of coins into Edwin's hand and walked away. Suddenly he turned back to Edwin and said, "You realize that now you have to start all over again. Next time we meet

I shall want another riddle. I shall be sharpening my wits in your absence. Do not expect to meet with the same success again any time soon."

The brothers bade one another a fond farewell on the road out of Winchester. Then the group of horsemen split, with Edmund and his men riding east into Wiltshire and Edwin heading south-west for Wimborne with Buntel and Bert. How long the road seemed to stretch between Edwin and Molly! How long would they be travelling before they reached home? The forest seemed to go on endlessly; but at last the trees gave way to open heathland. They passed a night in a sheltered hollow on the heath and were up early, eager to continue on.

As they passed through Wimborne and started up to the King's hall, without quite realizing it Edwin and Stig broke into a gallop: not the tight, desperate gallop of emergency, but the long loping joyful stride of man and beast eager for home. Edwin looked back. Bert could sit a horse pretty well by now, and was accustomed to old Red's big, rollicking gaits; but Buntel was bouncing uncomfortably on his pony's back, elbows flapping, nearly (it seemed) being thrown over Blackbird's neck at every stride. This paragon of hunting and tracking still had a few things to learn.

◆

Two days after the departure of Hana and the aethelings, since the weather was fine, Molly went for an afternoon stroll along the main road past the guard-house. Her excuse was taking Sebbi for a walk, but actually she felt a need to get out of the hall and away from its concerns for a while and take a breath or two of fresh air. The road was quiet; she did not encounter any travellers, whether warrior, pilgrim, or merchant.

In a wood she passed the swineherd knocking acorns from the high branches, which his grunting charges scrambled to retrieve. They made quite a noise as they went along, with the swineherd's knocking and rustling, and the hogs' excavations in the fallen leaves.

When Sebbi stopped to pursue something in the bushes, Molly dawdled by the bend in the road where a herd of cows grazed in a meadow. It was restful to watch such placid creatures and try to partake of their imperturbability after all the events of the past few weeks. Her head was still full of the aethelings' visit and Hana's words, not to mention the squabbles between Cuthburga and Winfred that looked like becoming a daily occurrence.

The cows at home had been chestnut-brown; these were creamy white with black noses and ears, and big, black-lashed brown eyes. She offered one a sprig of grass over the fence. This cow must have been the leader of the herd; she was more inquisitive than the rest.

Just as the cow was about to take the grass, her ear twitched and she raised her head to listen. At the same time Sebbi let out a joyful bark and took off around the bend.

Then Molly's ears caught the sound of hoofbeats coming closer—a small group, but approaching fast—and she had a pang of anxiety at the thought of another royal party descending without warning. Thoughts flashed through her mind in rapid succession: Sebbi recognized the sound—could it be? Can't, won't get my hopes up—too late! And then they were there before her eyes. Edwin (his arm in a sling—what had happened?) leaping one-handed down from a snorting Stig-rap, Bert scrambling down from old Red to catch Stig's reins, another man she didn't recognize, and now she had

Edwin in her arms again at last.

"Careful," was Edwin's first utterance, and Molly adjusted her embrace to avoid squeezing his injured arm. She revelled in the husband-smell of horses, sweat, and leather.

Now all three travellers had dismounted and Edwin introduced Buntel to Molly. She caught the lilt of his Mercian accent in his bashful salutation. Molly saw their looks and instantly sensed the bond between Edwin and this man, who had been unknown to him only a few weeks ago. Edwin smiled as he saw the hardened old poacher turn shy at the prospect of greeting his lady.

Observing the proprieties, Edwin and Molly walked sedately side by side back to the hall, Buntel and Bert following with the horses. Fram and Sebbi frolicked in the joy of their reunion. A gust of wind swirled the leaves and wafted the smell of wood-smoke and roast pork.

As they came to the yard Molly turned to the men and said that ale, bread and meat would be ready for them in hall shortly. Buntel took the packs from Stig's saddle, and Molly pointed him towards the reeve's quarters.

Over a hot supper and a few horns of cider, Edwin regaled Molly and Lullus with the tale of their adventures in Mercia, not omitting Bert's resourcefulness and Buntel's stalwart help. "So you see," Edwin concluded, "I am lucky to have come away as well as I did." Molly suppressed a shiver. She was glad, grateful, thankful that she had not known of it until she could hear it afterward from her own husband's lips; otherwise she could never have borne it. Edwin took Molly's hand and laced his fingers in hers. They made a pattern: his hard and brown fingers alternating with her pale and smooth ones.

Soon the others retired to sleep on their bench-beds in the hall and Molly and Edwin returned to their quarters, where

Henna was already snoring on her narrow bed in the corner. Edwin said softly, "Darling, you've done wonders around here."

"Thank you," Molly smiled as she pulled the pins out of her headdress.

"And what's this?" Edwin said, bending down to the basket of wool, where his sharp eye had caught the corner of a wax tablet.

"Never mind," Molly said quickly. "You are going to need my help getting your boots off. You can't do that with one hand."

"But I want to know—"

Molly put her finger to his lips. "Tomorrow," she said. "Tomorrow I'll tell you all. Right now it is time for weary warriors to get some rest."

"You are right as usual," he said, curling his good arm around Molly's waist. "Come, pillow-companion, and help me into bed."

"It's been a while, pillow-companion."

"Too long."

"We hardly had a chance to get started," laughed Molly, snuggling in under the covers.

"Shall we pick up where we left off?"

"No time like the present."

"Blow out that candle, then."

Historical Note

Although Edwin and Molly are fictional characters, the time in which they lived is a well-documented part of history. King Alfred and his contemporaries lived about midway in the Anglo-Saxon period. They could look back three hundred years to pagan ancestors who came to conquer and settle the land of Britain, forming seven separate kingdoms. Wessex was one of these kingdoms, a lesser star that for generations had been outshone by powerful Mercia to the north. However, from relatively humble beginnings Alfred's royal line would in time unite all of what we now know as England. By Alfred's time Christianity had been the religion of the land for at least two hundred years, and the culture of Rome with its books and monks had fused so effectively with that of the English culture of warriors and mead-halls that Jesus could be portrayed in poetry as a chieftain surrounded by his disciple-retainers. The next three hundred years of the period saw changes to society, laws, industry, and art that Edwin and Molly would not have imagined possible.

Alfred's time was characterized by regular Viking attacks, mostly launched from Denmark. This came to a climax in 878 when the Danish chieftain Guthrum, fresh from conquering the kingdom of Mercia, overran neighbouring Wessex and drove the young King Alfred into hiding in the marshes of Athelney. Rather than trying to buy off the Danes or engage in a doomed confrontation, Alfred launched a guerrilla resistance that eventually led to Guthrum's defeat in the battle of Edington. Our story commences with the kingdom of Wessex rejoicing in its victory and beginning to recover from the depredation it suffered in the wake of the Danish attacks.

Wimborne

Monasteries had their ups and downs in Anglo-Saxon times. In some generations monasticism was widespread and thriving; in others it went through periods of decline. One typical pattern inherited from the early Irish missionaries was the double monastery. This was a house of monks and nuns living in separate quarters and headed by an abbess. Wimborne in Dorset had a famous double monastery. In our story the abbey is located on the site of the present-day Wimborne Minster.

Wimborne was also a royal estate in the time of King Alfred, but where was this estate located? A short distance north of the town of Wimborne Minster is a stately home known as Kingston Lacy. The present house was built in the seventeenth century. However, there was a house and a royal estate on that site from medieval times, and the Anglo-Saxon name Kingston means 'king's enclosure'. Therefore, I have placed the royal estate of which Edwin is reeve at Kingston Lacy.

Mercia

Aethelred and the other Mercian noblemen and churchmen in the story were real historical figures. When Edwin and Edmund arrive in Mercia, they come to the once-great Midlands kingdom which had been vanquished by Vikings seven years before. King Burgred, who was married to Alfred's sister, was deposed and fled to Rome. In the intervening time the kingdom was ruled by King Ceolwulf II, an Anglo-Saxon who was put in place as a puppet ruler by the Vikings. Some time around 879 he drops out of the historical records, and a few years later Ealdorman Aethelred appears in those same records as the ruler of Mercia, but as a satellite to King Alfred of Wessex. Exactly what happened to Ceolwulf or how Aethelred came to power is not known. It is this tantalizing gap in the historical record that provided the setting for *A Council of Wolves*.

The names of Mercian noblemen from this period are chiefly known from charters drawn up by the king granting lands and privileges to persons and churches. All I had to work from were these charters and the knowledge of who came out as the ruler at the end of the story. Some names were present on Burgred's charters and also on Ceolwulf's. Why were these noblemen willing to serve both Burgred and his usurper? There are many possible reasons, some innocent and some not so innocent. Then there were names that appear on Ceolwulf's charters but not on Aethelred's. Where did these men go when Aethelred came to power? There were also a few names that appear on the charters of all three kings. Under what circumstances could a high-ranking nobleman preserve his position through that much turmoil at the top? These considerations prompted my portrayals of the Mercian characters.

Buckingham

Situated in a bend of the river Ouse, Buckingham is on the border of eastern and western Mercia. Given its strategic location, the town went back and forth between the Saxons and Vikings more than once. In our story, Aethelwulf's hall is on Castle Hill, where the Parish Church of St Peter and St Paul now stands. There was an older church to the south of Castle Hill, and that is where I have imagined the abbey. The settlement and the commons would be between there and the river's east bend.

Trial and Ordeal

The law was important to Anglo-Saxons, but they conducted their court cases differently than we do today. There was little emphasis on forensic evidence; the trial centred on solemn oaths sworn by eyewitnesses and character witnesses. Since law enforcement was not a public service, the plaintiff was responsible for exacting justice on the offender once that offender had been duly convicted in court. Thus the culture was geared to personal vengeance and feuding was common: just ask "those Ceaddings." Those who could not pay the fines owed due to their conviction, or who were guilty of serious but non-capital crimes, could lose their freedom and be sent into penal slavery—like Eng, if she's lucky. Hanging was the usual way for criminals to be executed.

The ordeal was used throughout Europe in the early Middle Ages. It was a last resort, a test of guilt in cases of serious crime when the usual trial method of witnesses and oaths was inconclusive and the accused person, like the hapless Cynric, insisted on his innocence. The process of performing the ordeal was very exact and the intent was not to torture the accused, but to appeal directly to the divine Judge to vindicate or condemn the accused person by a sign. Later, trial by combat (as portrayed to such dramatic effect in Sir Walter Scott's *Ivanhoe*) and trial by jury superseded trial by ordeal.

Edwin's riddles

Making riddles is a fitting pastime for a detective. The riddles Edwin presents to the King in this story (solutions: fish and cat) are my own inventions in the style of real Anglo-Saxon riddles. Many genuine riddles from the period survive in manuscripts. Usually the riddles take an ordinary object and describe it in an unexpected way, often in the first person as if the object is describing itself.

Names

As the Abbess says about Molly's name, there is not much that could be done about it: Anglo-Saxon names are notoriously difficult. Only a few survive in modern usage. My approach has been to choose more recognizable names for the main characters. Historical characters are referred to by their real names in a common modern spelling. The Anglo-Saxons were fond of nicknames, either shortening the full name with an i, or using a nickname based on some personal attribute. Molly's name (Molgifu) is rare. Some families (like Edwin's) bore alliterating names beginning with the same letter or sound. With regard to place-names, I have kept the modern spellings with the exception that the realm of Charlemagne's descendants is referred to as Francia, not France.

Further reading

If you want to get inside the heads of real Anglo-Saxons, it is possible to do so by reading the many original sources: historical accounts, poems, legends, sermons, riddles, laws. Translations are available in abundance. A readily available introduction to Alfred and his times is *Alfred the Great: Asser's Life of King Alfred and other contemporary sources*, translated by Simon Keynes and Michael Lapidge (Penguin).

The Icelandic sagas are also great original sources for the early Middle Ages. These are prose narratives that read very much like novels. They were written by Icelanders mostly in the twelfth and thirteenth centuries but set in the Viking Age, circa 800 to 1100. Egil's saga is a good one to start with. It is set in tenth-century Iceland with part of the story in England and a cameo appearance by Alfred's grandson King Athelstan. The translation by Christine Fell and John Lucas (Everyman) is recommended.

Secondary sources

There are many good books on Anglo-Saxon England. *Life in Anglo-Saxon England* by R.I. Page (Batsford) and *The Beginnings of English Society* by Dorothy Whitelock (Penguin) will get the interested reader off to an excellent start.

Reviews Appreciated

I'm delighted you chose to read *A Council of Wolves*. If you enjoyed it, please consider leaving a brief review on your favourite book website. Your recommendation will help other readers discover something new. *Ic ðancie þē* (I thank you)!

Latest news

To be the first to find out about Edwin and Molly's next adventures, visit my website www.elizabethspringerauthor.com. There you can sign up for my quarterly e-mail newsletter, a veritable treasure-hoard of news, reviews, and interesting facts about the Anglo-Saxons and Vikings. You can also find me on Facebook and Instagram.